The Cost of
Haven

Book 1 of The Great Cities

F. F. McCulligan

Order this book online at www.trafford.com
or email orders@trafford.com

Most Trafford titles are also available at major online book retailers.

Printed in the United States of America.

ISBN: 978-1-4669-8708-1 (sc)
ISBN: 978-1-4669-8707-4 (e)

Trafford rev. 03/26/2013

 www.trafford.com

North America & international
toll-free: 1 888 232 4444 (USA & Canada)
phone: 250 383 6864 ♦ fax: 812 355 4082

For Tolkien, Gygax, and other Rare Bastards

Preface

THIS STORY IS AUTOBIOGRAPHICAL. Sort of. I wrote this book when I was fired from my job. In the month that followed I split my time equally between writing and trying to get my job back.

Eventually, though, staying true to the events of real life impacted the validity of the story itself and I began writing it for its own sake. In the end I wrote it purely to discover what would happen next. I loved the process from start to finish, well the editing and formatting were a bit dull, but now it is done, and on the whole, even if I don't sell a single copy, it was more than worth it for me.

It takes place in a world where the greed and domination of humanity have reached their limit of efficacy and a primal force, un-united, and disorganized, has rebuked the realms of humanity on all fronts. The so-called "teeming forces of evil" is the fury of the wilderness, outraged at humanity's mistreatment and vandalism of the earth. I tried to make a point with this book. I wanted a world where nature was winning the war. I wanted a world where humans were the underdogs.

I dedicated the book first and foremost to J.R.R. Tolkien, whose very name gives me chills to write on this page. Rest in peace, Beren. No matter how I try, my work will never soar through the stars as yours does. I hope that one day, I may place a copy of this text upon your grave, a meager offering of thanks and of farewell.

Also, to Gary Gygax, I must tip my hat. When you left this world, I felt that I had lost an old friend. Much of my life has been well spent around a paper-strewn table with good companions by my side and my head in the clouds, and for that I will always be thankful. Without your influence, I would never have written this.

And of course, to the greatest fellowship on the planet, the MRB who share my passion for bullshit and imagination. You are the ones with whom I sat around the paper-strewn table. You are the ones without whom I would have walked alone.

My goals for this book are humble. I hope to break even in terms of coin, and I hope to see it one day, battered and well-loved, on a creaky, wooden bookshelf in my local used bookstore; just another paperback in the fantasy/sci-fi section. Whether or not anyone "gets it", at least I can say that I tried.

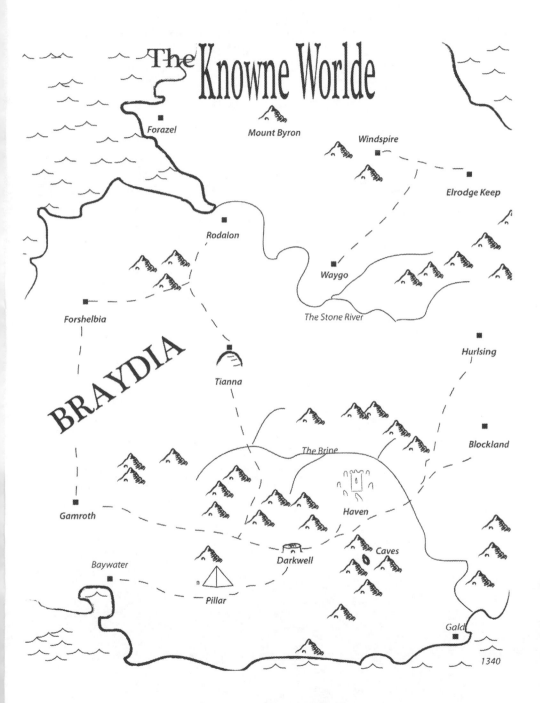

THE WORST PART ABOUT living in Darkwell was the smoke. Do not imagine the light and nostalgic aroma of a campfire, for that pleasant odor was lifted up and out of the city walls, and all that remained was the stink of wood that was burned green and never left to cure due to the onrush of necessity. And when it wasn't green wood, the fuel was peat, sliced from the dangerous bogs outside the city. When there wasn't peat, they burned dung. Pick it up from the fields, (at night if it isn't your field), stick it in the dung bin, and hope that the rats or the crows don't carry it off before you get the chance to burn it.

There were three great cities left standing on the continent of Braydia. Great is here used not as a judgment of quality, but of size, though in some sense of the word the cities maintained overtones of greatness . . . *Great* to visit but not to live there; *great* for meeting new people (thousands of them every day), and *great* for refuge against the teeming forces of evil that had already overrun the rest of the known world.

Darkwell's heart was a squat tower, its skin a high, circular wall. It contained a sea of smoke, like foam in a mug of ale. It was a windy, sunny day, which made the acrid smoke slosh over the wall in lazy gray waves. And blow out to the fields surrounding Darkwell, which lay between the wall and the ever-encroaching edge of the jungle. Of the three last cities, it was only Darkwell that was ruled by a king. Malagor was a true king (the word true here means descended from a line of kings, and is not meant to express any judgment of Malagor's character) and his reign extended far into the past so that he remembered many of the tragedies that had shaped the world into the frightening place that it now was. When Malagor came into power fifty years earlier upon the death of his father, there were more than three great cities in Braydia, and the fact that his city remained intact was a point of pride for him. Some of Darkwell's inhabitants said the satisfaction he felt regarding the destruction of his rivals was a dark and bitter vanity, which grew more dangerous as the greedy king aged.

Which brings us to Deagan Wingrat, who raised his ale in a salute to his own health, solitary as he was on a slipshod balcony that afforded him a view of the city he was sworn to protect: Darkwell. He was a tall, robust man in a suit of armor who wore his beard fuzzy, but not dangling. The whiskers of his chin were stark white, while the rest of his beard and hair was black. The knight used to be slim and athletic, but now he was thick and menacing.

He sat with his back against the hot stone of the city wall, looking toward the center of Darkwell from his lazy perch on a barstool forty feet above the street below. There were cracks between the floorboards of the balcony revealing other balconies and roofs below with sundry ladders and walkways connecting them. There was no movement that Deagan could make that would not elicit a creak or a groan from the structure.

"Another drink, s-s-sir knight?" asked the bar lad who had just climbed the ladder and couldn't remove his eyes from the precipitous drop below him.

As Deagan turned his head to reply, the floor creaked. "Aye, lad. Make it a stout."

"As you like, sir," he said, wiping a grimy hand on his apron. "Right away." Alone again, Deagan gazed out on Darkwell. The towers of stone looked like giants wading through the smoke, with over crowded scaffolds strung like clotheslines between them. The sun was going down.

The lad came back up the ladder and squeezed past the resting knight with a nervous laugh as he stepped over the jutting sword in its sheath. He set the drink down and took Deagan's now empty one.

"All's well with me, boy. You can take your leave." The floor creaked as he took the first foamy sip of his warm stout.

"Um," muttered the boy. It was obvious he wanted something, but was too afraid to ask. "What does it take to become a knight, sir?"

Deagan squinted at the spire of King Malagor, wondering if the king was home, and didn't reply until he'd taken another sip of his ale. "I don't know, lad . . ." he said lamely. Deagan turned to look at the boy. He had a young face with a big nose and shadowed blue eyes—a face that Deagan couldn't help but compare to Eli's.

"But," the lad went on, "You *are* a knight, sir?"

Deagan sighed, "If you must know, you need to do your time. You have to fight. You have to serve without ever asking for payment or praise. King Malagor has to choose you from the warriors, usually at a tournament, or a great battle against the forces of evil that he happens to hear about. But why do you want to go risking your neck in battle when it seems just as common to knight other sorts of folk, like diplomats or . . . minstrels?" He laughed quietly, "Do you hope for the glory of it lad? Tis not all swords and horses. Save your pay. Buy a harp. You're better off singing about heroic deeds than deeding them yourself, as it were."

"Oh," the boy said wringing his towel between his hands. Was he wondering if that rag was to be his lot in life forever?

Deagan smiled apologetically and said, "Go on, lad. This balcony's like to collapse with the two of us up here anyway."

He started down the ladder, but Deagan called after him. "Everything you've heard about knighthood is wrong, lad." He finished his stout in peace and climbed down the twenty-foot ladder and into the tavern window below. He paid the bar tender and went down the stairs to a door, that led to the street. The last scraps of sunset lingered.

Deagan sauntered through the winding streets and reflected on bad memories. He had a tendency to be a worrier, and tonight, since he'd been commanded to visit the duke, there was plenty to worry about. "Enough, Deagan. Just forget the past. Duke's waiting, fool; no sense feeling sorry for things you cannot change."

Duke Worth was a knight himself, but did not see the battlefield anymore. If he was your friend he gave the impression of being a loving, but demanding father figure. If he was your enemy he was colder than cold.

Though Sir Deagan had seen both of these sides, he was decidedly the enemy of the duke. Duke Worth. He always dressed as though he remembered he was a warrior once, but the chain shirt he wore was little more than a vest of wire that couldn't take a blow. That's what the duke's guards were for, and Deagan knew all too well what *they* were capable of.

He finally reached the cheapest stable in Darkwell, which was all his wages from the spire would afford. The horses were stacked four high, in stalls that were built one atop the other. Each stall was accessed by removable wooden planks that the stable boys would put in place for you. It took a brave horse to walk up the uncertain walkway to reach the second and third layers of stalls. It took a daft one to reach the fourth.

"The gray up there on number four, man. Mind the ramp and set it sturdy. If she falls, you'll be the one to catch her!" The three foot wide ramp was placed against the edge of the stall and latched in place. "Maggie, come here, now." He blew her a few kisses. She tossed her head at first, but soon tromped down the long ramp. A few other horses backed away from the gangplank, rolled their eyes at the long drop below and whinnied their dismay. Maggie walked on.

"That's my warhorse, boy. Mark her well. See that limp she has, though? Caught a pike right in the pastern when we went out trampling one day." Maggie balked as the planks bowed in the middle. Her ears were back and she stopped in place.

"Walk on, Maggie." He blew her another kiss. "Easy," he breathed. She made her way down the rest of the ramp and her heavy hooves found the sandy earth once more. The ground shook as she came forward. The stable hand gave Sir Deagan the bit and bridle and produced Maggie's saddle from a locked room nearby. Deagan prepared the horse for a ride.

He trotted her through the crowded streets having to duck under a wooden beam. The beam was part of a stack of platforms that rose up like scaffolding attached to the buildings on both sides of the street forming layer upon layer of slums. Someone threw out the dishwater from twenty feet up and it splashed the knight's horse and armor. Smoke spat and popped from all the cook fires above.

Deagan made it to the entryway of the Duke's abode. He hated meeting on someone else's turf because if Deagan wanted to so much as stand up from the table he would have to ask first. He was used to that being a knight, but it was an itchy feeling, much like wearing wool trousers with nothing else to change into.

Maggie's reins in hand, Deagan looked up at the façade of Duke Worth's home. It was unchanged from the time of his youth, and Deagan was suddenly overwhelmed with memories at the sight of the entryway before him that he had long avoided.

After only two and a half years of knighthood, Deagan was still a young man. He was slimmer and quicker to anger. He had good reason to be angry. The short fused knight planted his boot sole against the door to Duke Worth's hall with a boom. The doors slammed open and he stormed in, apparently startling a young woman who jumped giggling off of the Duke's lap. Guards followed Deagan in, calling for him to stop. But the young knight felt purple fire in his heart that drowned out his senses.

"How dare you, sir?" Deagan demanded.

"Pardon me?" The duke looked amused now instead of only shocked. He loved to put a knight in his place and it looked like young Deagan Wingrat would give him just such an opportunity.

"You left fifteen good men to die!"

"I have no idea what you are talking about young man, and I don't believe you do either," the duke said.

Deagan said. "I knew it was wrong . . ." his voice trembled with indignant anger. "I knew it would only end in death! There were good men, no great men among them! But you let them die while the rest of us—" he spat. "We told you this would happen so don't bother trying to weasel your way out of it."

"Calm yourself, Deagan," said Duke Worth smiling and glancing at the woman who'd been on his lap. Now that he'd given an order, Deagan had to risk insubordination if he wanted to continue. A sickening heat rose in Deagan's guts. Later he would learn that this feeling was telling him that he was about to let his anger get the better of him, and he was about to make a grave mistake. But at this young age, the feeling only spurred him on. He advanced on the duke.

"Admit you were wrong! Admit you were stupid! Admit that their blood is on your hands and that if you had left me there none of them would've had to die!" spittle flew from his mouth and landed on the duke's shoe.

Now the Duke was shaken, his mouth a flat line and his eyes old and frozen. "Guards," he said. And Deagan lifted his hands over his head, unwilling to harm any of the king's own men as they seized him. "Armor," said the Duke and the guards began ripping the armor off him, unbuckling, and finally scraping the metal of his breastplate across his face. "Shackle him to the post."

Wrists bound in iron, Deagan was tied in place. Duke Worth left the room momentarily, but returned soon with a long black whip. So this was what that feeling had warned him of.

The knight nodded his way past the guard and walked Maggie across the courtyard where he tied her up. He looked up at the terracotta building and exhaled. Why was he here? Usually his summons to the Duke would have had some explanation.

'Go meet the Duke to receive your orders, Deagan. Go meet the Duke to tell him what you saw in battle, Deagan.' This time it was only, 'Go meet the Duke, and don't be late, Deagan.'

He patted his horse and went up the stairs that led to the chambers of Duke Worth.

A pair of boots stomped down toward him on the stairs. They belonged to Sir Luthan. "Oh good Deagan, you made it. Brave days, I trust?" This was always how Luthan greeted his brother of the knighthood. Always these words, but after years of hearing them, this time they sounded dark and empty.

Luthan's voice came out in a grumble; his brows were furrowed and his eyes were down. "Look, Sir Deagan, honesty is one of the finest qualities a knight can possess. It pains me to be honest now though. I wish I could tell you everything is all right." Deagan searched the older knight's face for a sign of what was to come. What he saw there was pain and trouble. Sir Luthan went on, "It isn't as if you've had such a good year. Really, you've had a pretty hard one. Think of the Border Lands, brother. You must see that you were in the wrong." Bad news was coming and Deagan's heart felt crowded with so much emotion that his breathing was heavy.

Forcing himself to speak, Deagan said, "I did what I *had* to, Luthan. You would have done the same."

The older knight wasn't swayed. For some reason he still sided with the Duke, probably because he, like the duke, hadn't been there. "No, brother, you did what you *wanted* to. What you were asked to do in the Border Lands was the duty of a knight, nothing uncommon at all. Following those kinds of orders is the bread and butter of knighthood, Deagan . . ." Luthan was pleading now. "If you can't do it . . ."

Those three words echoed in Deagan's helmet. *Can't do it. Can't do it. Can't do it.* He squeezed the pommel of his sword, hadn't he proven he could do it yet? After fifteen years of loyalty and honor? How dare Luthan decide that all of a sudden Deagan was useless? *Then again maybe I am*, he thought.

"If you *can't do it* . . ." Luthan continued, "I must ask. Do you really want to be a knight anymore?"

Every mistake he'd made as a knight came rushing back to him—every moment when his urges had gotten the better of his oaths, each imperfection. The weight of them all filled his head until it ached. His vision went dark and his sword felt heavy in its sheath. Deagan had been complaining about being a knight for the last year. He'd been asked to do terrible things, forced to put his own beliefs aside. His life was hard and lonesome and he had no wealth to make it all worthwhile, no manor to return to. All he had hanging over him when it rained was his oath to the king.

"Deagan? How do you fare?" Luthan asked.

"Not well, Luthan."

"You have been a valiant knight, Deagan. The duke knows that. You can still change his mind, but I need to hear it from your mouth. And if you want any chance at all, you'd best say it *stronger* than the Duke's own trumpets. *Do you want to remain a knight?*"

Every hard, rainy ride on the king's business bubbled up into Deagan's head. Before his waking eyes, Deagan's lost brothers-in-arms lined up in order and died again. He relived the abuse he'd received from his superiors while forced by decorum to remain kneeling. He was truly speechless. More than anything he wanted to say yes, but he couldn't make himself do it.

"Deagan? My friend?"

"That's a question I've been asking myself a long time," Deagan managed. His power was sapped. If he was no longer a knight, Deagan felt he was no longer anything at all. For so long he'd defined himself by his sword and his oath. Now . . .

Luthan sounded disappointed, "Well, that kind of answer won't change his mind, brother." Luthan was an older knight and in many ways he was Deagan's superior and mentor. Now there were tears in his eyes. "Walk in that chamber with an answer like that and you're certain to walk out again, unbelted . . . What I mean to say is, the Duke is taking your knighthood away. I thought I would die with you in battle one day, my friend. And we could walk together into the hall of warriors, laughing at the duke and the king and all the rest of them."

Half in tears, Deagan laughed nervously. "You've an overdeveloped sense of glory, you old goat. That's all you can think to tell a friend at a time like this?"

"Take a minute," Luthan advised. "Compose yourself. The duke can wait another little while for you." One knight gave the other a reassuring pat on the shoulder.

K ELLEN WAYFIELD WAS NOT a nobleman, but he lived like one. Even in Darkwell and in times such as these, his manor was rich and well kept. Now in his study Kellen was sitting at a table strewn with papers, his gaze was lifted to a large map on the wall. The many realms and kingdoms of the Knowne Worlde were each bordered in dashed lines.

The map was drawn in year 1340 of the Braydian calendar. Since that date, nearly thirty years ago now, the majority of the map had been simply scribbled out. Windspire was crossed out with a quill and Kellen even took the trouble to illustrate heads on pikes surrounding its capital with trails of inky blood pooling on the countryside below. If the heads (one of them was meant to look like the king of Windspire Castle) covered the same amount of ground as shown by Kellen's drawing it would have taken all the horses in that nation to remove them. It wasn't a scale drawing, but Kellen Wayfield would be the first to tell you that he was not interested in such details; he was big picture oriented.

The big picture at the moment was grim. Elrodge Keep was crossed out with scorpions drawn climbing up its towers. A dragon could be seen laying waste to the good City Angorell. A great sinkhole was drawn on top of Hurlsing because the forces of evil had actually managed to tunnel underneath the city with huge worms or centipedes, and caused it to collapse on itself. He had drawn a snake with a long body; its head lay placidly in the West and its tail stretched over to the East. In the middle there was a large lump over what was once Forshelbia.

Tianna was under a dark thundercloud and burning, Gamroth was overrun by the undead, commonly referred to as dead men, rotters, or sarcophs, and Blockland just looked like a pile of dog shit. Kellen had actually drawn the dog shit when he was drunk one night before Blockland had been destroyed. This was because Kellen *despised* Blockland. Some of the names on the map were just furiously scribbled out. Roads were covered in X's if they were no longer safe and ports were sunken into the waves. Hand drawn serpents swam freely through the seas, and Kellen's poorly doodled dragons populated the skies like pigeons from the towers of Darkwell. One thing was clear on the entire blackened map: there wasn't much left belonging to humankind. Darkwell, Pillar, and Haven were three city-states all crowded together near the Southern border of the continent of Braydia. And like a looming cloud surrounding them Kellen had scribbled a vague, dark outline. Inside the line, around the three cities he had written, "Good Guys." Outside it he had written, "Teeming Forces of Evil".

Kellen sighed and leaned back in a fine leather chair. His wealth did not come from exploits of battle or from old riches in his family. In the truest sense, Kellen was a self-made man. He was a trader who used to travel the roadways himself with only one donkey and a small cart full of goods, but since that time he had grown his operation radically. Being surrounded by a murky sea of vile intent, however, was not good for trade, and the hey-day of his wealth was now over.

The books before him were logs of his accounts and expenses and they all pointed the same direction. He was losing money as quickly as humanity lost territory. He thought he still had a few years of the good life, however, and Kellen never did anything without a plan B.

He was slim and tall, in good health and only thirty years old. He was handsome, but the air of mischief about him was so palpable that it was not surprising he'd never married. Marrying a noble woman had been plan B for several years, but Kellen found out that it was a hard con to trick a mother into letting a scoundrel like him anywhere near her precious daughter. Kellen would have been a horrible husband and everyone knew it.

Closing his books, he finished his tea and handed the cup to Rory, his faithful butler. Rory was a few years younger than Kellen, and he was the finest butler in Darkwell. He had olive skin and a close and tidy beard. His hair was black and slick with grease. He was in amazing shape. Kellen allowed him to keep a training room in the back courtyard. Being a fantastic butler came with a lot of perks and Kellen would have been a horrible butler, so he appreciated Rory to no end.

Kellen trotted down the stairs and out through his fine red door and into the streets of Darkwell. He moved quickly and avoided bumping into the hordes of people on the streets. He had a meeting with the leader of his main caravan. The man's name was Jorn Kahorne and they were to meet in the square by the fountain.

The sun filtered through the smoke. The steady trickle of the fountain occasionally made itself heard over the din of voices and chickens being sold at the market. People were gathering their drinking water in buckets from the fountain. Some were bathing there too.

Nobles tended to stay away from there, or when they had to pass through they would cover their noses with those obnoxious cloths they always carried. If he married a noble woman would Kellen carry one of those, too? He suspected he wouldn't make a very good noble, but he *liked* the smoke of Darkwell, even if he was the only one. He breathed it in deeply and leaned against the stone of the fountain. His faithful caravan driver, Jorn was nowhere to be seen.

Kellen waited by the fountain. If Jorn arrived now, he would be early as he usually was. But time passed as time always does, and Kellen took a seat with still no sign of the man. Now, if the caravan driver walked in he wouldn't be early, but he would certainly still be on time. Jorn did not show up however, and with nothing else to do, Kellen continued to wait. Eventually Jorn had charged straight into the realm of tardiness and still did not appear. Kellen waited until Jorn was positively late for there was still no trace of the man. Kellen yawned.

You don't become the head caravan for Kellen Wayfield by being late. Darkness fell such as it did in this city square. Lamps burned dimly to fend off all but the darkest shadows and still no sign. He trusted Jorn . . . and his intuition told him something was amiss. No. Amiss didn't begin to cover it. His intuition told him Jorn Kahorne was dead.

A MORE RECENT MEMORY WHISKED Deagan away. *The clangs of hammers on dented armor rang out into the war camp. The dry smoke rose from the cook fires and drifted through the jungle. Deagan was shirtless and sweating, covered with sun-browned hide and striped with pink scars. The sun would last another hour and a half. After the day's ride, Maggie the gray mare was chewing on some jungle grass within the reach of her lead rope that was tied to a tree across the camp from where Deagan now stood. Four dozen of the king's soldiers were grouped together and making ready for battle on the following day. They were miles from Darkwell, in what was once considered peaceful and civilized territory, but was now called the Border Lands.*

A young man with a nervous frown sat on a tree stump sharpening his sword. He was wearing his armor even in the close heat. The shirtless knight addressed him, "Sir Deagan's my name, little brother. Sir Deagan Wingrat. Would you care for a game of sticky?"

Unwilling to refuse a knight's wishes, the young man stood and sheathed his sword. "Aye, it sounds like fun." He tried to sound braver than he felt. Deagan threw his apple core on the ground and picked up a pair of equal length sticks that had been cut and piled as the campsite was constructed. It was common practice to cut saplings out of the way when a group this large made camp, both to clear land and to invite warriors who may have grown rusty to indulge in a game of sticky.

Deagan pulled his helmet down over his head and buckled the strap under his snow-white chin. Then he picked up his shield and strong looking stick. He didn't bother putting his chain shirt on, he didn't expect the lad to hit him. The lad followed suit; he hefted the ill-fitting helmet from the stump and unbelted his sword to let it rest on the ground while he sparred.

He followed Deagan out to the center of camp. They squared off and with one resounding bang, Deagan rapped on his own shield with the stick. It was a call to fight.

Deagan stood there with his blue eyes locked onto those of the younger man. He was relaxed and didn't move. The lad took a step forward, cowering even as he advanced. He looked over the edge of his shield with intense concentration. The lad stepped even closer, now within inches of swinging distance. Deagan moved his back foot forward, not even enough to change his posture, then crack! The young man went reeling from a blow to the temple. He hadn't seen the strike coming; he didn't react.

"Come in swinging this time lad. Don't get in swinging distance if you don't intend to swing yourself. What's your name?"

"Eli," he said raising his guard again.

"Did you see me move my foot, Eli?"

"What?" Crack! Eli was hit again in the temple, by the same trick. He was quick to raise his guard again and this time he came in swinging. Deagan turned from side to side on the balls of his feet, moving his whole body behind the shield that bore his coat of arms, a single sword. Eli produced a predictable pattern of strikes that fell reliably on Deagan's shield. Then Deagan stepped back twice to draw the young warrior into a rapid charge. Eli took the bait, and when the young combatant was between footsteps, Deagan advanced half a step and raised his shield to connect with that of the charging youth. The boy flew off his feet and looked up to find the knight standing over him. Deagan leaned in and slowly dropped his stick on the boys face. They were both laughing.

"How did you do that?" Eli laughed as he took the knight's hand and rose to his feet.

"That my young friend, is the question you should be asking." He explained the feint and told him how the charge had been broken. As the pair fought on, Eli showed fast improvement, but nevertheless, his stick never touched the knight's skin. The coaching session went until they could no longer see. Others had joined in and played sticky as well, more still watched from the sidelines. Soon the sport was done and the entire company was gathered around the campfires and they brought out the liquor and ale. It was water for Eli, though. Nothing else passed his lips.

Deagan's sweaty bulk glistened in the sunset. How many times had he shared tales around fires on the eve of battle? It was comfortable to him, even though he knew he might not live another day.

"You're water-sworn, eh?" Deagan asked as Eli sipped water from a clay jug and kept his distance from the revelry by the campfires.

The boy looked up and replied, "Yes, sir I am." He sounded apologetic, his tone saying that he was aware of how foolish he must seem to such a brave and beer-guzzling knight like Sir Deagan.

"Why?" Deagan asked.

"My father was water-sworn. It's how I was raised. I took the oath when I was three."

"Straight from breast milk to water-sworn! That's quite the raw deal. There are many drinks in the realms that could tempt you away from your oath. How do you stay strong?" Deagan asked.

"I'm not tempted. I like water," Eli answered simply. "Those men don't make the harder drinks look too appealing," he said pointing to the rowdy band of miscreants.

"No they don't," Deagan agreed. "I wish I had your self control, Eli. You are the smartest man here by far, present company excluded of course," he said pointing to himself. Deagan watched Eli's laughter rise and then fall as the boy's expression faded from congeniality to dread. He sipped from the water jug and stared down into it. It took strong resolve to last so long on water alone, but he was too young to be out here.

"Do you live with your parents still, Eli?" Deagan asked.

"I'm looking for another place," he answered.

"Your father is a good man. He raised you well," Deagan said. "That's not something to run away from, nor anything to be ashamed of! You'll find what you're looking for, lad. But in my experience, you always find it once you give up on looking."

Eli clearly didn't understand, but he nodded as though he did. Deagan left him to think about it. What he really wanted to say to the water-sworn *boy was, run now. Go home. Don't die for this pointless mission,* but since he knew Eli was too brave to turn back his words would have been wasted. It was a lesson the youth would need to learn for himself if he survived long enough.

Some distance away, the other warriors told tales of heroics that would come on the following day. They bragged of their exploits and got each other's blood up, as was said in Darkwell. Deagan alone remained solemn. Against the evening's chill, he belted his tunic tighter with a strap of white leather. Around his neck, there hung a golden chain. He leaned back on a tent pole and let the firelight wash over him from a distance. The shadows of the encamped warriors interrupted the fire glow as they rollicked about, engrossed in conversation.

"And I believe *what I've heard about these bastards!*" said one man. "They keep witches in their cabins with them. Witches of great beauty, but never let them speak for a spell will be woven over your very heart. They wear armor. And they carry steel."

A second voice rose out of the tumult to answer the first, "Well, the king didn't leave a lot up to the imagination when he gave us our orders regarding any witches we *might find. Did he boys?*" They all laughed drunkenly.

"Those ignorant bastards won't even see us coming!"

When the boastful banter reached its zenith, one warrior challenged the rest of them to a game of "torchy" and brandished a burning torch, Deagan rose and left for his blankets under a low canvas tent by the stream. The Border Lands could be dangerous even in such numbers. He washed his face and rested on his back, but could not sleep for a long time knowing that if danger arose it would fall to him to put all to rights.

"Go and think it over," Luthan said with another clap to the shoulder.

Deagan shook himself, driving the memories from his mind as he looked up into Luthan's face again. He nodded, left Luthan's company with a firm hug and went back outside to think for a time. Could this be happening? Of course it could. *After what happened in the Border Lands how could any king want me?*

He slouched down the stone stairs of Duke Worth's manor, and went down to his horse with a furrowed brow. He reached up and rubbed Maggie's cheek. She was perpetually shedding, and inch-long hairs flew away and found Deagan's face. "They want to get rid of me, girl," He said softly. He rubbed her down and scratched her withers. "I think I'm about to be banished." Maggie dropped her head as if to join his sorrow.

Deagan tried to clear his head, but he could barely hold his gaze on the images before him. Unchangeable memories and unknowable futures whirled through his mind faster than he could keep track of. So many troubling images went by him that he couldn't make any of them out, nor see, nor even think. Then his eyes rose up from her well-shod hoofs (he paid only for the worst stable in Darkwell, but he did not mind the cost of the best farrier) up her front legs and to her strong, stocky neck. She was not fully armored now, those heavy plates waited in his rented chambers. "I am such an idiot," he sighed.

"How can they do this?" he asked himself. "There must be a way that I can fight this! There must be some rule or decree that says I get another chance. Why should I need another chance any old way? I did the right thing. It just didn't happen to be what the duke and the blasted king wanted. Could be it's them who ought to be unbelted, not me!" He knew this thinking would get him nowhere.

The knight gazed up at Maggie's long-lashed and expressive eyes. Upon seeing those clear hazel orbs, a terrible realization hit him that made his heart sink: Maggie was the king's horse. *No!* He thought. *Good Gods, no!* He reached for her and held her snout to his breast as though someone would pull her away from him if he let her go. What he realized then, he tried to suppress, locked in his heart never to escape lest he crumble right there on the cobbles. He wove his fingers into her close-cropped mane and laid his cheek between her two eyes. Her sweet breath rose up around him in invisible clouds.

"I won't let them take you, Maggie. I won't let them take you, big girl. It's all right Mag. It's okay," he said frantically working his thick fingers into her mane. Her smell took him back to every battle he'd fought by her side ever since she was given to him as a gift in his third year of knighthood twelve years ago. All but one of those battles had been victorious in the service of the king. *The service of the king,* he thought. *Nothing more. I was but a slave. A tick mark in his books.*

Maggie was the king's horse. And when he lost his knighthood he would no longer be entitled to ride her. His vision darkened, but he kept his feet.

"Luthan said there was a chance I could change Worth's mind. I promise you Maggie, that I will do my best. It don't matter how hard I've had it. You're worth *all* the duty and *all* the suffering and *all* the Gods Damned . . . *bowing* that comes with it. I tell you what. I'm walking up these stairs, Maggie. And when I come back down, you'll still be looking at SIR Deagan Wingrat *the knight*! And I'll take you to the stables and get you some good oats, huh? What do you say, Mag?"

Hot as the emotions boiling inside were, Deagan knew from countless dealings with his superiors that humility and deference were better than defiance. He might get away tonight with a harsh tongue-lashing or additional watches at the gates. He would take whatever they had to give him and he wouldn't complain. Maggie was all he had. The only part of being a knight that was still worthwhile. He composed himself as best he could. Tears still stained his eyelids red, and yet he managed to calm himself. For Maggie's sake he had to win today, even if it was the hardest battle he would ever fight.

Deagan climbed back up the stairs of Duke Worth's manor, swung open the great wooden doors to Duke Worth's hall and entered a large room with windows looking out on the countryside. Deagan's old friend, Sir Luthan standing off to the side greeted him with a nod as Deagan stepped forward onto the large red carpet. A fireplace burned on the far wall behind the Duke's chair. The king would have killed him if he'd had the audacity to call it a throne. Duke Worth had made himself a miniature of the king's own throne room. It was less grand, but upheld the same aesthetic.

The duke was standing with his hands behind his back, looking out the window. He wore a rich silk tunic held at the waist with a belt of white leather—one of the marks of knighthood that would soon be stripped from Deagan. *No. Not if I can help it,* Deagan thought. He straightened and approached the Duke's left side. He kept his distance, and bowed. "M'lord," he said.

"Hello Sir Deagan, I trust you are well?" The Duke did give him the service of a handshake after his prolonged bow.

"Aye, Lord, I'm well enough. And how is m'lord fairing?" Deagan had ruffled Duke Worth's feathers before with his lack of formality, but had no desire to do so now.

"I am well," the duke said flatly. "Deagan, I know that Luthan has told you why we are meeting tonight, yes? Indeed. As I understand it, he put some sense of hope into you regarding my decision, but . . . well I see a very real weakness in your judgment. An unacceptable weakness."

The word weakness was like a knife in Deagan's heart. He felt the weight of his belly and neck. Indeed he was weaker than he once was. He thought of Maggie and grew determined once more to see this through with integrity and to fight the decision if he could. "M'lord, can we not start this conversation with a list of all your woes against me? I'm powerful certain I could put your mind at ease if given the chance."

The Duke stared back at him blankly, showing his age all the more due to the lifeless expression that he wore. Sir, Luthan sat to the side, with his eyes downcast, his arms wrapped tightly around himself, his face red. "I don't believe the onus is on us at this point to prove anything. I believe the onus is on you." He sat in silence, fixing Deagan with that lifeless stare as the candlelight flickered off of his bald forehead, Deagan thought desperately, but had no answer. Had the Duke even asked a question?

"Look out this window, Deagan," said the duke. The window was little wider than an arrow slit, but afforded one of Darkwell's finest views. The duke's manor was built directly into the city wall, as some of the older, and grander buildings were. It had been something of a defense tower, though it could not be seen from outside the city. The arrow slit opened out to a view of the countryside. There were humble peasant's cottages lit with dim radiance in the fields around the city. There was a red clay road, the West road that led into the forest where a lumberyard still operated under the watch of a thousand soldiers. The stars shone out over the hills. Directly below the window was the foul water of the moat. Far out at the edge of sight was the looming jungle. These days those woods would be too dangerous to travel unguarded, even within the sight of the city.

The Duke went on, "Do you see that far rim of jungle, Deagan? When I was young it was nothing but farmland all the way from here to Haven. As a boy I made the journey by myself without a second thought. That *thicket*," he spat the word, "was once civilized and safe. It was once *ours*. There were actual *people* there, working, building, living like they were meant to under the protection of Darkwell and its king. Why then has all this changed? All that stands between the darkness and this city is the knighthood. You understood that once. Why have you forgotten? What you did in the Border Lands was unforgivable."

All he wanted to do was yell at them, to tell them that they couldn't do this to him, that it was unfounded and unjust. He wanted to tell all the tales of his valor and heroism, but they all faded from memory and all he could see was the hopelessness of the situation before him, and the disapproving gaze of his superiors.

Then he thought of Maggie and he remembered some scrap of his courage. He squared up to face the Duke. "I have been a loyal servant to his majesty for the last fifteen years. I've bled on his majesty's battlefields. I've slept out in his majesty's rain. I am not so much younger that I can't remember those days as well, when the children ran free where now they be menaced by dark forces. And I *have* stood between the darkness and this city—aye—and without faltering." His voice grew weaker as he saw how utterly unmoved the Duke truly was. If anything, the older man's contempt grew.

"I am a good knight, my lord. I . . ." Trying to show courage, he looked into the Duke's face again; what he saw there was unyielding authority. "I . . ." He looked to Luthan, and saw nothing but disappointment and some inner anguish, that Luthan had never shown before. "I think . . ." he sighed. "I think I see the way this ends. Tell me what I must do, lords. You'll be wanting my sword back I should guess." He started undoing his belt of white that held the king's sword. He removed the gold chain.

"Stop, Deagan," The Duke said, looking as disgusted as a king who visits the dungeon to witness the suffering that he has ordered upon his own people. "Finish these details with Luthan. I must step out now for I have other business that demands my attention." He was looking over Deagan's shoulder.

Deagan turned around and saw one of King Malagor's advisors. A newer one named Jatham Holmin with a bald, shining head. The man was a coward and Deagan cursed himself for having forgotten his place once or twice in order to tell him so. He was a coward, but he was shrewd and he was close to the king. Jatham had a smug look on his face. Clearly he knew what was happening to Deagan and did not mind at all. It had been Jatham that ordered the raid in the Border Lands. Jatham who Deagan had disobeyed.

Duke Worth rose so quickly that he seemed fearful to keep Jatham waiting. "Good evening, Deagan." He marched away with the bald adviser.

Luthan stood and offered Deagan his hand, but Deagan couldn't look his old brother-in-arms in the face as he clasped it. Without the weight of his sword or his chain, and also lacking the white belt that used to slap his knees as he walked, Deagan felt somehow freed. All the duties and oaths that had kept him on the borders of misery for the last year were finally broken. He knew he'd been pushing against his oaths when he acted so rashly in the Border Lands, but at that time the crisscrossing scars on his back from the duke's whip were aching again, and his allegiance to the crown was as threadbare as an old tunic.

Luthan's hand stopped Deagan on his way out the door. Deagan turned. There were tears in Luthan's red eyes, and his bearded mouth struggled to stop trembling. In his fist was Deagan's sheathed sword and he firmly punched his knuckles wrapped around its hilt, into Deagan's breastplate, over his heart. "*This* is still yours," he said. Did he mean the heart or the sword?

"I can't take this Luthan. It was never truly mine. It was made in the king's smithy and meant for the king's armory."

"Aye, it was crafted in the king's forge, but it was *made* on the battlefield, no other can wield this, Deagan. You are a good man."

"Thank you," he breathed as he took the sword.

"If there is anything I can do to aid you, lad. Only ask and I'll give you all I can." Deagan smiled at him and got the hell out of there.

"**I**'VE ALREADY TOLD YOU *the truth of it Lord Saxus," the towerman in the steel cap replied, his voice echoing off of the walls of the throne room. Guards lined both sides of the hall in perfect discipline, their armor utterly black except for the golden tower that marked their breastplates, and the golden stars that adorned their large rectangular shields. Even their faces were completely obscured by black wire mesh that covered the tower shaped opening, through which they motionlessly watched the throne room.*

The hall was large and square with high windows allowing yellow sunlight into the chamber illuminating walls decorated with tapestries depicting agrarian scenes—picturesque farm fields woven in thread of gold, rich blues, and deep greens—and around the top of the walls marched an endless parade of livestock, relief carved into marble friezes. The walls were painted with labyrinthine patterns that reminded Saxus of the arithmetic of bookkeeping and the elegance of well-tilled earth.

Royal Lord Saxus was not descended from kings, but from farmers. It was through agricultural innovation and success that his family in the ancient past had accomplished the construction of Haven, which sprang up around their magnificent farmlands piece by piece; first a market and a granary, then tradesmen and lesser farmers, builders and entertainers flocked to the promising young community. With the expanding wealth of the Saxus line, they were able to acquire, tame and claim lordship over the vast fertile valley surrounding Haven, declaring their descendents for all time to be the Royal Lords of Haven, for no mythological reason such as the divine right, but rather because they had so much wealth that no one dared to argue with them. This all happened a thousand years gone, and so of course no one alive today thought it at all strange that the ability to succeed at farming had resulted in a millennium-long dynasty of rulers.

Kein Saxus sat upon his throne, clean shaven and middle aged in a light linen tunic that kept him cool in the jungle heat. He was accompanied by several of his esteemed advisors, who sat nearby in lesser seats made of wood and carved to resemble implements and tools used in gardening and raising animals. One such seat was empty, though—the seat of Lord Othar. Lord Othar often preferred to stand during court and that was why his chair was empty. The newest addition to Haven's council, a fidgety man with much to say, was dressed in a black tunic and green leggings and a white fleece hung about his shoulders.

There was also, old Lord Hardeen, who would ascend to the throne if the unmarried and childless Kein Saxus should unexpectedly die. Kein hated the thought, for Hardeen was far too ambitious, and would no doubt muck things up, as was his tendency within his own household. Beside him sat Lord Himmon Burra, a trusty vassal, and good knight, and on the far side sat Lord Death, who insisted that it was in fact pronounced DEETH, but at opportune moments, Kein found it amusing to forget that.

"If Your Lordship doubts the man, why not send a small troop to investigate?" suggested Lord Othar in response to the testimony of the pleading towerman. "Perhaps ten or twenty could ride out and find the answer to our riddles and return with more . . . reliable tidings." A look of dread colored the kneeling towerman's face.

"Yes," Saxus replied, "Make it so. I'll hear no more unsubstantiated legends in this court today. You are all dismissed." First Guard Androth's boots rang on the floor as the knight crossed over to the towerman in his blue tabard and silvery steel armor to escort him from the throne room. The towerman quaked at the mere proximity of Androth in the black armor, with no face save a black mask, and he did not tarry as he gave his final bow and marched briskly from the chamber with a black knight on his heels. When the man was finally gone, Saxus noticed a change in posture in the rest of his royal guards; they breathed easy, as they often did when no one but the royal lord and his advisors were present. Even their relaxed state still looked like utter discipline compared to most guards, and that made Saxus proud.

The advisors stretched, stood up, or bent over a parchment to record the notes from the day's happenings. A good farmer keeps good records, and that tradition had carried on for ages in the throne room of the royal lords of Haven. Always a scribe bent scribbling on vellum or parchment with a pile of fresh quills in front of him.

First Guard Androth did not pause for a break, but instead walked straight to Saxus and kneeled before him. "Rise, Guard," Saxus said. "I've no more need of these advisers, but wish to speak with Othar in private. Have your guards see these counselors safely home and you alone will remain to stand watch in this chamber."

Androth nodded, stood and spun to face the other guards. With a series of gestures, but not a word spoken, the guards were all organized, two with each council member and silently escorting them to their chambers. Androth alone remained, and as was the custom of the guards, stood still and silent, close to the door once it was closed and barred behind them.

Lord Othar sat down at last, but not in his own chair, in the chair beside the royal lord. "What would Your Grace require of me, Royal Lord?" he asked.

"This business with the dead men . . . I just don't know if we are safe. Sooner or later something must be done. And when that time comes the people will look to me for the solution."

"And if that day comes then you shall have it." The dark clad man replied.

"I wish to be seen to be doing something about this. Perhaps that will buy us time." Saxus declared with confidence he wished he felt.

"The key, Lord Saxus is your Dragon Riders. They could solve this little disturbance in a heart beat, but that is not what Your Greatness desires, is it?" he purred.

"No," Saxus admitted, rubbing at the stubble on his chin. "No it's not."

Lord Othar looked at the guard who by now had become nothing more than a fly on the wall to Saxus. "Are you certain we can trust this guard, My Lord?"

"Othar! Don't be ridiculous! They are all sworn to silence, sworn to the Cloud Tower, and completely loyal. Androth here is my most trusted one of them all, the chief of them in fact. You need not fear the Royal Guards, lest you be an enemy of mine," Saxus added with a cocky chuckle.

"Very well," Othar said, unconvinced. "Your key is the Dragon Riders. Send them out on a mission of indeterminate duration, post them in a neighboring city, send them to survey the far north. Anything to keep them occupied and show the people that their lord is doing something about the issue." It seemed well to Kein. Soon he would have what Othar had promised him and this would all be over.

"With all due respect, Your Grace, I would much prefer if you would send this guard away," Othar complained, itching at his arm.

"Othar, you overstep your bounds!" Saxus laughed. "The guard stays. At any rate, I will send for the chief of the Riders and let him know that he will be moving his force to Darkwell . . . for extra defense, let us say. It always did cheer the commoners to see the muster of the dragons above the city."

"Quite," Othar said, still glancing at the expressionless mask of the guard by the door. "I have never seen it with my own eyes."

"Guard," Saxus boomed. "Get Oscar." The black-clad figure nodded and left the room. "Don't know what it is you fear with the royal guard, Othar. When you're not in front of the other advisors you're a hopeless coward sometimes."

The great doors swung open and in strode a tall, elder knight along with the first guard. His white mustache was crisp and clean, and his thin white hair flared out at his ears and at the nape of his neck. He was thin and fit for his age and he wore a long tunic emblazoned with a red dragon breathing fire, a short sword hung from his belt. He was one of the few who Kein Saxus allowed to carry steel in his presence for he had been a staunch defender of Haven for over fifty years.

"Your Grace," he said bowing to Saxus.

"Sir Oscar," Saxus greeted.

Then the Dragon Rider turned to Guard Androth with a smile, and said, "I have never seen your face, nor heard your voice, but nevertheless

I have seen your work with a spear and it is truly unequaled. Would that you could train my men even for one hour." He clasped Androth's steel-clad upper arm and gave the guard a friendly punch to the breastplate, a greeting, one great warrior to another. Androth nodded slightly as the older man walked past and approached the throne, ultimately coming to a crisp stop and genuflecting humbly with his arms out to his sides.

"Sir Oscar!" Saxus said, "Rise, Sir and stand tall as the honored guest of this throne room that you are."

"Too kind, too kind, Your Grace."

"Not at all. I have a plan laid out for you. Would you like to hear it?"

"Most eagerly, My Lord," Oscar replied.

"You will muster all the Riders and take them on patrol. Search the Western Shore for signs of trouble, then report to Darkwell to bolster our ally's defenses for a time. I will send for you when and if you are needed back here in Haven."

"Uh . . . understood, My Lord." Sir Oscar said. Lord Othar, was watching everything intently, most of all the guard by the door. "When must we depart?" Oscar asked. "And will there be arrangements made for provisions and roosting space for the mounts? I daresay the city of Darkwell is crowded enough already."

Saxus was uncertain. He stammered for a moment before he looked quickly to Lord Othar whose sharp, impatient nod, spurred Saxus to answer the question, "Yes, yes of course."

Androth twisted the long spear, grinding the butt of it into the dusty stone, which made a gritty sound. Othar lunged forward, "My Lord, I must again request that this guard be placed outside the door or dismissed entirely for the day."

Saxus considered for a moment and Sir Oscar turned with a surprised look to laugh at the absurdity of the suggestion and shake his head, but Saxus said, "I simply refuse to send away my bodyguard, Lord Othar. That is the end of it."

Othar's eyes were locked on the guard's mask. "I need assurance that this man won't repeat any of what he has heard or seen. I need absolute proof." Saxus buried his face in his hands in embarrassment. Would this paranoid coward never cease? Lord Othar's face moved and twitched with a dark intensity in his eyes as his mind raced underneath. "A ha! I know just the thing," Othar said.

"Finally, some way to put your anxious mind at ease. What is it?" Saxus asked.

"Order him to take his mask off."

Saxus saw the black helmet move back and forth minutely, saying no.

"And how will that—"

"Once I see his face, My Lord. He will know to keep silent." There was a threat in Othar's deep tone.

"Othar, the guards are sworn to silence as I have already explained, their only interest is to keep me alive and maintain the safety of Cloud Tower. They have no political ambitions, no one to talk to even if they did. Why, Androth here has seen and heard many of my dealings, and my most embarrassing moments. Let it be enough that I trust the royal guard even if you do not."

"Of course you do," Othar said, "But you are right, I don't. If they are as honorable as you think, then it would be nothing at all for this one to take off his mask and show his face, for he will never tell a soul and therefore nothing will ever come of it." Othar was trying to sound reasonable, humble even.

"Othar, please let this go," Saxus said, and was glad to see Sir Oscar nodding fervently in agreement.

"I am afraid I cannot, My Lord." Othar said sharply. "I don't feel I will be able to help you any further unless I have some assurance of security."

"Won't be able to help me? What nonsense."

"If that is the way Your Grace feels, I'm afraid I must be going," Lord Othar took three steps to the door.

"Is that a threat?" Saxus asked incredulously.

"No." Lord Othar replied turning to point at the royal guard, "but he is."

"Wait, sit down," Saxus said and a look of victory began to form around the corners of Othar's mouth. This man with such big talk was as needy as a child. Of course how well did Kein really know the guards? Perhaps it wouldn't hurt to put a little fear into this one to put Lord Othar's mind at ease. "Guard Androth, forgive me. But nothing ill will come of this since I trust you completely and I know you'd never speak a word of this to anyone. Go ahead. Remove your helm."

Oscar the Dragon Rider breathed a sigh of regret, sucked his teeth and gave Othar a look of contempt, which the intent man ignored as he worried the fleece upon his shoulders with his bony fingers. The guard hesitated for a moment, but could not disobey a direct order from the Royal Lord, as humiliating as it may be. Placing the long spear against the wall, Androth pressed both gloved hands onto either side of the polished black helmet, lifting it free.

Oscar gasped, Saxus nodded, looking at the other two, and Othar's face brightened into a smile of triumph, releasing several clucks of laughter. Saxus had seen the guard's face before and was therefore not surprised, but the other two were shocked. Othar edged around his table and came close, presumably to inspect the knight more thoroughly or perhaps to gloat.

"What is your name, guard? Your true name."

"Enough!" Saxus bellowed. "You've had your wish, now let us return to business. Androth, put your mask back on and let's have done with this foolishness."

"No matter," Othar said quietly. "I will find the day of your induction to the order in the books of the scribes. I will find your true identity. And I'll learn about your family, oh yes, friends if you have any, lovers . . . I trust no ill will come of this, will it guard Androth?"

The black mask turned to stare Othar full in the face, and Saxus supposed that the muscles under that armor were poised to draw a weapon and kill the man. Though no indication of this tension was evident on the surface of the steel shell, Othar stepped back with alarm as though he felt the animosity nonetheless.

"Sir Oscar, until your Dragon Riders depart one week from today, keep yourself out of the Lower Quarters will you?"

"May I ask why, Royal Lord?"

"It is not your place to do so," Lord Othar replied.

"You are dismissed, Dragon Rider," Saxus said. Having received his orders he turned away. As he walked by, the old knight gazed deep into Androth's mask, trying to see through the wire mesh, then becoming aware of his staring, the honorable Dragon Rider broke his gaze with a forced smile and hurried out of the room without a word.

T HE SMELL OF SMOKE drifted in through the white curtained windows as Kellen sipped his tea. He sat on a round backed chair and gazed out the window into the town square that held the fountain—the meeting place where he had expected his head caravaner two hours before. He filled the small porcelain teacup with more steaming water. Where the devil was Jorn Kahorne?

The square was full of oil lanterns that glowed in the night. A few city guards wandered around the square, but as if they were ghosts, they went in and out of focus as they passed through the pools of light, trapped in their cyclical duties, but longing for something more.

A few beggars and refugees littered the cobble stone streets; the planks of wood that made their meager roofs rattled slightly in the evening wind. Kellen had chosen this spot not only for watching the square, but also for thinking, though he was finding the task more difficult than ever, being so shaken at the disappearance of his finest minion.

I really shouldn't think of them as minions, should I? But what could have happened to him? I'm sure that he had enough guards with him. No one has reported any large bands of evil roaming the road to the city of Haven lately. Where is that blessed wagon driver? If anything happened to him, then something must have happened to the rest of them, and the shipment. Of course my people are more important than the shipment, but still, it's never good to have missing cargo.

Kellen wasn't the sort to worry much about things he couldn't change. He liked to keep charging onward no matter what was chasing him. But if those men all lost their lives doing his bidding . . . He put the thought from his mind. He was still waiting for Jorn. Jorn was late, not dead.

Or what if his men stole the cargo and remained in Haven? Kellen didn't think so because he paid his men well and Jorn best of all. You can steal cargo once and get away with it, and yes you'd get rich enough to gamble to your heart's content or pursue whatever earthly pleasures the Great Cities could offer you—for about a month. After that you'd be either working or stealing again. But still, what if they had stolen the cargo and Jorn wasn't coming here at all? He'd have them all thrown in the dungeon, that's what. And Jorn, who of all Kellen's loyal minions—er—employees should *know better*, would be thrown in the darkest one.

An old woman refreshed Kellen's tea, but he didn't think he could stomach any more of it. His tongue was already throbbing from the bitterness. Then a figure stumbled out from the east entrance of the square and lurched forward until he reached the fountain, where he slumped to a seated position. His leg was stiff, his arm looked broken.

Kellen's heart leapt and so did the rest of him. He left the tea shop and rushed out to the square. He could see that it was a man dressed in travelling clothes. He got closer still and saw that it was indeed one of his men, but not Jorn.

"Beam!" he said when he reached the wagon driver. "Are you all right? Where's Jorn? Good Gods *look* at you! What happened, Beam?"

"Oh, it was dreadful, sir." The man's body was wracked with a horrible coughing fit. Blood spotted his pale lips.

"We must get you to the barber's, my good man. Up with you now!" He lifted Beam gently and started to guide him through the streets. "Where are the others, Beam?"

"They didn't make it, sir," he said through wet sobs. Blood dripped out of his mouth and he grew heavier on Kellen's shoulder.

"Hold on, man! You're going to be fine! What happened?"

"Tram ... pled ..." he breathed as he fell to the ground.

"Help! You damned worthless guards! Can't you see a man is dying? HELP!" The guards came rushing in and helped Kellen carry the man to the nearest barber. A cylindrical sign of red and white stripes marked the barber's shop. The guards took their leave and Kellen went inside hollering for the proprietor to come and assist him at once.

The barber's chambers were like a dungeon. And Kellen hated bothering barbers at night. They were bad enough in the day, but at night, the jars of potion and the bowls of leeches took on an extra patina of nastiness that almost made one's scream-and-run reflex go off unexpectedly.

"Easy old boy," Kellen breathed as he placed a damp cloth on Beam's forehead. Don't try to speak just yet." The worst part was the waiting. Why couldn't Elbor just wake up and save a man's life like he was supposed to?

Kellen felt something tugging at his trouser leg. "Ah!" he cried. He stood up to get away from the rat and hit his head on a cage hanging from the rafter. Behind him, a tray of sharp implements clattered to the dirty floor. The black rat ran under Beam's bed and disappeared. The solitary candle attached to the wall cast many shadows. The cage he had hit still swung back and forth. Beam groaned.

Kellen bent to collect the cutting tools from the tray. "Easy, Beam. It was just a rat. Don't get too excited now. Calm down."

Beam groaned again and started convulsing in his bed. "Easy now lad!" Kellen was by his side in an instant, but he checked under the bed for any rats before he knelt down. Beam was still moving violently when Kellen finally saw why. A two-foot long snake had landed on Beam's chest and was staring him in the eyes. The glow of candles started moving down the stairway heralding the barber's arrival. Another snake dropped out of the sky and onto Beam's leg. Kellen looked up and saw the now open cage swinging in the candlelight, more snakes coiled on top of each other inside. The first snake slithered onto the floor and Kellen shrieked. But the second one stayed there menacing both of them with a hood of scales, stretching out to either side of its head. Kellen heard shuffling footsteps coming down the stairs. "*Get away from there!* Is that you Elbor? *Shoo!*"

An old man's voice answered, "Of course it's me, young master. If you've made a mess of my surgery table it'll be the end of you do you hear?" He laughed four barks of laughter.

"Help us, old man! The snakes are loose!" Kellen replied.

Finally a white haired and bent old man with a peg leg came into the room bringing with him a great deal of light and a sense of hope. He set the candelabrum down and hurried with a *click, click, click,* over to the two men. The snake hissed and lunged for Beam's face, but he moved away just in time. "Gotcha!" cried the barber as he gripped the snake with a pair of tongs. It coiled upon itself and writhed to get away, but he lifted it carefully into the cage and closed the lid.

"Here," he grunted as he dropped the tongs into Kellen's hand. "Go catch the others." Then he set about the healing of the wagon driver.

Kellen went out on the hunt, treading lightly and slowly. Over his shoulder he said, "He said he was trampled, barber."

Elbor held up a curved blade and brought it down close to Beam's throat. The breath caught in Kellen's breast. *Rip!* The front of Beam's tunic flopped open to both sides of the table. There was a large round bruise over his heart. His arm was poised unnaturally in the air and the hand was held up in a quivering claw.

"When did it happen?" Elbor asked.

"I don't know . . . could have been days ago."

Elbor took some leaves from a jar and lit them on fire. He then placed leeches on Beam's chest that affixed themselves happily and began to swell.

"My wiles can sustain him for a short time. After that he will die."

"Please, master barber, you know that I can pay."

Elbor laughed. "I know ye can, son. But, paying *me* won't save his life. Go to the healers and pay *them*. You know as well as I that they deal in more than silver, though." Kellen gulped. "If you'd save his life, get the healers. I'll tend him such as I may. Ride, my boy! But do not assume this man will live."

*D*EAGAN ROSE BEFORE THE *sun. He carried buckets of water up the banks of the stream and into the war camp for the others in order to pass the time. On his third trip to the main camp he was no longer able to resist his temptation. Deagan suffered from a constant urge for food that had left him in his current pudgy state. When he passed one of the supply horses on his way back to the stream, he opened the small jar of honey that they had brought with them and unearthed a paddy of butter. He gorged himself on a mixture of the two of them as he huddled by the larder. When he heard other soldiers stirring in the morning air, he got rid of the stuff as quickly as he could, back into the saddlebags they came from. He stood up and his stomach bulged as if it held a stone. As usual, the food he had eaten still didn't satisfy him. He went back to carrying water, the bags under his eyes were dark and felt heavy after a sleepless night. His back felt like it was on fire.*

In time, the whole camp awoke and broke down the tents. Most of these soldiers had been city guards with a minimum of combat experience and had never seen war. In fact, Deagan was the only belted knight in the company. The next most experienced leader among them was a warrior in the king's service for eight years. Korvis had ridden against the darkness before, but never at the head of the charge. He was still young.

"Sir Deagan," Eli called to him. "It is a good day to die, wouldn't you say?" It was a common warrior's greeting, or at least non-warriors thought so for it was used often enough in the plays and the puppet shows of the streets.

"Eli, let us hope that it is good enough for our foes, but let's you and I keep waiting for fairer weather." The knight tightened Maggie's bellyband then turned to Eli in full. "Make me a promise, lad."

The boy seemed taken aback, "What would you ask me to promise, sir knight?"

"Swear that you will live by chivalry."

"What is that, m'lord?"

"If your enemy drops his shield, you drop yours. If the enemy drops his sword, give it back to him. Do you follow?" Eli nodded. Deagan grabbed Eli's breastplate from under the armpits and pulled him so their noses were an inch apart. Into Eli's eyes, he said, "And if your enemy is a good man, well maybe he's no enemy after all."

Eli was frightened. "Aye m'lord. I understand."

"You understand better than that Duke Worthless," Deagan spat. The knight released him and went back to readying Maggie's barding, "I'd not fight beside a man who did not uphold chivalry. Stay with me. The rest of these soldiers care for nothing but power and cruelty. They aren't evil quite, but the king sent them on this mission for a reason and me with them. I don't yet know why—other than to dishonor me, on a common raid when I should be out fighting the real enemy."

"Deagan. Eli. Good Morning." It was Korvis sitting all armored upon his mount. "The men are all but ready. We ride as soon as all are horsed and gathered." His face was not like those of the other fighting men. He'd seen war, and this wasn't it. He turned away from them and gave the word to the rest.

Soon the company was underway and they rode down one of the king's roads. They needed to be wary; these roads were no longer safe, but a number such as theirs and armed so bristlingly could at least fight their way through to the other side of any trouble that arose.

After half a day's ride, the jungle birds, monkeys and other animals went oddly silent. The dusty air grew thick with humidity and the sky darkened rapidly.

Plink!

A raindrop splashed off of Deagan's helmet.

Plink! Plink! Plink!

Soon the rain was falling in sheets. Later, when they reached their turning point, Deagan and Korvis nodded to each other at the front of the group and turned the entire company into the jungle and off of the road. There was an unmarked track there leading away from the road and up a hill. It was difficult to see, overgrown as it was with leaves and shrubs. It was slow going. Finally it became so dense that they had to walk their horses that were slipping with every step on the bright red mud.

By day's end they had halted at a massive tree that blocked the sloping roadway. They were close to their destination anyway so the obstacle didn't bother them much. It gave them some cover from he rain, for it's massive, curling limbs still clung to life, and were sheathed in greenery, straining for sun. Korvis and four others crept up to the top of the ridge and left their horses with the main force.

The rain let up a bit while they were gone and Deagan could not wipe the squinting look of disapproval off of his face. What enemy awaited them at the bottom of the next hill? He hadn't wanted to ask the others since he was higher in rank and station and did not want to show signs of ignorance. But why hadn't he been told? The order was given by the king himself, but it was that rat, Jatham who'd given the plan of attack.

"Rape, pillage and burn!" he had said, "They deserve nothing less."

In Deagan's opinion, if Jatham got what he deserved it would likely involve a noose. Why had he agreed to this march? After a year of pushing boundaries, maybe for once he just wanted to do what he was told. Or maybe he didn't have the will to push back anymore. The scouts returned. One with greasy black hair and thick heavy muscles made it back first. He was well liked by the other soldiers because they thought of him as fearless and experienced. He'd been a jailer for his majesty's dungeon and he'd seen death. Some men would be humbled by it, but others grow prideful.

"Rape, pillage, and burn eh boys?" the jailer laughed. "They won't even see us coming!" The group cheered softly. Deagan had found out that this man's name was Colstin. If this jailer was good for one thing, it was that he could get men's blood up. He looked to Deagan with a crazed, wide-eyed laugh. Deagan only squinted back as torches sprang to life on all sides of him.

The sky over Darkwell was dotted with clouds that were lit from below by the blazing torches and lamps of the streets, and from above by the white moon. The stars sparkled in complete, pure, freshness. It was a new sky for Deagan Wingrat, former knight of the king.

What could he do next? He hardly had the capacity to imagine a future for himself, but the stars, the moon and the clouds held quiet hope. He did not want to cry, he did not want to rage. All there was left for him was to despair and reflect detachedly on the events that got him here.

It was true that the unending demands of his knighthood had become a burden of which he had wished on more than one occasion to rid himself. It was also true that he could think of nothing more comforting or perfect in this moment than to go home to his loving wife and explain everything. Unfortunately Wingrat had never taken a wife, or a wife taken him, and he had no such comfort awaiting him at the cramped chambers he called home. He walked Maggie back to his room where the king gave him shelter in exchange for his service. Luthan had explained that he had a few days before he needed to return his steed or vacate his premises. That he should take his time. But what good was time without an oath to uphold?

The blue-white stars glittered above him and for a span of minutes it was all he could do to hold Maggie's lead rope and stare at them all. He couldn't have said what they meant to him if someone had asked. They were significant. They explained everything.

Maggie stirred in her harness and tossed her head. She had never liked standing still for too long. Neither did Deagan. He walked on, attempting to keep watching the sky.

"Och." he laughed at himself. "Of all my troubles, the worst one is my need for a new belt." He didn't like the way his armor felt, without the added cinching of a well-tied belt—preferably a white one.

He wandered at first. Wasting an hour, then another. No true thoughts occurred to him, only impressions. He stopped again to look up at the stars. He was up on one of the refugee platforms now, perched between two blocks of stone towers. From here he could see the king's tower in the center of Darkwell, with its torch lit parapets and its glowing arrow slits. He could also see the dark rim of the high city wall that blocked the lowest stars by creating a man-made horizon. Perhaps from the top of King Malagor's spire, in the center of the city, he could see all the stars at last. Such was the benefit of being a king, but Deagan would still crane his neck if he wanted to look upon the levels of the city where he would never dwell or the barriers over which he would never see.

He'd long dreamed of a day when no one had to hide behind the walls while legions of Evil could walk freely outside them. For all the goodness of human kind, still they couldn't band together enough to mount a true offensive against the darkness. King Malagor was too busy with his 'rebels'. Everyone had something more pressing, some excuse. That was why as Deagan gazed up at the sky, he knew that only that small portion of it encircled in the wall was truly his. Only the circle of sky owned and protected by the king had ever belonged to him or to any other knight, for the other stars could only be seen when camping in the wild. And that often meant sleepless anticipation of ambush.

Deagan didn't want it to be that way. He had visions of becoming a warlord and taking back the land from the darkness, but those were only boyish fantasies. Black smoke was rising in the north.

Deagan stopped at his room to collect a small barrel of beer that he'd been saving for a special occasion. He might not have a wife, but he did have a friend. He tied up the barrel, and rode out into the streets heedless of any onlookers.

BEAM WAS STANDING IN the gray swaying grasses of an endless rolling plain. No trees were in sight, only the lifeless grass under a billowing gray sky. He looked down at himself. His tunic was unharmed and clean as it had never been before, but the grayness of the grass moved forward from his surroundings and into the fabrics of his clothes. The colors were muted, but everything was clean.

He looked around him at the vast meadow country. The last thing he remembered was the barber's surgery bed. A snake had fallen on him. Then all was pain. But there was no pain here. All that existed around him beside the warm breeze and the dark clouds and the landscape, was a pile of black rags behind him and far away. He could only see the rolling dark shape from the corner of his eye. He tried to look closer, but everything inside him seemed to want him not to, so he ignored it. He walked for several minutes through the soothing country of his death.

The black shape was closer now. Still as in a nightmare, he couldn't look right at it. This was not supposed to be a place of fear. It was supposed to be a place of peace. Yet he feared that shape, not knowing what it was. The pile of rags drew closer still and when he looked away, he was certain it would leap on the back of his neck and seize him with cold oozing fingers.

He ran. Looking back, the now vivid shape was closer. It rose up from the ground forming the figure of a man, but lacking a mouth. Instead its eyes drooped down its entire face. Its eyeballs were elongated and slimy. The skin that should have been eyelids hung loose, revealing red flesh beneath. Beam ran faster, but the shape was beyond speed, it was beyond escape.

Beam turned again and the face loomed directly over his shoulder. "No!" he screamed.

Then he turned again and the slippery pile of rags was back on the ground, a puddle of wavering dark cloth. He wasn't running anymore. That flabby, oozing face bubbled to the surface of the rag pile and it held such terror and wrongness that he couldn't move or look away.

You can undo your crimes, said a voice in his head.

"What crimes? I've done nothing."

You can be forgiven if you come with me, the voice persisted.

"I have nothing to be forgiven for. I have been both honorable and true!"

The face grew angry and the pile of rags surged forwards. *Fall into me. You will begin anew. The weight of your crimes will make you burn forever in this place. I will free you.*

There was a burning in Beam's throat so intense that he thought it might kill him. Smoke rose from his mouth and even the vapor burned his eyes. A pressure on his back grew. Was he lying down? "No, you have the wrong man!" he said in protest, trying to hold the rag-monster at bay only to find that the death country was gone and pain of life had returned.

When he opened his eyes he was looking at Kellen Wayfield squeezing his hand tightly with a concerned look on his face, an old hag, quietly corking a bottle, and a very frightened looking barber.

T HE SENSATION OF A torch passing in close proximity to your head is almost like living an entire day. The heat and the light pass from one side to the other and when they are gone they leave you cold and blind. There were men rushing past him. Already the charge had begun. Deagan carried no torch; he only mounted Maggie and blew her a kiss to urge her through the dense jungle. Stalwart as ever, the warhorse bore him forth, a tall sentinel amid a sea of shorter figures that stalked up the rise and crested the ridge. The rest of the men left their horses behind because they were not trained to remain calm in battle as Maggie was—the king had not seen fit to supply this raid with any of his best horse, nor his best men for that matter.

The gray glow of the sky outlined the nearby ridge, and red firelight gave the trees their shape as men passed below their twisted branches. A muffled roar rose before them. The men in front had made themselves known with a war cry, "MALAGOR!" he heard. "FOR THE KING!" Deagan could not yet see the enemy, but clearly those in front were already engaged in battle.

He kicked Maggie to a trot and she powered up to the top of the hill to finally crest it and look down upon a downward slope that led to the enemy camp. There were low stone huts, and many old decrepit stone fences. The windows of the huts were aglow with firelight, but there were no combatants in sight. The only soul he could see other than those he came with was a woman running into a cottage carrying a basket. No doubt the men believe she is one of the so-called witches, he thought bitterly.

The knight rode down the hill and quickly gained on the mass. They could rush in like fools, but Deagan would take a wider view, seeking signs of ambush, evaluating the enemy. The warlord in him sprang closer to the surface, but he did not yet seek to take charge, only to aid, watch, and see. Perhaps they were fools, but it was still Deagan's responsibility to keep as many of them alive as he could. Chivalry.

Maggie's hoof beats thundered through the center of the village. There was a larger building in the center of the town. He rode close by it on the right side and he saw into three windows in quick succession. The first two windows showed him different views of the same room lit by candles and the glow of a fireplace. His first glimpse told him there was a sizable group inside, peasants. The second window showed him that there were both men and women, and they were reacting to the raid they were now sieged by, some looked worried, some cried while others tried to maintain order or make a plan. The third window, the final open one, was on the second floor, and it showed him the face of a woman. She was handsome and gray haired, lean, beautiful, and strong. The light from the fireplace behind her made some loose hairs glow like a halo. There was no fear in her face. She stared the knight in the eyes and slammed the shutters closed.

Deagan circled around behind the building. He had still seen no armed combatants, but behind the woman . . . hadn't he seen the glint of steel in the corner of the room? He couldn't be sure. He rode around the back and past the other side of the building, but the windows were already shuttered, and he could see no more than the glow of the fires. A small wooden door interrupted the rear wall of the building. The hinges were on the outside. He found a nearby handcart full of wooden poles and dismounted long enough to brace that door shut.

He looped around the entire village spying the perimeter of the jungle that encircled the cluster of buildings, and saw no sign that anyone was outdoors to oppose them. All he had to do was reconvene with the others, secure the area and capture one cottage at a time. And he mused that he'd need to gag all the women to assure his company that they'd not fall prey to witchery.

By now Maggie was blowing great steaming clouds out of her nose as she surged through the rain. She leapt a low fence and brought Deagan back in sight of the charging men on foot. Deagan watched as a torch flew through the air and landed on the thatch of one of the huts. "NO!" Deagan roared.

A man was holding the door to a cottage closed and another guarded the window. Another torch flew. And another. Deagan found Korvis. "Hail, brother! Bring men to secure the large building. Hold the doors shut. Burn NOTHING! Do you hear me? Nothing! And it should only take three men to hold each cottage, but get twenty for the big one!" He'd spent as much time as he could. Now it was time to control the men.

Screams tore from the cabin. Flames grew as they fed upon the grasses. Most of the men stood about watching the fire, holding their torches in trepidation, but those who had already engaged themselves to holding the cottage shut were still holding strong. Deagan moved toward the fire.

He passed an open door with movement inside. He was startled, but remained calm. Inside the door was a tall muscular man whose hands were at his waist. Was he loosening his belt? The door swung shut and a woman screamed.

He kept on toward the fire. To his left a group of men were advancing on another cabin torches raised. They had secured it similarly to the first. "Stop!" Deagan ordered. "Do you not see that they're unarmed?"

One of the men looked back at him, abashed and lowered his weapons. Even as Deagan thought he had gained some control, another man yelled, "Ye're not in charge here! The king's man was clear enough! They're evil! Rape, pillage and BURN!" He threw the torch on the roof and others followed him, setting two more cottages ablaze. Deagan wheeled Maggie around to see a fourth cottage ignite, its inhabitants screaming.

Beside him, Deagan saw Eli, sword drawn and turning about as if enemies swarmed him from all sides. Deagan dismounted, grabbed the bar across Eli's helmeted face and pulled him until their helmets clashed. "Do you see any combatants here?" Deagan yelled.

"N-no, sir."

"Then sheathe. Your. SWORD!"

The barrel of ale sloshed happily on Deagan's shoulder. Such somber memories shouldn't trouble him now. If possible he would try and celebrate, but he would settle for plain old company if he must. He tied Maggie to the post, for at last, he had reached Kellen's manor.

Having needed some way to keep both his sword and his trousers up, Deagan now wore a belt of thick rope. He knocked at the door and felt bad that Rory would need to wake up in order to let him in. Or would he? Though it was late, many lights were lit, and a loud ruckus drifted from the windows.

K ELLEN COLLAPSED ONTO HIS bed in the middle of the
night. He had just said his last farewell to Beam, the
caravan driver that he had tried to save. Unbidden
shivers still jumped down his spine from the brief and unsettling
interaction, he'd had with one of the Healers. Clearly the hag was
no longer fully a part of this world, for her eyes wandered into other
unseen realms . . . and she spoke to things. Even Kellen would berate
an inanimate object from time to time. But the Healer hag not only
spoke to things, but also listened. He had tried to charm her, and
perhaps he had made her feel somewhat girlish again, but his tricks
would do no good. She simply would not do him a favor and work
for free.

"*I can't make him live again, trader,*" she had said. "*Not for one such
as you who forgets so easily to pay his debts. Hush, little trinket, I know
what I'm about.*"

He had hoped that the healer wouldn't know about him, about
his history with the Healers' order. He finally swallowed his pride
and admitted defeat; the hags were his last chance. "*Whatever I owe
you . . . double it, just bring him back.*"

"*Something wicked stalks this man. I can't bring him back for you
Davis Keel. He knows I'm not interested in coin, trinket, yes.*"

"*That's not my name*"

"*Neither is Kellen Wayfield,*" she said with a revolting grin, looking
first in Kellen's eyes then back down to the strange doll she called trinket.
"*I can't make him live, but I can make him stop being dead . . . for a time.
And yes, Keel, consider your debts doubled.*"

Kellen got up and poured himself a goblet of wine. And a second one for Rory, his butler, even though he knew that when the butler refused it, Kellen would drink it anyway.

"Rory, my good man. Wine?" he called down the hallway.

The sharp click of Rory's footsteps accompanied his answering call, "Not tonight, sir, if it is all the same to you." On the word you, the young, healthy and well-dressed butler rounded the corner into Kellen's room. "I thank you for your generosity, however."

You won't be thanking me for my generosity for long, Rory. Kellen thought darkly.

"Do you need anything before I go to my training room for the evening, sir?"

"Not at all, Rory. I can take care of myself for an hour or two." Kellen said this as though he was trying to convince himself that it was true. "You are, as they say . . . a free man."

Rory smiled and gave a quick bow, "Very good."

Kellen's wine glass somehow progressed from full to empty as he thought back to the healer and her pawing, groping hands. His nose filled with the acrid stench of the burning liquid she'd poured into Beam's dead throat. The hag, the barber, and the trader had all fallen silent when Beam's eyes shot open and he drew breath. "*No, you have the wrong man!*" was the first thing he had said.

"*Ask him your questions, trader. He is not long for this realm. And remember the price we agreed on. Your debt may be a heavier one than you think! Two favors, my grandson. Two favors!*" And as her laughter died away Kellen lost track of her. He didn't know if the hag had crept slowly out of the barbershop, or if she had sunk into the very shadows around her.

Kellen walked over to the books on his desk and hiccupped as he opened the most recent of his accounts and thumbed through the yellowed pages of the small book that served as his inventory. Once his quill was inked, he started carefully crossing things out.

"Should I count the horses lost? He didn't say anything about the horses. Well, yes to be prudent I should. I don't know where they are after all and if that doesn't make them lost, what does?" He made a definitive line in his inventory, crossing out an entry that read, *12 horses*. "Hay and grain supplies are still good, though. Proportionally to my fleet of steeds . . . I'd say they're outnumbered by their feed!" He made himself laugh. "Aye, I can certainly *feed* the *steeds*. But who *needs a greedy steed?*"

The barber's hands had started shaking, splattering beeswax onto Beam's bruised chest. Kellen had turned up his nose with a frown. He had to make the most of it. *"Beam? Can you hear me?"*

"Yes I bloody well can, sir. I've got ears haven't I . . . haven't I? I can't feel anything." He had looked as far to the left and right as he could, he even stuck out his tongue to reach for them. He was paralyzed from the neck down.

"What happened to the caravan, Beam? How did you get trampled? Were there any other survivors and where are they now?"

"The sky was dark as we traveled south to meet you, sir. And sturdy though the horses were, they started to jump at the littlest sound. A fell stench arose from amidst our feet and a dense fog twisted towards us from the trees. Laughter, sir. Yes, laughter came rolling in from a realm other than this. We armed ourselves, and drove on into the afternoon. The sounds and the stench followed behind us and when we were in sight of the city wall from the top of the hill called Hagrock, we were beset by creatures both ghastly and strong. Their very will was enough to choke a man's life out. Their very intent was enough to darken your heart, sir. The guards clashed against them, but they were dashed to the ground and the creatures feasted on their still living bodies. In the confusion one of the horses trampled over me, but I was too shocked to feel the pain of it. I tried to get away, but a hand grabbed me by the leg. I hacked off the hand, so quickly in fact that I did not have time to see whose it was. Jorn Kahorne, my own leader, lay handless and deranged, crawling on the ground. His eyes had gone all white and instead of his usual confidence, I could feel from him the same

maddening glow of evil that hovered about the other creatures. He had become one of them. I made it all the way to Darkwell before I realized that his hand still clutched and scratched at my leg, until I pried it off at the city gate. It may be there still, or it may have crawled away. The pain is returning now, sir . . . My chest! Can't breathe!" Kellen still thanked himself for not correcting the man. Technically Beam hadn't been breathing at all since the hag had served him that potion of acid.

Kellen had held Beam's head as the eyelids fluttered one last time. He'd missed seeing him die the first time, so he relished the chance to do so now. *"You were a good man, Beam!"* he'd whispered. He placed a coin on each of his closed eyes and pressed his own sheathed dagger into the man's hand . . .

It was becoming clear. No matter how many times he checked his work, the answer was always the same. He still had two running caravans, one of them was en route to Pillar, the other was waiting for its new cargo so it could sally forth to the same destination as Beam's–Haven, but of course that trip would have to be cancelled. What he had left were two caravans capable of making two or three trips a month. Even if he sold the extra hay and grain, and even if he reduced the number of guards with each caravan, he'd still come to the same end eventually. Kellen never usually had a hard time doing what needed to be done, but this time, he could do nothing but hesitate.

He picked up the goblet for Rory and stopped before taking a sip. Instead he walked out of the room and down the hall. Even the road to Haven was dangerous now—deadly even. Why had he not heard that it was a problem? Come to think of it he hadn't heard anything from Haven at all.

He entered Rory's training room to find him shirtless and lifting himself repeatedly on a steel bar. His muscled body was quite a sight. "You should have been a gymnast, old boy!" Kellen said, setting the wine down on a wooden bench.

"Oh, thank you sir, but I am more than happy to be your butler. Is there anything I can do for you?" He walked over to Kellen and controlled his breathing.

"Well I don't know how to do his, Rory, it's just that . . . it seems the old well has dried up so to speak . . . I mean you've been a damn fine butler, Rory . . . Really you have." Rory nodded graciously. "I just . . . you understand. I'm terribly sorry to have to do this, but I can't seem to find any other way around it. I can barely afford to pay myself these days, let alone continue to live the luxurious lifestyle that I have grown accustomed to. A butler is an expense that I can no longer . . ."

"Not following you, sir," Rory said patiently.

"The north road is closed, Rory."

"Yes, sir? I didn't know."

"And overrun, it would seem, with *evil* forces."

"Yes, sir."

"And, you see, some of my caravans have for the last six years operated solely by traveling that same road to transport rare and exquisite merchandise between us and Haven."

"Indeed, sir."

"And now the caravans are forfeit. And if I understand correctly, my men are now among the ranks of the . . . er . . . *undead.*"

"Oh dear," Rory said, awaiting the point if there was one.

"Blast it Rory you're the best butler in the city . . . I just. I can't afford to pay your wages any longer."

Rory, finally beginning to see the signs, rocked back on his heels and the smile faded from his lips. His posture slouched and he broke his loving eye contact as he furrowed his brow.

"Terribly sorry, my friend, if there is anything at all I can do to help you, only name it and it will be yours."

For a long moment Rory's face appeared to wilt, and tears twinkled in his eyes. He heaved a great breath and then, finally straightened with great energy. He mustered up his resolve and looked Kellen in the eye again. Then in an unprecedented burst of butlery willpower he said, "Very good, sir. I will ready your tea and an evening bath. In the morning we will break our fast with eggy bread and fresh honey. Will that be all, sir?"

Kellen sighed and rolled his eyes, "You don't understand my dear man. I can't pay you. You aren't my butler anymore. It's over—"

"No *you* don't understand!" he took a step forward. "I am a *butler*. My father was a butler. His father before him was a butler back in a time when butlers were unheard of in Darkwell. It is who I am, sir. It is what I am. When I wake up every morning, do I cook and clean and go to the market with the weight of chains upon me? No. When I fold the napkins for your guests to look like little birds, am I thinking about my pay? No. You said it once this evening, sir. And you were right. You told me I was a free man." The tears came back, but not out of sorrow, only out of love. "I always have been." Rory picked up the goblet and drained half the wine. "I will see to your bath, sir."

Kellen was truly moved. "No bath tonight, my friend. Tonight, we celebrate! If you are staying . . . then I am the luckiest man in Darkwell! Huz*zah!* Come here you stiff backed acrobat!" He pulled the younger man into a strong embrace. Laughing, they went up together and tried to finish the wine.

H IS BRIEF FORAY INTO the cold, painful world of the living was over and death took Beam once again. The caravan driver lay in the grassy field, but he couldn't see. There were things on his eyes, heavy and cold. He sat up and two silver coins fell from his face. He clutched them in his hand. In his other hand there was a dagger in its sheath. The grass brushed his face.

He stood up and walked a ways clutching the dagger in one hand and the coins in the other. It was soothing to walk. There was no pain and he felt that he could walk forever. He looked behind him and saw the black pile of rags. It didn't hold the same terror for him since he held the knife and felt ready, but still it seemed wrong that he was not alone. This place was meant for solitude, and the dark shape took that solitude from him. Its very presence violated him. He just kept walking and this time the pile of rags kept its distance. Way ahead, there were two sparkling points of white light upon the field. Without knowing why, Beam smiled to see them and walked closer.

He thought to breathe deeply and enjoy the feeling of clear air in his lungs, but found no need to breathe and that his body was comfortable, full of energy, as if he had already taken a satisfying deep breath, a thirst quenching sip of water, an outstanding night of sleep and a perfectly nourishing meal all at once, but unlike in the living world, these sensations did not fade away. The only thing he did not have was a sense of safety, because the black rag-thing dogged his steps.

As he drew closer, he found they were horses. A white stallion and a white mare they were, unsaddled and unshod. Beam was a horseman in life, and had never seen their equal. His heart grew stronger and richer, just for having seen them. They stared him squarely in his face. Behind them there was a golden archway that housed a strong wooden door.

Was he a warrior? Thought the stallion in Beam's mind.

More likely he was a thief, that dagger was never meant for combat, only for dealing death in the night, replied the mare.

Then how did he find us? Asked the stallion.

Yes, how did he find us?

"I–I–am a caravan driver. My name is Beam. I came from Darkwell. I was killed by a horse, but I came back to the living realm for a time. When I woke up here the second time I had these." He held out the blade and the coins.

The mare tossed her head. *You went back? You should have stayed in the land of the living. We do not want you here.*

Hush, sister. He was brave in life.

"I had no choice," the dead man pleaded. "I was dragged back somehow, it burned my throat."

How did you find us? asked the mare suspiciously.

"I walked freely, with neither map nor track to follow."

This is a warrior's realm. The mead and ale flow freely herein. It is paradise for those who have fallen in battle. Immortal feasting and telling of tales await you if you enter. But why have you come here if you were a caravan driver in life? Thought the stallion in Beam's mind.

Beam looked down at himself and reflected on his life. Now detached from the day-to-day events of life, he watched it play out before his memory as a heroic saga. Each day he rose early to tend the horses. He sacrificed his entire life to the keeping, training, and driving of horses. He never demanded more from a horse than he demanded from himself, and yet at times, a horse would push through a dangerous climb, navigate a deadly cliff for him, or endure the longest drives for him without the slightest complaint. They were brothers in arms. "I have a warrior's heart," he answered confidently. "I suffered no evil to go unchallenged in my presence. I carry steel even now."

The dark rags crept closer.

Then surely you may enter. Step forward. Said the stallion.

Something isn't right, the mare thought as she stepped forward, blocking the door.

Come, sister, he has proven his quality.

No. Do not let him in. She gazed over Beam's shoulder then let out a deafening squeal of anger. *You were followed! You led the enemy to our doorstep! I knew you were not worthy!* Then she reared up and advanced on Beam, her sharp ivory hoofs flailing toward his heart. Beam retreated, but finally she clipped him with her toe, and he fell backward, experiencing the shock of being head-bashed. The light appeared before his eyes and the dizziness came, but there was no pain. He suddenly got the sense however, that he could very certainly be killed, whether he felt the pain or not.

He ran, leaving the door and the horses behind. He was soon lost and tripped on a tussock of grass. Sickened by a sudden presence, he looked around him, feeling violated at his lack of privacy. This was his death after all, and it was very bothersome to have it interrupted. The dark puddle of inky fabric slithered closer. Again the dribbling face surfaced from below.

They turned you away for your wrong doings in life. I am your last chance—the voice thought in his head, but before the monster could finish its sentence Beam lunged at it with the dagger.

"You have ruined me! You have driven me from paradise!" He sunk the dagger into the body of the puddle. For the first time, a flabby, bloody mouth appeared on the face and bit, Beam's arm to the elbow. He screamed in panic, but the flesh and robes of the monster's body soon muffled the sound as he was devoured forthwith, and killed, even in death.

B EAM OPENED HIS DRY eyes. Little bits of light sloped in upon him even though he was in a box on the back of a cart. Though he was oddly numb, his skin felt raw and painful as though he'd been squeezed through a hole, and something didn't make it through the hole with him. His soul was gone. Though he still had no need to breathe, the feeling of satisfaction he had enjoyed in the death world was gone, instead he felt tortured by the lack of air, desperate to drink water, and . . . hungry.

He pushed on the lid. When he tried to speak, only a groan of agony escaped his lips. First he would feed, then he would travel to Haven, see the Master, and receive his orders.

H E WAITED FOR A time then knocked again. This time a clattering rush of footsteps approached the door from the other side and the door was pulled open. Rory grinned at Deagan though posed, somewhat less steadily than usual, in a butler's doorway pose. His lips and teeth were purple from the wine. "Come in Sir Knight, master Kellen would be delighted to see you."

A roar came from Kellen's bedroom, "Make your way up the stairs Sir Deagan! That's it, no time to waste! It is the best night of your life and you've already missed most of it!"

Rory laughed behind him as he trudged up the stairs. "Rory, are you not wearing a shirt, lad?"

"Right you are, Sir Knight," he said giggling. Deagan didn't press the issue.

All he said was, "Ah."

Deagan thumped the barrel on one of Kellen's nice chairs before properly looking up and around. Kellen had tied the curtain out at an angle and stood with one foot raised on the back of a chair. He had tied a cravat over one eye and was just as shirtless as Rory. "Ahoy, matey!" Kellen called out.

Rory fell on the floor laughing. He beat the floor with his fist in protest against the hilarity. A smile wormed its way onto Deagan's tired face. "You make a good pirate, Kellen," said Deagan.

"Oh come now, Deagan we needn't bore Rory with that old story."

"Another night, perhaps," Deagan agreed.

"Avast!" Kellen cried and Rory echoed him, as if to say, *Avast! Can you believe it?* And continued to succumb to the laughter. "Tap that keg, cabin boy, before I become angry and plank the plank with you!"

Rory kept laughing and stumbled out the door. He howled all the way downstairs.

"Well, this is just what I needed," said Deagan, "I've had a dastard of a day." He could not hide the sincerity.

Kellen leapt from his sailboat and ripped off his eye patch. "What are you saying, O Knight? What fate has befallen you?" Kellen grabbed the white chin of Deagan's beard. "But first it is *excellent* to see your fuzzy, ridiculous face, old dog! Have a drink! Cabin boy!" he bellowed down the stairs. "Tap this keg on the double!

"In the mean time . . ." Kellen said as he entreated Deagan with a goblet of wine. Deagan set it down and picked up the whole bottle, one upping him.

He drained a good portion. He wasn't a wine drinker on most occasions, but for crying out loud, Kellen was a pirate again and that called for some extraordinary measures. "In the mean time," Deagan said when he was finished. "Arrrr."

They laughed together late into the night. Deagan began calling Rory a cabin boy as well—as affectionately as possible, of course. Deagan then called Kellen the cabin boy by mistake, which caused an uproar. And by the end of the night they were arguing bitterly (between drinks and between guffaws of laughter) about who really *was* the cabin boy at all? And just *what* were his *duties?*

For the rest of the night, whenever Rory spoke he blinked too much and left his mouth wide open between phrases. This was evidently the way he thought pirates should talk. Deagan closed his left eye and for the life of him could not open it again. Kellen threw him on the bed, and both he and Rory pried his eye apart, but as soon as they released him, it shut again.

Deagan's shirt came off. The three of them sang sea shanties and rocked back and forth in each other's arms. Kellen only stared out to sea from time to time, then gave a crazy look to Deagan and tackled him to the ground yelling, "Abandon ship! Save the cabin boy!"

Rory fell asleep laughing on the floor. And that left Kellen and Deagan to discuss the matters at hand.

Deagan explained the situation of his discharge, "Mayhap my grumbling and complaining finally caught up with me. Of course one of the main things Duke Worth yelled at me about was the raid in the Border Lands. Curse 'em all. If I wanted to go out on raids like that I'd be living out in the wilds with the Gigants and the Wolfmen and all the rest!

"Worth then went on and on about how when he was a boy he could travel from Haven to Darkwell with nothing but his fancy clothes to protect him, and essentially blamed everything that's happened on me!"

Kellen asked, "What do you mean everything that's happened?"

"He pointed to the hills as if it was my fault that the teeming forces of evil were taking over our lands in the first place!"

"I hadn't thought of that, but he might be right," Kellen said sarcastically.

"And Luthan let me keep the sword, but I need to give Maggie back. You know how much I love that horse, Kell." He looked down at the floor and held back his tears.

"Look Deagan, it's not as if you were all that great of a knight," Kellen said conversationally. That certainly got Deagan's attention—so much so that Kellen had to dodge Deagan's thick fingered hand as it reached for the scruff of his neck.

"I mean, you let *me* get away with thievery for years without ever so much as *asking* me to stop!"

"Look, that was a very specific situation. Lots of motives to juggle, and lots of possible . . . buffoonery . . . to sort out. It gets to a certain point when if I *had* said something or thrown you in the dungeon or killed you, then it would have been obvious that I'd known all along and this whole thing would have probably happened a lot sooner."

"But it's stealing, Deagan! Aren't knights of the realm supposed to, I don't know, despise all thieves in the king's domain? Aren't you supposed to disapprove of that sort of cabin boyishness? Ha!"

"Ha. You're practically begging me to turn you in! If it means that much to you, go turn yourself in!"

"No, no, no. I couldn't possibly."

"Besides," Deagan continued. "You were one cabin boy that always had a good reason for doing what you did. You did it, and had a reason. That was what made you not just any thief, but a good thief. You were always somewhat heroic with your burglary weren't you? If it wasn't complete balderdash I would have joined you and we could have been thieves together!"

"I would have liked the company," said Kellen wistfully. "There you go again. What kind of knight would wistfully dream of giving up his order to become a simple thief? And then, of course, there was the whole incident with the churchman."

"Oh yes. That was a bad incident and that was a bad man."

"And what did you do about it? It's the middle of the night. And you storm in. And you have your sword out and you just start yelling at the top of your lungs! 'Hey you Cabin Boy, quit cheating with all the church money!' you said. And then you said, 'Give back the church money to the church before I give you some *duties* you're not soon to forget!'

"And what did he do?" Kellen asked rhetorically. "He picked up a crossbow and shot you with it!" He had to take a break so he could laugh properly while Deagan rubbed the sore spot on his arm where the bolt had pierced him. "So what did you do? You show up with him tied in his own bed sheets to the king himself, and you throw him on the ground and of course you're bleeding all over the place. And you think the churchman is going to the dungeon, and you're going to get about five thousand medals and awards, but no! The churchman goes free and the king says:"

Deagan chimed in and they both said the next bit together, "Stop bleeding on my floor?"

Deagan burst in, "and all I wanted to do was yell at him and say how hard it was to catch the churchman with a bleeding arm and how it isn't all swords and horses being a knight you know, and how he should really stop being such a *cabin boy* and get to his *duties* every now and again. But all I said was, 'I'm sorry, your majesty, I'll clean it up right away.' And then I spent an hour washing his blasted floor!"

They laughed. "Why didn't you talk me out of knighthood in the first place?"

"You were too much of a cabin boy to listen. And besides you loved it! Really when it came down to it you loved being a knight. And you were a damn good knight. The best one I ever met. I mean you came back to the city with such tales of excitement and such spirit! Never mind that you allowed a mad burglar to walk the streets! You were valiant and true and incredible! If the king were half as good a man as you, we wouldn't be in this mess."

"You're too kind, old friend. Well, at least now that I can't lock you in irons in the course of his majesty's justice, you don't need to keep lying to me about the fact that you're a smuggler. I'm no more threat to you than any other accomplice you've had over the years."

There was a long pause as they both drifted in thought. "Duke Worth was the one who fired you, right?"

"Yes."

"So you can be knighted by the king, but a Duke can un-knight you? Doesn't that seem wrong?"

"Exactly what I thought. He had no mark of the king; he had no letter. In fact he never even said the words, I un-dub you knight. It was just assumed and then he walked out with that stinking rat Jatham."

"I wonder if the king even knows about this. You should march in there and ask him for your gold chain back!" Another pause as they both imagined the scene. "You don't really think I'm a smuggler do you?" Kellen asked.

"I do. You've been a criminal your whole life, and I've allowed it. I'm sure you only kept it a secret from me so I'd have a free conscience, but the minute you told me you'd take up honest work for once and lead the life of a simple trader, I knew exactly what you meant. Once a pirate, always a pirate. A smuggler is a trader of sorts, so I must thank you for never lying outright."

After a smiling, but intense stare down, in which Kellen tried to think of a way to refute it, he chuckled and gave up. "Yarr," he said. "Once a pirate, always a pirate."

T
HE DRAGONS HAD LEFT *Haven the night before, spouting their flames into the sky as they rallied before their departure. Saxus and his sycophantic yet indispensable adviser Othar had been right, the commoners cheered them on as the Riders put on their display.*

Saxus had begun to see Lord Othar in private more frequently and had left the other advisers out of his planning. This upset Lord Hardeen most of all for his ambitions were like a thirst that was hard to slake, but Saxus knew that whatever petty dreams the lord held to would not matter in the end.

He had not seen reason to hold court for four days, instead remaining hidden away in his throne room, or in his personal chambers, working out the final preparations for his plan. He kept Guard Androth alone as a personal bodyguard for Othar trusted no other, and in fact had threatened to abandon Saxus altogether, to instead spend his time on a more trustworthy partner, King Malagor perhaps. Whenever they could get a moment away from Guard Androth, they fought like bickering children unable to share their toys, except the object of their disputes was more sinister. Othar wanted to have the royal guards killed.

"Sooner or later they will turn on you, Lord! You say they have an oath, but their oath is to the city, to the throne, not to a man, even one such as yourself!" he had said.

"You don't know them, Othar! You are a damned fool to think they would be easily gotten rid of even if I were to consent to this! I should send you into their chambers with a dagger and make you do it yourself. Then we'll see what they think of your little plan, how would you like that?"

They left the argument unresolved and that night Othar had ridden out of Haven to who knows where. He often did that, not always out of anger, he just disappeared to go and do his work and returned in a day or three. This time, Saxus wasn't sure the man would return, and had the cruel realization that his city had hundreds of issues that demanded his attention. If his gambit failed, he'd have to go back to tiresome old rulership, counting coins, passing judgments, listening to suck-ups and all the rest. He remembered why he had aligned with Othar in the first place. He was done being a mere lord . . .

"My Lord," the servant Berr, said bowing. "Lord Othar waits in the hall."

Saxus jumped up, having not seen the adviser in a week, "See him in!"

When slight framed, dark-clad Lord Othar walked into the room, Saxus thought he saw his First Guard move a bit. It didn't surprise him; Androth had every right to hold a grudge after the unmasking.

Othar's face was a mask of contempt. "Have you reconsidered what we spoke about?" He would not bow. He would not even greet the royal lord.

"Androth," Saxus sighed. "Leave us." The knight hesitated for the first time in Saxus' memory. "Go," Saxus said with a thick demanding tone. With that, the black statue, which so permanently adorned the corner by the door, was gone.

"I have thought of a plan. If you will stay and provide your services, I will see this . . . thing done which you requested. Perhaps you were right all along," he said thinking of how moments ago he had witnessed the first disobedience however slight from one of his guards.

Othar smiled. "Good. Then you have come to your senses. My services are yours, Your Grace," he bowed and the two of them sat down to write the letter.

T HE VILLAGE WAS BURNING and Deagan couldn't stop it. Korvis' men had surrounded the town hall. One of the cottage's doors opened and out came the jailer, all sweating and muscled. He dragged the body of a dead man out into the night. He bent down and lifted the corpse over his shoulder and yelled, "He tried to fight! He tried to fight and look what happened to him!"

Deagan rode closer to the jailer, he wanted to keep trotting onward and cut the insolent braggart's head off. He was the king's man though. And the last thing they needed was fighting amongst them.

A line was forming. The inhabitants of the cottages that were in flames were now all dead, so the men who had been holding the doors shut were free to come forward, becoming a mob behind the jailer. There were still plenty of torches in plenty of hands.

"How many in this one?" Deagan asked Korvis, pointing to the large central building.

"I would guess a hundred. But they are silent."

"Have they tried to get out?"

"Yes sir, but we have kept them in. What should we do?"

Deagan rode forward to the mob. "We'll wait here! Go and get logs to barricade them in. Soon we will have them captured, and can return 'em to the king."

"Ha!" laughed Colstin the jailer. "I've escorted dangerous men before. It takes two to move one prisoner. We don't have the numbers to capture them all and escort them back to the king. What would he say? He'd say, 'I told you to kill them, not take them on a nice little walk!'" The rest of the men laughed.

Rape, pillage and burn, Deagan thought. That was indeed what Jatham had said.

"Come on then! Let's follow our orders, boys!" A torch landed on the big building's roof, then three more. The men cheered and after the jailer, they rushed in to hold shut the doors and the windows. Eli, the water-sworn youth held back.

Korvis yelled, "Wait!"

Soon all the cottages were up in flames.

"Is this what you wanted, Your Majesty?" Deagan whispered as he watched it burn.

Deagan awoke from his dreams to three very alarming sounds.

One: carpenters on the street below hammering nails in to the frame of what would soon be a new refugee platform that they were building onto the wall of Kellen's manor. This pseudo-rhythmic sound had infiltrated Kellen's dreams in the guise of fifteen tap dancing skeletons singing sea shanties to which he couldn't remember the words.

Two: Rory singing very badly in the kitchen downstairs while making eggy bread

Three: A dragon landing on Kellen's roof and everyone on the street below screaming at the sight of it.

The dream flitted away and Deagan came to his senses. His senses were telling him that he'd be better off dead than so badly hung-over. Without lifting his face from his arm he said, "What is going on . . . it sounds like they're yelling, 'Dragon,' out there." This didn't stir Kellen.

"I'm sure it will sort itself out," Kellen mumbled.

"You're probably right," Deagan replied, and went back to sleep falling back into his dream.

Smoke drifted high into the air. The black, stinking stuff wheeled up from the village in twisting columns, filled with angry red sparks. The first cottage to be burned was now dying down, its stones cracked and walls caving in. The big building in the center of town was surrounded and smoke

poured out of the shuttered windows and chimney. The firelight was almost as bright as day, but sinister, for it was fueled in part by the still living inhabitants of the village.

Deagan would not resort to killing the king's own men, besides the only two that would fight with him were Eli and Korvis. The three of them would be outnumbered fifteen to one.

"Yah!" he spurred Maggie to a gallop and looped around the building. Only a few stood at the back, mostly watching, but also waiting with their hands on the door that Deagan had barred. He looped around to the front again and saw no real change. Korvis stood back and watched, shaking his helmeted head that shone in the firelight. Eli stood beside him, sword sheathed. There was nothing left to do but watch it burn.

"Master Kellen," Rory called softly waking Deagan from his memories.

"Mff?"

"Knight here to see you, sir. Says he's from Haven. He seems to have landed his dragon on your roof, and would like to make arrangements with you for its safekeeping."

"I am a pirate, not some cape-wearing hooligan's stable boy! Who does he think he is?"

"Wake up, ye crooked rascal," Deagan yawned. "You're bound to profit if you're shrewd."

"Would you like to get yourself dressed, sir or would you like me to help you?" Rory asked.

"What do you take me for?" Kellen rose from his pillow and attempted to look poised. He could not pull it off and instead he looked poisoned. "Come and dress me, now, that's a good lad." He hoisted himself off the bed and Rory propelled him through the difficult routine and escorted him down the stairs. Soon enough he was presentable and opened the door.

"Good day, Sir Knight. Please, come in," Kellen said as he bowed to the figure standing before him.

"Thank you, sir." He was a tall and slender knight. His armor was woven of cured leather and looked light. His shoulders and chest bore metal plates, and his helmet was smooth and emblazoned with golden flames.

"To what good fortune do I owe the pleasure of meeting one of Haven's finest warriors, pray tell?"

"I am sir Oscar. We are here for additional defense. Sent by Haven's Royal Lord Saxus. We have been flying around all day looking for anyone who might have received word from His Lordship that we'd be arriving. We were told there'd be accommodations for the mounts, but high and low we have searched, and no one has heard any word or whisper."

"Did you say *flying* around all day? Of course you did! When I saw you I didn't realize you were one of the Dragon Riders from Haven. Well finally you have come to the right place. I am Kellen Wayfield. I am the one who was to accommodate your dragons!"

"I am so relieved!" The knight said. "So what is the plan?"

"Well, sir, dragon keeping is an old and dangerous art, and surely your order is the only one who now practices it. In fact, judging by your bearing, you must be chief among your Riders, and a true master of the beasts. I, knowing very little of dragons myself, have not made much preparation. So please, great Dragon Rider, name your mounts' desires and I will begin the labor of making them welcome."

"Thank you, gracious host. Your name will be held in high esteem among my men."

"Thank you, sir." Kellen bowed with mock humility and said, "First off, sir Oscar, what do they eat?"

No. DEAGAN THOUGHT, I can't allow this. *Maggie shook the ground as she carried him to the back again. Eli and Korvis ran after him, but couldn't keep up with the warhorse.* When he got there, a few men still held the door.

"To the front!" he roared. "To the front!" *They took their hands off the door.* "Are ye daft, fools? The enemy is at the front. Go now!" *The men at last moved in that direction, they took their hands off of the door and turned around the corner of the big central building at a run.*

Deagan dismounted and pulled the beams away, tossing them on the ground. He knew he didn't have a lot of time. Eli and Korvis would be here soon. When the last brace was gone, the door fell open; a dead or unconscious man who had been leaning against it collapsed into the red mud. Behind him, all was tumultuous black smoke.

Deagan called inside, "This way! Come on!" *And before he could fully get out of the way, the throng of people ran out the door, coughing and staying low. Women and children made their way out. Old men who looked like farmers hobbled past. Everyone who was able carried supplies not for war, but for settling. They looked like any other bunch of refugees fleeing from the forces of evil. Except this time they were fleeing from King Malagor, and they'd find no refuge in Darkwell.*

Deagan was pushed aside by the rush. He turned quickly to see Korvis and Eli, panting behind him, looking on in shock. Many of the villagers near the back of the crowd were armed and armored in the manner of Haven's soldiers. A sword connected with Deagan's shield. "Go ye fool," *the knight barked.* "I'm not your enemy!"

The man came on anyway. He slashed and jabbed at Deagan and the knight defended himself. Eli and Korvis were by his side in an instant.

Trading swipes with the growing number of fleeing fighters. Eli took one step too close to the enemy, and forgot to come in swinging. His young life was ended before he hit the ground. Blood flowed freely down his neck painting his armor "No! Run, you bastards! Can't you see I've let you free?"

The last one to come from the building wore fine ceremonial armor. When the fighters saw this knight, they looked at the darkened face of the helmet and waited for directions. The chin lifted and the spear pointed, indicating to them they should run off with the rest of them. They did so. Korvis dropped to Eli's side in order to help him, it would take Korvis another few battles before he knew when a brother-in-arms was beyond help and it was time to help himself.

The helm was seamless and polished black, the face of it was split by a dark gap, the space there was in the shape of the Cloud Tower, the palace of Saxus, Haven's Royal Lord. Behind this heroic mask no face could be seen inside, for the space was covered with black steel mesh. The warrior carried a black shield that was wide and tall, marked by a single gold star, and couched a long spear inlaid with gold lettering. A crimson sash circled the belt, and the breastplate came to a ridge in the front that bisected a shining tower of black gold.

The warrior raised weapons at the ready and quickly engaged Deagan in combat. He parried the first thrust of the spear, and then the second, but the third jabbed him square in the face. The point of the spear was less than an inch from his eye, but could come no closer, for the gap in his helm was too narrow and the wider part of the spear's blade was pinched in the wounded metal.

The faceless warrior tried to retrieve the spear, but found it utterly lodged. Deagan's opponent crouched low and twisted at the waist to fling Deagan to the side. As sturdy as Deagan was, he couldn't resist and was pulled violently to the side, jarring his spine and stretching the muscles of his neck. Instead of being knocked down, Deagan dove in the direction he was being pulled, and in one quick motion he removed his helmet and rolled away. He lay on his back and laughed in the other knight's face. A brush with death always gave him a sudden sense of humor.

"What do you have to say now, mister pokey stick?" he taunted. Nothing apparently. The other knight shook the spear to remove the ungainly helmet from its point, but it didn't work. As Deagan regained his feet, the spearman quickly pinned the spitted helmet onto the wet ground with an armored boot. Even after a powerful yank, the spear would not come free. "Run off with your friends, sir Knight. I didn't save your life just to have to kill ye."

The knight bowed and ran away. A few seconds later, soaring out of the dark beneath the trees, Deagan's dented and scarred helmet came sailing through the smoky air. It rolled to a stop in a shallow red puddle of mud and ash. Chivalry, *Deagan thought, gazing after the mysterious knight. Something other than chivalry awaited him on the other side of the town hall however—something completely opposite.*

Deagan pulled his shirt of chain mail over the quilted, stinking robe that kept him from being pinched by his own armor. A few buckles over his trousers kept his leg armor in place, and then the collar of steel went around his neck. He slipped his head into the hood of chain, and then put on his heavy, cloth baldric, that bore his coat of arms. It was a field of deep red, with a simple embroidered sword that was once white, but had long since been dirtied to a sweaty brown. He tied the thick rope around his waist to hold up his sword and looked into the eyes of his dented helmet for a time before putting it on.

His footsteps rattled down Kellen's stairs and soon he was out on the street. Kellen and sir Oscar were talking merrily in the kitchen. Only Rory saw him leave.

"I won't soon forget last night," Deagan said as he went out the door.

"Nor will I, Deagan. I am sure your kegs of beer will be welcome here again whenever you like."

"Aye, and I can think of no better cabin boy to tap them for me." With that he left to tend his horse. Before he made it to her though, a fleeting and gigantic shadow passed over him. He looked up to see a preening dragon, perched on Kellen's roof. He marveled at its elegance. It sat like a long-legged dog on the rooftop armored in dull azure scales. Its wings were wide and leathery, stretched across shafts of jointed bone. Its long neck was serpentine and its head was like a crocodile's, flat and wide with protruding, yet heavy-lidded eyes with vertical slits for pupils, with a horn on its nose sharp and curved.

Still looking up to the majestic beast, he brushed Maggie's gray fur thoroughly, flicking the course bristled brush at the end of each stroke. He scratched her withers and she soon fell asleep standing. Other horses traveling by stiffened and turned away when they saw the dragon, while Maggie was relaxed as could be as Deagan massaged the long, firm muscles in her chest and her shoulders. To quench her thirst, he walked her to the nearest well in the street and drew up a bucket of water. Others were waiting to use it, so he didn't drink any himself thirsty though he was, and he poured the water in a pail for her to slurp quickly.

The sun was shining on the street before Kellen's manor and the fresh scent of milled lumber mingled with the percussive ring of hammers. The saws' teeth sliced the boards to length as men framed a refugee platform against Kellen's wall. The excitement of the dragon kept everyone lively and the chatter around Deagan was fast paced and completely devoid of fact. It seemed that the world sailed by him as he brushed and brushed his good horse. He had been planning on returning her to the king's stables today.

Deagan finally saddled Maggie and put her armor on. He slung his shield on her and then rode slowly through the streets of Darkwell, looking as magnificent as he could, all armed as he was and on such a steed. Her roached mane bristled under his fingers as he passed the shops and slums, the cook fires and gutter drains. He did nothing but saunter on, alone in the misery of parting with an old friend.

There was some undertone of grace to the way he was leaving the knighthood. He was unhappy with the duties he'd been given, the barbarism that had taken the place of chivalry. And yes there had been times when even Maggie herself had been a great bother as she refused to travel past puppeteers, or to eat her food if she hadn't been brushed. There were times when he had been so saddle weary and injured that he wanted to collapse on the ground, but always, his duty was to Maggie first, and then to himself. He grudgingly lifted her saddle from her and brushed her. He painfully dragged her the water, and tossed her the hay. And then if she acted up or refused to eat, he sometimes even yelled at her, which made her ears go back, and then she wouldn't listen to a word he said for a day or more.

"Tis a pity that horses must get tangled up in the affairs of men. That you can be traded to and fro, driven into battle . . . given and then taken back." Tears welled up in his eyes.

Like so many times before, she carried him into the doors of the king's horse barn. It was furnished with the best of attendants. And other knights rested their steeds here. There was energy in the place, and the sweet smell of horses in sunshine. Sir Luthan was there, unarmored, but carrying steel, and he was brushing his fine gelding named Luka. His brow furrowed when Deagan dismounted and led Maggie into the stalls.

"Well met, Deagan."

"Luthan, I am here to return the king's horse," he walked past the knight and into the back of the barn where he hoped to be alone. He tied her lead rope to the bar in front of her and removed her armor and saddle. "Well, let's call it a day, girl." He moved to take her saddle off, but she refused. She nibbled his hand with her lips, which always meant she wanted to go out and run. "No, girl. We have to call it a day." She finally relented. He brushed her again and he was transported back to all the thousands of times he'd done it before.

"You might not ever understand this Maggie, but I'm not . . . not going to be your rider anymore." His voice wavered. "I am no longer a knight, Maggie. I don't agree with the reasons . . ." In order to control his voice he had to lower it to a whisper, "But I have no choice." He sobbed for a minute. "Don't you realize I would not leave you if I didn't have to?" She looked at him with her big brown eyes. Maybe she smelled his tears and it made her sad, but beyond that she didn't understand.

"Maggie. I told you that I'd never leave you. You saved my life too many times to be given away. I was sure that if you were g-g-gone," he paused. "I'd have nothing to live for. And I promised you that legends would spring up about your name and you'd become the greatest warhorse in all the world. You still may, big girl . . . but I won't be there to see it happen." He could not speak because his back was shaking and his lips were pressed tightly together and trembling. He feebly tried to brush her, but knowing it was the last time he'd do so made him collapse against the stall's rough-hewn wall. He threw the brush on the ground with force and held his head. When he was finally able to speak again, this is what he said: "*I love you more than I will ever love myself.*" And he was taken by grief completely. She nuzzled the brush back to him and forced her head under his arm. He sniffled and gave a little laugh. Finally, he was finished. Maggie pulled at her rope and stamped her feet, singing out a deafening whinny as he walked away.

The rest of the day was filled with pain that he knew no drink could assuage. He waited in the bright sun for something, anything to happen to him. But in agony, he wandered the city, rusting the inside of his helmet with tears. There was no comfort and no cure for this wound. The pain was worse than any he had suffered in battle and Duke Worth had dealt the blow. Not for the first time, Deagan got his blood up thinking about the man. He got his blood up *hot*. No rage could fill the emptiness inside him, though, and each memory that trotted past was another twist of the dagger in his heart. "Maggie," was all he could whimper for the rest of the day, until he was exhausted and fell asleep in his lonely room.

"THE REASON YOU ARE all gathered here, my fine guards and drivers, is because we have a new and unexpected change in our enterprise," Kellen announced to all his assembled laborers. "Jorn Kahorne and his entire caravan were waylaid by evil forces and were all slain." A rowdy whisper thundered through the small crowd. "It saddens me deeply to bring you this news and being their employer, I cannot help but feel responsible for this tragedy. I am sorry to all of you who knew those brave and stalwart men, and to those of you who would have known them, but will never have the chance. They were noble to a man, and they fought valiantly before being overtaken by the enemy's greater numbers. They were sarcophs, living corpses that struck our caravan. They were probably workers like Jorn and the others in life, but were corrupted to vile ends by a diabolic will.

"So today we must not grieve only for Kahorne's troop," (when he planned this line of his speech, he struggled to avoid rhyming mourn with Kahorne, so he changed it to Jorn, but still it rhymed. Finally Kellen had settled on changing mourn to grieve.) "But also for those who were forced by whatever malignant entity to take their lives. A minute of silence, please."

When the touching silence was over, Kellen broke in quietly, "I will no longer risk any of your lives as you travel the dangerous roadways. Each one of the horse drivers may keep one horse if they wish. The rest will be sold and I encourage you all to make me an offer if you'd like to buy any of them, I will not drive a hard bargain. It will be sad to lose the rest of the horses, but you will see that we cannot keep them, nor would it help us to do so.

"Our business will change dramatically at this time, but I believe it is for the best. For the safety of all of you, and for the safety of this city, our new venture will be quite different from what you are used to. When you hear my proposition, you will be free to stay or leave as you will, but the pay will be good, and the cause is worth working for."

"Tell us, Kellen, I can see that you are eager to win us over with your new scheme, so please, get on with it! What is this new business?" This worker had a Baenish accent, song-like and steeped in a language far older than what was spoken in Darkwell.

Kellen glanced at Rory, who smiled. "Gentlemen. We are now dragon keepers!"

Every one of them looked around at each other in shock. Soon the looks of surprise gave way to impish grins. Each and every one of them was on board, excited for a change, and devoted to their daring leader. "But we don't know the first *thing* about dragons!" Someone protested.

"Neither do I, my good man. That is why we have *him*." He opened a door to reveal an armored and mustached man who was using the blade of his sword to butter his toast. He beamed at them and bowed grandly with his arms out to the sides. "This, my friends is Sir Oscar, Knight of Haven and Chief of the Dragon Riders! And he informs me that dragons, in fact, eat hay."

T HE HALL OF THE Royal Guard was the only place in which a Guard could be out of uniform. It was a chamber that lay buried deep within the Cloud Tower, at the end of a well-guarded and poorly lit corridor with only one, small secret entrance. The corridor terminated in an ordinary wooden door, but on the other side, the accommodations were more than adequate. Saxus had been inside but once, and had no need to return. He had servants for that. He handed the letter to Berr, who was one of the few servants in Cloud Tower permitted to enter the hall of the royal guard, he was educated, trustworthy, well-paid and sworn to maintain the secrets of the royal guard on pain of death.

To the Royal Guards,

Your presence is required. Tomorrow night you will have the delicacies and drinks that you have up till now only salivated over while I feasted other men. This is in thanks of your loyal service, which I can never repay. Only your own servants will attend, and the way in shall be guarded, the windows blocked so that you may remain anonymous.

Royal Lord Saxus

The letter had been delivered yesterday and now the throne room was adorned in all its finery. Torches lined the walls, and candles adorned the tables, but the windows were covered in heavy curtains as promised to ensure that no one would see the faces of the guards. The servants had finally made all the preparations, and the meal of many courses filled the chamber with rich smells of meat, bread, drink, and pies.

Saxus tried to compose himself. Lord Othar of course was too cowardly to see his deed done and said he would return on the following day. This promised to be the most uncomfortable feast of all time, its guests sworn to silence as they were. It almost made Saxus laugh, but instead a dark smile crossed his face, deepening the wrinkles at the corners of his mouth and eyes. "It will all be over soon," he said, pushing the curtain aside to look out the window at the expansive view of his city.

"My Lord Saxus, I announce the Royal Guard!" the servant by the door called into the dead quiet of the throne room. In marched a row of black armored warriors, each one carrying a full array of weapons, and helmeted with impenetrable black masks of wire mesh. It was truly silent.

"Welcome!" Saxus greeted them with a forced smile. "Come, and seat yourselves. Be easy and have a toast with me."

The only part of the instructions they would not obey was the "be easy" part. No Royal Lord had ever feasted the Royal Guard in the history of Haven, and they didn't have any training in table courtesies, but nevertheless, they sat on the chairs that surrounded the table, arranging their swords on their belts to hang them out of the way. Then one by one they removed their helms, and the faceless, immortal soldiers of the royal guard became human before his very eyes. Some of them looked afraid, others utterly stoic. Their hair had been brushed and dressed nicely, and their faces were washed and well cared for.

They had all raised the goblets of wine in a toast by the time, Saxus realized that the guard seated closest to his right did not take off the black helm, or raise the glass. The defiance of it boiled the royal lord's blood. "Remove your helm! Or I'll have you back out on the streets where you came from!"

The guard signed with both hands, a message that meant. "I will keep watch while the rest drink." Some of the other guards looked uneasily at one another. Saxus eyed the guard beside him.

"No need, Guard. Just remove your helm and share the toast. You are not on duty just now." There was another moment of hesitation, but finally the two hands lifted the helm to reveal the human face underneath. "For

Haven," Saxus nodded at the guard and then put the goblet to his lips. The rest of the company followed suit. "Go on, then. Eat!"

The feast began. The sound of forks on plates was deafening without the chatter of voices to overpower it. The guards ate slowly, keeping an eye on the door, or checking to see that their swords were secure in their sheaths. They seemed to be doing all right, and Saxus watched them intently. When suddenly he got the notion that one of them was missing. His gaze drifted from one end of the hall to the other and he counted them. Nine. He counted again from the other side. Nine. Who was missing? He spent so little time looking at their faces that he couldn't remember which one was absent. He tried to remember if one had stepped out to use the privy, but no.

Suddenly he stood up and gasped, "Where's Androth?" The sound of forks ceased and all eyes turned on him. Some were defiant, some frightened, some apologetic, but none of them Androth's. His breath came quicker, and his face flushed. His knees felt weak and he sat back down. "Servant! Berr, come here." He said and soon the serving man was beside him and at his service. "Go and find Guard Androth, now!"

"Yes, Sire," the man said with a bow. When he was about to leave the chamber to carry out his orders, one of the silent royal guards was up like a flash. He was a man in black plate, with a short brown beard and flowing brown hair held back in a piece of twine, and his hand was upon the door barring Berr's exit.

"What is this foolishness? Let the man go and do his duty!" The guard didn't turn to Saxus, but only stared in Berr's face, and the smaller man backed away.

"Guards!" Saxus screamed as he ran to the back of the room. The main door burst open and all of a sudden the towermen were upon them. Their blue and silver baldrics depicted an outline of Cloud Tower where they served, and they wore silver helmets and chain mail. The first towerman in the door swung at the bearded royal guard, but he deftly dodged aside and drew his own sword, chopping off his assailant's arm in a single upward stroke to the unprotected armpit, killing him. By then the rest of the royal guards were on their feet with weapons drawn and had formed a wall of spear heads, which several of the towermen promptly killed themselves upon before they broke off their charge and squared off in a large mass just outside the chamber doors. A stale mate.

In that moment of silent stand off, a drop of blood hit the floor. One of the royal guards had a bloody nose. Another drop and then another splashed onto the stones. The towermen looked on in disbelief as blood poured from all of their opponent's noses, then their mouths. A sword clattered loudly to the floor as the bearded man's hand began convulsing violently. The tremor moved up his arm and seized his whole body, until finally he lay still on the ground, with foam bubbling from between his chalky lips.

Second Guard Traleen raised a shaky sword and yelled, "For Androth!" And with the final charge of the Royal Guard, many Towermen were skewered. As the battle raged in the doorway, one of the royal guards stumbled back toward Saxus, with a blade drawn. "Stand down!" he said, brandishing his own sword and fumbling for the handle on the wall behind him. The heavy footsteps of the royal guard were uneven and desperate, but the bloody-nosed face was resolute and calm. The guard was only steps away from him when Saxus screamed knowing the end was at hand. But then the tremors came, the foam belched from his mouth, and the black armored soldier collapsed before him, twitching on the ground. Saxus kicked the sword away from the pain-wracked claw of a hand, and dropped the sharp edge of his sword on the defenseless guard's neck. He hacked at it repeatedly, terrified of his own brutality, yet exulting in the moment. He realized at last that he was laughing, and that he was alive.

By the time he looked up, he was the only one left standing. The servants had all been killed along with his double garrison of towermen. And the only Royal Guard with a wound from a weapon was lying dead at his feet, the others having each fallen prey to the poison. Saxus jumped up on the seat of his throne, then stood with his feet on the arms of the great chair gazing out over the dead. The job was done, except one corpse was missing from those at his feet. He thought back to when his adviser, Lord Othar had demanded that First Guard Androth be unmasked. And now he was one of three people living that knew the face of the one he needed to kill.

G WYN STALKED INTO THE squat tower that held the throne room of Darkwell's King Malagor. Prior to passing over the deep moat and in through the nigh impenetrable gate this morning, she had never been to Darkwell before, but now she was forced to come here as an ambassador for her people. It was possible someone else from her group of survivors could have come into the city in Gwyn's stead, but Androth would hear no argument on the matter.

Gwyn was both meek and bold in her demeanor, as unassuming as a peasant, yet as commanding as a queen. Some people had magnetism, but Gwyn had gravity. No guards had yet been born that could refuse the beauty, elegance and power of a woman such as Gwyn, except perhaps, the Royal Guards of Lord Saxus who were silent and foreboding, and did not yield to cunning.

Within an hour's time the clever woman was in the audience of the king himself. His hall was rich with tapestry and furs, and it was as warm as a summer day despite the evening chill. A blur of movement at the far end of the large hall caught her attention. A figure quietly slipped behind a curtain as she entered, but she pretended not to notice. What coward would run and hide behind a curtain upon the entrance of a simple serving woman?

Seated on a large throne, in a formal cape of fur and with a golden crown upon his aged brow, was King Malagor. Gwyn kneeled and bent forward putting her forehead to the floor in the most subservient of bows. A flickering rosy light came from the bases of the six pillars that upheld the ornately painted ceiling. The deep, circular pits into which these pillars were set apparently contained fires, but little smoke entered the hall, so Gwyn guessed that the pillars acted as chimneys as well as supports. Woe to the man who stumbles into one of those fire pits, *she thought.*

The far end of the hall was indented by yet another fireplace, the light of which silhouetted the royal throne. Guards stood nearby, clad in armor and bearing swords and round shields.

"What is it?" the old king demanded.

She said, "It is an honor to gain your audience, Sire. I have news from Haven and would tell all that I know to a wise and gracious ally of my city."

"Rise, my child." King Malagor intoned impressively. "Why has Lord Saxus sent one such as you to bring this news?" He meant, why did he send an aging servant instead of a messenger, knight, or lord?

"I am not here on the errand of the Royal Lord, nor on the request of any other. I am here because in my station I see much, and that which has befallen Lord Saxus worries me deeply. I am here to request aid from Your Highness." She took a few steps forward. "Will you hear what has happened to Haven, Sire?"

First he glanced to the curtain where the figure had vanished earlier, and then a smug look settled on King Malagor's countenance. Gwyn detected a vague approval in the King's face as if he was somehow glad to hear that Haven was in peril. "Get on with it then," he said.

"Thank you, Your Highness." She bowed again, not as low. It took all her will to keep her eyes from drifting to the curtains where she knew a presence still lurked. "As you may know, the city of Haven is war torn. The stolen lands to our south are now peopled with shambling corpses. Dead men, that exist only to feast on the living. I fear that soon all will collapse, but still Lord Saxus hides in his chamber and sees no one. He sends bands of men against the assailing force of sarcophs, but always he sends too few. As if he means for them not to come back."

"Indeed, you do see much as a servant to the Royal Lord . . ." the king chuckled.

Ignoring this she continued. "I have left his service because I saw him no longer fit to rule the city and no longer able to protect it. I ask you then, Sire for two favors." Her voice was strong now, hiding none of its dignity. It had the timbre of an ancient language. The song like tones of Old Baenish, which Gwyn spoke with her family when she was a girl. "The first is to shelter all of those I came with in the walls of Darkwell. There are some hundred and fifty of us who fled from Haven. We escaped with little more than our lives. Haven is not safe anymore and we need the protection of your walls if we are to make any kind of a new start. I don't ask for much. Better to be homeless on the streets of Darkwell than a landed noble in Haven these days."

"I see," said the king. His face giving no hint of whether he would oblige.

"My second request is for you to send word to Lord Saxus. To appeal to him yourself and convince him to fight the oncoming forces with all the might and vigor of his youth instead of lazing about his chambers in solitude, hiding from reality."

"You would have me tell the Royal Lord of Haven how to govern?" asked the king amusedly.

"Your highness, I would have you kill him and take his place if it would end the scourge on my homeland." Gwyn knew that kings couldn't resist flattery.

King Malagor leaned to the side in his throne to get a better view behind the curtains as he laughed at Gwyn's suggestion. Somehow I'm playing into one of the king's plans, Gwyn thought. She didn't mind that one bit. The maneuvers of an old and greedy king did not concern her. If it was one of the king's advisers, why wouldn't he stay out in the open?

"Please," Gwyn begged; she also knew kings loved begging.

"Go and wait outside these doors, content yourself for now, and let me think on your requests." Again he glanced at the curtain. "By the end of the day you will have your answers."

"Thank you, Sire," she said, and she bowed before him. She backed away five steps, then turned without looking up and left the hall. Two guards opened the doors for her. Then she waited.

A well-dressed courtier of the king came to Gwyn in his finery. He showed her no respect and disdained her simple frock, but nevertheless gave her an almost imperceptible nod. "His Majesty, King Malagor has decided *what he shall do. There is not enough room in the city and your people will have to find lodging in the nearby abandoned village that was once called Oxham. It lies away in the Border Lands. The buildings will need new roofs, but there should be enough space there once you get that small detail sorted out." He showed no signs of continuing.*

"Thank you, sir. And what of my second request? Will his majesty appeal to the Royal Lord of Haven?"

"Such matters are best left to those who understand such things," he said, meaning not you, peasant. And don't ask again. *"Do you need any help finding Oxham? I believe some of the peasants on the streets will know the way. Good day,"* he said, and walked away.

This wasn't far off from what she was expecting. At least no one could say she didn't try to use the diplomatic approach before taking matters into her own hands.

G UARD ANDROTH?" THE MAN greeted his new leader with cautious respect from outside the canvas tent. He had forgotten that the faceless guard was always silent and of course wouldn't answer him. Knights and their oaths had always puzzled him.

"It's me, Durvish, captain of the South Towers." *The South Towers,* he thought. *Now I am captain of nothing.* He thought back to the stink that had risen about his towers and heard the fell laughter of the dead in his ears as if it were still following him. He shivered. It was a warm night, and there were fires in the camp behind him, but this group had been through far too much in such a short time. Even King Malagor was now their enemy; Darkwell's ruler had made that clear enough when he sent that troop of men to burn them all alive in the night. That raid was a month ago now. Durvish's troop had been hiding in the jungle ever since.

The city-state of Haven was built in a fertile river valley about a day's ride North of Darkwell. Jutting up from the rich earth, there were massive points of stone littering the countryside like crooked teeth. The standing stones had been carven into watchtowers. Durvish wore a blue baldric over his armor and it carried his coat of arms: a large horned bull flanked by green trees. In one of the South Towers a banner bearing the same standard hung ragged over a quiet and lifeless field.

The rotter invasion began almost two months ago. There were rumors of strange happenings coming from the outermost villages and farms—'*Grandma went missing from her coffin in the back room!*' Or, '*The old blacksmith appeared to me, but he was not the same. Dead and stinking he was, and covered in the dirt of his grave.*'

The rumors troubled Durvish and the towermen, but from their outposts, there was nothing to be done for no order from Cloud Tower had come. One day, the stench arose. Then the laughter . . . Durvish sent word to the Royal Lord via his swiftest rider. The dead that they didn't have time to burn only rose up and joined the fight, slamming their unfeeling fists into the heavy doors of the South Towers or just wandering through the fields, looking for flesh to consume.

Durvish had gotten no word since the invasion began. For all he knew, the Dragon Riders, the inner city, and the Royal Lord Saxus himself had all been devoured just like the fertile countryside around the South Towers that he'd tried to defend.

Alone and without help the dead men that littered the farmlands and fishing villages below them would have pinned the towermen in the Towers until starvation set in. But help didn't come. Guard Androth came in its stead.

The flap of the tent opened and Guard Androth, still, as always, in full armor, allowed the captain to enter.

The Royal Guard gestured to a spot for Durvish to sit down. Candlelight glowed warmly on the white canvas. Durvish pressed his pommel down and kneeled on the grass inside the tent. He gazed down at the vellum and saw the map of the Knowne Worlde. There stood Haven, Darkwell and Pillar, three circles left in a world overwhelmed by darkness. He let out a sigh of despair and looked up to the Royal Guard, who sat straight backed on a tree stump. The knight pointed a gloved finger at the mark that represented Darkwell, then slid it to the east and tapped the word *caves*.

"Are we traveling there, then?" Durvish asked, looking up. The black-faced helmet nodded.

"But, pardon me, lord. Didn't Darkwell's king send those men who raided our camp? Didn't we get refused when we asked to stay in their city walls? Clearly that city harbors no love for our cause . . . or us. Why then should we travel so close?"

The finger again tapped the map. "Aye, lord." We will make ready immediately and wait for your command." The helmet nodded once.

Durvish exited the tent. The rest of his people still looked grim and determined even though many had lost loved ones and friends. The fires of Malagor's army had taken thirteen of them. And they had not been swift deaths. Many of them still had nightmares about the raid, and many more relished the chance to face that force again, and leave them all dying in the rain to contemplate their own cruelty. Except that one man . . . the one with the white belt and gold chain who wore a sword on his baldric as a coat of arms. The one who fought Guard Androth and lived. No, no one wanted him dead.

Durvish gave the orders for his towermen and the villagers from the lower quarters to ready themselves for travel. "I know *where* we are going but I do not know *when*." He smiled at the gathered people who laughed knowingly. They knew that Androth would not speak, and therefore the details of certain orders were left unknown. This uncertainty had become usual and comfortable for this group from Haven. Following the cryptic orders of Guard Androth had kept them alive, and they wanted to stay that way.

Strange folk, these Royal Guards, Durvish thought. But what could Durvish call Androth now? For the knight had left the guardianship of the Royal Lord behind along with the winding alleys of Haven.

T HIS WAS THE BEGINNING of Kellen's list of needs that he would send with his men to go and procure:

400 sheaves of hay
25 wire brushes
25 lengths of heavy chain, ten feet each
50 pounds of nails
43 large water buckets
75 logs of sturdy wood
250 gallons of oil

They were trading men and knew that if Kellen could find better prices than they could, their pay would be docked, so all over Darkwell, men in the employ of Kellen Wayfield haggled for dragon supplies. Apparently the thing to do was to lash three logs together in a wide open triangle on a high exposed location, build a platform or a walkway around it for the dragon rider, and then allow the dragon to build its own nest there. On top of Kellen's house, the first roost was constructed. It had a sturdy ladder that led in to one of Kellen's windows, and it had a decent view of the city. Sir Oscar with his dragon, Pete was able to lift the logs into place for the first roost while Kellen's' men secured them in place with ropes and nails. The men on the street below looked on in jealousy as they constructed their platform by hand.

Soon Pete was hard at work making his nest. He howled as he returned after each trip into the city with his mouth full of tree branches and his front talons gripping vines covered in colorful grapes or clotheslines still adorned in people's garments. If they were careful, they could build one more roost on top of Kellen's manor. And with Pete's help, they did so. Then they built another one in the top of his ancient oak tree. This was the kingliest of roosts, and the easiest one to build. It seemed that Kellen's crew was growing more adept with the process. Pete didn't get jealous though; he liked his brightly colored nest with Kellen's chimney poking through it. He curled around the chimney and took a nap after two hard days of labor.

Kellen got Sir Oscar to invite two of his dragon rider friends over to take up residency. There was a red dragon named Ero, ridden by Sir Johan, and there was a green named Warmaker ridden by Sir Goodsing. "Tally ho, Sirs Knights." Kellen greeted them warmly. "Welcome to Dragon Manor." He gestured grandly to the sign above his door, which indeed did say Dragon Manor.

"Well done, for just two days work Kellen, old boy, but there are 22 more of us still perching from night to night in the belfries and battlements with nowhere proper to rest! What'll you do about that?" Sir Oscar asked Kellen in the tone of trying to stump him, but he was starting to realize he was dealing with a man who could not be stumped.

FINALLY, THE LID OF the coffin came free. Beam's body lurched out of it. He saw the back of the cart driver's neck and didn't hesitate to descend on it. The man screamed and tried to fight him off, but Beam's body didn't feel the blows. A warm surge of blood filled his mouth and he drank greedily, but even as his dead belly filled, nothing could satisfy it.

He gnawed and gnawed, until a strange sensation occurred. His head fell off, literally. Or rather his body fell off, leaving his head still latched on the dead cart driver's neck. Beam's eyes rolled in their sockets, but could not see the swordsman that had bebodied him. He worked his tongue in the man's wound, but could get little more sustenance, finally his grip loosened and his head rolled down to the street. His vision was a spinning blur as his eyes collected dust from the road, the bumps and scrapes that would have rattled him in life held no sensation for him now. He landed face up, and looked into the cloudy evening sky. Two heavy boots approached and suddenly he was looking up into the face of a very serious looking man with a dripping sword and a beard with a white chin.

D EAGAN SPEARED THE HEAD on his sword and slammed it on the roadway until the tip of the sword pierced through the back of Beam's skull. Blood dripping everywhere, Deagan walked over to the cart, overturned Beam's headless body and hauled it, kicking and struggling down to the street. He threw it on the ground face down and stepped on its back. He squeezed the cart driver's hand saying, "Hey. Old man. Can you hear me?" The cart driver's face fell forward to rest on his chest with blood seeping through his beard as Deagan shook him by the shoulder. "Didn't think so," he sighed.

As reverently as possible, Deagan picked up the driver's corpse and placed it on top of the body of the sarcoph. "Forgive me, old man," he muttered. Then, one foot bracing the bodies, Deagan put his weight on the pommel of his sword and drove the blade through the back of Beam's head, through the cart driver's torso, and finally through Beam's wriggling body. It was an old knight's trick. He only had to hope no more of them came around because he was all out of swords.

He looked around him; no particular reason brought him here other than the urge to get a better view of the dragons flying above the city. Then he heard a man's scream coming from Flag Street and he had come running. A bent old man stood nearby watching Deagan work. He wore a tattered robe of brown and carried a clay jug at his side with a thick leather strap around his body. His head was shaved in the manner of the water-sworn. *Eli* . . . Deagan thought.

"You don't look like a knight," the old man said in spite of his missing teeth. Deagan grunted as he turned away to search the cart.

Beam's coffin was there, its lid forced open from the inside. "So what are you a guard? Off duty and out of uniform by chance?" He raised his eyebrows as he took a long drink from his clay jug. Behind the old man stood a small crowd. Some of the men were holding clubs or daggers, but most of them were simply listening. Still others looked on from doorways, or windows. He tied the horse up to a nearby post, and then turned to face the bystanders.

"I'm no knight. I'm no guard. Just someone who'd rather see the likes of these taken care of." He gestured to the corpses pinned to the ground. The writhing of the decapitated Beam was unmistakable, and even skewered as it was, the eyes and the lips were still moving. There was a murmur of disgust in the crowd and most of them stepped back. "It's alright," Deagan assured them. "I've handled their kind before. The curse don't spread into living flesh. It may soon take a hold of this unlucky fellow, though. You lot be careful. And start burning your dead."

"We owe you, Sir." the old man said. Deagan favored him with a relieved smile. The mob heeded this man's words and seemed more certain of Deagan's character. "What do you need?"

"You owe me nothing, my friend," Deagan said. He stuffed all the remains into the coffin, pulled his sword free and cleaned it on a rag that he found. He stood on the coffin still in the back of the cart, and nailed it shut knowing it wouldn't hold long since the nails had been pried loose once before, so he tied a rope around the coffin, it was wrapped many times and tied tightly.

Deagan untied the horse, sat on the driver's seat of the undertaker's cart and took up the lines. "Where are you going with those?" the water-sworn elder asked.

Deagan smiled. "There's enough smoke in Darkwell as it is. And there's firewood to be had out in the jungle."

"You'd risk the jungle?" the old man said with a smile and another gulp from the jug. "You put more faith in your sword than I would have thought."

Deagan nodded and thought for a moment. "I put faith in little else," he said, and the cart took him down the road. If he upset his cargo and left it sprawling on the streets of Darkwell, it could easily be the end of the city. The affliction would spread and the city would crumble. He had seen it happen before. He went on a campaign once to the city of Gamroth, which had had a bit of a zombie problem. Comfortable though he was *slaying* them, Deagan knew he had no *solution* for them, at least not on the grand scale.

He had a solution for this rotter and it's soon to be rotter friend though, and that solution involved firewood. He drove the cart out through the city gates; the guards there recognized him and he didn't know whether they had yet heard about his discharge from the knighthood. He let them keep believing he was *Sir* Deagan Wingrat for now and he rode out into the forest, where he started collecting firewood—collecting it just as fast as he could.

GUARD ANDROTH'S PEOPLE ARRIVED at the caves and lightened their loads by laying packs and baskets down. The cave's mouth was even darker than the night around them and they kept their distance. It was a moss-laden mouth in the earth, which exhaled unpleasant cold breath that smelled of death, awaiting them like a ready-made grave. Without resting more than a moment, the black clad Androth walked to one of the baskets on the ground while the other travelers collapsed after their long night and morning of bushwhacking through the jungle. The black knight struck a torch, and lit two others off of the first, then gestured to Captain Durvish who watched intently.

"You don't mean to charge in there, do you? These folk haven't had a rest, yet." All eyes were on the black knight, the black cave, and Captain Durvish sitting on a black rock. For the first time, the people questioned Androth's leadership. "Can it wait until we've had a—"

The helmet shook back and forth.

"Gods its hard to reason with someone who don't reason back," Durvish said, and he stood up, noticing the pains in his feet and his knees as he straightened to hand the torches to two of his towermen, keeping the third for himself. They were Darby and Kilter, two veterans of the sarcoph invasion who had served bravely.

Torches in one hand, swords in the other, they walked forward into the cave with Androth behind them.

The firelight reached out before them in an advancing wave, lighting the recesses of the cold cave. Kilter gasped at the sound of something clattering loudly across the floor, "What was that!" he whispered hoarsely.

"It's okay," Darby answered, "I just kicked something."

"Shhhh!" Durvish shushed them. The four of them stopped to listen, unsure if something deeper inside had heard the sound, but despite waiting for a long time, they heard nothing but the drip of water and their own breathing.

Breaking the tense silence, Durvish asked, "well, what was it that you kicked, Darby?" Androth's black-gloved hand pointed to the floor, which, of course, was covered with dusty bones. Some of them however, were stripped of their meat only recently. Lying against one wall, among some of the older bones there were piles of armor, not unlike that worn by the knights of Darkwell. It reminded Durvish of the man who had freed them from the raid, for there was a belt of white leather lying in the dust.

"Do you think a bear lives in here?" Durvish heard himself ask. "Could a bear do that?" his voice dully petered out in the tomb-like cavern as they crept further in. No one answered him. He hoped it was a bear.

The cavern narrowed around them, until they stood in an opening to a large cavern that a torch would not illuminate fully, leaving vague, wet darkness before them. They stayed in the choke point, not wanting to venture into the unknown. Kilter's panicked breathing rattled next to Durvish's ear, making it hard to listen for danger. Androth took the torch from Durvish's hand, took two steps forward and threw it into the cave. It flew end over end through the blackness, the speed of it almost blew the torch out. It glowed enough to watch it fly, but it didn't light the room. It bounced off of something near the top of its arc then careened down to the left and found a resting point on the floor. Now that it was stationary, the flames regained their strength and slowly Durvish's eyes adjusted. There were rocks littering the floor by the torch, large boulders actually. His mind indulged in many illusions, but he convinced himself that the bears and the faces that he saw in every shadow were only his imagination. He swatted at his neck. He hadn't noticed until now that there was a drip from the cavern roof landing on him. For a split second he had made it out to be a poisonous spider biting at him, but he soon found relief, knowing it was water. He moved to the side.

Androth searched the darkness, and blended with it so well that the knight was little more than a vague outline. Durvish put a hand on the black armored shoulder before him, saying, I'm still with you. Another drip landed on Durvish's neck and he moved further to the side to avoid it.

Androth's boot echoed through the cave even though the step was slow and careful and made only the sound of grit on stone. Durvish took a step forward to keep abreast, and to keep his hand on the doughty shoulder of the Royal Guard. A splash of liquid oozed down Durvish's shoulder and back, some seeping through his tunic. He jumped and uttered a sound of disgust, "Yech!" *shouldn't cave water be cold?* He thought, wiping at his neck. But the first two drips hadn't been cold either, not as cold as they should have been.

"What?" Darby demanded, in a low growl. "What is it?" But Durvish didn't answer for a sudden fear had burst from his heart and leapt through his whole body, paralyzing him. Somehow he forced himself to turn around and slowly look upward.

His eyes widened, and at once the other towermen followed his gaze, but it was too late. Above them, a great fleshy arm dangled from a stout, hairy shoulder. The massive hand was just feet over Durvish's head. The figure was still as a statue, was it dead?

"NO!" Durvish screamed as he ducked and rolled away. Darby only let out a wordless, gargling shout. There was a huge, ugly face, with drool dangling in a sticky rope from its lips, and above that there was a single eye, with a brow furrowed in concentration. The hand snatched at Kilter's panic stricken form, the man was gone, pulled up into the blackness, screaming. Until his scream was muffled as his head entered the drooling mouth, and then silenced with a crunch. Before the towerman's dead hand dropped the torch, it shone upon the sickly figure of a grotesque giant that was somehow crouched above them on a ledge of stone, or wedged inside a burrow of its own making.

Durvish picked up the torch and the three of them fell back into the tunnel. Durvish glanced over his shoulder to the torch that Androth had thrown. Standing over it there towered a Cyclops, three times the height of a man.

"Androth!" screamed Durvish, "I think there are two of them!" And from behind them came the sudden rush of labored breathing and the charging foot slaps of gigantic bare feet. It sounded more massive than an elephant. Its sickly breaths were irregular and wet, and its stumbling rage was as fierce as a swarm of killer bees. Into view came the hairy-skinned form of a giant Cyclops. Its belly rippled as it rushed, and it's bulging arms held a club. It breathed through its flat nose, for in its mouth it still held Kilter's body, sucking on the bloody head and neck, black blood dripping down its sagging paunch.

Its equal in size and strength, another Cyclops came running behind it. "Oh Gods. Oh Gods," Darby said between panting breaths as they ran. Then one set of footsteps suddenly ceased. The Royal Guard had turned to fight.

"Androth! There's no chance," Durvish begged, but his voice was a gasp. Nevertheless, somehow, Durvish turned to fight too. They may not be much, but they were the only thing standing between these things and the rest of the camp. Darby came back to join them in disbelief. He held his shaky sword in front of him. Androth took a deep breath, spear raised, shield held tight against the body, and then stepped forward to engage the monsters toe-to-toe.

Durvish advanced, terrified, his heart frozen by how surreal it was. And then the silence of battle closed in, for it had begun. The clubs swung around and around, but Androth dodged them handily. The strength of the beasts was such that the stone of the cave shook and crumbled as they slammed their weapons against the walls and floor. If one of those blows hit its mark, certain death would follow. And yet, the Royal Guard remained calm, moving only far enough to get out of the way, saving energy and allowing the savage clubs to come within inches.

"Alright boys, let's give them a taste of steel!" Durvish said, wondering if he would walk out of this cave alive. Darby advanced with him. It was lumbering above them, focused myopically on Androth. The black knight dodged a blow of the club, but the swing carried Darby with it, crushing him against the cave wall and leaving him breathless, and desperate to crawl away on his broken limbs. Another thump with the tree trunk demolished his legs.

With a lunge, Guard Androth was suddenly between the two giants. "No, you damned fool!" Durvish protested, but already the black knight was surrounded by legs like the masts of ships and covered in the shadows that they made. The Cyclops in back grinned maniacally and bared its yellow teeth as he took a massive two-handed swing, thinking Androth was trapped, but looked aghast when the blow landed instead on his compatriot, causing the other monstrous creature to cry out in pain and clutch its arm, doubled over to cradle the wounded limb close to its body. Durvish from behind it went in to swing at his flanks, hacking with all his might. Bloody streaks like lashes from a whip colored the giant's backside, its hairy legs.

"Take that, wretched beast!" he cried. With a frustrated grunt and howl that may have been some form of language, the Cyclops turned to face the torch bearing Captain Durvish with a devilish belch.

Durvish stepped forward to prove his mettle. Then, blossoming from the Cyclopean eye was the gold worked spear of the Royal Guard.

The monster shrieked and bellowed with the pain and the sudden blindness but not for long, for he toppled backward dead. When his massive corpse fell out of the way, his shadow went with it, a curtain parting to reveal Androth sword in hand. The black figure darted under the other giant's legs while slashing ferociously at any exposed flesh. The slashes were so rapid and they cut so deep that Durvish almost felt sorry for the brute. The blood rolled down the Cyclops' legs and finally the beast dropped its club and backed away. But Androth had cut off his escape, forcing him up and out instead of back into the cave where it made its home. His lips hung slack, and his single brow was twitching violently in fear.

The armored form moved decisively reaching out to strike with hard stabs at the cowering giant's toes. Durvish advanced again, hoping to slay this thing from behind. As he was working up his courage, Androth became a flurry of movement, and somehow pushed the giant backward onto the body of the first. The still vertical spear, steadily braced in the dead giant's skull was waiting for the Giant's tender back. It was sheathed anew in blood as he finally came to rest, looking up with his one eye at the last thing he would ever see, the gold inlaid spear of a Royal Guard of Haven.

Androth couldn't pull the spear out. The torchlight played upon the Guard's blood covered armor and dripping weapons, but it didn't show the face behind the black wire mesh. The two of them walked out of the cave. The Royal Guard wordlessly ordered the tower men to get ropes and pull the bodies out of the cave. This was where they would wait for now.

Durvish, in a battle-drunk haze, felt that his whole body was buzzing with sensation. The after effect of mortal fear was exhilaration and utter gratitude for the chance to keep living. Smiling and regaining his breath, Durvish looked out at the valley that stretched below the high entrance to the cave. He hadn't noticed it until now, but looking down from the clearing at the cave's mouth, he could see the lights of Darkwell. There were shapes circling above the city and at times they lit up like fireflies.

"WHAT THE HELL HAPPENED to you?" Kellen asked as Deagan walked into Dragon Manor, smelling of foul smoke and covered in scratches. In answer, Deagan laughed and immediately began removing his armor. "Don't just toss that on the floor, you're filthy!" Kellen complained.

"I'm tired, hot, and I just found a rotter *inside* the city. If it weren't for me, half the damned town would be walking around like your grandma trying to bite each other's faces off by now. So I'm *sorry* that your precious floor is getting dirty from my armor, but right now you'll just have to monkey up and deal with it." He dropped a bloody gauntlet on the floor. "I'm not the one who invited half a dozen dragons into your damned bedroom."

"Wait a minute, for your information, the dragons aren't sleeping in my bedroom, you oaf. The Dragon *Riders* are. Do you even know how late it is? Did you say you found *rotters* in *Darkwell?*" Kellen's jaw dropped. "Answer the second question first," he finished.

"Try listening for once you daft old burglar. I found *one* rotter in Darkwell. And I killed it—killed it a few times actually. And no I *don't* know what time it is but if I were to hazard a guess I would say bed time," Deagan whined as he pulled the armor off his legs.

"Where the devil did you get that horse cart outside? And what about the horse?"

"Kellen, do I have to explain everything? Use your imagination!"

"So you *have* turned to a life of crime!" Kellen gasped hopefully.

"Chivalry doesn't just disappear because a duke takes my knighthood away. I'd never steal a copper, even from the richest bastard in the three cities. If you must know, the man who owned that cart was an undertaker. Other than that I've no idea who he was. I was out in the streets when along came this cart with a coffin in the back. The lid popped off and—you may have put two and two together by now—that was the rotter coming out to say hello. I couldn't kill it before it got the undertaker, but then as a precaution I staked them both to the ground, hauled them into the coffin and tied it shut. Then I borrowed the undertaker's cart and burned 'em out in the woods."

"Oh come on, you're telling me you wouldn't even steal from the most evil dark wizard? Even if it was in order to save Darkwell? You wouldn't steal the dark wizard's wand?"

"As usual you're missing the point." He moved to the curtained window that was perfectly clean and hung in picturesque folds due to Rory's incredible butlery. "There could be more of them."

"But you didn't see any others?"

"No."

"And you didn't try to find out who the undertaker was before you burned him and stole his horse? I thought you said you'd never steal."

"Och, I'll give it back to his family in the morning. There's no more I could have done."

"You'll be a criminal before the end, Deagan. I just know it."

"It's just as likely that you'll become a knight," Deagan scoffed.

GWYN WADED IN THE stream by the cave. The corpses of the Cyclops removed, it was now safe to reside there. Some of the villagers skilled in herb lore, survival, or hunting were able to start foraging for sustenance and setting up a more appropriate camp. Baskets of fruit were shared from campfire to campfire and the sweetness of the wild food lifted everyone's spirits—so did the slaying of the one eyed giants. There was a palpable relief that accompanied the slaying of evil. It was enough to make one believe that the world was just a little bit safer now. Besides, the way the Royal Guard had handled the two behemoths was quickly growing from rumor to legend. In truth, Androth had barely survived, but these people dearly needed a hero.

Gwyn's heart was broken in three places. It broke when her family was taken away in her childhood and her uncle sold her into the service of the Royal Lord. It broke a second time when she had to leave Haven. It broke a third time with the realization of what she had to do next.

The towermen understood her loss the best, and gave her a wide berth as she washed off the dust of travel. The rest of them eyed her without any understanding, like she was from another world. And in some ways she was.

She scrubbed her face with the cold water and blew air through her lips to keep it from running into her mouth. She poured water in the palm of her hand over the back of her neck, the muscles in her arm rippling. The questions still troubled her. Why would Malagor have sent Gwyn and her people to that ragged village

Oxham in the Border Lands only to order a savage raid against them several days later? Who was behind the curtain in the throne room?

Over Darkwell, Dragon Riders were soaring in great wheels spouting flame to illuminate the night. Dragon Riders of Haven. Why would the Royal Lord Saxus send away his fiercest warriors at a time when the sarcophs, the dead men, gained territory in the outer lands?

She suspected he sent them away for the same reason he abandoned the South Towers: he had turned against his own people. He had stayed hidden in his keep, taking no audience but that filthy advisor, Lord Othar. Even the Royal Guards were sent outside his doors to patrol as if they were mere footmen.

Haven would not fall while Gwyn drew breath. She had to return there, but without help, charging into the palace to bring the Royal Lord to justice would be to no avail.

With help on the other hand, much could be gained. That was what Gwyn was counting on. She stood up, her old, strong back creaking slightly. And she knew that her time to rest was over. She needed to find the Riders. Wordlessly she dressed herself and walked through the camp. She handed a note to Captain Durvish, and left down the path to Darkwell.

KING MALAGOR LOOKED OUT of his high window onto the city of Darkwell around him. He had no grand view of the countryside, only the cramped squalor that lay inside the high wall. But he could see *all* the squalor. It was his—Malagor's and no other's.

He was old and infirm, but it seemed that at least for now, he was the ruler of the greatest of the last great cities—even if luck did have something to do with it. For Darkwell, unlike Haven and Pillar, had never had its walls tested. Darkwell had never been attacked. Whatever the reason, he had the upper hand on Haven, and it would soon be his. It was a pity that his throne room had no view of Haven, for he very much would have liked to gaze upon it and slowly form his aged pale hand into a fist as he imagined crushing it and taking it for his own.

There was that troubling detail of the rebels from Haven who had tried to gain entry into Darkwell. What was her name? Gwyn? She was a handsome woman, queenly, but of course, some scullery maids took on airs when they got to a certain age. They got trapped in their work and their gossip. Their lives were so narrow that they thought they'd seen everything. Well . . . she had seen much had she not? She had known about Saxus sending the Dragon Riders away. She had known about the Royal Guard leaving . . . but Malagor wondered, did she know about the Royal Guard being poisoned? It didn't seem like it. That Gwyn knew too much, and that was why the raid on Oxham had been necessary. It was a clever plan by Jatham, Malagor's advisor and confidante, sending them to the village as a gesture of goodwill then sending men to do away with them.

It was a pity that they hadn't had the decency to die properly. In fact they not only survived, but disappeared. Malagor furrowed his brow in worry. He hoped the servant woman and all her fellow rebels had been eaten by denizens of evil that wandered around the outskirts of the realm. There were plenty of nasty creatures out there by which their meager numbers would be swiftly digested. This convenient demise was what Malagor had assured his men had befallen the rebels, though he had no proof. It was that proof for which the Darkish King dearly longed.

That failure in the Border Lands was in large part the fault of that peon Sir Deagan Wingrat. It mattered not, Jatham had seen to it that the knight's belt was taken away and he was no more threat now than any other commoner in the realm. Certainly Deagan wouldn't be fouling up any more of King Malagor's ambitions. No, the king had a new knight to replace the old. Colstin was his name. He'd been a guard for Duke Worth long ago, but had shown a certain aptitude for dealing punishment, so he had become one of Malagor's own jailers. He'd been loyal in the raid in the Border Lands even when that fool of a knight had not been. Jatham of course would have had Wingrat put to death, but perhaps there was some shred of mercy left in the king even now. More likely than that, Malagor just wanted to get his way for once! Jatham certainly was helpful and respectful and all the rest, but he did have a way of overstepping his bounds and needed to be reminded that a king was a king and an advisor was not. Speaking of that bald sneak of a man, where was he?

"Jatham? Come in here, Jatham," Malagor called.

"I am here, Sire," Jatham answered as he bowed from the entryway. "What does Your Majesty need?"

"Send another troop to find those rebels. It is most unfortunate that they got away the first time. I have a king's sense of justice and it does not endure going unsatisfied."

"Indeed, Your Highness. I will ready a group of hunters and footmen."

"Footmen?" Malagor asked. "Why send footmen when you can send wing-men?" He laughed at his little joke, and said, "What good are Dragon Riders if not for securing the king's realm from dangerous rebels, Jatham?"

"My King, they are both fierce and loyal. It would be wise to pit them against your enemies, forgive my stupidity in suggesting mere footmen."

"Yes, yes," the King said dismissively. "See to it, Jatham."

Jatham stammered and his face took on an expression of shock. "S-s-sire? I mean no disrespect or ill will, but I'm afraid that I shall need to attend to other matters. Your Highness may need to—if it pleases Your Highness of course—to give the order yourself, or appoint another of your men to do so."

Malagor's face turned red and his brow became a ledge of stone overhanging his eyes. "What the devil has gotten into you, Holmin? You'll do it yourself and that's final! Whatever else you're working on can wait!"

"I'm afraid that this is out of my hands, Sire. It is simply not in my power to give this order to Sir Oscar. Sir Oscar was close to Lord Saxus. Perhaps Your Highness can see my predicament now?"

Malagor thought for a long uncomfortable moment while his advisor wrung his hands and peered into the king's eyes with a twitching lip. Jatham was right again. It would be most unfortunate to slip up now. Especially since they were so close. Damn him for being right all the time. King Malagor sighed, not feeling much like a king at all. "Very well, Jatham, you're dismissed."

In answer, Jatham only bowed as he backed away, a smile on his face and sweat on his brow. He was a coward, that Jatham. King Malagor looked back out the window at his domain and stood up straighter, trying to reassure himself that he was still in control.

Yes, Kellen, tis a fine manor, but it seems to have something of a *dragon problem* wouldn't you say?"

As if he hadn't heard the nobleman sitting across from him, Kellen went on. "Look at the sweeping roofline, the woodwork around the doors, the cleanliness of the steps! I've the finest butler in Darkwell, you know. Wait a tick! Did you say dragon *problem?* What do you mean?"

"I mean there are two dragons taking up residence on your roof and a third is perched atop your tree! If that isn't a problem then I am sorely mistaken!" The speaker was Rond Hollow, a nobleman who wasted most of his time sucking up to more powerful noblemen. His bangs reached down to his eyebrows and he had no neck. He wore fine velvet clothing and golden rings on his fingers. He was rich, and owned land, that was why Kellen was speaking with him.

"Mistaken you are, sir, I insist. Not to be rude, but you don't know the first *thing* about dragons do you?" Kellen smiled apologetically as if he had just exposed a nasty secret of Hollow's.

Needing to save face, Hollow replied, "Of course I do. I know they are dangerous and a great nuisance! Why do you think we're off slaying them all the time?"

Kellen chuckled knowingly. "Dragons aren't a nuisance once you learn to master them. It is a sign of a great man to be able to tame and handle the beasts. Look how serenely they wait on the rooftop. Look how majestic they are and how they add such grace to the lines of the building. There is a reason they sometimes carve them out of stone to adorn the houses of the wealthy. Because dragons are beautiful, they're cunning, and they will defend their master to the death." Kellen allowed some very convincing tears to well up in his eyes. "I'll never be the same man again after working with dragons. I'll never be the weakling I once was."

"Well, humph, how did you come up with these dragons?" the nobleman asked. "Where did you get them?"

"I daresay you've noticed there has been quite a flush of dragons in the area of late haven't you? Well they came from Haven. They were sent here for extra defense. It turned out that I was in the right place at the right time and I was charged with finding the dragons their accommodations. You can't bring them to a regular stable of course!" Kellen laughed, bringing the nobleman in on a joke. "They'd eat all the hay!" he concluded. The nobleman laughed heartily, but was not sure whether this Kellen Wayfield was being serious. Either way, he was certain that he was dealing with an experienced and reputable man, a man who could tame dragons! Well, something about him *did* have an allure most uncanny. Was it the vitality of the dragons being transferred to him?

"Well that seems to have been a lucky happenstance indeed, that you landed such a commission. You must have dealt directly with the Royal Lord Saxus, I should think."

Kellen had done nothing of the kind. In fact he had made the whole thing up. "Well, I dealt with one of his loyal advisors. Did you know the dragons will build their own nests if you let them? All they need is a trio of good logs to be put in place and lashed together. We built those three platforms in less than two days. And oh they look grand. My men are getting quite adept at putting them up . . . tis a pity . . ."

"What's a pity?" Hollow asked.

"Oh it's nothing. What of your affairs? I trust the royal court is as stimulating as ever?"

"Never mind that, what's a pity, Wayfield? Go on."

"Well I can't fool you, my boy," Kellen said with a smile. "All I was saying was that it's a pity I have so many dragon supplies, and so many dragons thank the Gods, and I seem to have run out of roof space! There's nothing like the feeling of truly bonding with them, you know. Much like a loyal and noble hound, or a great steed. I'm sure you are a horseman of great renown, or so I hear. Hm. You'd probably have a fairer hand than I at dealing with the beasts, being such a gifted rider. I envy the lords of horses . . . but there is no horse that equals a dragon in *power!*"

"Do you think I could really tame them? Do you think I could have the touch for it?"

Kellen looked the man squarely up and down. "Yes, I have a hunch that you could." He looked out the window at his manor again and sipped his tea. "They are damned expensive though."

"I wonder how well such a platform would rest upon my own roof," the nobleman mused.

"I have seen your roof, sir. It is a magnificent one. I should think that not one but several roosts could be maintained there." Kellen then looked as though he had just had an idea, though he'd had it long before. He snapped his fingers and said, "Wait! Are you proposing to help me house some of these dragons? I would be much obliged and grateful for your service! I could have a team of men at your castle—"

Flattered, the nobleman interrupted Kellen with a laugh, "Castle! Ha. Oh tis far humbler than that, call it a . . . house, or a manor. Castle indeed."

"As you like, sir. I could have my team meet you there today to see what potential your grounds may have for dragon habitation."

"Well, what will the cost be, Kellen?"

"That all depends on the number of roosts you are able to sustain. I still wish I'd been able to fit a fourth, maybe if I wasn't so fast to build the first one I could have thought it through . . . Should I send my team m'lord?"

"I believe you should, Wayfield. It will be my delight to have them all come in and join me for supper when their surveying is done."

"As you wish, Rond. I can't believe the service you are providing me. I am honored to have help in this endeavor of dragon keeping. It'll make a strong man out of you, but be warned, you will never want to get rid of them once you start in!"

They shared another laugh and already Rond Hollow had begun to think of himself as a dragon tamer. His step became nobler, his chest more full.

Kellen had already surveyed the nobleman's abode the night before and estimated they could put five dragons there and two more on nearby treetops. The work would begin soon, tomorrow if the Gods willed it, not that Kellen believed in them. He finished his tea and waited. He had arranged to meet with a nobleman from the Southern side of Darkwell in this same tavern in half an hour's time.

D EAGAN PICKED UP HIS *muddy helm from the wet ground.*
*The rain stopped. A few of the King's men came back
around the building and saw that the door was open with
smoke pouring out of it. Deagan stood there, watching them cautiously,
sword drawn. Rain and sweat matted his short hair to his head and rivulets
of the mixture curved down his face only to drip slowly through his beard.
The men looked back at him in shock and mistrust.*

*He whistled for Maggie and she walked to him. He mounted her and
rode back. Eli lay dead under Korvis' touch. A pang of guilt washed over
him. If he hadn't opened the door, Eli would be alive now.*

*Korvis had torn off his helmet and now wore a severe expression as he
closed Eli's young, dead eyes. Blood spilled from his hacked apart neck. It
was not the first time Korvis had seen death, nay, he'd even dealt it, but he
looked up at Deagan in a fury nonetheless, shaking his head in disbelief.
Korvis rose to his feet with his sword tip resting on the ground.*

*Soon the rest of the men had gathered around the back of the building.
Perhaps they noticed that the screaming from within had stopped. Perhaps
one of the men had gone to the front to tell them what had happened. They
were all there under him and drenched in water and firelight. They squeezed
their weapons and torches. They had their blood up for killing, and hadn't
yet gotten their fill of it.*

*A murmur moved among them. They said harsh things, Deagan knew,
even though he couldn't hear them. He tried to put his helmet on, but found
it was too badly dented and he threw it in his saddlebag.*

*"It is done!" Deagan yelled to the crowd, fearful that he would be
the next to join the dead, but refusing to show any weakness. "They were
innocent. That Jatham was wrong about them. They were no threat to us*

or to Darkwell. We can report to the king himself that our mission was successful. He need not fear these people any longer, and we have driven them from the Border Lands."

"Shut yer yap, you fat, stinkin' knight!" the Jailer bellowed. "We had 'em where we wanted 'em and you let 'em go for no damned reason! You're a coward and every one of us is a witness to it!"

Korvis looked wrathfully at the Jailer. He was shaken by the tragedy of Eli's death, but he had now returned to the moment, realizing the mounted knight may be in danger. "Do not speak that way to your betters, jailer." Korvis ordered.

"What are you going to do about it if I do, huh? You gonna kill me? Throw me in the pile with that kid on the ground?" He pointed to Eli. "Is that what happens to the king's men who try to follow orders around here? You make me sick. You'd stick up for a coward just because of the color of his belt! If you're not with us, you're against us!" He screamed. He walked toward Deagan and Maggie. A few other men surrounded Korvis, blocking Deagan's view of him.

"In fact, if he's not man enough to kill the rebels, then I'd have to say he is a rebel himself, wouldn't you, boys?" He laughed. "You know what Holmin told us to do with rebels. Rape, pillage and burn 'em! So which one would you like to try first, eh, Sir Knight?" A few other men laughed.

Deagan charged Maggie straight for the advancing man. His blood was boiling with rage. He knew he'd done the right thing. He knew he'd saved lives. This man was insulting him unjustly, and all the way to his core. It would take a lot of willpower to keep from killing the jailer. Instead Maggie plowed into Colstin's chest, avoiding the man's sword. The smell of burnt horsehair billowed around him, for the torch he held had struck her side as the jailer fell to the ground.

The man rolled from side to side to get away from Maggie's pumping legs. He thrust the torch underneath her belly so she was standing above it. Deagan almost fell from his saddle as Maggie reared up to get away before the flames could hurt her, but this gave Colstin time to regain his feet.

The jailer was finally upright when Deagan was upon him again. He lashed Colstin's back with his sword, wanting so desperately to take the frightening man's life with that swing, but he held back, still unwilling to kill the king's own men. The jailer screamed in pain as his free hand grasped the shallow cut on his back. The crowd of men pressed in upon Deagan. It was time to go.

Colstin had other plans however. His hands covered in blood, the jailer jabbed hard at Maggie's side with a rusty sword. Deagan kicked the blade away with an armored shin then disarmed the man with a hard chop of his sword. He spun the horse about with great skill and she forced the ring of men back with her hindquarters, knocking several of them into the red mud.

Deagan saw an opening in the ring around him. It was his best chance. A torch struck him in the back, and burned his neck. Men laughed. Had the torch fallen away, or stayed put upon the saddle behind him? He urged Maggie through the gap in the ring, but she didn't have enough space to build up a proper charge. Nevertheless she lunged forward in a burly trot. Most men got out of the way, but one had decided to try and fight. Deagan was beyond compassion for these men now, though not without mercy. The man raised his sword to stop Deagan. There was a thump. The severed sword hand fell to the ground as a scream came unbidden from the bleeding man's throat. Then at last, he was free to ride away from the first battle he had ever lost.

His memories had distracted him, and when he looked up it took a moment to recognize his surroundings. Deagan remembered that he had been wandering the streets for two reasons. He needed to find Luthan, and he needed to make sure he'd seen the last of Darkwell's rotters. He made his way from the stable to the barracks and back again. He even chanced a pass by Duke Worth's place. He hadn't seen the duke however, which he was thankful for. The duke still made him sick.

Kellen had done a good job of spreading the word about his dragons. Already some other nobleman had erected six roosts on his property. This city was getting crowded indeed. If only Kellen could convince some rich noble that it was fashionable to take in some of the refugees that populated the slums.

Finally Deagan decided to make for the courtyard where Luthan sometimes practiced. He passed through a cramped alley filled with potted plants and small stacks of firewood to the hidden courtyard between the backs of four buildings. Some of the training gear was laid out here. There was a rope strung across the courtyard like a clothesline with shorter vertical ropes tied to it at odd intervals that held suspended orbs of clay. Deagan went to the far end of the courtyard, reached up to the main rope, and wrenched it back and forth erratically to send the clay balls swinging, jumping, and colliding with one another.

Deagan grunted as he charged into the swinging obstacle course with his sword and shield raised. For him it never felt like practice. Each session took on the importance of true combat. The fifteen-strike combination that he performed was difficult enough in an open space, but now it had to be modified on the fly in order to weave through the swinging balls without touching any. Dividing his focus, Deagan was aware of the ball behind him even as he swerved past the one ahead. He crouched and spun under the jostling main rope, cutting down an invisible foe with his twelfth shot. His sword hit an invisible combatant in the back of the leg, and then the gut for the thirteenth and fourteenth. Now past all the balls and unscathed, the bulky swordsman imagined his 15th shot taking off the top of Duke Worth's head.

Deagan's hard breathing reminded him of how long it had been since he'd done such a routine. In the far corner of the courtyard there was a plank of wood with three holes in it. He carried it over and placed it in its stand in front of the still swinging clay orbs. Again he reached up and shook the rope, but this time he picked up the blunt practice spear from the ground and dropped his sword and shield. Periodically, the clay balls appeared through the holes as they swung on the other side. He stabbed with both hands. He sunk the wooden spear cleanly through the holes in the board but wasn't able to strike the clay balls behind.

He thought of the knight he'd faced behind the town hall in the Border Lands raid. The black knight's spear was neither short nor light. And when it struck, it dealt a heavy blow, but all this had been done while the knight wielded a great shield in the other hand. Curses why couldn't he hit the orb behind the board? He'd never been much of a spearman. The balls slowed until one of them all but stopped and he managed to strike it with ease.

Then Luthan walked in wearing his full armor and carrying all his weapons. Deagan dropped the spear and stomped over to embrace him. Gods that old knight was a sight for sore eyes.

"What's the idea, Deagan? Doing some training for the forces of evil?" Luthan asked.

"Aye, and what's it to you unless you're here to do the same?"

"I am here to do the same," Luthan said with a smile. "It's always more fun playing sticky with a partner."

"Sticky is it? Well I could be convinced to partake of a game." Soon the two warriors were fully armored, wielding sturdy rods of wood, and beating the living daylights out of each other while laughing hysterically.

Luthan paused and then panted, "Watch this." And he strode forward with a weaving combination of strikes that left Deagan guessing to the last. He deflected the first two, but he was soon forced to retreat. In a quick effort he tried to peel away from the assault by darting to the side, but Luthan was upon him again and had him blocking blows in desperation. Luthan drove Deagan back to the wall and once there he slammed his shield into the former knight's body, crushing him against the bricks. This however was not a legal finish to sticky. One of them had to die. And being pinned was not the same as being killed.

Luthan tried to deal the final shot to Deagan's helm, but it was blocked and their wooden blades were locked against each other, hand to hand. This didn't happen often, and no one really preferred the arrangement because either blade could slip and when it did, either man could die. Rare as this blade lock was, these two had practiced it against each other many times. They pushed and swiveled their blades, able to tap each other's helmets but not with enough force to deal a killing shot.

Finally in a moment of distraction, Deagan looked to the side. He was aligned with the opening of the alley that led to the street. A woman walked by. *Gods she's beautiful.* Deagan recognized her from somewhere. The town hall in the Border Lands! She was there! She was the fair damsel, well, fair *dame* who had closed the shutters. She was the lady with no fear in her face. "Luthan. Did you not see that fair damsel?" Deagan asked.

"You think I'll be so easily fooled?" Luthan asked.

Clunk! Deagan's stick finally landed on Luthan's helm and the two of them disengaged. "Well I suppose I was so easily fooled after all," he said, saluting Deagan with his sword.

"I must go after her, Luthan. Thanks for the match. It's been too long. Wait here, brother, I've news that will chill your blood." Deagan jogged toward the exit. "You could use the practice anyway," he added as an afterthought. A stick hit him in the back of his helmet almost knocking him off balance and he turned to give Luthan one last good-natured grin.

The street was full of colors and various cooking smells that made the air almost pleasant. "Fresh fish!" called a peddler at the street level. He pushed past some sad and hungry looking men—men of Elrodge Keep to judge by their garb. It was a city Deagan would never visit, having been sacked. Had these men been there when it fell?

"Pardon," Deagan mumbled as he shuffled past. A man carried a basket up a wooden ladder that led up into more slum platforms above the street where metal braziers stood scattered upon them, holding the ever-burning fires of Darkwell.

He took a gamble and guessed she wasn't heading into those slums above him, but he scanned them anyway as he passed underneath their shadows. People were sleeping in the corners, building small crafts from their homelands, sharpening weapons. *No, not weapons,* he told himself. *Knives are tools, and they're used for cooking. Not everyone is a warrior.* Besides, many refugees were disarmed by the Darkish Guards upon reaching the gates, it was the only way Malagor would allow them in.

He sped up for he hadn't seen her yet and reached the next square, a courtyard with statues and trees, populated with more peddlers and entertainers. He could see her nowhere, and now had no confidence that he'd find her. There were a hundred directions she could have gone.

He walked back to where Luthan was training. The knight was practicing the same combination he'd used to pin Deagan. "Luthan," he said. "I lost her, but she's out there somewhere in Darkwell."

"Ah. That happens, brother. Keep looking."

"I will."

"And what was it you wanted to tell me? The news that'd make my blood run cold," said the Knight.

"I killed a rotter on Flag Street not three days ago," Deagan answered. "Have you seen any others?"

"**R**ORY, MY DEAR BOY, I have a summons to the king it would seem. Some sort of mission no doubt." The Dragon Rider sighed through his mustache and looked to the floor. "I'll be back in the evening. And if possible my friend, I will tell you all about it." Sir Oscar had a fatherly look.

Rory, the butler looked up from sweeping the kitchen floor. He laid the broom leaning perfectly in the corner and came forward to the knight at full attention. "Very good, Sir Knight. Can I have anything prepared for you or your mount upon your return?"

"A hot slab of pork would do quite well I believe, if you'd be so kind?"

"Of course, sir," Rory replied, overjoyed to be of use. "Anything else?"

"No, no that will do. Well, wish me luck!" And with that Oscar climbed the ladder out of the window and mounted his dragon. The house creaked a bit as the beast leapt from its perch. This worried Rory and he made a note to himself to reinforce the rafters tonight. There was plenty of lumber to be had after all.

Rory looked down at the plate that Oscar had left on the table. Toast again. Crumbs were everywhere. He may be a Dragon Rider, but he was no butler.

It was a short flight to reach the spire in the center of Darkwell where King Malagor resided. Oscar pulled out the written summons that he had been given by a messenger earlier that day. Sure enough it asked him to meet on the spire's roof. It was opportune enough for Oscar, but he hoped the stairs didn't make too much trouble for the elderly king.

Pete alighted on the battlements and Oscar leapt from the saddle without hesitation, still reading. A group of guards gawked at the creature and kept their distance. One of them led Oscar down a trap door. He was conducted into a small room where the king awaited him.

"Sir Oscar!" Malagor greeted him. "How good to see you."

"And you, Your Highness," Oscar said bowing.

"I have something of a mission for you, my boy. A bit dangerous perhaps, but nothing you can't handle."

"Anything, My Liege," Oscar said.

"You will fly out tonight, gather the other Dragon Riders, and scour the surroundings of my city until you find the rebels. When you find them, kill them all and report back to me. Is that understood?" the king asked.

"Understood, Your Highness. May I ask where they were last seen?"

"Oxham. It is a small town in the Border Lands. You'll find it on any map. Perhaps they are still there? You will find out."

Oscar understood that it was time for him to leave, so he bowed and said, "Of course sir, we will leave immediately." Then he backed away in a bow until he turned and went back to the roof with a furrowed brow. Pete carried him away into the night, flapping his wings only a handful of times as he glided down to Kellen's manor.

GWYN WALKED THE STREETS of Darkwell, she had left the rest of her people from Haven at the cave and she now sought sir Oscar. She knew he would be here somewhere. In Haven, there were three compounds where the Dragon Riders kept their steeds and all the weapons and supplies that were needed to do their unusual and dangerous job. These were called dragon hutches and they were made of the same columns of natural stone that jutted out of the countryside to make the South Towers. They were pocked with carved roosts that the dragons decorated after their fashion and they had elaborate staircases that gave access to all the roosts.

In Darkwell, however, it seemed that the nobles allowed the beasts to roost directly on their own homes. Gwyn was taken aback by the cavalier way that one nobleman she saw approached the steed of one of Haven's most prized knights. He *patted* it on the nose! This would have been unheard of in Haven. The Dragon Rider stood idly by, looking nervous.

Gwyn had gone no closer for she did not want to risk being spotted by anyone other than Sir Oscar himself. And none of the six dragons perched on this nobleman's house were Oscar's dragon, Pete.

There must be another hutch somewhere in Darkwell. They couldn't be forcing the poor dragons to circle endlessly above the city. Then again, with Saxus' lack of concern for his own people, it seemed likely he'd give much less consideration for the dragons. It was possible he'd sent them here without making arrangements for their stay at all. She had seen one dragon plop tiredly onto the tower of a small temple, only to be met by an uproar from the crowd below. It slipped on the smooth rocks, its tail and one of its back legs dangled over the side and it breathed heavily, but the surface was too small and too slanted for it to truly rest. Finally exhausted, unable to keep its footing, and agitated by the people below, it took off to the skies again, circling.

Gwyn rounded a corner and the sounds of hammers and saws came drifting up the hill to greet her. A platform like many of the others she'd seen was being built against the wall of one of the stone manors. She walked closer to see the dragon roosts that Kellen had built.

There were three roosts, one in a tree, the other two on the roof, but there were only two dragons sleeping there. The empty roost had a unique look. In its center, the chimney of the building rose through the woven covering that the dragon had made. She had to get closer to be sure, but this looked like it could be Pete's handiwork. She remembered his affection for bright colors, and the nest was lined with brightly colored laundry. She climbed onto the platform nearby and got a better look. Yes, she thought that was Sir Oscar's handkerchief draped over what must have been the dragon's water bucket. She decided this was the place to wait. Sir Oscar would be with Pete so it was no use going in there to find him now.

Perhaps at last, the group of Haven rebels had the aid they needed in overthrowing the Royal Lord.

D URVISH GRUNTED WITH THE effort of lifting the massive beam into place. He'd been tasked with crafting the defenses of the cave. The Royal Guard's written instructions had told him to fortify it inside and out. There were some tools that he wished he had, but with the kits that the tower men had brought with them he was satisfied well enough.

The South Towers had needed serious repair when Captain Durvish had been given their command. His inventive nature, strong knowledge of rigging and carpentry, and passion for building siege weapons, were all part of why he'd been given the job. He outfitted the South Towers with all sorts of long-range weapons and other defenses that he and his towermen built from scratch: ballistae, catapults, trebuchets, traps, locking gates that could not be battered down and escape tunnels that led to hidden outposts. Durvish loved drawing and redrawing pictures of his inventions. He loved practicing with them even more. Since the clearing at the entrance of the cave was relatively small, he decided to craft a ballista, a huge mounted crossbow that could be aimed and shot by a single man, but would take two of them to load. Around the ballista, he ordered the construction of a dry stacked stonewall.

While some worked on the defenses, others of the towermen and a few villagers worked together to make a tunnel system that would bring water into the cave in case they were trapped there for an extended time.

"Take care and mind this boulder here!" Durvish ordered. "We'll shape the wall around it that's all." He was like a child building castles on the beach. Marching around and checking his plans, Durvish oversaw the rest of the preparations, but was most invested in building the ballista—not just a decent ballista, but the best ballista of his siege weapon career.

He hoped that the fort would be ready by the time Guard Androth returned, for when it was, it would be a real beauty.

GWYN KEPT HER FOCUS as she watched the roost from her seat in the tavern across the street. Darkness fell before Pete finally set his great talons on the edge of his colorful roost and Sir Oscar climbed off him. She watched in sheer joy and anticipation as the familiar knight wire brushed the dragon's dark azure scales and oiled him liberally. Pete absolutely gleamed when the careful knight was done, and he curled up to hold the hay bale in a coil of his tail as he ate. Sir Oscar climbed down a ladder and Gwyn paid the bartender for the drink she had nursed since late afternoon. Then she left through the door and passed under the platform.

She knocked on the door that said Dragon Manor over it. Though Rory had been in the other room, he opened the door instantly, surprising Gwyn. "Yes, M'lady? Is there something I can do for you?" the butler asked, showing no sign of being shocked by her shocking beauty.

She bowed, "Yes. I seek Sir Oscar. Is he here?"

"I shall inquire about your request."

Gwyn was impressed with his manners. She noted that he never gave her any clue about whether Oscar was there in the first place. Perhaps he had the instincts and the training required to be a Royal Guard. She waited on the doorstep patiently, certain that soon she would be closer to her ultimate goal of bringing the Dragon Riders back to aid in the freeing of Haven.

The door opened again, "Please come in, M'lady. Sir Oscar informs me that he would never keep a beautiful woman waiting on the doorstep. This way, please," Rory said. He stood to the side and she entered the best-kept manor in Darkwell. It was devoid of dust and clutter and it was impeccably arranged. The fire was burning brightly in the next room, yet no scent of smoke could be detected. Instead the aroma of roast pork and herbs filled her nose as she walked on the fine red carpet and into the abode of Kellen Wayfield.

Gwyn entered the main room where Sir Oscar was still unbuckling his light riding armor. The white haired and slender knight turned to face her when he heard her light footfalls behind him. When he saw her face, his jaw dropped open and his breastplate fell to the floor. He hurriedly knelt before her and lowered his eyes.

"Guard Androth, I did not expect to see you here!" he stuttered. "Rory, do leave us dear boy. Nothing personal," Oscar said knowing that Gwyn might not speak openly unless they were alone.

"Of course, Sir Oscar," the butler said bowing out of the room.

"Rise, Oscar," Gwyn said. "I need your help, and I would not ask you lightly. We have much to discuss, so I hope that you have some time."

"Time, I'm afraid, is something I could use some more of, Guard. The king has ordered me to ride."

"YOU SAW A DAMSEL, eh, Deagan?" Kellen asked.

"No, she had a nobler face than any damsel. In my old age I've found that a young woman just cannot impress an old man! Ha. They could have the finest features and the best figure in the world, but something about 'em looks . . . doughy. Like they haven't come out of the oven yet. A woman needs thirty odd winters on her before she'll be to my liking," Deagan declared.

"Suit yourself, hag-lover," Kellen said.

They were outside Kellen's abode and it was night. From the hedge popped Rory.

"Wah!" cried Kellen. "Get out of that hedge, man!"

Rory didn't budge. His mouth was a straight line. "Master Kellen, is there anything I can do for you this evening? Sir Oscar and his guest are already inside at supper."

"Guest?" Kellen asked, amused. "What guest?"

"Her name is Gwyn and judging by what you said Deagan, she'd be much to your liking . . ."

Rory almost cracked a smile but decided against it. Why was the butler's head so low over the waist high hedge? Was he standing in a hole?

"Do get out of that hedge, Rory. It can wait until the morning."

Still the butler didn't remove himself. "The hedge needs trimming *now* sir. There will be other tasks for me in the morning."

"If you like," Kellen conceded giving the butler a suspicious look. Kellen and Deagan entered the house.

Sir Oscar leaned back on two legs of his chair and chewed the pork slowly and with grave consideration. Sitting by him was the woman that Deagan had seen on the street. He gasped. She turned to see the former knight still armored as he was after a day of patrolling for the undead. The white patch on his chin and the crow's feet aside his twinkling eyes were unmistakable. He let his smile grow freely.

"You were at the raid," he said at last.

Kellen swept forward and lifted her hand to his lips for a brief kiss. He introduced himself, but Deagan didn't hear for he was shocked to see this lady before him. She wore the firelight like armor and like a gown. The gaze of her eyes drifted to Deagan even as Kellen's grand and showy greeting washed over her. She did not blush with his wiles. She made no motion to show that he had won her over. Words were cheap to her, Deagan felt. He hoped that being in the presence of the man who'd saved her life in the Border Lands cheapened them further.

D EAGAN HAD JUMPED THROUGH many high and flaming hoops to become a knight. He trained with Luthan, went to tournaments, volunteered to fight for King Malagor's wars, which turned out to serve only his insecurities and ambitions and were never intended to defend the people themselves. It was strange how the perspective on his life's work could change with something as simple as the loss of a belt and chain.

He remembered being knighted however, and how that moment had made it all worth it. *Shocked at being asked to the king's court, where he had never been before, Deagan bathed in the stream and bought clean clothes for the occasion. When the time came, he was called forward to stand in front of the king and Malagor made a brief speech about his exploits.*

Deagan now wondered whether it was the same speech that he delivered every time he knighted someone, but at the time it was the most marvelous thing that had ever been said about him. He glowed with pride.

"Honor!" the king bellowed. "Seek it out, and you will find it in this man. Courage! Ask any who has fought beside him, and they will tell you the tale of how Deagan Wingrat saved the lives of two fellow soldiers with no concern for his own safety. Chivalry! This is a heavy word and yet, this man carries it with him wherever he goes, acting in the most valiant, just, and loyal manner in all that he says and does."

Luthan, who had given him the majority of his training, came forward, smiling broadly and dressed in his finery. Draped across his hands was the white belt. The young niece of the king, Princess Breya stepped up from behind her father and opened a long wooden box. She gleamed with pride as she pulled out the chain of gold, handed the box to an attendant and raised the necklace to put it over Deagan's head. Everyone laughed when the young princess had to pull Deagan down by the front of his shirt in order to reach for she was less than ten summers old.

As Breya stepped back, the king came forward again. "Kneel," he said impressively. "I dub you Sir Deagan Wingrat, knight of Darkwell!" The sword tapped him once on each shoulder, blade down. It was sharp, so he certainly felt it, but he made no indication of pain. He was humbled by it even as he was honored. Deagan kissed the royal ring. "Now, rise," Malagor said.

Finally Deagan turned away from the king to see the assembled courtiers and knights behind him. They cheered, one and all for his accomplishment and it gave them all heart to see a strong new warrior added to the esteemed ranks of the knighthood.

Then the king had turned him back around and said, "Let this be the last blow you receive unanswered." With surprising strength, the king delivered a punch just as powerful as his speech into Deagan's chest. The force knocked him backward, but the rest of the knights in the hall were there to catch him. Again everyone cheered and Deagan could tell from the looks on the other knights' faces that this had happened to all of them too.

Had he really done anything so wrong? In the king's eyes, yes, saving the lives of those he was trying to kill was more than certainly an act of treason. Though, no longer a knight, Deagan clung to the life of chivalry for that concept was easy enough for him to grasp. He likened it to fairness, decency, doing your best, honesty, and never giving up. Deagan didn't see actions as lawful or unlawful, however, especially not his own. It just wasn't the way his mind worked. He was raised in the squalor of Darkwell, a place where survival mattered more than law.

Now he shared food and company with one of the people for whom he threw it all away. Oscar had introduced her as Gwyn. The way he looked at her seemed familiar making it clear that they weren't strangers. Deagan hadn't been this close to one of the so-called rebels since he had fought with that brave spearman in the Border Lands behind the town hall and seeing this Gwyn alive and well rather than devoured by creatures in the jungle meant Deagan's defiance of his orders at Oxham had done some good after all.

He decided Gwyn was worth it, if only so he could look at her stupidly with nothing to say, which was exactly what he did.

Deagan was speechless and she was tongue-tied as well. The two of them would have made quite a pair, staring at each other on the street. He was glad he hadn't caught up with her. Eventually, as the conversation continued, Deagan stopped gawking and went about removing his armor, stealing glances in Gwyn's direction as often as possible and thought perhaps she was doing the same. She was probably the only one in the city who would truly appreciate the story of his discharge. It had been for her and her people after all. To her, he might even be a hero.

"These are good men, please explain to them all you have told me; they can be trusted," Oscar said, urging Gwyn to speak.

The woman said nothing, but patiently looked at Sir Oscar who sighed in exasperation as though she had put him through this silent treatment many times before.

"Well, gentlemen, Gwyn has been searching me out in Darkwell for three days. I wasn't aware I was so hard to find! Anyway, as I understand it," Oscar began, "The Royal Lord Saxus has been—blast this is a crime just to speak about—he has given up his defense of Haven. Evidently the men from the South Towers were overrun . . . With sarcophs were they?" Gwyn nodded. "Right, rotters. The towermen were left to defend themselves for over a week and Saxus sent no help. The undead have taken and wiped out the lower quarters as well."

"How do you know that Saxus isn't *trying* to get rid of them, but he can't do it?" Kellen asked as he poured himself some wine.

"Well, Kellen," Oscar continued. "The Dragon Riders have been ordered to stay away from the lower quarters for the last month and a half. We easily could have slain the undead for as you may know the dragons have been known to breathe a bit of fire from time to time," he said proudly.

"When you were ordered to stay away from the South Towers, were you given any reason?" Kellen asked.

"None," Oscar replied. "None at all, even after I inquired about it several weeks into the ban, he would tell me nothing. In fact Saxus refused to see me at all, even though we have always been good friends."

"When was the last time you saw the Royal Lord?" Kellen asked.

"I saw him at about the time when the sarcoph raids began in the South. His last order to me in person was to stay away from there. Ever since then, everything has come through that advisor of his Lord Othar and he has stayed perpetually hidden in his throne room, with only Othar for company. At around the same time, even the Royal Guard was sent outside the throne room. Which, for your information, is unheard of. The Guard has never left the lord's side in the history of Haven." He glanced at Gwyn. "Apparently the Royal Lord Saxus has needed more privacy of late."

"Why?" Kellen asked.

"I don't know," Oscar answered.

"So what is the theory, now, that Saxus is evil? How do we know he is even alive if no one has seen him in, what, a month?" Kellen raised his eyebrows at both Gwyn and Oscar, daring them to prove him wrong. "So we don't know . . . This Othar you speak of could be running the show and the throne room could be as empty as Deagan's coin purse!"

Deagan laughed nervously. Kellen could never hold his tongue when there was a beautiful woman around could he? Deagan sat at the table with them, and served himself a modest haunch of meat from the pork plate before him. He scowled and tried to think of some retort against Kellen, but as the seconds went by, his opportunity was lost and all he could do was blush as he ate the pig.

"What's to be done about this?" Kellen asked heroically as if they'd come to the right man for the job.

"Hold up a bit," Deagan said. "Lady . . . er . . . Gwyn I saw some of your men wearing the garb of Saxus' army. How is it you got from Haven to the Border Lands, and where are your people, now?" Deagan finished. He looked at her with honest concern, but still she didn't speak.

Instead Oscar chimed in after a moment. "The men you saw dressed in the manner of Saxus' army were the towermen, guards assigned to watch over the South Towers. The Towers are surrounded by farmlands called the lower quarters. The lower quarters are a part of Haven, but not within the city proper. Gwyn and the villagers from those farmlands were forced by the rotters to leave home and so they fled here to Darkwell for refuge.

"Gwyn went to speak with the king, to ask him for help, and a safe place to stay," Oscar said.

Deagan stopped eating, a wad of meat still in his mouth, to look up at Kellen. Then Kellen said what they had both been thinking. "Pardon me, but did you say she went to *speak* with the king?"

"Ah, yes." Oscar said, realizing the confusion. "She only speaks when it is absolutely necessary."

Deagan and Kellen nodded as though that explained everything. Oscar continued, "So when she asked for help, the king sent her, the towermen, and the villagers to a place in the Border Lands called Oxham. Which turned out not to be any help at all."

The *king* had sent them to the Border Lands? Deagan's fork clattered to the table. Malagor sent refugees into unsafe territory and then by the Gods he had the gall to order not only his goons, but a knight to go slaughter them? Deagan stood up, with his cheeks flushed and his nostrils flared. "Oh this is ripe news." That sick, purple feeling rose in his throat, warning him that he was about to lose control. "An *evil king*. You know what? I don't regret a moment of it! If I was still allowed in the king's court I'd . . ." He threw a plate against the wall and it broke. Rory's head popped up from the window. "He's heartless! How could I have been such a fool? Some of your people were killed, nay burned alive!"

Just as the butler was about to chastise the former knight, Kellen interrupted, "Rory, leave him be. Come in here. There is trouble brewing in Haven."

And the head lowered, until only Rory's eyes could be seen scowling at Deagan. He paused there then Kellen continued, "Get in here, Rory, I have need of you. Leave the hedge to its own devices for the night." A brisk bow showed that Rory understood and would obey, and within a moment the butler had vaulted smoothly through the window and closed it behind him.

Deagan lowered his voice to a hoarse whisper, "I can't believe this! I served the dirty bastard for too long. Fifteen years!" He picked up another plate and drew back for a throw, but instead he squeezed it so tightly that it looked like it would crack.

Without interrupting, Rory snatched the plate from Deagan's grip and immediately set it on the table. The former knight stormed across the room with a grunt.

Kellen explained what Oscar had told them and Rory looked shocked at all the news. He couldn't believe the vast change in Deagan's demeanor. There was severity in the large man's bearing. "The hedge can wait for the night, Master Kellen. I think I should like to hear more about this," said Rory.

"Sorry about the plate, I've got a short temper sometimes," Deagan said.

"Forget it," Rory said. "Just a plate."

"Is there anything I *can* break?" Deagan asked and they both laughed.

Sir Oscar had cleaned up the shards of the plate, and the beautiful woman sat as silent as ever.

Oscar spoke up as he placed the last of the shards on the table. "Deagan, before you and Kellen came home, Gwyn told me more about what happened in the Border Lands. I am grieved to hear that the king would demand such foul deeds, but I am honored to share a meal with a man so chivalrous as you. Please lift a glass with me, one and all, for tonight we dine in the presence of a hero."

"Huzzah!" Kellen cheered drowning out Deagan's quiet and surprised thank you.

"Now there is a troubling detail that I have not yet shared," Oscar said. "Today I was ordered by the king to go and seek out these "rebels" and destroy them all! He must be troubled that you let them escape Deagan. He must be troubled indeed."

Deagan could see why such a woman should be feared, but by a king? "King Malagor is hungry for control. I have always known this. If anyone disagrees with him, it tends to be their last mistake as a part of his court. He gets rid of any who threaten his authority. If only he had such ambition when it comes to ridding the world of dark forces, but nay he never did. More than half of his attention is used up on keeping his own people under his thumb. And he *hates* refugees sheltering in these walls. He sees them as dirty and dangerous. Malagor wants to remain an idol of authority, the pinnacle o' grace and dignity, and the fearsomest king in the Knowne Worlde. He was always afraid that his men would lay their weapons down if they thought they were fighting for a weak king. So rather than being weak, he turned to evil," Deagan spat on the floor in disgust. "Sorry," he said wiping it up with his sleeve. Gwyn smiled down at him. She must pity him, unable as he was to avoid making an ass of himself in front of her.

"When did the king order you to fly, Oscar?" Kellen asked, changing the subject. The edge of a plan was forming behind his words.

"Tonight, Kellen." The Dragon Rider admitted solemnly.

"Do any of the other Dragon Riders know of this plan?" Kellen went on.

"No, I have yet to muster them all, and give them their orders."

"Good," then we have nothing to worry about."

"What do you mean nothing to worry about? There is a very *dark* conspiracy going on here!" Deagan protested.

"Yes there is, my friend, but at least we can buy some time. Listen, Oscar, this is all you have to do . . ."

R EGRETFUL HE COULDN'T LET Pete rest longer, Oscar climbed up the ladder and saddled the dark blue dragon lovingly. Pete shook his head from side to side as he woke up and howled a greeting to the caring old Dragon Rider.

His acting would be put to the test. As he took a deep breath before stepping into the stirrup and mounting his dragon, the silence surrounded him. Then ever so faintly boiling up from the chimney came Kellen's voice then Deagan's. He couldn't make out what they were saying, but it sounded like another one of their incessant arguments.

He patted the dragon's neck and said, "You heard it all, didn't you, Pete?" he chuckled, as the dragon nodded sharply. It was the gesture he'd been trained meant agreement to humans. "You won't tell anyone will you?" The dragon grunted, but didn't move other than to lift the knight's weight with the action of its breath. "Pete," Oscar said in a warning voice. "Don't tell the other dragons, and that's a command."

The dragon shifted from side to side and howled in protest. "Pete!" the Dragon Rider scolded. "Listen to me! Not a word, you understand?" Pete howled again at the sky, then he gave his sharp nod that lurched the knight forward in the starlight. "Good. Now, fly!"

The dragon leapt from the roof in an elegant arc. He dropped down toward the street below, but his massive wings exploded to the sides at the last second and they carried him upwards. He soared low until he reached the outer wall. The Dragon Riders had found that at this time of night the thermals were best in that part of town.

When they got there, the dragon, invisible against the sky except for the stars that he blocked, rose up in lazy circles over the city. "Now call them, Pete!" Oscar commanded.

Pete let out a massive howl that rattled Oscar's helmet. A spout of flame jetted from Pete's straightened throat. The light of it was enough to illuminate the rooftops below. Then, Pete careened up through the heavens even further, and the grunts and howls from the other dragons soon came up to join him. In a quarter of an hour, the entire company of twenty-five Dragon Riders was amassed in the dark quiet air above Darkwell, only the air wasn't dark or quiet for long, for when the dragons muster after a lull of inactivity, they grow wrathful with glee at seeing their old friends. Some of them needed to be scolded for breathing too much fire or trying to wrestle with their companions in mid air. This was all part of being a Dragon Rider, Oscar knew, and though he'd been at it for over thirty years, he still loved the little pleasures about it. In fact, it still thrilled him to death.

What he needed to do now, however, was give orders, and fast. Being a slave to chivalry for so long made him a terrible liar so he hoped the excitement of a mission would help his men believe his word. It was now or never, he supposed. "Dragon Riders!" he roared through his helmet's grating. Pete translated for him into Dragon. Anyone who couldn't hear Oscar would at least be able to hear Pete. "Tonight we patrol the lands!" again the dragon roared and squealed his own version of the words. "We will scorch the earth in the Border Lands, to scare off the darkness!" Pete roared. "We will let the enemies of Darkwell know there are Dragon Riders to be dealt with, and that we don't take kindly to *nonsense!*"

Not taking kindly to nonsense was one of Oscar's least effective motivational catch phrases. What Oscar didn't realize was that Pete's translation into dragon of what he was saying was, "ROOOOOOOOOOAAAAAAAAAAAAAAAAAARRRRR RRR!"

And it turns out that this is one of the dragons' very favorite inspirational catch phrases. In fact it was the only one they needed. The rest of the dragon's joined Pete's cacophony and tumbled through the air with sheer exhilaration.

Full of fire and ready to sally forth, they sallied forth. There was a village called Oxham that, according to Kellen Wayfield, could use a good torching.

J ATHAM HOLMIN AND KING Malagor stood side by side at the window in Darkwell's throne room watching the muster of the Dragon Riders. It filled them both with a sense of accomplishment and invincibility. All it took was a word, an order, and even these mythical beasts would drop what they were doing and bow to the king's wishes. Soon the rebels would be dead once and for all. The two men smiled at each other, trying to show approval of the other as though they were appreciative equals in the same cause, but underneath, they both feared each other and wanted the other one dead. King Malagor sensed this undertone in Jatham's gaze. *Well,* he thought. *Agree to disagree.* And the two of them laughed as they clinked their goblets of wine.

"Sire, I must be going soon," Jatham said. "I have important business in Haven, that will finally ensure its downfall. I may be gone for as long as a week. That is of course, if Your Highness has no further need of me."

"Of course, Holmin, I understand completely. There is much to do in Haven, yet." Then after a bit of thought, he said, "How is my old friend Saxus looking these days?"

"He looks like death, Your Majesty," Jatham laughed. And so did the king.

"Take your leave, Jatham, report to me when you return triumphant."

"Thank you, Sire," and with that, Jatham left the throne room at a fast walk.

The fireplace burned warmly and the fires at the base of the pillars gave a beautiful glow as they crackled and popped in their alcoves. Malagor walked the perimeter of his throne room reflecting on the carved stone scenes of his forefathers' days. He saw the old beautiful days when civilization covered the Knowne Worlde. There was an image of his great grandfather, Malgon, smiting the evil from the far distant lands of Prynn. He saw the Ten Thousand Horse Charge from the days long ago, when the king had sent this great number to rescue a foreign city even though there was no chance for them to return. So much had been risked before his time, yet Malagor had never risked anything not even so much as the disapproval of his people. In a way comparing himself against his forebears filled him with regret, but he also knew that these were darker times than those of the past and if he risked too much, then his reign could end very quickly, in fact, the civilized world could end if he made but one mistake.

This fear had paralyzed him from the time of his youth as he watched cities crumble on all sides, but now, a new fear took his heart. Hadn't Jatham been Saxus' closest adviser too? What was to keep the darkness that he wove on the Royal Lord from also entrapping the king himself? All Malagor had was the word of this mysterious adviser and no token more reassuring than that. Perhaps letting that man into his domain had been the last mistake he would ever have the chance to make. He didn't know what to do, never had, and he didn't have the energy left in his old bones to stop it now. All he could worry about was sticking to the plan, swooping in to save Haven at the last minute, and taking control of it. He would be remembered at least as the king who saved a neighbor in a time of need. Unfortunately, he was forced to remember that he had some part in bringing about that need in the first place and no matter how he was remembered by others, that guilt would plague him forever.

Again Malagor convinced himself that he was too old to worry about it or change things now. Chivalry was a young man's province, not that of kings who needed to make the hard decisions for the greater good. How long could Saxus have lasted anyway? Men wouldn't fight for a royal lord they would fight for a king. Malagor was doing the civilized world some good by giving them something to believe in. He was reassured by this thought as he sought his feather pillow and fell asleep on the second most comfortable bed in Darkwell. The most comfortable of course was Kellen's.

ORY HAD TAKEN THE time to secure the rafters more firmly in preparation for Pete the dragon's take-offs. He had built in triangular bracing throughout the attic to reinforce the entire roof. When Oscar and Pete left that night, the house did lurch a bit, but not nearly as badly as before. Rory looked pleased with himself as he stood in the room listening as the schemers continued.

The woman visitor looked very deep in thought. Her eyes moved from side to side under a furrowed brow. Beads of sweat glistened on her forehead and finally, as though she was letting out a breath that she had held for far too long, Gwyn spoke for the first time in Deagan's hearing. The sound was like the rhythmic and lilting accent of a farm girl, but it was tarnished with many years of wisdom and hardship. "M'lord," she said, looking at Deagan. "Your oath to the king was taken away from you against your will. You've done nothing wrong and you've done many things right."

Deagan blushed, but said nothing. He wasn't sure he could agree with her on that point. He had made many mistakes. Though maybe he never truly did something *wrong*.

She went on, "Well, your not alone as far as oath breaking goes. I left the service of Royal Lord Saxus, and if I had not done so, you'd not be hearing my voice now, for I was sworn to silence. I was entrusted with many of his secrets, and I was present at many private meetings, which is why I was forbidden to speak, in case I told something to the wrong person. But now it seems that sharing the secrets of Lord Saxus may be my only chance to save Haven.

"My name is Gwyn Androth, I was one of the Royal Guards of Haven's Cloud Tower. Deagan, it was I that fought you at the back of that town hall in the Border Lands. You put up a decent fight. I knew even then that if I had to kill you it would be the end of a good man who did not deserve it. And when you no longer stood against me, but for some reason decided to let my people free, I could sense that it was against your orders. I didn't know if your own men would let you live."

"You're a Royal Guard?" Deagan asked in shock. He wanted to bow down before her. They were some of the most feared knights in the civilized realms. Truly he was lucky to have survived their duel.

"I am no more a Royal Guard than you are a knight at this point, but that was a title I wore for many years," she answered.

"Are all the Royal Guards women?" Deagan asked in awe.

"No, not all, but Lord Saxus prefers the company of women. Besides that however, he believes that women give wiser counsel. I do not know if this is true, because I've known some daft women in my time, but like I said, he trusted me with many secrets and took my advice in his affairs. I always strove to guide him toward the good, but like many rulers, his heart is easily won over by greed and temptation."

"Wait a minute, you keep talking like he's still alive," Kellen said. "But you haven't seen him in a month or more. He may have been greedy, but why should he simply abandon the defense of his city? Leaving the South Towers to be overrun? What could he stand to gain by letting rotters rule the farms on the southern borders of Haven?" He stood there smiling in disbelief.

Rory added two crisp logs on top of the andirons in the fireplace. Deagan thought to himself, unable to see any gain in the realm of finance, strategy, or competition with other kings. He squinted into the fire and tried to make sense of it all. "Lady Androth . . . you tell us that Saxus will trust ye. Is there any way you could enter his chambers and sway him to stop his . . . madness?"

"Ha!" she laughed. "I didn't just leave on a whim, giving up my life and home. I don't take oath breaking lightly, and neither do you. But the look in his eyes told me all I needed to know. He was under a spell, or driven to madness.

"I do not think that now there is much hope to sway him. I left when I felt I had to. I tried to convince the other Guards to come with me, but they were too proud to leave. I believe that by now they have all been sent to their deaths at the hands of the enemy, or they've been poisoned or worse. I don't know this to be true, but if I know Lord Saxus as well as I think I do, he won't take the chance of allowing anyone so close to him to live. Some of them may have survived. Marguerite was on her guard and swore to me that if one more thing went wrong she'd run." Gwyn looked off into the distance and clenched a fist in her lap.

Kellen chimed in again, "Lady Androth, you say that he banned the Dragon Riders from the lower quarters as soon as they were attacked, yes?"

"Yes, at just about the same time, and that was the last time he was seen."

"And now he's sent them out of the city entirely. Do you follow, Deagan?" Kellen asked his old friend. Rory looked intently at the two of them.

"Blazes! Haven's got to be under attack right now! With a Royal Lord who'll do nothing to stop it!" Kellen burst out.

"I know," Gwyn answered. "That's why I came. I saw the Dragon Riders over Darkwell, and knew Sir Oscar would be here. We need him to come back with us to retake the South Towers, and from there to mount an offensive against whatever other force might present itself at Haven's walls. There isn't much time. They call me a rebel," she smiled, "with no good kings left in the realms, I would call myself nothing else." Gwyn stood and she slung her pack over both shoulders. "I'm going back to my people. When Oscar returns, tell him that we make for the South Towers in the morning."

Deagan stood as well. "Kellen, it'll have to be you that tells the Dragon Rider what the plan is. I'm going with Lady Androth."

Kellen stood next. "Rory, I'm afraid I'll be going too. I have a feeling that the Dragon Keeping business is about to go belly up. Do mind the manor while we're gone. And help me pack!"

"Very good, sir," Rory said, but something about his tone of voice made it clear that he didn't feel very good at all about being left behind.

Gwyn's voice came forth reluctantly, but when it did she said, "There are caves to the east of here. There is a path that leaves from the main road not far into the jungle. My people are there."

Deagan gripped her arm as she moved to leave and in a warning tone he said, "I've been there before. It's no place for weary travelers to rest, Androth. Last time I was there, most of my troop was slain. One-eyed giants in the deep. With enough men they can be beaten, but . . ." It had been for his insolence to Duke Worth over the decision to fall back that he had been whipped long ago. The scars burned him still, especially when agitated. He was that way now.

"Do not fear, Wingrat. The giants are no more." She smiled and left Deagan with a thump on the chest—a warrior's farewell. She had to make haste while the two men prepared themselves. The heavy armor on Deagan's back made him an imposing sight once more, a stern warrior carrying steel. Kellen came downstairs in a thick suit of cured leather armor. It was lighter than metal, made for fencing in fact, and Kellen's hair was in a braid behind him. He wore high black boots with the tops turned down, and at his waist was a beautiful curved saber that glowed in the firelight like polished silver. No doubt Rory had polished it in the display case once a week for the last five years.

"Let's go and retrieve two of my horses, we'll catch her up on the road." Kellen said. And the two of them left to do just that.

THE SMOKE LAY HEAVY that night around Darkwell's ankles. Walking through it was like wading, although the opaque gray matter did not offer any resistance like water would. The fires of the city burned normally, but instead of the smoke rising, it sank in that hot night air. The torches of the streets left beacons to see by, and it was by these that Jatham Holmin made his way to the guardhouse where he would talk to the gatekeepers. He shadowed his face in a cloak of black oilskin.

"What news from the gates?" Jatham asked through a small barred window in the door to the Guardhouse.

"Who wants to know?" the guard replied.

"It's Jatham, my friend, no need to be sharp with me."

The guard stammered for a moment, but finally he came back around. "M'lord," he said as he hurriedly pulled back the dead bolt that held the door shut. "Please come in."

"Thank you," Jatham said. "I forgive you for not recognizing me at first. What news I said, what news from your gates? Have you seen her?"

"She never came in today, sir."

"Are you sure? She is the rebel leader. She may have wiles that you would not guess. She may have guises or entryways unseen. So tell me, captain, can you be sure she is not in the city?"

"I assure you, sir she didn't come in through this gate," the guard answered confidently.

"I see. Keep a watch for her." He looked out the window to the gate below, when he ducked away from the window with a gasp. "If she never came in, then how is it that now she is standing at your gate, waiting to be *let out*? Tell me that my guardies!" They looked down at her waiting by the gate. She looked around and finally turned her stern but radiant face up to the window above her where the two guardsmen were crowded and looking down. Jatham punched one of them in the stomach and he said, "let her through you fool."

One of the guards protested briefly, but a sharp look from Jatham silenced him. He went down the stairs with a key and unlocked a small door beside the gate. He allowed her to leave. A minute or two later Jatham came down the stairs with a key of his own, and he left through the same door to follow her.

His footfalls were silent under the blanket of the wind, just as were those of his quarry that gracefully loped before him. She had neither smiled at the guard nor thanked him as the door had been opened. Her disguise was imperfect. She acted like she was above the guards even while masquerading as a peasant. Jatham knew her for certain now. She was Guard Androth, chief among the Royal Guards of the Cloud Tower, and against her there would be no chance of victory should it come to a contest of arms. Yet she could be outfoxed, and already Jatham had planned her downfall. He knew that she and her band had escaped from Oxham, for the raiding party reported failure—all because of the heart of a knight. Jatham had seen to that Deagan Wingrat. His heart was now broken he was sure, but it was a pity that he hadn't been put to death thanks to the stubbornness of a doddering old king. Oh well, the knight hadn't been seen at court since the raid. He was probably begging on the streets.

Androth stalked forward before him and he ventured from shade to shadow along the road. Few traveled this late, so he did not fear being spied by passersby, yet the senses of the Royal Guard were wickedly sharp, and he knew that she would recognize him in an instant. Which is why he had hidden behind the curtain when she had come to King Malagor for succor. She of course would know him as Lord Othar, but it made no difference, for even though it might take her some time to realize his part in all this, her hesitation would not be long enough for him to escape her alive. The downfall of her city was his fault and what kind of guard would she be if she forgave him for that?

The road twisted on into the East, but Androth stopped suddenly. Like a dart, Jatham thrust himself into the darkness beside the road and got low. The eyes of the guard scanned up and down the track for a time. Jatham dared not even peek at her again. Finally he looked up to see that she was gone from view. She must have left the road.

He crept closer to where she had been. The jungle was now closer about him, for each step took him away from civilized country and into wilderness and the bleak desperation that was now the surrounding environment of the realms. So she was hiding somewhere in his territory was she? Perfect.

But Jatham was no fool. One way he knew this was because he knew what he didn't know. He knew that he didn't know exactly why Androth had left the Guard. He didn't know how many men she had with her if any. He didn't know how long she'd been in Darkwell, or why. These things put sobering fear into Jatham's mind. He lived in fear, he slept wrapped in its discomfort and wetness. He bathed in its filth and he spoke its malicious language with every word. Fear was his cloak, and though it was his weakness, he could also use it against others.

The place where she had left the road was a narrow, dirty path. Jatham hopped the ditch to reach its entrance. He went forward, following cautiously and listening intently. He heard nothing, and fear gripped him. Could it be that she was waiting for him with her gold worked spear pointed at his heart? He convinced himself that if he continued he'd make a mistake and be found. Then he would be sent to the other world with no coin and no steel. He'd been there that way before, but if he was sent there against his will . . .

He inhaled deeply into his nose, trying to breathe away the terror of death that gripped him. He waited for a time, listening. Then he turned and left the path to get back on the road. The sight of the city walls looming above him was comforting. He returned to Darkwell, his gait ever quickening as if the spear tip was gaining on him. He let himself in through the door and went back to the guardhouse.

"You let her get past you once, gentlemen. Do not let it happen again-" he said through the barred window of the guardhouse door. The guards inside turned to look at him, and he saw that these were not the same men he'd left an hour before. The guard had changed. They looked at him quizzically and he left without another word.

He waded through the smoke until he reached the king's tower. This was where Sir Oscar would report when he returned from scorching the woman's camp and people.

Jatham did not sleep. Instead he thought of two things, and both of them had to do with Guard Androth. The first was why had she been in Darkwell. The second was what a fine addition to his collection she would make.

WOAH, PETE, RIGHT THERE, old chap. Attaboy." Oscar directed his dragon as the beast alighted on the tower of the king of Darkwell. He looked out at the city's many lanterns and fires as he reflected on the sorry state he was in. He hadn't had much practice in treachery before, and thought the experience was extremely nerve wracking. He took off his helmet and patted the dragon gently on his flank. Of course the dragon and rider were both unhurt, for they had only been embattled against a few empty huts in the border lands that had already gotten a good scorching once before and not too long ago from the look of things. Oscar wasn't a tricky man, and had little under the surface besides chivalry and care for his beast and his Riders.

"Well met, guards of Darkwell," Oscar greeted. "I'm here to tell His Majesty about our successful ride."

"Yes, sir," one of the guards said and he went down the trap door. Oscar sighed and made himself ready for a meeting with the king, trying to keep the lies straight in his head—the lies that Kellen said would work like a charm.

Light came up from the chamber below and Oscar heard voices. "No, you fool I shall speak with him myself." The voice said. And then a man climbed up through the trap door and appeared on the rooftop. He approached Sir Oscar eagerly, wrapped in a black coat.

"What news Dragon Rider? What news from the skies? Have you caught our band of rebels and put them out of the king's realm forever?" the concealed man asked in rapid succession.

"Aye, lord," Oscar said. "Indeed, they are no more. It was not difficult for my Riders to do them in, and not one of us was harmed, but it was hard on the soul to see some of Haven's own men and women go against the crown and be forced to die."

"Yes, of course," the cloaked man said, trying to conceal his excitement. "And where did you find them, sir Knight?"

"It was strange sir, it took several passes to confirm that it was them, but they had taken up residence in a small town in the Border Lands. From what the king told me sir, it was Oxham, the town they tried to stay in before. My Riders went there first to look for signs of their passage, but instead the rebels themselves were there. So we of course followed through with the king's wishes my lord." Sir Oscar bowed and Pete scratched his chin.

The shrouded man fell silent for a moment. He'd seen Androth take a path into the jungle. Indeed that was proof that her people hadn't camped at Oxham or anywhere near the Border Lands. The Dragon Rider's lie was apparent, and now that he looked closer, he could see the signs of it on his face.

Sir Oscar was uncomfortable not being able to look the cloaked man in the eye. Did he recognize the voice? Someone from Haven perhaps.

The cloaked man brightened again in posture, stepped forward and took Oscar under his arm. "Sir Oscar, you must celebrate with the king for this is a great victory! He is already asleep, but for night owls like us there must be a pint of ale in these halls!"

"Sadly, sir, I must attend my mount, for he has flown hard and needs rest, though he is unhurt. Perhaps we could celebrate another time?" Oscar asked. He struggled to keep himself from being pulled to the trap door.

"I insist sir, your dragon can wait. Look he is already asleep! Come with me."

"Right. Of course," Oscar agreed, looking over his shoulder as the cloaked figure walked him to the hole in the tower's floor. They both descended the stairs to the guardroom below. This was a circular room above the king's quarters that had a good view of the surroundings.

There were always guards positioned here. There was only one exit and it led to a corridor that surrounded the King's bedroom.

"I bet you that these fine men know where to find some wine at this hour!" said the man jovially. He approached the guards and they snapped to attention. He whispered to two of them. They stepped forward and in the blink of an eye, they seized Sir Oscar by the arms.

"What is the meaning of this?" Oscar demanded. "Unhand me you fools!"

"Who is the fool now, Dragon Rider?" Jatham asked, pulling the hood from his bald scalp.

"Othar!" Oscar gasped. "What are you doing in Darkwell?"

Ignoring the knight's question, Jatham continued, "I know that you didn't find the rebels. For they are no longer camped at Oxham. You are a terrible liar, Oscar, I love dealing with knights for that reason. They can't lie." He gloated with a fearful grin for a moment then he barked, "Take him away! To the dungeon!"

"No! I implore you, not there!" Oscar begged, but he didn't struggle for he was outnumbered and already captured. He was unbelted and all his weapons were taken. The guards took his armor and his shoes, leaving him helpless.

He thought back to when all this began. He knew that it was a despicable shame that had brought him to such ends as lying and turning against his orders. But who should be ashamed, he or the king? Oscar would not struggle against capture because he had dignity, not because he believed he was in the wrong. He walked freely to the dungeon surrounded by the guards, but not in their grip, and once there he bowed to the guards and stepped into the dark saying, "I know that you men are only carrying out your duty, so I hold no grudge against you. But know that you are putting in prison a Dragon Rider, a knight, and a man who did his best to help the great cities."

The guards looked at each other uneasily and with heavy hearts they closed the door and locked Sir Oscar away.

R ORY SWUNG HIMSELF AROUND the bar with ease and grace, faster and faster until he released and vaulted himself through the air. He landed a forward flip on the ground with his feet together. He was coated in sweat, and still filled with disappointment and hurt. He did not like being left behind, but if Kellen thought it was best, he'd grudgingly abide. He told himself that surely there was plenty to keep him busy with three Dragon Riders living in the house, and plenty of work left on re-enforcing the roof. Still, he wouldn't mind working out more of his frustration through some of his training. He lifted weights until his muscles felt like they would burst. When he felt that he had done all he could do, he heard the familiar sound of dragons landing on the roof. He washed up and quickly got dressed to go upstairs and attend to the Dragon Riders' needs.

He climbed the stairs to Kellen's bedroom where the Dragon Riders now slept, and he called to them from the hallway, "Hail masters, is there anything I can get for you before you slumber?" It seemed that nobody heard him, for two of the knights from Haven were talking in the room, and didn't reply.

"That's a trifle strange, that. Pete comin' home all suddenly an' Oscar nowhere to be found? I've never heard of something like that happening before."

"When did you first see Pete?"

"He was standing on his roost wailing when me an' Warmaker landed. He's still got his saddle on. You think Oscar's heading out for another ride tonight?"

"Could be, he was being mighty secretive during that raid."

"Well I'm sure it's over our heads and none of our business, don't you think?"

"Aye. We're not his keepers nor his superiors. In fact it's the other way around! I'm guessing if he knew we were worried he'd have himself a good laugh at us, he would!"

The other laughed, "I'm sure he would. Oh, my back gets sore with some o' those longer rides, don't yours?" And the conversation went on as Rory listened with a furrowed brow.

Rory had known what the plan was since their conversation with Gwyn downstairs. Oscar was going to take the Dragon Riders on a wild goose chase and then report back to the king that they'd found the rebels and scorched them where they lay encamped at Oxham. What if something went wrong? Whatever had happened, Sir Johan and Sir Goodsing were completely in the dark about it. At least Oscar had kept the news from his own men, would Jatham believe him? Rory didn't think so; he hardly believed the man was capable of lying in the first place, and unfortunately, it was Oscar's ability to lie upon which this whole plan relied.

Rory again called in, "Good evening Sir Johan, Sir Goodsing. Is there any way at all that I may be of service tonight?" He looked at both of them expectantly. These were not men who were accustomed to being waited on.

"Nay lad, off with you," Sir Goodsing said gruffly.

"What he means, dear Rory, is no thank you, and good night." Sir Johan corrected him.

"Of course. Good night . . . say, you wouldn't know what's become of Sir Oscar would you?" Rory asked.

The two Dragon Riders exchanged an unsure look, then sir Johan answered, "He just stopped at the tower to report back, he'll be here soon."

"Very good," Rory said. "Good night."

"Good night," Goodsing said.

"Oh," Rory said. "Is there anything his dragon will need before he returns?" Perhaps I could brush and oil him while we await his master?"

"Ah, well, let us take care of that, now Rory. As much as we both appreciate it," Johan elbowed Goodsing who was scowling. "There's a certain routine to it you understand."

"So you are going to brush and oil him I take it?" Rory asked.

"Yes we'll go up there in just a moment."

"Oh not at all, not at all. I have watched the three of you tending your mounts countless times since you've moved in. I understand you've just been out on a raid, and after each of you has already tended your own dragons, I'm sure you can't be thrilled to tend a third. It is no trouble at all I assure you."

Rory, who was already half way out the window heard muffled protest from the knights below capped off by Goodsing yelling, "Well don't let him eat you, then!" But he was used to such protests, they had never stopped him before.

He got onto the pitch of the roof and walked over to Pete's colorful nest of laundry and tree branches. He stirred at Rory's approach and the butler slowed to a standstill.

"Easy, boy. Easy," Rory uttered deeply. Pete's head rose from the platform and hovered like a snake high over Rory's head. He tipped his crocodile head to look at the butler through one brown eye and snorted smoke from his nostrils.

Rory bowed to the beast. "Good evening, master Pete. I am here to give you a brush and an oiling. But first I think you need a drink." Rory picked up the two buckets and went down the rear ladder to Kellen's well in the yard below. He hauled them back up on the pulley system that they'd built for just this purpose then tied off the rope, to let the two buckets hang there like cherries thirty feet off the ground near Pete's nest. Pete extended his long neck and stuck his snout into one of the buckets. Steam rose instantly with a *hiss*. It soon died down and Pete finished the water. He reached out to the other bucket with a claw and pulled it closer to him to drink.

Rory waited until he was done then refilled the buckets and hoisted them again. The dragon drank again, but did not finish the second bucket. He howled down at Rory. The other dragons reacted with snorts and howls of their own. All three of them, Warmaker the green, Ero the red, and Pete the dark blue had their heads lifted and looked at each other as they talked in a language of their own.

Rory climbed the ladder and he got his balance on the catwalk that surrounded Pete's nest. He stepped over the thick, heavy tail and came to the dragon's side. He unbuckled the three buckles that held the saddle on and lifted the heavy piece of leather to the side. Heat escaped from below the saddle like it did from an oven door, which made the butler squint and draw back. Rory found the wire brush and took it firmly in his hand. He took long hard strokes all down Pete's neck and back. The beast was large, and the brushing took a long time. Still no sign of Sir Oscar.

The brushing done, Rory picked up a bucket of oil and a rag with which he buffed the dragon's scales. This too took a long time, but Pete fell into a hypnotized state of relaxation, so Rory had to assume that the dragon was appreciative. When he was finished, he put away all the implements in their places on the catwalk, and walked back to the ladder that would take him down to the yard.

Pete woke up and uttered a low bark through his nose. Rory turned to look at him. The other dragons woke up and barked back, getting louder and louder until they were howling and yapping at each other excitedly. For the second time, Rory wished he could understand what they were saying.

"Pete?" Rory asked. The dragon stopped and looked at him.

"Can you understand me?" he asked cautiously. Pete gave one of his sharp downward nods, then his snout bounced back up to the level.

"Where is Oscar, Pete?" with that, he began howling at the sky loud enough to wake up the neighborhood. Several people opened their windows across the street and yelled at him to see if he would

"Silence his beasts!" of if he'd be so kind as to "Keep it down out there!" Rory did his best to bow to them all and acknowledge them as appropriate, but he was interrupted by Pete's muzzle pressing against his back. He was surprised, but didn't jump. Instead, he slowly turned.

"Yes, Pete?"

Pete answered in a low and meticulous grumble with defined syllables and rhythm. Rory shook his head still not able to understand. "Perhaps I'll get the Dragon Riders," Rory offered. He climbed down the front ladder into Kellen's bedroom and asked the Riders to come up with him on the roof. It didn't take much convincing to bring them up, for all Rory had to tell them was that Pete could tell them where their leader was.

In a few minutes, the three of them were gathered around Pete and he was grumbling in his language to the Dragon Riders.

"I can't make out everything he's saying. But I know he can show us where Oscar is if we follow him, right boy?" Pete nodded at Johan.

"Well what are we waiting for then?" Sir Goodsing asked. And they saddled up and flew away, leaving Rory behind yet again. He watched from the roof however, and he saw the three dragons with Pete at the lead heading toward the center of Darkwell.

"YOU EVER BROKEN ANY bones, Kellen?"

"No. Well nothing more than a finger. You?"

In answer Deagan only laughed as he rode beside his friend through the stinking smoke. Deagan always held a gloved hand to his nose on nights like this. Kellen always breathed deeply. It showed a fundamental difference in their characters, for Deagan always wished to be free of the walls and in the fresh air even though he knew that his sword would be his only protection. Kellen, on the other hand, always wanted as much stone and as many men standing between him and the darkness as he could get. "Aye, I've broken many *other* people's bones. And they've managed to break three or four of mine."

"Why do you ask?" Kellen said.

"It's just that here you are going out on an adventure. We're not even out o' the walls yet and your arse is so tight you're likely to rip a hole in your saddle!" Deagan laughed.

"Spare me, Deagan. How tight was yours when Gwyn only did so much as look around the room?"

"Well, I'm not thinking of dying out there tonight, you rat," Deagan said. "I'm thinkin' of her."

"And I'm thinking of being eaten alive by who knows what. I'm not even sure what our actual . . . ah, quest *is* at the moment, are you?"

"I'm not sure what it'll end up being, that's true. I think we're off to kill Lord Saxus, from the sound o' things." Deagan grinned in disbelief. "No more moping around here for me, searching the streets for rotters that aren't there. It's time to do something. We'll know more when we get up to that cave I was telling you about."

"Blow me down," Kellen said, swaying on his horse. "Killing Saxus? That's bound to be the dumbest thing we've ever even considered doing."

"Dumber than posing as some kind of Dragon Keeper? Or better yet, dumber than becoming a knight?" Deagan challenged.

"Well when you put it that way. Maybe it's number two or so." The two of them laughed and recounted stories for the rest of the ride to the East gate. Once there the guards let them out and they went on their way.

The night was crisper and clearer outside the walls, but the air still held moisture that would make it a sweaty ride. The road stretched out through the farmlands ahead and the little houses each had lanterns of their own. Deagan thought he could remember the way back to the cave, and he hoped the path would afford him less fear this time knowing that the Cyclops were dead. The rebels must have found them dead in there when they arrived. If Deagan told them half the stories he'd heard of what happened there it would make their blood run cold—good men chewed to pieces, used as clubs against each other. Sounded ugly. There were few survivors. Deagan's back ached.

"Will you stop that, Kellen?" Deagan complained. "You know we have all we'll need, Rory packed it after all. And you checked it yourself."

"Hey, there's no harm in being sure is there?"

"You're missing your feather bed already aren't you?" Deagan joked.

"Well, there's nobody in it to miss, friend. Anybody in yours?"

"My good old pad o' straw never saw anybody's backside, but mine, thief."

"I didn't know you took an oath of celibacy." Kellen said. "Oh, that's right, you didn't" Kellen joked.

"Who needs a wife when I have you?" Deagan answered. And he threw his apple core at Kellen's face. The two of them rode along the dark twists and turns and the company they shared kept their spirits high and kept Kellen's mind off the grisly horrors that undoubtedly awaited him. Until they came to the path Gwyn had taken leading up a hill to the side of the road, at which point the grisly horrors became the only thing either of them could think of, except Deagan who also thought of Gwyn's fair and handsome face.

Deagan went first up across the ditch and up the hill into the jungle. He didn't notice Jatham's tracks, nor did Kellen. But they would be at the caves in a couple of hours. Maybe they'd catch up to Gwyn. Until then, they would be on their guard and they wouldn't laugh much at all.

S IR OSCAR SAFELY TUCKED away in the dungeon, Jatham returned to the streets. He was full of fear and anxiety now. Had the Dragon Rider met with Androth? Why would he lie? Why else would he even think there was reason to lie other than if he knew the woman who he had been ordered to kill. He felt that all eyes were on him. Every refugee in ragged clothes seemed to stare him down and mock him in his finery. Well, it wasn't his fault they were paupers. He'd had nothing to do with the fall of the various cities that left them all destitute and homeless on the streets of Darkwell.

The bloody knight was probably sitting up straight and waiting to die properly down there even now. Jatham couldn't believe the audacity, nay the gall he'd had to bow to the guards that locked him away. What disrespect! Jatham hoped he'd rot slowly in there, but in the meantime he had Rebels to attend to.

He made his way to the king's stable and pulled out his ring of keys. His hands were shaking as he struggled to find the right one. He groaned in rage and threw the ring on the ground.

A voice came from behind him. "Why in such a hurry, Jatham?" It was one of those knights—Luthan was his name. He was holding the lead rope to his warhorse in one gloved hand.

"No matter. No matter, good sir. Just need to ride. Need to ride now," Jatham hissed.

"Allow me to assist you," the knight said. "I haven't so many keys to choose from." The knight quickly found the one and let them both into the large barn doors. Luthan went about his business unsaddling, watering, and brushing his horse. He let out a tired yawn or two as he did so and massaged his back between chores, all in all he didn't pay much mind to Jatham, but nevertheless Jatham was as suspicious as a cat that's been stepped on too many times.

Did he follow me here? What does he know? I could kill him now and take him for my own. He could lead my little raid tonight. Yes he could. The old man won't see it coming. He thought this, but he didn't really believe he would do it. He had no reason to. But nevertheless his fear was getting the better of him and he needed something running through his head in order to keep from being paralyzed by it.

He made his own horse ready, but it picked up on his anxiety. It bucked and reared in the stall, crushing Jatham against the boards. He pushed the beast away from him and backed away from it. He could see the whites of its eyes. Jatham looked around him and could not see Luthan anymore. Where is he? Where is he hiding now? Jatham thought. He went back to his horse and soon calmed it. He saddled the gelding and hastily picked up a bag of oats to feed it later. He led the beast out through the stable doors by his lead rope, still having no sign of the aging knight.

Then a figure approached him from the side. "Ahhh!" Jatham screamed as he stabbed into Luthan's gut with a knife from his belt. The old knight caught Jatham's incoming wrist, then he dropped a fist on the man's arm, almost, but not quite breaking it. Jatham dropped the dagger and yelped in pain. Blood dripped from between Luthan's fingers, and he let go of Jatham to squeeze the wounded hand with the other. The knight looked at Jatham in disbelief. Jatham mounted his horse and spurred it out of the stable leaving the door wide open. He rode away as fast as he could, galloping smoothly through the torch-dappled streets of Darkwell.

"The gates! The gates!" he cried as his horse circled in front of North gate. The guards obliged him as quickly as they could. As soon as the portcullis was high enough, he spurred his gelding out of the city and onto the North road that led to Haven. He rode as though his life depended on it.

There is much to do! He thought. *Much to do and I can't do it here. To Haven then, my horsey. Let's ride to Haven.*

D EAGAN AND KELLEN RODE single file up the dirt path to the caves. They'd been on the trail for less than an hour, but the time dragged on.

"Remember when we bought that goat?" Deagan asked. Kellen could hear the smile in his voice though he was only looking at the warrior's back. "And you thought you could keep him in your manor without Rory finding him?"

"Well I think we all know how that played out. We could have gotten away with it if he didn't stink so frightfully. Of course that's what you get for buying a billy goat instead of a—what are they called? A sissy goat or some such?" Kellen bantered back.

"Nanny is the word you're digging for, mate. And you never even tried my idea, and to this day I'm telling you it would have worked like a dream."

"Um, like a dream *come true*, were your exact words I believe." Kellen corrected him.

"Aye . . . But it didn't come true because you were too much the coward to try it."

"Deagan, I'm not about to dress a goat to look like Sir Gregory! It's insulting to think you'd even imagine Rory falling for it anyway."

"Not to mention the goat," Deagan laughed.

"What do you mean?"

"Well, wouldn't it be insulting to the goat to compare his uhhh . . . countenance to that of sir Gregory? They've formed a guild, those goats. Haven't you heard? Everyone's got a guild these days. And they don't stand for being slandered, insulted, or compared to naught but the noblest o' creatures. Now, if you dressed Old Cranky up like a dragon . . . the Goat's Guild would be fine with that I'm sure."

"And what about the Dragon's Guild?" Kellen retorted. "They'd hate it wouldn't they? Some goat strolling around, getting into the garbage . . . It just wouldn't do, Deagan. It wouldn't do at all!"

"Where is Old Cranky these days?" Deagan asked, genuinely curious. "*That's* not him I hope!" He turned and gestured to Kellen's white horse. "Thought there was something a bit odd about that horse, Kellen. Passing a goat off as a horse . . . you're always trying to cut corners."

"I've got to think of my bottom line Deagan. Besides, a goat makes a better horse than a horse does any day. Ever since that Horse's Guild came around . . . Besides you're not riding much better," Kellen chided.

"Oh *this?* He's a pig!"

"Really? Could have sworn he was a goat!"

"Nah. Pig, through and through."

"There's no Pig's Guild, I hope." Kellen mumbled to himself.

The horse hooves thumped on into the black jungle ahead of them. Kellen looked back periodically to guard their rear and their flanks, and Deagan kept his head forever turning, scanning the front and the sides. On they went, over a hill and down the other side. If Deagan remembered correctly it would be only a few more of those hills and they'd be at the Caves. He hoped that Gwyn had had enough time to tell her people that they were friends. His heart was beating in the anticipation of his reception when he arrived, for here were the only people who'd consider what he'd done in the Border Lands to be honorable. His honor was gone back in Darkwell, and that might have been the one thing he missed most, even more than Maggie.

He hoped his trusty warhorse was well taken care of by the next knight to ride her. He'd thought of asking if he could come and simply brush her for a morning, when he'd played sticky with Luthan. He knew in his heart that Luthan would be forced by the precepts of the duke to say no, and he didn't want to ask, and thus put himself in the position of hearing his old friend say that. Understanding it didn't make it easier. The 'pig' he now rode was satisfactory, but he had no bond with it and he was Kellen's horse, not Deagan's own. Nothing had ever really been his own.

"Say." Deagan said. "What do you reckon would happen if I just marched up to Duke Worth and asked for my belt back?"

A pause filled with night sounds and hoof falls transpired before Kellen's reply. "It would take a great deal of courage. After everything you and Duke Worth have disagreed upon. Are we going to the same caves that you yelled at him for ten years ago or more?"

"Aye the very same. I suppose I'd have to apologize for what I did. I'd have to . . ."

"That's it, go on."

". . . Not yell at him."

"Good start, good start," Kellen urged him.

"I'd probably have to let *him* yell at *me.*"

"Yes, yes."

"But if he raised a hand against me I'd be swift to chop off his—"

"Wrong, you'd do nothing of the kind. In fact you'd bow and scrape and carry on until he were finished, then ask him for your belt again and tell him you were a new man."

"A new man?" Deagan asked.

"Yes I like the sound of that. A new man." Kellen looked off into the dark suddenly to his left. Had he heard a twig snap? "But it begs the question, Deagan. Do you really want to be a knight again?"

Sir Luthan visited Deagan's thoughts, asking him that same question. He remembered the hesitation in his answer, and the weakness of it. But that was before he lost it all. He had still been shocked then, and losing Maggie hadn't yet broken his heart, left him debilitated for an entire day, and crestfallen for the rest of that dark week. When Luthan asked him that question in Duke Worth's Manor, he didn't have a good answer. When Kellen asked him, he was sure that he did.

"Aye." He said with finality. "I was born for it. Service to the city, courage and chivalry—they raised me better than my own mother. Riding into battle on Maggie's back, knowing she'd see me safely through to the other side or die trying—those are the things I miss and the things I once lived for. I'd be flogged again by the Duke to have it back."

"I know you would, Deagan. You were a good knight. Would you really want to work under the duke? And King Malagor? If I recall correctly, it was only a few hours ago that you declared him to be evil. He'd be your master again. Could you trust him?"

This gave Deagan pause. He heaved a great sigh and looked down at his hand as he rearranged the reins between his fingers. "You're right, you old scoundrel. The king gave up on me, and I gave up on him. It was a fool's hope anyhow. No duke worth his weight in duck shit would go back on such a decision."

"Duck shit?" Kellen asked.

"Since I was discharged from knighthood," Deagan answered simply. "I just can't help imagining Duke Worth covered in the stuff."

The two of them rode on and the path passed above a cliff that dropped off to their right. The fall would be crippling, the distance was long, and it ended in craggy rocks below. Deagan's horse balked at the sight and backed away. The view from here included Darkwell's outer wall, and the glow of the lights within. The city hovered like an island in the sea of farmland and roads surrounding it. They hadn't traveled far at all yet as the crow flew.

"Easy, horse," Deagan said in a soothing tone. "Easy, now." The horse stamped its feet and backed further away, finally bumping into Kellen's steed. The upset horse was not listening, and threatened to lose control. Deagan dismounted into the shadow of the jungle and went to the horse's head to hold the reins as he looked into its eyes. "Kellen, why don't you go first, maybe Piggy will follow once you get to the other side."

Kellen nodded and kicked his horse to a walk. He passed on Deagan's uphill side, or his left, and followed the curve of the path above the cliff. The dragon keeper disappeared along with his horse behind the curve of the mountain. "Come along, Piggy," Deagan urged. The horse stood still. The sound of Kellen's passing faded and Deagan was left with the tree frogs. "Walk on, Pig," he tried again. Still the horse wouldn't follow its companion. Deagan tied the steed to a tree and walked forward to meet Kellen. Behind him he heard a low moan and thought it must be the whining horse.

The curve around the mountainside was longer and more treacherous than Deagan thought it would be. It took him a few minutes to catch up with Kellen on the other side. He was sitting on his horse, eating a hunk of bread, and looking out into the dark. "Kellen?" Deagan asked.

"Yes, sir?"

"Come help me will you, this isn't going to work. I figure that if you take the reins I can push him from behind and as long as he doesn't kick me off the cliff, we'll get him over here eventually," Deagan turned to go back to his horse, knowing that Kellen would be right behind him. Again the two were separated by the curve of the rock.

Deagan came in view of his horse and moved to its head cautiously not wanting to spook him. He untied the reins from the tree branch they were dangling from, and he checked the horse's saddle and straps. There was something making noises in the jungle back toward where they had come from. The horse rustled and shook its head, and the sound drowned out what Deagan had heard. "Silence, beast!" Deagan demanded, and in another minute the horse was still. He heard nothing this time, but kept listening anyway.

"Kellen, where are you?" he called. No answer.

Then he saw shapes moving in the dark. They were gray shapes, shambling. He counted two, four, six figures coming closer. The trees broke the moonlight into shards and it betrayed his eyesight. He hurriedly grabbed the reins and tried to lead the horse forward. It refused again. A vile stench arose, and with it came an otherworldly laughter.

"Gods, you've chosen a perfect time to be stubborn haven't you? *Hyah!*" He cried as he whacked the horse's flank. Piggy started and walked three steps forward, but wouldn't keep going. Deagan looked back to the approaching figures. What had been half a dozen was now a horde. And those closest to him had faces now. Dead faces?

"Hail, night travelers!" Deagan called to them. "My horse seems to have lost heart here at the cliff. What brings you to this . . . path . . ." Rotters.

The lead one had white eyes and a filthy, long beard. His hand was wrapped stiffly around a meat cleaver. Deagan being made primarily of meat, thought this was concerning. The rotter kept walking forward with an ungainly gait, but certainly not slow. A roar of threatening and hungry groans arose from the mass of dead men, their voices were thirsty and dry, though they still achieved a gurgle in their throats.

"KELLEN!" Deagan yelled. And he yanked once more on the reins unwilling to leave his horse to be eaten alive. Kellen finally came edging around the cliff and into view. His face was a mask of fear and concern.

"I'm here old boy, what's the hurry?"

"THEM!" Deagan pointed back at the mob. They would be upon him soon. "It's *your* damned horse, so do something about it, and the next time we go to your stable, I'll not be so foolhardy as to trust you." He drew his broadsword and turned to face the throng that was steps away. Rotters had little combat prowess, but they had tricks that could make a dead man of you all the same. One of those tricks was that, being dead, they were nearly impossible to kill.

Kellen approached his horse and took the reins. If Deagan had Maggie under him, it would be easy to charge through them, turn around and maneuver that cliff path to be on his way. But now, he faced a great lot of sarcophs unhorsed and alone.

In preparation, he lifted his shield so the point at the bottom was in line with his front knee and held his sword up across his eyes, so that if he tilted his head, he could look through the triangular slot between the top line of his shield and the bottom line of his sword. This was the stance that he took when standing in a shield wall. That formation required many men armed with sword and shield. He had a hard cliff on his left and a sheer wall to his right. Perhaps they could be his allies.

The first rotter lifted his cleaver as Kellen tried to pull the horse to safety. It dropped on Deagan's shoulder, but the former knight was fast, and shifted slightly to keep the blade of his sword between his flesh and the sarcoph's weapon. He twisted in the hips, and keeping his elbows close and his defenses tight, he struck the dried, yet oozing flesh of the bearded rotter's neck. The head fell to the side, but wasn't severed. He took a downward chop and cut off the rotter's hand. Then another dead man rushed forward past the first.

This one wore no clothes and lacked a scalp, it had only one eye, but it carried a pitchfork. It tripped forward in a powerful, but unbalanced lunge. Two of the four tips were dancing before Deagan's eyes, having made it into the slot between sword and shield that he peered through. This pinned Deagan's sword hand. He swept the sarcoph's feet with a kick to the ankle and the monster fell to its side even as a third one advanced, followed closely by the rotter that was almost beheaded, and another unscathed one.

Deagan skewered the newcomer with a hard jab, but it had no effect for its heart had already stopped beating and its lungs were already empty as old grain sacks, but Deagan now had a grip on the thing. He dropped his center of gravity and from his knees he twisted and forced it off the edge of the cliff. It tried to grab onto the sword for balance, but only lost fingers as its hand slid away. This rotter struck the rocks below, and immediately tried to straighten its mangled bones. It latched onto a jutting stone with a deformed paw and pulled itself upward.

Kellen had brought the horse forward a little farther, it looked like soon the mount would get the hint and keep walking on its own. "Come on Kellen!" Deagan yelled.

He had better luck with the next dead man, severing the top half of its head, including the eyes, then swinging back through to take a leg off with the next chop. It collapsed to the path, then in a blind, biting lunge for Deagan's foot, it went over the edge.

The one with the floppy head and the missing hand advanced on Deagan as he regained his stance. It had picked up the cleaver in its other hand and now walked at Deagan backward for that was the only way it could see. The cleaver bounced off Deagan's shield once, twice, and when the third identical, backward chop came in, Deagan stepped aside and pushed the animated corpse down the cliff. In the descent its head pulled away from its shoulders.

Then Deagan advanced on them, tired of being on the defensive. He struck at their putrid heads with his heavy, dripping blade, confusing them, driving them back. Two more dropped to the ground, disabled and thrown off their feet by his maneuvering. He stepped back to his defensive position and risked a glance over his shoulder to see where Kellen was. He was out of sight, but the horse's backside still appeared around the curve of the mountain. He would have to hold his ground a bit longer in order to give Kellen enough time.

"Who's next?" he challenged them. He had a hunch they couldn't understand speech, but thought it was worth a try. The stench was overpowering and he tried to snort it out of his nose. The next row of rotters were now making their way over the crawling corpses on the path. He couldn't help but admire their tenacity. Deagan exhaled preparing for the assault.

An undead body stumbled toward him wielding an axe over its head. Deagan sidestepped a rapid downward swing and came back with a sword blow to the temple, but the rotter brought the axe back up on guard and deflected his shot. Another corpse lurched forward with a rusted scimitar that Deagan turned away with his shield. He took two careful steps back to get out of the scimitar's reach while dealing with the axe man. The axe thudded off his shield and smashed into the rock to Deagan's right. He plowed his armored body on top of the axe, pinning it to the wall. He struggled for a few moments with the sarcoph, without being able to get a shot. Then the rotter's filthy claw uncurled from the weapon's shaft, and it lunged at Deagan with an open mouth full of maggots. Deagan was almost sick inside his helmet at the smell. He slashed its chest, driving it back, while the one with the scimitar came in again. He blocked the sword with his own, but was forced back a step. The axe clattered to the ground and the rotter picked it up again.

In a flurry, Deagan charged the two of them. Shoved the axe man off his feet with a shield bash that caught him fully in the chest, and chopped the scimitar wielder's sword hand in half, leaving the sword dangling from a thread at the end of the rotter's arm. He found a crawling hand on the path with his boot, which he crunched into jelly. The rest of them were still coming.

Something struck Deagan in the face and sent him reeling. The edge of his boot was suspended over open air. A hand flew past his shoulder as he regained his footing and retreated a step. The stench thickened inside his helmet and would not dissipate. A writhing, pulsing snake of intestinal tract squirmed through the air at him. They were throwing their severed parts. This would be a tale for the mead hall if he lived to tell it.

Deagan chopped at a few more, a line of three of them now confronted his solitary shield wall. He hacked, kicked and struggled until his lungs heaved in his armor. before he realized he had been hearing Kellen's voice. "Deagan, come on!" he called.

Deagan booted the closest sarcoph in the chest, sending him back into those behind him. And he turned to navigate the cliff-side path. He rounded the bend and found Kellen waiting for him on the other side. An undead child was scrambling after him, holding a buckler in one hand and a knife in the other. Its hair was unkempt and filthy, and the dirt of its grave clung to the corners of its eyes and mouth. The lips hung loose to reveal straight healthy teeth—baby teeth. He jumped toward it, and swept it off the cliff with his sword. Though here it wasn't so steep or so tall and he knew the child would return.

"Is this horse ready yet, Kellen?" Deagan asked hurriedly as he panted.

"Ready as it's likely to get. You go first."

Deagan kicked the horse to a trot, and finally Piggy went. Deagan couldn't have explained how relieved or thankful he was that the beast had obliged. He may have come away from the skirmish unharmed, but he was growing tired. If he needed to keep that up much longer, eventually he'd make a mistake.

Deagan and Kellen were soon galloping into the taught jungle. Every time a branch touched them they thought they were again beset by the undead. It was a rapid and terrifying ride to make it to the caves that night, but before them, sure enough, the campfires and torches of the tower men lit up the night, and hope was kindled anew in their fast-beating hearts.

G WYN REACHED THE CAVES late that night now in the dress of a Royal Guard, having donned the armor that she had stashed on the path on her walk to Darkwell three days earlier. She entered the firelight with her spear held aloft and the black gold star on her breastplate shining warmly. Durvish was there at the entrance to the cave. He sat by the fire in his armor, modeling some mechanism or other with some sticks he'd found in the jungle. He looked truly alive.

And it appeared he had been busy. The cave's mouth had been furnished with a grand double door made of fresh hewn wood that glowed whitish red in the firelight. Beside the entrance stood a partially completed ballista. Eight of the tower men were working on carving long spears. At their butts however, were large feathers, presumably those of the large bird that was now roasting naked on a spit.

She nodded to Durvish and his towermen all went back to work as he approached her with a bow. "Guard Androth," he began, unable to hold back a smile. "The defenses are well underway, Sir. As long as we don't get attacked before tomorrow night, we should be able to make this a fort to be proud of. Come, let me show you around." When Durvish's gloved hand gripped her armored shoulder, she knew that the captain believed her to be a brother-in-arms.

The camaraderie Gwyn felt for other warriors had always been cheapened by her oath. Even now as Durvish touched her, the sensation should have been rewarding, but was instead empty, for Durvish did not know who or what she was. To him she was a man, a strong fighter, disciplined and trustworthy, but all these things were drilled into her, forced down her throat like fish oil until perhaps there was nothing left of the girl she had been.

She had told that charming knight Deagan that she was no longer a Royal Guard. Then weren't her oaths now broken? She thought of taking her helmet off, and speaking to Durvish face to face for the first time. She wanted friendship—not for the achievements of her spear, but for who she was at heart. Instead she clapped Durvish on his shoulder, and nodded in silence.

He went on, "Excellent. These men here are carving bolts for the ballista up there. These turkey feathers are still a bit small perhaps for the fletchings but they don't have to fly far. That's why we made them so heavy." Durvish led her up the bank and behind the cave to the ballista. "This is the ballista," he said with dear admiration. "The last one we built lacked a bit of oomph and it needed a bit more swivel to it. Well this one can turn in a full circle." He stood behind it and gripped the handles as men who were still working on it stepped aside. Durvish demonstrated its full range of mobility. It was surrounded by a low wall of large stones, and more men were bringing stones forward to continue to build it up. "See that? We could shoot at the moon, or we could shoot at our own toes if we wanted to!"

He turned the weapon to face one of his men. "*Pow!*" he laughed. "If I actually shot Wyll here, I'd send him all the way back to that tree. Run Wyll!" he shouted, laughing. He had an easy rapport with the towermen. They wouldn't be called disciplined by the standards of any other fighting men. Spirited would describe them better.

Gwyn shook her head from side to side and let her shoulders jump as though in laughter. She nodded to Durvish and gestured that she'd like to see the rest. He took her down to the gates. "Now these are coming along mighty good, y'see. He knocked in a special code on one of the doors and it swung forward. It was very thick, and balanced on its hinges so that it would swing freely. The outside of the gate was hewn flat, but on the inside, the curvature of the vertical logs could still be seen. There was a locking and barring mechanism that depended on ropes, pulleys and thick sturdy bars. There were several tower men working on the locking mechanism. "When they're done it'll look something like this," Durvish said as he held a wooden component in place. These men are trying to affix it to the door, still. It can be barred already though, don't worry."

The towermen had also attached torch sconces to the cave walls and cleared out all the bones and refuse. The hallway sloped downward. Gwyn and Durvish started down. They climbed through a rough window that had been made as another defense. It was built of logs and bolted to the cave so that the opening, which was once large enough for a Cyclops was now only fit for a person to squeeze through, much like a wider version of an arrow slit. There were men here too, working on a crude shelf that was attached to the downward side of it.

"Just a simple squeeze hole, here." Durvish said, still proud, but not as thrilled to explain it. They came down further and there were men working on some planks that were built into the floor. They passed by the men and continued on. Another squeeze hole was built into the wide tunnel below the first, this one had three openings, all of them were at a level you could step through and had the same dimensions as the first one. There were towermen working here too, some on either side of the wall.

Captain Durvish led Androth through the center hole and chuckled as he pointed up and said, "heh heh, watch your head." She looked up, and found a guillotine like blade, secured over the entrance. It looked like a sword that had been bolted to a wedge shaped block of wood. Above the other two holes there were a log and a boulder. "See, the log is rigged so it'll swing in from the side and clobber 'em. If there's one thing I've learned about traps, it's that you want to keep your enemies guessing. One of them kills you from above, one of them kills you from the side, and the rock swings down and kills you from the front. Watch this," he said and checked to make sure no one was in the way. "Rock test!" he called.

"Clear!" came the response from the men who stood back to watch.

"Here we go!" Durvish dropped the palm of his hand onto a wooden lever that held a rope and the boulder that had been affixed to the ceiling swung down in a smooth arc. It passed cleanly through the left most squeeze hole then the rope hit the top of the opening and the rock's course was quickly turned upward. Gwyn imagined the stone easily lifting someone off his feet and bodily throwing him back amongst his own ranks. The rock swung a few more times, each time with a little less of what Durvish called oomph. After three swings, Durvish called, "ready!" and he gripped the rope. Other men held it too. On the upswing of the fourth arc, Durvish ordered, "Now!" And the group of men pulled on the rope, catching the boulder and hoisting it back up to the ceiling with great effort. Then they worked together to lower the rope into its holding place at the base of the wooden lever, and Durvish flipped the switch that held the line.

Panting, the captain continued, "It seems like we're consistently getting about four lethal swings out of it before needing to reset. In order to get our own people through these we decided not to do any trip wires or anything else that's triggered by the victim. Unfortunately that means we need people to stay here and watch the traps while we're being attacked, but I wouldn't mind being that man. It would be a good show, even if it were the last thing I saw. The good thing about all of these is that once they are tripped, they will eventually block the squeeze hole. The one with the falling blade will be blocked off instantly, but the rock and the log take a little while to stop swinging. When they do though they settle in front of the squeeze hole and then our men can stand there and chop their fingers off when they try to push their way through!"

Gwyn was impressed. For all her time spent in Cloud Tower, she'd never seen defenses such as these. She clapped her gauntleted hands together in admiration for their work, and nodded to Durvish especially. This wasn't bad for three days work.

He led her further down, and found finally not another squeeze hole, but a door. Gwyn walked past it at first, for it was mounted in a hollow of the stone cavern, and hidden in the shadows. Torches in their sconces went on down the tunnel into darkness. They had been arranged so that the shadows were deepest surrounding the hidden door. "Right here, Guard Androth," Durvish beckoned impishly. "We found a side passage and turned it into our living quarters. Some of the villagers are in there now, working on making it comfortable."

Gwyn heard running water as she passed through. The darkness enveloped her for a moment, but there was light ahead. She heard people talking merrily about everything that had gone on. There were many villagers here tending fires, the smoke from which exited through a hole in the ceiling. The sound of water grew louder in Gwyn's ears. There was indeed a pool of water filling on the far side of the chamber.

"It'll never overflow! Want to know why?" Durvish asked expectantly. When Androth answered with a nod, he went on, "We can shut off the flow from above ground. It takes a little while to get everything plugged up and taken apart, but we can do it at need, and for the moment its being used faster than its filling up."

She was impressed yet again, there was a reason this man had been entrusted with the defense of the South Towers. The three cities needed more men like him.

The door to the corridor behind them slammed open and a helmeted man entered in a hurry. Gwyn knew the look of urgency in messengers' faces well enough and she saw it in his. She had already taken several steps toward the door by the time he finally spoke. "Captain," he panted, "There are riders above! And the legions of death follow close behind them!"

Without another word Durvish and Androth made there way back up through the tunnel and through the various defenses. The planks that Gwyn had seen on the floor were now clearly trap doors that led into pits, the mechanisms for which were being fitted and finished by several of the towermen posted there. Gwyn hopped the edge of one of these pits and kept on behind Durvish to the mouth of the cave.

The cave spit them out into the camp. All were standing and at the ready, two men sat astride horses, bearing weapons, but not wielding them. The battle lust showed in the eyes of some of Durvish's men. Gwyn recognized the mounted men at once as Kellen and Deagan, for she had arranged to meet them here tonight.

She slowly lowered her hand as she approached the men, and in response, the towermen let their spear tips ease toward the dirty ground. Some of them were loathe to do so, but nevertheless, they obeyed. She extended her hand to Kellen, and then to Deagan.

"Hail, Guard Androth," Kellen intoned grandly. "We bring news from the jungle both insidious and dire. Arm yourselves and make ready, for upon our trail their now advances a host of death." The men gasped in horror and groaned in weary dismay, only now did Gwyn notice the blood dripping from Deagan's sword. "We have joined battle with them at the fell cliff not two miles west of here. If the legends are true, they will sniff us out before long. They will smell our lifeblood—our very breath."

"How much time do we have? And why did you lead them here?" Durvish demanded.

This time Deagan spoke up, he urged his horse forward to get the man's attention. "They would have come here whether we'd met them or no. They had their heads down as if for a long march when I saw them first. They were just as surprised to see us as we were to see them. I was at Gamroth for two months before it finally fell. I have hunted these things and lived in their shadow. I am no stranger to their ways."

"Then, brave warrior, help us to ready ourselves for their arrival, and when will they get here?" Durvish replied.

"You ask for aid and you shall receive it. We have less than a handful of moments to prepare. I see this cave is fitted with a door."

"Aye, it lacks a lock, but may be barred." Durvish replied.

"Then leave me with twenty shield men up here . . ." Deagan trailed off as his gaze rose above the cave's entrance. Seeing what had caught his eye, Durvish smiled knowingly. "Does that work?" Deagan asked.

"Oh, aye."

"Then we need enough men up here to use it. Do you have shovels?"

"Err—yes, but what for?"

"Burn pit," Deagan replied. As the two of them continued, Gwyn worked on forming a shield wall with the twenty that Deagan had requested, and had sent the rest inside. "Get as many men as you can spare to dig a burn pit as deep as a man is tall, and many yards across, fill it with firewood. Sir, Oscar can handle the rest . . . where is he by the way, surely he should have made it by now?"

"Sir Oscar of Haven? The Dragon Rider? If he's coming here then I like our chances!"

"He's not here yet?" Deagan asked again. He looked out to the skies and saw no sign of him. Then a wave of stench rolled into the camp, like the foul breath of the great maw, which issued forth the hideous laughter that accompanied it.

"Do not flag!" Kellen hollered from the back of his horse. "Do not fear!" He raised his saber. "We have something to live for, but they have only hunger. Keep killing until they must crawl over the corpses of their dead!"

Some of the men roared with battle fury. They wanted someone to get their blood up, but the dignified Kellen Wayfield was not their leader. Durvish who had just loaded the ballista and now commanded a view of the clearing from behind its handles, bellowed, "Alright, boys we've been through this before! Kill as many as you like, but LEAVE SOME FOR ME!"

The men roared with laughter and called out their own taunts to the still unseen force ahead. The stink grew thicker and the laughter louder. Then the first of the undead appeared. They approached in a mob-like cluster, most of them crowded next to each other on the path, but many more spread out into the trees on either side. At last Deagan joined the shield wall, on the far right end. His breath was coming deep and regular, though somewhat hurried. His sword hand itched with anticipation. To make his presence known he grunted as he slammed the left edge of his shield into the man to his left. They nodded at each other grimly, then shared a moment of death defying laughter. Was there something larger than the rotters lurking some distance behind the trees?

Deagan counted his breaths, *five, four, three, two . . .* . The battle began. Weapons, claws and undead skulls surged against the center of the shield wall, but the formation didn't buckle. A heavy creaking, *Punk!* Came from behind them and one of the ballista's spear sized bolts flew over their heads and pierced two of the rotters, sending them back into the night. Durvish laughed as he and an assistant reloaded the weapon.

Kellen rode back and forth nervously, unable to join a shield wall, having no shield, and waited for a chance to step in. Deagan watched him from time to time, knowing that it wasn't his first battle, but that the old bandit might need some looking after before the end. Since no monsters assailed him yet, Deagan waited and glanced up to look for Sir Oscar.

Gwyn posted herself behind the row of shield men, and lanced the brains of the monsters again and again as they drew close. The eye, the forehead, the mouth, these were her targets, for she knew that she couldn't stop a heart from beating that was already dead. She dropped the rotters again and again, her count climbed from ten to twenty in as many minutes of bloodshed.

The sarcophs still poured into the clearing and showed no sign of slowing down, the mass that attacked the center of the shield wall spread out to both sides forcing the battle closer to Deagan. Only a few feet away, a man was killed by a crudely thrust sword in a decrepit hand. The men on either side of him hacked the offending monster mercilessly. Finally a charging corpse confronted Deagan, and he parted its arm from its body in one swing. As it regained its senses and approached again, Deagan dropped the weight of his broadsword down on its crown. He freed his weapon from the rotten skull, and chopped downward into its upper leg. His approach was to disable the head and at least two limbs in order to stop a sarcoph. Even then it was best to do more, but when time was short, the head and two limbs would suffice.

More rotters charged him, and now he was in the thick of battle just as the center of the shield wall was before. He knew what it was time for. He did his best to chop both feet off of the fallen sarcoph in front of him before he abandoned his spot. Another bolt from the ballista took care of two more dead men. From behind the moaning hoard, the sound of loud grunting and snuffling was finally loud enough to be heard above the din of combat. A large dark shape loomed behind them outside the torchlight sending a chill through Deagan's spine. *A living, breathing thing approaches, evil enough to keep such company as this.*

"Killing pocket!" Deagan ordered. He pulled men back from the shield wall, moving them into position. "Killing pocket!" some of them knew what he meant and helped (between sword swings) to arrange those who didn't. Soon enough, what had once been a flat shield wall, was now curved inward, so that any sarcophs trying to get to the men in the center would have to get into the pocket, and more than one sword would be in reach enough to kill them. This slight retreat was enough to provide the dead men with level ground on which to fight, rather than in the pile of writhing body parts that were their fallen fellows. The footing was temptation enough to bring the first wave of rotters into the killing pocket.

Sarcophs were not renowned for their awareness, their cunning, or their ability to work as a unit. Therefore, any tactics at all were better than none, and the killing pocket worked like magic. They stumbled forward only able to focus on one enemy at a time, and then before they knew it they were flanked by men who did not hesitate to take them down. Unbeknownst to Deagan, however, the formation of the killing pocket did not work perfectly, for a gap had formed on the left branch, and Deagan was now returning to the right one to retake his position there. He began killing from there, one, two, three next! One, two, three, next! And on and on, but the gap remained and around its fringes, men were dying.

Gwyn saw the weak point and so did Durvish. The captain launched another heavy bolt into the gap, it was enough to discourage an all out breach for a few seconds, but it only pinned one of them to the ground, and only by the leg. Even if the rotter had to gnaw it off, he'd soon be advancing again with the rest. In those extra seconds that the ballista bought, Gwyn charged in and filled the gap of four men. She stood in place as a sentinel at the gates of a city. She was instantly rushed and outnumbered. Being outnumbered was one thing she was used to, but never was it so uncomfortable as now. She held her spear over her head and stabbed down with it, wrenching it back from whatever innards it had been buried into just in time to stab again. They kept coming. Her breath was fast and labored, and sweat poured down her body. *Die,* she thought repeatedly. *Die, die, die!*

Her spear tip plunged deep through the misbegotten rib cage of a small rotter with a black tunic and a battle-axe. Somehow, the weapon was finally stuck. She tried to pull it free, but only yanked the still active foe closer towards her, she pulled again, and the rotter was closer still, but her spear showed no sign of becoming dislodged.

The battle-axe swung at her, aimed directly at her helmeted temple, she closed her eyes, but never felt the blow. Instead, the axe was knocked aside by a gleaming polished saber. Kellen, on foot now, stood beside her, and took two short yet powerful slashes into the thing's upper arm. The dry muscle tightened on either side of the wounds like a sausage cooked over a fire and the arm fell inert. The dead man looked up from its limp hand in time for its lidless, dust-glazed eyes to see Kellen's saber come in to behead it. Kellen joined the shield wall, but had no shield. His left hand, however, held a torch.

"This is my last one!" shouted Durvish as he sent a ballista bolt into the fray. It ricocheted off a tree and knocked a group of sarcophs backward, but none of them were pinned or disabled.

"Open the gates and get the men inside!" Deagan ordered making eye contact with Durvish. There was a moment of protest in the captain's eyes as he looked around the battlefield and gripped his short sword, but soon he nodded and gave the order.

His assistant went down and knocked the code onto the door, it was opened from inside while Durvish yelled, "Retreat!"

Marshals of the Captain repeated his command *Retreat! Retreat!* and the shield wall backed away. Deagan parried a couple of shots from the closest enemies, but didn't swing for a killing blow which would risk his sword getting lodged in one of their wretched bodies as the men to his left flank disappeared into the cave. He wanted to buy them as much time as possible, but he knew after years of experience that you could always expect at least two men to die in a retreat: the one who tries to buy more time for his fellows, and the one who stays to avenge him. Deagan had been through plenty of battles so far without being either one of them, so he left the job up to the towermen. He blocked another blow with his shield then disengaged and ran for the door.

"Hurry! Fall back!" Durvish called as he held the gate's open edge apparently determined to be the last one in. Deagan brought up the rear of the company and slipped inside just steps before the horde of sarcophs that rushed behind him. He bent down to peel the fingers of a corpse's hand from his ankle as Durvish shut the great door behind him.

"Move, sir! Get out of the way!" Deagan ducked under the beam and laid a hand on it as if to help, but the group of towermen handled it easily enough. The bar slid into place on its brackets and the only sound now was men breathing in a close tunnel.

"We'll make for the first squeeze hole, and hold it for as long as we can. Send the wounded down into the caves where they can rest and be safe. And if it comes down to it, they will defend the villagers there." Durvish hustled his men into position and Deagan followed his lead. He marveled at the freshly built squeeze hole that he could barely make out in the torchlight below. He waited for his chance to take Durvish aside.

"Do you know how many we've lost, man?" asked Deagan, sword sheathed.

"Ten dead, several more wounded," Durvish answered. "It could have been much worse if it weren't for your command . . . you say you've taken to the field against their kind before?"

"Aye. But there's something in their ranks against which I've never been trained or tested. It looked like some great beast, though I can't say what ilk."

"I saw it as well," Durvish confided. "The door was meant to keep out men. If I'd had more time we could have built a stronger one, but as it is, it won't be long before that thing batters it down."

"Well, let's get to the squeeze hole with the others then. We'll cut its arm off when it reaches through." The two of them clasped hands and then turned to follow the others downward as the first *cracks* of weapons against the door resonated through the cave as though it was the stretched goatskin of a drum.

When they got to the barrier, it was Kellen's hand that helped Deagan through the opening and onto the other side. The men huddled all battle ready and breathless, clutching their weapons and shifting to get the best advantage. Some of them started to believe that the gate would hold them off, so they began to rest their weapons on the ground or on their shoulders. Then a great *boom* sounded from above accompanied by rushing air and splintering wood.

Another *crack!* and the gate was gone, looming on the other side was the great beast all coated in black, oily fur, with huge hanging arms and short powerful legs. Its head drooped below its shoulders and on it there was a huge jaw with rows of sharp teeth.

From both sides of this monster, row upon row of dead men advanced and shambled towards them—pouring through the wreckage that was the doorway, and into the sloping, torch lit tunnel.

"Steady," Deagan breathed. "Killing pocket again. Not a deep one, there, like that. Now get ready!" The first of the sarcophs crawled through the squeeze hole with a grunt. Three swords rose and fell upon it before it could swing a weapon. Two others followed behind it and were defeated handily. Soon the bodies of the dead stuffed the squeeze hole to bursting, but the timbers remained strong. Then, in a horrific movement, the bodies lurched backward. They were writhing and therefore still animate, but it was through no will of their own that they were dragged away from the front line, even as they continued to scrabble for purchase, reach out with maimed claw-like hands and gnash their rotting teeth at their prey. When the squeeze hole was mostly clear, except for a severed leg stuck in a lower corner, the assault resumed, a wave of lifeless flesh breaking against the barrier as carelessly as the stormy ocean battering the rocks.

The towermen held their own, losing not a man. Their swords hacked and slashed as though they were gardeners hoeing weeds. Again the bodies filled the squeeze hole and were yanked back where they came from to get discarded on the floor by their fellows. Then it grew quiet enough for the defenders to hear themselves breathe in the echoes of the dank cave. The rotters held back some fifteen feet from the opening. "Steady," Deagan warned the others.

Then one staggered forward quickly reaching the doorway. He was about to come through, his gray wrinkled skin held taught against its stiffened face, but instead he threw something at the tower men. It was a severed arm, bloody stump on one end, a jagged gash on the wrist, but still attached to a hand. The limb immediately started dragging itself toward the towermen as the rotter stooped behind the partition.

The first one was joined by several more and a volley of body parts came flying through, landing at unnatural angles on shields, helmets and shoulders. In profound disgust, the men tried to rid themselves of such grisly adornments, but in their distraction, an axe flew through the hole and slammed into a man's face, taking him down screaming. The sarcophs threw torches next—they must have wrested them from the sconces on the walls. Gwyn held her spear one handed, butt resting on the floor. With her free hand, she caught a spinning torch that whooshed through the air in her direction. She looked over her shoulder to see Deagan watching her. His face lit up suddenly with the spinning fire of an incoming torch, and he raised his shield to keep the thing at bay. He didn't steal any more glances at her for the nonce.

"Sorry, rotters! Nothing to burn here!" Durvish taunted. "Just keep all these torches out of the way men," he ordered.

More weapons were hurled through, but the shield wall stayed firm. The throwing slowed down after a time and the stalemate went on unhindered. This time however, no one lowered a sword, waiting. Then, through the squeeze hole they witnessed the running approach of the behemoth monster.

Slam! All they could see were its surging limbs and bulging stomach. The structure did not budge at first, but dust fell from the roof of the cave. It laid its paws against the wall and heaved.

"Stand back," Deagan called and he backed away from the doomed structure. One man charged forward with a yell and reached with his sword out through the squeeze hole, he stabbed into the creature's knee, but as he did, the wall finally gave way and crushed him to death. The clatter of rolling logs and falling posts deafened the men and even killed one or two, as they retreated to the next squeeze hole.

The towermen weaved through the pitfall traps and Deagan and Kellen followed suit, stepping only where the men before them did. Durvish brought up the rear and was the last one through the triple squeeze hole.

"This one will stop 'em boys. Don't worry about that!" Durvish cheered. Deagan looked up to the array of traps that hung overhead ready to be sprung. He liked these towermen. "Stay back boys, we've gotta save these traps for that big thing. We'll let the undead through and kill them the old fashioned way, and when the big one shows up we'll see if we can lure him through the holes."

"He can't fit through the holes!" Kellen protested.

"His neck can," Durvish promised.

The line of towermen was ready and waiting when the undead began to haul themselves through the three openings in the wall before them. They formed a shield wall five rows deep that spanned the entire width of the tunnel. Deagan was in the first row Gwyn and Durvish were in the second, and Kellen was in the back.

The third stage of the battle was joined. The stench and the laughter poured in amongst them and Durvish wondered if the villagers inside the hidden chamber could hear the fighting.

The shield wall held strong and wouldn't be broken. Deagan dropped many, and Gwyn, who could reach over the front line with her spear killed many more, though her weapon could not cleave off limbs, it seemed that enough blows to the head would accomplish just as much.

The men felt confident, but also grew weary. Their shield arms drooped and their swords struck less hard and less often. Deagan killed on, not slowing yet despite his fatigue.

Noisome dark blood seeped down the corridor and lapped at their boots. Limbs dragged themselves between the men's legs to grapple with their scabbards, or claw them.

A towerman screamed and swiped his blade down his belly trying to scrape away a grasping hand. In his moment of distraction a rotter with one arm lunged at him, sinking its jagged teeth into him and bowling him to the ground. Another towerman, spinning to reach the claw that scratched at the back of his neck was beheaded by a rusty axe and silenced.

"Don't look down!" Deagan ordered. "Just stomp on them! Crush them if you feel 'em!" The men took heart and did as they were told, stomping madly while they fought.

The onslaught slowed, and the otherworldly laughter quailed. Finally the gargantuan beast peered through the center hole. Its huge yellow eye searched all sides for combatants or dangers, and then it straightened and backed away. Kellen noticed bits of dust falling from the ceiling.

"It's pushing it down!" he yelled. Gwyn didn't hesitate, she charged forward through the mass of unliving flesh and Deagan chased after. Durvish was soon behind them and then the rest of the towermen advanced, their shield wall dissolving. Deagan hacked the enemies before him making space for Gwyn to push through.

Gwyn lunged. Her spear tip passed in between two of the great beast's ribs. She twisted the haft and yanked it free. The beast clutched the wound and bellowed. It backed away from the wall. Gwyn crouched between the center hole and the far right one. The swinging log was suspended over her head. Deagan guarded her flank as several sarcophs tried to attack her. *Clang! Slap!* It was a bitter struggle to keep the monsters away from her. By the time he could stop to breathe, Deagan found that an armless rotter on the floor had latched onto his boot, the sharp teeth gradually tightening, grinding through the leather. He shook his foot to get it away, but it did no good. And a battle axe crashed into his shield, taking his focus away from the monster on his foot,

There was a deep resounding grunt from the other side of the wall, and a few pebbles fell with sounds like rain drops on Gwyn's night black helm. She spun out from behind cover, and Gwyn's spear found the creature's belly. This time, as it reeled in pain, and the spear came free, it plunged one great groping claw through the hole.

"Now!" Gwyn yelled. Her woman's voice sounded foreign and beautiful in the halls of stone surrounding the battle, but the urgency and command within it were undeniable nonetheless. Durvish who had situated himself by the triggers, threw the lever that would send the log swinging from one end to slam into the beast's forearm with the force of a battering ram. Gwyn flattened to the ground, and the log missed her, connecting squarely with the black furred limb.

The arm withdrew and still the battle raged. Deagan kept the rotter at bay, its nasty wounds would have been mortal if it were a human foe, but as it was, the deep lacerations to the abdomen and chest only slowed the monster down. Deagan took his chance to try and pry the heavy creature from his boot, but the jaws only tightened, a hard ache crept into his toes. The standing one advanced again, putting Deagan on his guard.

For a time it seemed that the giant had retreated, but then, the other arm came in, grasping for any enemy it could reach. It reached into the center hole, and when Durvish saw this, he released the guillotine from its mounts and it slid downward onto the back of its saber clawed hand. Deagan yanked Gwyn out of the way landing with her in a heap amid the writhing fallen foes. This time as it recoiled in pain, the monster left two fingers behind that lay still.

"Ah!" Deagan grunted as the teeth of the sarcoph finally breached his boot leather. The pain doubled and gurgling purple fluid oozed from the stinking face of the biter. Gwyn drew her short sword and wedged it into the corpse's mouth to pry it away. Deagan felt a slight release and tugged his boot free bringing several teeth with it, but the vile rotter did not give in, it lurched forward and landed on top of them bleeding on them, wriggling closer to any exposed flesh. Gwyn's sword stabbed and stabbed while Deagan held a dead man by the throat. This one had no legs, but it reached for Deagan, finally able to grip his throat with surprising strength. Gwyn was still on top of him, pinning his legs while she hacked at the armless rotter's head. He tried to get her attention, to get her help, but a strained, unintelligible noise was all that came from his lips.

The great yellow eyes and giant maw came roaring into the opening. Gwyn stood, threw the corpse to the ground and nodded to Durvish. Gwyn dodged the boulder as it arced downward and passed cleanly through the doorway. It slammed into the monster's face and then rebounded, killing a rotter in an alarming explosion of guts on the backswing. Thrown from its course, it slammed the wall, jounced erratically on its rope, until the fibers snapped and it fell, rolling toward Deagan. He put a boot on the side of it as it rolled toward him and it pushed him backward. He tried to kick it away, but it was too heavy. His vision was growing dimmer, and his lungs were on fire. Gwyn jumped out through the hole and his eyes went wide. He punched the rotter with a gauntleted fist and bones crunched, but the grip did not lessen. All Deagan could hear was the pounding of his heart. His attempts to fight back became feeble and the rotter pulled itself within inches of his face.

Then a spurt of blood erupted from the dead man's head. Kellen grappled with the thing and pried its fingers from around Deagan's throat. "You alright Deag?" Kellen asked patting the former knight on his cheek. Without taking the time to reply, Deagan stood up and found his sword. Gasping and sputtering, he threw off his helmet and stumbled toward the squeeze hole.

There stood Guard Androth, her foe lying unmoving on its back. Kellen then looked around him. The towermen surrounded the few remaining rotters. Kellen strode over the corpses into the ring of destruction behind the wall. Then, with his saber he dispatched the final off-balance sarcoph by beheading him from behind. Gurgling voices, emptying guts and writhing fingers remained, but the laughter from the otherworld was gone. It was now a matter of cleaning up the mess and rejoicing with what little ale and mead the Haven folk still had left.

I N ANOTHER WORLD, A black clad specter waited in the grass. Always, they arrived to the death fields with that look of surprise, as if they were waking up in an unfamiliar room after being so sure they had been safe at home. They almost always felt themselves and looked down at their clothes next, looking for wounds, the demon supposed. And then without a single exception, they all started walking. It was then that the demon could win them over. He liked to follow them, and allow their boredom to grow and give them time to wonder if this lonely wandering was all that lay ahead of them. It certainly wasn't, the demon knew. He had seen those star-horses guarding the entrance to the Hall of Warriors . . .

There were fewer dying this night than he had expected. Deaths had been arranged, why had they not yet occurred? The monster in black kept waiting, afraid to miss his chance.

Then more appeared. Warriors from the South Towers he'd wager, just as he had planned.

He crept closer in the grass, watching the surprise fade to peace on their dead faces. Feeling so eager to harvest them, the demon did not wait for them to begin their march into the unknown, but rather he took the form of a man, or as close to it as he could manage, and he allowed the men to see him.

Their armor was polished and clean, their clothing immaculate, and they looked at him with eyes filled with fear, but also defiance as they gripped their weapons and stared wordlessly at the grotesque, approaching shape.

Welcome to the fields of death, the voice said in their minds. *More's the pity you're here too soon.*

The warriors looked at each other, one reached out to another's shoulder with a gloved hand, but both of them were immaterial and they both gasped when they couldn't feel the contact that they had expected.

"This isn't right," one man said to another.

It isn't right that you should be here. You are too young and have much left to do. You left people behind, and you have left work undone, oh yes. But I can take you back. You can do more for your people. You can do more for yourselves.

"What do you mean you can send us back?" one of the towermen asked.

Just reach out your hand, thought the wicked voice. The words echoed through the plains, and thundered from the sky. Though still afraid, the first man stepped closer. He slowly lifted his arm.

Reach out your hand . . . your hand . . . your hand. Came the echo in their heads. The suggestion was strong, but one remained unconvinced, and stared the demon in his drooping, sloppy eyes.

"No, brothers," he said and reached out, not toward the creature, but to pull his fellows away. His hands passed through them.

The demon reached forward with a black fold of cloth only inches from the fingertips of the towermen. *Reach out your hand, that's it.*

When they were about to make contact, the towermen started to change. It wasn't a rapid change, it began with an orange glow.

Their fingertips shone with a warm light, which distracted them from the cajoling creature before them. The demon backed away, terrified, avoiding the burning light.

The glow spread up their arms and legs, until every part of them glowed like fire.

Then as the demon cowered in his puddle shape, the towermen rose higher, out of the monster's reach. A look of understanding came over them, and they clasped their hands over their hearts with the sword hilt upon their breasts. They sailed together in shining red warmth, floating off toward the twin horses and the hall of warriors. The demon knew this meant that in the living world their bodies had been burned which told him the mortals were taking precautions against his game.

If they'd had time to burn the bodies, didn't that mean that the battle was over? And a mere handful of dead had appeared in this world. The rebels were more formidable than he had surmised, and evidently he had underestimated them.

I must have greater numbers, the apparition thought. *And these damned rebels just won't die.* A dark and wicked thought occurred to the twisted creature—a gamble. He set out, his figure a spiraling whirlwind of black cloth and rotted, swollen flesh. He followed the flying dead, careening over the gray grasses, for the towermen would lead him to the greatest source of dead warriors he could ever hope for. The Warrior's Hall.

THERE ARE POINTS IN history that are remembered forever, woven into the tradition of the land. The charge of ten thousand horses against unbeatable odds was one, and the legend said that no one who was there lived to tell the tale . . . how then did the tale get passed on? It is a mystery, like many other questions in life. The wide-open sky above Darkwell was the perfect canvas on which to paint the next epic. It would be a tale of courage and a tale of dragon fire.

The gleaming lights of the streets and buildings gave the circular stone wall a warm glow, the pillars of smoke were like the prayers of its inhabitants, rising gently yet urgently up to the Star Country.

It wasn't King Malagor's doing that had put Sir Oscar the Dragon Rider into the dungeon. It had been his trusty adviser, Jatham Holmin who sentenced the foreign knight. Would the record show how greed rather than malice had guided the king's hand? Would the dangers of vanity and temptation receive their full measures in the legend to come, or would the simple and undefined 'evil' again be the villain's only qualifier?

For Malagor now served the teeming forces of evil, but the nuance of how this came to be was the greatest and most interesting part of the legend. For once upon a time, Malagor was a good man. In his youth he was cunning and brave in his warrior's training. He was a rule follower and a natural born leader. He was fond of hunting, but also of the natural pursuits such as gardening and woods lore. There seemed to be no discipline, study, or art that young Malagor could not master. He was favored by the courtiers as the rising star of Darkwell, the future king who would carry on where his father Barthus had left off.

When Malagor took the throne, he lived up to the dreams of his subjects. He freed many lands from the clutches of evil, he defended his people and his neighbors. He even ripped the foreign nations of the North from the grasp of dark forces, where all resistance had been destroyed. He was a warlord more than a politician. But what the historians may one day forget is that in those days, being on the side of good was *easy*.

Malagor's father had already engaged Darkwell's army in the above undertakings, and thus Malagor's duty was to clear them up before any new pursuits were begun and that was what he did. A fortunate turn of chance gave him victory in one battle, an unexpected and favorable wind afforded him the advantage in another. The people started to believe that Malagor could never lose. That he was blessed by the King of he Star Country, and that his coronation marked the beginning of a new era, so much so that some wished to begin the calendar anew with the year one being the same year that he took the throne.

The forces of evil receded slightly. Still the map was blackened by their dominance in the vast majority of the Knowne Worlde, but now Malagor and his armored knights had kindled hope in the hearts of human kind. When the new king had finished with his father's old business, he turned his attention toward home. He became entrenched in the day to day operations, the minor disputes, and the intellectual debates of the wise. He believed that with such great success in war, he could apply all he knew of war craft to the taming of Darkwell, leading the great city into an age of prosperity and peace that would be rivaled by no other. The world had conspired to make the great king vain.

It had been so easy to follow the course of war that his father King Barthus had laid out for him, that he found his own subjects far more difficult to work with than his enemies had been. With trolls, there was nothing for it but to slay them, and thoroughly, but with the likes of human kind he found that he had to give something up every time he wanted something in return. At first he likened this compromise to the loss of men while fighting in war. But he found that the loss of his dignity, the minute chips of his mental well-being were harder to withstand. The slow wearing down of his self worth was worst of all, for when he failed to arrange a treaty, a trade route, or a plan, his sense of failure was staggering. He no longer remembered the man who he had once been except as a phantom to mock the failure he had become in his middle age. Darkwell did not prosper. Nor did its neighbors.

Malagor became ruthless. He made decrees instead of consulting others. He made demands on his allies instead of negotiating. For the dream of Darkwell's greatness he once held had been twisted into something dark and vain. The groping reach of his tax collectors squeezed money from the peasants and the dealings he had with other nations were underhanded. He had become willing to take any measures just to pursue Darkwell's greatness. And when at the end of his days Malagor had failed to *lift Darkwell up*, he began to toy with the idea of bringing his neighbors *down*.

It was this insidious motive that Jatham Holmin appealed to. He had information, plans, and influence in Haven. Ultimately, Jatham Holmin revealed that he also had another gift. He had powers. He had walked in the land of death . . .

The historians however would not remember Jatham's name. They would not remember his tendency to hide behind the curtains when people sought audience with the king. The reason that he would not be remembered is because Jatham was not truly a man. His former self was lost in the shadows of the long and horrific paths that he had traveled to arrive on Malagor's doorstep. It was fear that drove him, fear that someone *knew* about him. *He knows! He knows! I'll kill him before he tells.* These were the thoughts that ravaged the hollow recesses of Jatham's soulless mind. And they drove him to do terrible things.

One of these things was to throw Sir Oscar into the dungeon, where he would soon die of thirst, starvation or sickness in the dark and moist catacomb of stone that snaked under Malagor's spire. Yet if death called him, Oscar intended to sit up straight to wait for it, poised on the stone bench by the gate he'd been locked inside of. He had been there mere hours when thunder shattered the very dust from the walls of his prison. It was the crash of dragon fire.

Oscar stood up and gripped the bars of the dungeon, the vast unknown stretching back behind him and the light, barely out of reach and locked away, before him. He stared through the bars with his heart thumping in excitement and confusion. Tonight was the night in history when instead of Malagor sending his men against unbeatable odds and winning, his men *were* the unbeatable odds and the small force assailing them stood little chance, but tried anyway. Though it was Oscar's first notion of any upheaval, the dragon fire was not how this story began. It began with a conversation at the spire's gate.

"Good afternoon, spire guard, I am Rory, loyal butler to Kellen Wayfield and loyal servant to the king. His Majesty has requested my services this night, that I might prepare for him a breakfast feast for the morrow."

"He's got servants for that," the gruff guard replied, holding his pike casually.

"Of course, master guard. And I've been told that they are very skilled in the kitchen arts. But I have been trained since I could walk to prepare the finest of meals in all the known cooking traditions. My plan for the morning is roast duck, and it will take me hours to prepare. I must begin within this very hour to have it done in time."

"Grizelda makes a fine roasted ducky! I've never known the king to need such as yourself when he's got perfectly able servants to do his cooking."

Before the guard could say, "Be off with you!" which he was certainly about to say, Rory interjected, "I'll bet my coin against yours that I can best Grizelda's roast duck any day. I'll be sure to bring you a plate of it in the morning to your guard post." As he said this he produced a golden coin. "Of course, in full confidence of my skill, I would leave this coin with you tonight."

The guard looked at him suspiciously, as all guards should, but he accepted the token, and furtively stored it in his pouch before standing aside and letting Rory through the smaller servant's gate of the spire. It was a tiny hatch in the back of the castle. It was well fortified and out of the way, but if a guard let you into it, you need not worry about fortifications.

Rory carried the following things in a basket: three ducks, herbs and spices, a bottle of mead, a loaf of bread, seventeen gold coins, a scroll of parchment sealed with wax, a sock filled with stones, flint and steel, and an oil soaked rag. Rory had set out on foot, and the Dragon Riders went by air. The dragons were now perched on one of the scaffolds near the spire. The inhabitants of this particular slum were uneasy and didn't cause any trouble for the knights. A wee lad in his long hanging tunic and bright shining eyes came toward them to meet the dragons. The Riders obliged him, and as they waited tensely, the youth's curiosity and innocence gave them some reprieve from the anxiety. When the signal came, they would no longer be welcome in these walls, instead they would be corsairs harrying the king's own men with flame and thunder. So even as they played with the boy on the scaffold, they watched and they waited.

Rory continued on through the dark corridor within the servant's door. He followed the turns and looked over his shoulder once or twice. He was not sure where the entrance to the dungeon would be, but he felt fairly secure in thinking it was below him. Before long he found an unadorned and unlit stairway leading down. The smells of cooking were heavy in this part of the spire, also there were scents of perfumes and soaps for the king's bathing and laundry no doubt. Rory recognized the smells of all the spices, meats, and breads. He could tell that the sourdough had been left to rise too long, and that the venison had been burnt. If he ever did cook these ducks he would indeed wager they'd surpass those of this Grizelda, whoever she was.

Rory dismissed his day dreams and descended the dark stairs. His crisp, dressy boots clicked on the large, flat stones, but he feared no unfriendly ears, for up till now he'd done nothing wrong, other than bribe a guard, and what guard could object to that? He still had sixteen coins left to bribe with, hopefully getting him all the way to the dungeon.

The stairs turned to the right and Rory had little choice but to follow them. He saw the first glimmer of torchlight below. He stopped to smooth his hair, then took a deep breath to muster his willpower and walked down.

The hall he entered had no smells of wash or food, but only the scents of slime and dark places. Molds grew on the walls, putting forth their stuffy, fresh scent. Rory knew that smell could poison him, so he covered his nose and kept going. The torchlight was closer now; it was a solitary light in this long tunnel. As he drew closer he started to make out the thick carpet of dust that lay on the floor.

His breath caught in his throat and he nearly dropped his basket. A shiver of terror raced through him. There was a figure beneath the torchlight. There was a man there, crouched or crumpled against the wall with his hands outstretched. The frightening thing was that Rory hadn't seen him until he was too close. He had been looking so intently at the flame, that the figure beneath it didn't catch his attention. Now Rory himself was at the edge of the torch light. And he told himself that he couldn't turn back. Then there were voices, light and boot steps behind him. Men were coming down the stairs. His eyes widened and his breath quickened. He was caught. Well at least there was a chance that he could get past the sleeping man; the awake ones wouldn't be so easy.

He tip-toed down the hall further into the torchlight. Now he could hear the guard snoring. The men behind him grew louder and gained on him, for while he crept carefully, they stomped heedlessly. Still they were on the stairs, but soon they would be in this hall. He placed a boot beside the man's hand, stepped over his knees, lifted up his basket and slowly crossed over him. Now the other men were in the hallway, coming fast. Their voices echoed down to him, but Rory did not pay attention to what they said. Rory put two gold coins on the ground near the man's feet. Then he left the torchlight and came to a fork in the tunnel. Just as the new guards reached the sleeping guard and booted him awake, Rory ducked down the left passage.

He heard them chiding the sleeping man, and soon they argued over the coins at his feet. He couldn't tell how many of them there were. He shuffled quickly down the corridor away from their voices. The sounds of the men behind him covered his rapid retreat. He did not know where he was going, but the smell of evil was thick in the tunnel. Soon the boot steps advanced again. Rory felt the walls for any exit or alcove he might conceal himself in. Finally his hand found a gap in the stone, and he squeezed into it. He forced his body back further and further into the crack, but found that he could not completely hide, it was too small. And he had now wasted precious time. He dropped two more coins on the floor and continued on, the torchlight felt so close that it burned his neck. He stalked down the hall.

"What's this, more gold!" cried one of the guards behind him.

"This time we split it down the middle, I say," replied the other.

"Why? I found it!"

"Yes, but you aren't clever enough to explain how you got it, and you know full well that these don't belong to you. If Garret finds them in your pockets during inspection he'll have your head. These aren't even Darkish coins! And you've never left the walls in your life. Everybody knows that!"

"If Garret finds 'em, I'll know whose face to break in for telling him about it," threatened the first man.

The second man sighed exasperatedly. "Always the first thing you think of is to threaten somebody. Why not work together here? Garret needn't find out at all, if we keep our story straight he won't suspect a thing and we can spend it all in the Guild district before he knows we've got it."

Rory crept on, but he kicked a stone that made a sound. Instead of waiting for the men to find him, he allowed himself to be found first. "Hello?" he called to them. "Is there someone there? I'm lost."

"Who's there?" the guard demanded, shoving the coins into his purse. Rory walked toward them composing himself.

"I am Rory, butler to Kellen Wayfield. I was sent—," the guards seized him and pressed him against the wall. He let out a grunt of discomfort as they lifted his arm behind his back, wrenching his shoulder almost to the breaking point.

"Who are you?" they demanded again. "What are you doing here?"

"I am here to cook for his majesty. This is my first visit to the spire and I had a difficult time finding the scullery. Can you help me find it?"

"What the blazes are you doing down here?" the second man asked and his arm was lifted even higher behind his back.

"Ah!" he called in pain, "Look through my basket, there is a scroll, I'm here to cook ducks for the king, nothing more! Just lost."

Roughly the man shoved his meaty hands into the well-packed basket while the butler was still held against the wall. The rummaging sounds went on for a few minutes. "Oy, comere," the searching guard grunted.

The guard holding Rory, let him go and carried the torch over to shine it on the basket's contents. Each man held a halberd, a long hafted axe with a spike on the end and a matching one on the butt. The man who'd searched the basket now let it lay on the floor.

Rory turned around and saw his Halberd was leaning against the wall as he held the scroll in both hands, trying to unroll it. Rory knew that once he opened the wax and looked inside he'd see that it wasn't a summons from the king or any other official document, but a blank page. So just as the seal was broken, Rory bashed the armed guard in the face with a tightly balled fist, and then in the confusion of the torchlight falling to the ground, he snatched up the great halberd, and brought its haft forcefully up into the reading man's crotch dropping him to the ground. Rory reached into his basket on the floor to pull out the sock full of rocks. He swung it down into the floored man's temple. The man stopped writhing and slumped completely. The man he'd punched was on his feet, but badly dazed, he braced himself against the stone wall with one hand.

"Forgive me," Rory breathed as he 'socked' this man as well. He fell to the ground landing on the torch with his arm. Rory quickly snatched the flame from under him and held it aloft. No one else seemed to be coming. Breathing hard, but now strangely calm, Rory packed up his basket and searched the men for keys. There were none, but he did take back Kellen's coins.

Rory trotted down the corridor full of confidence. *Perhaps I'm suited for this hero business after all!* The torch in one hand and his basket in the other he came to another dim fork. The stench of evil was stronger coming from the right hand side, so that was where he went. It wasn't just the stench of evil. It was the smell of death.

Rory sensed that he was close, so he laid his torch and his basket down. He got out from within it his sock, and stowed in his pocket the rag and the flint and steel. If the torch lasted long enough, he wouldn't need to use the flint and steel, but he brought it just in case. Carrying the weight of the three ducks had grown unnecessary. There had been fighting now, so what good would his story do?

Now it was time to signal the Dragon Riders. They had agreed to circle the tower every few minutes to look for it. There were iron barred drains that led from the streets down into the tunnels below.

What their purpose was, Rory couldn't guess, but for him, they would be his way to signal the Riders. He listened for the sound of water, and when he heard it, he turned toward the trickle. It was slight, but it echoed enough that he could make it out. He followed the sound, with his hand outstretched, until finally he felt the tiny waterfall coming from a grate that led to the street. Above him there was a ten or twenty foot tube that was the drain. He could not make out any starlight, or sound coming from above, but he knew it must lead to the street. The entrance to the stone passage was only two and a half feet across, and even on his tip-toes he couldn't reach it.

He felt a moment of panic, for the plan had been to reach up and tie the rag to the bars, light it on fire and then move on. The storm drain above him though offered no such ease of access. Rory spent a moment of indecision, gazing about him in the dark.

". . . So I walked into the middle of the damn thing . . ." Rory caught snippets of a conversation and more boot steps coming from the corridor ahead. ". . . Half a goose still roasting . . ." Guffaws of laughter. They were getting closer. ". . . hail to King Malagor and all that . . ." Through the mumbling echoes of the stone he could not make out all that was said, nor did he care to. It was surely vulgar and uncouth, not much to Rory's liking, and it was a wonder he could make it out at all over the pounding of his heartbeat within his ears.

He knew that there were no alcoves or hiding places behind him, he'd come from there, and hadn't seen any. And the guards still advanced. He thought of fighting them off again, but having the luck of one of them laying his halberd down was not apt to happen again, happy fortune that it was. He doused the torch in the trickle of water and tucked it next to the wall, so they wouldn't trip over it.

There was little chance to think, and little time to act. The first orange gleams of torchlight licked the craggy walls ahead. He took a deep breath and leapt for the tunnel above him. His hands struck the wet insides of it and he found that his finger tips brushed what felt like a lip of stone he might be able to hold onto.

". . . great . . . varmints . . . nothing like the old days," Rory heard. If he could get a little higher . . . the torchlight bathed the far end of the hall now. Rory launched himself at the ceiling again, visualizing the lip he had felt. This time he caught it in his fingers and swiftly lifted himself up into the opening. He pushed his back against the tunnel and inched his way higher. He found another handhold and latched on. Below him, his feet were kicking ineffectually to and fro, the barest glint of his polished leather shined out, the reflection of the torchlight. If the guards saw him, and came upon him here, they would quickly skewer him with their long pikes. There would be no defense or escape.

With all his considerable might he hoisted himself in. His boots disappeared into the murky blackness of the drain and he braced them against the walls of it, securing himself into place. Still he strove higher in the channel until finally he reached up and gripped the iron bars of the drain and held himself there. Now he could hear the sounds of the city and it gave him comfort and respite from the damp and dread of the deep dungeon.

"Turny told me I'd been asleep for three days, that he'd never seen the like and couldn't for the life of him wake me up! This was a lie, of course and it had been just an hour, but he dressed me for the wedding just as quickly as possible and made me eat and drink before making me run to the blasted castle!" Both men were laughing. Rory wondered if they'd be laughing for long. The rush of light and noise passed under him at last as the heat and smoke from their torch rose to meet him in his hiding place. It happened so quickly that it seemed neither of them suspected his presence in the least. But it would be only so long before they found his basket of ducks. What had he gotten himself into?

Rory braced himself with his feet and tied the rag to the bars. The quarters were small so it was difficult to strike sparks with his flint and steel, the sound scared him as well for he did not wish to give himself away. He told himself, "Rory, you've come here to do something and you'd best get to it. If you get scared now there was no point in all the rest of this foolish adventuring. Now strike that spark!" He slammed the steel into the flint and sparks glowed brightly as they landed on his clothes, he tried again, the *click* of the fire starters was loud in his ears, but he tried a third time and this time the rag caught a large, bright spark. The cloth smoldered for a moment then a reluctant lick of flame sprung up from the edge of it. The heat continued to build however, and the flame came to life. Rory descended to avoid the fire and stowed the flint and steel in his pouch. A feeling of satisfaction and fear mingled inside him and he watched the sky, squinting past the flaming rag. After a few minutes, two huge, fearsome figures swooped over the drain. People in the city screamed or jumped with terror as the dragons descended. Rory alone took heart to see their coming.

He crouched hidden above the tunnel, but then a crash of dragon thunder smashed the keep. Confusion swept the halls of the catacombs, distant yells rose up. Loudly now came more breaths of fire, surely landing on the streets above the dungeon. Rory's life flashed before his eyes. "How did it come to this dear Rory?" he asked himself. "You've beaten guards, hidden in a filthy drain, now you fraternize with dragons and make war against the king. Once you were such a fine butler! And before that you were such a polite and earnest boy, so innocent and unassuming." His reverie went on as the distraction built up around him. Three guards with lit torches stormed past him. One of them held the three ducks in the basket. "It's now or never you hapless servant." He said to himself. "Goodbye, Darkwell."

He dropped silently onto the floor of the dungeon and ran back the way the guards had come. He stepped lightly, but his feet carried him swiftly. Now his heart was lifted on the tide of his excitement and for the first time in his life, Rory got his blood up. A guard surprised him, coming around the corner. The guard seemed to be moving in slow motion in his heavy armor while Rory felt free and light, his speed gave the blow from the sock enough force to slam the guard's head into the wall of the tunnel and knock him out.

Rory didn't slow down. He could smell death ahead and he went toward it. He came to a section of tunnel where many torches gleamed from the walls. The corridor was wider here, and at its end there stood a guard. His back was to Rory, and his gaze faced into the bars of the strong door. In fact he appeared to be arguing with someone on the other side.

"They *are not* dragons!" the guard roared at the darkness. "We are not under attack. Control yourself, prisoner, and leave me to my business."

"Believe as you will, friend." An unseen speaker muttered from the other side.

By now Rory had crept up behind the guard. With a flourish, he spun the man's halberd from his unsuspecting grasp and pinned him to the door with its sturdy haft. He lifted a knee into the man's groin as he tried to yell in protest.

From the other side of the door a hand gripped the face of the guard's helmet, trapping him in his pinned position. The guard managed to slip away from Rory's hold and slide his head out from his helmet, "Ha!" he said as he turned around.

"Ha *ha!*" Rory replied and punched him in his unprotected face, leaving him dazed and slumped against the dungeon wall. Rory scrambled for the jailer's key. He found it affixed to his belt and turned it in the massive iron lock. The door swung open and Sir Oscar strode out to meet him wearing the smile of a free man.

"Rory! It's you! Oh you have truly outdone yourself this time old boy! What the blazes are the dragons doing out?"

"Rescuing you, now come on!" at that moment another man emerged from the dungeon, the knight and the butler were taken aback. He was huge and his beard was short. Even next to Deagan he would have been an imposing figure, his garb was all black and his face was covered in soot and grime. So filthy and unkempt was he that both the other men were offended with the sight of him. Under his eyes hung dark circles and around him there hovered a malignant aura. His gaze was sickeningly depraved, inhuman. And as he moved, his powerful form was so full of sickness and fatigue that he pulled himself out rather than walking from the dungeon. His appearance was all the more horrific to Oscar, who had never once seen the man while he was imprisoned, but he must have been there all along. He now thanked the stars that he held out and did not sleep.

"Who are you?" the knight asked.

"Can you not see?" the large man rumbled in his dry and stinking throat. "I am a criminal against the crown. Like yourself, I was forsaken. Like yourself, now I am free."

The man wandered away down the tunnel and the two of them hoped that the guards would not let him out alive. "Unsettling as that man is," Rory said as he closed the dungeon door and locked it, "We must follow his lead and rid ourselves of this place. That distraction you hear above will keep them busy, but we must hurry, or risk your saddle-fellows being skewered by the king's arrows."

IR Goodsing and Sir Johan soared valiantly around the tower. They had seen the light of Rory's signal and had begun their assault instantly. They struck out at the walls, but as soon as the first balls of fire impacted the stones, a hail of arrows issued from the many arrow slits and turrets of the citadel. The king's archers were not trained to shoot at flying targets and scores of arrows flew wide of the mark. The townsfolk took shelter as best they could, but who could say whether one or two of them may have caught an arrow in the confusion.

And confusion it was. Men on foot poured out from the castle, horns sounded in the heights of Darkwell, and the army was mustered with startling speed. Soon spears were hurled from the top of the tower. These too were poorly aimed and left the dragons unscathed as they swooped away from the tower then came back in to strike again. They were not trying to harm anyone, which made the battle hard indeed for it was not their custom to leave opponents standing after a flight.

Goodsing called to Johan, "Are you unhurt, brother?"

And through the whistle of the wind in his ears, Johan yelled back, "For now!" And they dove again on the spire of the King. Two more assaults found them still unharmed, and they thought that time was wearing thin. A group of dragons, riderless probably, had risen to circle and watch the scene. If they descended on the tower in concert, and not knowing the plan, surely lives would be lost and all of them would be exiled from the city or put to death. So Johan kept a weather eye on the circling troop above to ensure that they kept their distance.

"It's time!" Goodsing yelled as his dragon, Warmaker banked to the right and left. What he meant was it was time to get Pete, eldest and largest of the dragons. Goodsing hurtled through cramped city streets, dodging the clotheslines, the beams upholding the scaffolds and the close hemmed buildings, and he landed next to the rooftop where Pete lay waiting. The dragon nodded his great head and arose in glory to join the fray.

Pete followed his sharp nose and found Rory's scent. He knew the human's plan had been to escape through the same way he'd entered. And he gave wonderful brushings so he was certainly worth keeping around. The trail led to a strong door that to Pete looked like little more than a plank of wood hinged with string. He built up and pressurized his fire into a massive and terrible ball. He unleashed it on the doorway, which broke to cinders and blew apart.

Unbeknownst to any of them, a man standing on the other side of that door was the only man killed by their assault. Pete fell to earth by the door and began to guard it, his heavy claws raking the cobbles and leaving their mark, daring anyone to cross that line. He roared his challenge to the night. The dragons, even those high above, took up his chorus, and Ero and Warmaker redoubled their fury as their waves of flames crashed upon the stones of the streets around the tower and the bastion of the tower walls.

Soon men set upon him, laying their lives on the line to secure the doorway that had been blasted apart. But deadly as he was, Pete would not kill them, the knights had forbidden death dealing, and he would obey for as long as he could. They had him surrounded and he could not take off, not without his master.

CAPTAIN DURVISH AND THE tower men rallied together in brotherhood. Their music was joyous as well as tragic as they saluted their fallen out on the sacred funeral pyres. Deagan who had never known any of them by name, but who had seen friends die before was moved to grim tears as he watched them send their dead to walk in the other worlds. Nevertheless, he worked tirelessly to clear the tunnel of the still grasping hands, the still wriggling legs and the biting heads of the undying foe they had beaten. It was impossible to count the numbers of their attackers, for they were now all in pieces, but Deagan estimated two hundred, plus the one monster for which he had no name.

The burn pit dug and chocked with sticks, Deagan led a group to scour the area for any remains, which they piled into the pit. The mass grave was lined with towermen, each one was prepared to herd the body parts and keep them down where they belonged. The fire was lit even as towermen continued bearing corpse-pieces into the blaze.

Durvish officiated over the fallen towermen, speaking of their grand heroism and the glory they would enjoy in the Hall of Warriors when they crossed the vast plains of the other world and made it to the Star Country at last. When he was done speaking he watched the warriors armor fall apart, wreathed in fire. Tears filled his eyes, but he could not stop looking in wonder at the helmeted head of Guard Androth, whose voice he had heard for the first time. He approached her.

"Guard Androth," he said quietly. She turned to him, her black war-mask holding the crisp fire. "These men fought bravely, but none so bravely as you. We are again indebted."

"You owe me nothing," she said, her feminine voice sending waves of confusion and disbelief through Durvish's head yet again. "Your defenses held, Captain, as I knew they would. Be proud of your achievement. While we know nothing of how the people of Haven are faring, at least we know that Durvish can keep his people safe." She clasped his shoulder in the warrior's way. He did not hear her words, but only her voice, which was like a country wife's lilting song, but sterner, and steeped in the wisdom that came from long silence. Her touch now had a different meaning to him. She who he would have sworn was a man.

"You've broken your oath," he said in awe, looking back up to her face.

"When I left Saxus that oath was already broken. He broke it by leaving the South Towers to be destroyed. Yes, now I may speak, but I am not fool enough to hope that my words can change what is to come."

Durvish nodded. He adjusted to this new identity before him. He let go of his desire for her to have kept her secret and accepted that she was still the slayer of the Cyclops and the defender of his people that she had ever been. They had traveled far together and weathered the raid of Malagor's militia. His respect for her grew. He bowed before her. "What do you command then, Androth? The enemy is repelled for now, and now our location is lit by many bright fires. If there are more of them they may soon arrive. Should we rebuild the defenses?"

"No, Durvish we're not staying here any longer. Keep the people safe and inspire them to endure. As you do so, however, ready them for travel."

"Where are we going?"

"Back to Haven."

"To what end?"

Gwyn looked North and said, "Mine or the lord's."

I N ANSWER TO THEIR leader's roar, the dragons descended one by one. Johan looked up and rose to meet them. As one of them glided down to join the battle, Johan guided Ero upward and under the drake's belly, a clear signal to cease its advance. When the outraged dragon, plunged further, Johan put a hand on its under side and shoved it away.

"No!" he yelled. "Back up with you! And tell the others to do the same! I'll explain when it's done you horrible worm! For now just go back up!" The dragon whined in protest and tried to sink again. Without being urged to, Ero lunged up and nipped the other dragon's neck, warning him to do as he was told. Whining louder the dragon winged up into the sky.

"Goodsing!" Johan called, but his friend was too far below him to hear. He sped away, blocking the stars as he herded the other dragons back up into the sky. None of them had riders, or even saddles. That would make this far more difficult. Other dragons responded to Pete's roar, and dove on the tower. Ero and Johan spread the message that this fight was not theirs. They turned another dragon back to the sky, but it would not be long before there were too many falling to Pete's aid for them to repel. This was not how Johan dreamed Darkwell would one day fall. He was determined to stop them. As he surged around in circles, grappling with the beasts in mid-air to get enough time to reason with them, the first spits of fire landed on top of the tower, and spear hurlers were put to death.

"*Hurry, Rory!*" Johan hissed.

T HE TWO OF THEM hurried on through the stone walled tunnels, each one now bearing a torch. Rory now felt much more secure with the protection of Sir Oscar close behind him and they felt confident that any guards they found could be easily dealt with. Oscar carried the jailer's halberd as he trotted the loathsome corridors, ready to wield it for his freedom's sake.

Rory led them down the hall where he'd fought the first two guards. Still they lay there, but not as they had been left: unconscious and on their backs. They lay one on top of the other, their faces devoid of color, their heads at unnatural angles from their bodies. "I did not do this," Rory told Oscar in grave concern. "I left these men alive, but unmoving."

"I believe you. No time to worry about it now," Oscar advised, sensing the defensive fear in Rory's voice. The two of them continued past them and then ascended the stairs. More shocks of dragon fire blasted the spire, thumping into the old stonework. When they reached the top of the stairs, the smell of cooking was gone. It had been replaced by the acrid stench of dragon breath. A slippery haze filling the halls of the spire parted as they stalked through it.

When at last they reached the door that Rory had entered, they saw that the stalwart barrier had been lifted off its hinges and laid smoking on the ground. On the far side of it, a great tail slashed back and forth. They peered through the door to see Pete the dragon holding a ring of the king's guards at bay. He slashed with his claws, breathed fire, and lunged. He spread his wings and swept them away with his wind. Trickles of blood flowed from arrows that stood impaling his wings, one had buried itself in his neck, and many more lay broken on the ground around him having struck his scales.

"Go on!" Rory said, pointing to the saddle on Pete's back.

"What about you?" Oscar asked. "Do you have any way out?"

"I'll find a way."

"Nonsense!" he gripped the faithful butler by the hand and pulled him out into the fray. The guards yelled in protest and an archer, his bow at full draw, turned to aim at Oscar and Rory. He was the second man Pete would kill that day. Fire consumed him and his arrow never flew. Pete hunkered down and the two men climbed aboard. Oscar kicked him to action and the beast flew skyward.

He roared triumphantly. Sir Goodsing joined him in a steep upwards climb. "What's going on here Oscar? What were you doing in the dungeon?"

"There is much to discuss, but let's not do it here!" Up into the higher reaches above Darkwell the two of them hurtled. Rory's heart was again gripped with fear, the wind was cold, but such heat radiated from the dragon's back that he was comfortable. When his heart finally unclenched he was awestruck at the beauty of the city from so high, but even more life changing than the view, the butler marveled at the sensation of flight.

Pete reached the dragons now and roared their retreat call. In relief Johan shouted, "*That's* what I've been *telling* you! You daft lizards! Welcome back to the skies Oscar. Did you have fun underground?" The dragons' chorus shook the air, and they rallied in a hot, turbulent mass.

"Go back to your roosts," Oscar ordered. "Go back and keep your Riders safe! Saddle up and follow! We ride to the east!" With that he banked to the side and flew off. Johan and Goodsing were close behind him. They traveled to the lair of the tower men. And though their mounts could breath fire, it appeared that the tower men had already started fires of their own, and large ones.

K ELLEN AND DEAGAN STOLE away from the group when the body parts were well sorted. They watched the dragons over Darkwell in curiosity as they spoke.

"Well, how did you like your first ditch battle?" Deagan asked.

"It wasn't that bad," Kellen replied.

"I couldn't help but notice you stayed mostly at the back," Deagan goaded him.

"I couldn't help but notice that I saved your life. Besides, you know as well as anyone that I would have been up front if I could have been, but the way the shield walls worked out, it just didn't make any sense for me to be up there, it would have ruined the formation. It's a pity I didn't get to spill more blood."

Deagan laughed, well you got that last one. He was a scary one too. Good thing you were there to take him down. He never saw you coming . . . of course that might have been because he was trying to run away . . ."

"Are you crazy? He was going after the towermen when they were least expecting him! If I had stayed my hand, I would not be able to live with myself, for human blood would have been spilled due to my negligence, mark my words."

"Well it was a good shot, you took off his head. Let me see your sword there."

"It's a saber," he said unsheathing the slightly curved blade.

"It's light," Deagan commented. "Balanced."

"Yes, and it's sharp as well, Rory saw to that, no doubt. It's light because when I first started carrying steel I surely didn't need any more weight that might sink me in the water. I was one of the few pirates who took the trouble to learn how to swim."

"I know a little swimming," Deagan said, "but only enough to prolong the drowning process. I couldn't swim to save my life, I mean."

"Not in that, you couldn't." he knocked on Deagan's helmet. The two of them threw pebbles into the gurgling stream.

"Do you believe in spirits?" Deagan asked.

"Like water spirits?" Kellen said.

"Aye, or phantoms."

"I've seen one, Deagan, of course I believe in them."

"You have not." Deagan dismissed him, but he was looking to the camp where Gwyn stood by the funeral pyres.

"I have seen a ghost. It was deep within the watches of the night, and a fell sound arose from the walls of my manor. Rory was asleep in his chamber, and I was alone in mine."

"A common condition."

"For you and I both. The sound happened again. I heard it. It was like a muffled thumping as if someone were trying to get out of my closet."

"You lie," Deagan challenged, but a shiver had started to toy with his spine.

"The handle moved, and I felt all the warmth being drawn out of me. Then a voice said, 'Listen,' cold and far away. I wasn't afraid. I knew the spirit only wanted to be heard."

"No. It didn't say listen," Deagan protested.

"I swear that it did. And the door opened, but no one was there. From the closet came nothing but a dark breeze that put my candle out and a groan like this," Kellen imitated an unearthly groan and Deagan shivered again.

"Then in the dark I gripped my dagger to my breast."

"I thought you weren't afraid!"

"I was *then!* I took the dagger in hand and I heard footsteps. I felt a presence in the room. It was much like a father coming to check on his child in the night, but it was a father with lost intentions and an empty mind. I didn't feel watched after. I felt accused. My wrong doings passed through my head, and it seemed that the specter could sense them. I could hardly breathe, and then, a weight pressed down on the edge of my bed. I felt a person sit there." Deagan gasped. "I felt a cold hand resting on my forehead. Another one pressed down on my chest. Again I heard the groan." Again he mimicked the sound he referred to. "And the phantom remained there, unmoving, holding me down. I didn't sleep that night. I laid still until the morning light dispelled the presence and I was alone again."

There was a pause. The story was over. "How can you still sleep in that room?" Deagan asked, unsure if he would ever sleep again.

"I had the ghost taken care of. Have I ever told you about my friend the barber? We met when I sought him out to sort out my spirit." Kellen explained. Again Deagan gazed over at Gwyn in her war gear.

"There is a way to get her attention, you know" Kellen offered. "Standing at a distance with your only friend and casting glances at her isn't it."

"What do you suggest?"

"It's called talking."

"I'm going to kill you," Deagan replied. Just then, three dragons landed in the vicinity, startling all of them with the formidable wind that uplifted the dust, stirred the foliage to show the white underside of the leaves, and fanned the flames on top of which the corpses had been thrown. Oscar dismounted, and Rory hopped down behind him. The towermen and villagers were from Haven, and had seen the dragons flying above the city, but never so close as the three massive lizards now sat. The butler steadied himself against the dragon's flank and then looked out at the people around him, not knowing any of their faces, nor they his.

"Rory!" Kellen and Deagan yelled together. They rushed down to the clearing and found the butler still shocked from the flight. "Rory," Deagan said. "Is that dirt on you?"

"Yes it is," he said excitedly, and launched into a modest version of his tale. Soon all those present were listening to his account of the plan, the escape and the battle in Darkwell. Oscar chimed in with praise now and again for Rory's cunning and prowess. Neither of them mentioned the other escapee, the large, disturbing man who refused to identify himself by name.

Oscar had often wondered if by doing good one also committed a portion of evil. If his escape yielded any such evil it surely was the death of the guards and the escape of the frightening man from the dungeon. But now, like the rest of them, Oscar was made a fugitive, which he had to admit was better than dying in the deep tomb under Malagor's keep. So exhilarated was he by the second chance he'd been given, that he picked Rory up and cheered loudly. Everyone laughed and merriment again overpowered the gloom.

Then Durvish, Rory, Oscar, Kellen, Deagan and Gwyn held a council around a campfire, other warriors came and went, but they did so with great respect and deference to the leaders and heroes gathered there for conversation.

It was Durvish who spoke first, a jungle fruit in his hand and firelight dancing over his face. "Surely you are well met, Sir Oscar of the Dragon Riders. I have heard of your fame long before today. But what's to be done? We have all journeyed far, and yet it appears that another march lies ahead, back into the dangers we have only narrowly escaped. Now, Androth has spoken to me in confidence about our future plans. They involve you, Oscar, the other Dragon Riders as well. Is it a good time, now to bring this mission forward?" He turned to the knight, expecting no more than a nod or a shake of the head.

Instead she lifted her helmet off and spoke, the crowd gasped as one. "The difficulty in being a thief is that the more you steal, the heavier your purse becomes as you run to escape." Kellen nodded knowingly at her words. "Saxus became greedy in the pursuit of wealth. Instead of a lord, he acted as a baron of thieves. His army became a plundering horde of raiders, and I, as his Royal Guard, was forced to ward against his victims as they returned to claim what he'd stolen from them. He is a disgrace of a man. And a villain. His villainy will be his downfall. His greed will be his weakness."

There was a pause. "We're all in agreement to bring him down. We just need to figure out how." Gwyn finished.

"But what about the rising undead problem? The threat is spreading." Kellen said. "They killed my caravan drivers not to mention all the guards I sent with them. They took the South Towers of Haven, and now we've been attacked here! I'm starting to think I'm bad luck."

"It's not you that's sending the monsters against us. I don't know what is. But I feel that the answer to that riddle lies in Haven," Gwyn answered.

"The other Riders are going to be here soon," Oscar said. "I'll need to outfit myself with weapons. I've been robbed by the jail guards."

A heavy fog then fell on the camp that swirled about them in the jungle heat. The stink of burning bodies now settled instead of rising. The discussion continued into the night. By the end, they had all agreed to travel to Haven over the mountains rather than by road so they could arrive in the South Towers without being accosted by any sentries or patrols. They decided to leave soon lest the sarcophs came back to the caves.

As the group packed their things, Durvish stood in the clearing and gazed at the broken doorway he had built. The logs that they had chopped down and hewn to size had granted the entrance such order, had made this desolate cave into a home for his people. Now it was stove in, useless, never to be repaired, and bathed in the smoke of Durvish's burning enemies. This wasn't the first thing the sarcophs had taken away from him.

"Ready sir?" asked one of the towermen breaking the captain's dark concentration. He nodded and joined the group, not taking his eyes off of the carnage until they had marched out of sight.

S IR LUTHAN, HIS HAIR in grey ropes, his mail worn down where the plates slid over each other, climbed the familiar stairs to the throne room of King Malagor. He knew this must be a busy and confusing morning for the king, what with the unexpected dragon attack of the night before, but he knew that his tidings must be heard this very minute or else it would be too late. The knight's hand was wrapped in a white bandage, staunching the blood from Jatham's knife cut. Should he tell the king about that too? It depended on the old man's mood, and judging by events of late, this tidbit would need to wait.

Finally the guards let Sir Luthan into the second highest chamber in the spire. He bowed before the king, but Malagor paid him no heed. He had walked into a conversation between Malagor and another of his advisers. Not Jatham.

"And what of the other 'Riders, they too have abandoned us I presume?" The king demanded crossly.

"Your Excellency is right again, sire. Vanished in the night shortly after the attack. Their current whereabouts are unknown," the adviser said.

"Then it shall not surprise you to hear I want a reward for dead dragons, or dead Dragon Riders. No one attacks the spire and lives. Send word that a handsome sum, say one hundred and fifty coins will be paid for the Dragon Riders, and 200 for the head of a dragon. With such rampant desperation in the city, surely someone will be fool enough to try and kill one of them, and even if he doesn't, the hunt may at least yield some clue as to where they have gone."

"Very good, Sire." The adviser said.

Luthan cleared his throat. The king was clearly in a rage, this news would not cheer him.

"What do you want!" he barked, rubbing his temple.

Luthan rose at last to his feet, trying not to allow the pain in his knees to show, and holding the wounded hand behind his back. "Sire, I have news from the lower levels of the keep."

"Get on with it, man," the king urged him.

Malagor had started to severely offend Luthan. "It seems that some of your prisoners escaped in the night, My Liege."

The king threw his breakfast plate on the floor and a servant rushed in instantly to gather it. "What!" he hollered, as Luthan winced.

"The dungeon guards report being ambushed in the midst of the dragon fire. Apparently a small troop of men made an attack on the dungeon and opened the door. The guards have conflicting stories of what occurred. One man told me he was knocked out by someone claiming to be a duck chef of some sort. Another, who was very nearly killed, says he was stabbed in the back by that thief, Assadon. Another told me that he was bowled over by five or six men in black, wielding clubs and hatchets."

"How many dead?" Malagor asked, sick of the details.

"Only five sir."

"And how many prisoners escaped?"

"Only two, sir."

"Two?" the King roared. "Last I knew there was only one living prisoner and that was Assadon. Did that worthless debtor, Halmor come back from the dead? For surely he was the last one sent in there, and it was weeks ago."

"Your Highness would be right, but it seems that your faithful adviser Jatham saw fit to sentence someone to the depths of the Dungeon, My Liege. So say the guards."

"Who did Jatham send to the dungeon? Who was this other escapee?"

"It was no other than Sir Oscar, chief of Haven's Dragon Riders. He was locked up yesterday, and within hours he was freed. Know you not what crime he committed?" Luthan asked.

"The last *I* knew he'd been sent to locate and assault the rebels. No one knew where they were, so no one expected him back so soon . . ." The King pondered a moment. "Are you certain that it was he?"

"I am, Sire," Luthan replied.

"Then the only crime he could have committed would be insubordination to the crown . . . It is fortunate we have Jatham on our side, Luthan, he is a shrewd man and would not place someone in the dungeon unwarranted." The king muttered something to himself then broke off. "No matter," he finished as Luthan clutched the bandaged hand behind his back. "You heard me issue the reward for the Dragon Riders, no doubt? Let us hope that this measure is enough, especially if the lot of them have turned against us."

"Of course, Sire. Are there any other preparations you would like to order to ward off another attack on the spire?"

"I would, except there was no attack in the first place," the king mused. "It was only a diversion. Yes I see it now. Only a diversion to rescue the knight from my dungeon. If the dragons wanted to kill, they would have gotten more men than they did. They would have torn this spire apart and we both know it. I actually must applaud them, for they got their man back with the fewest deaths possible."

Luthan was not sure how to react. He was a noble knight, but he was a yes man as well. And a yes man is always struck dumb when agreeing with the king means agreeing that he was fooled. Luthan stood motionless, waiting to be dismissed.

"Now you may go, sir Knight," the king said at last for he had much to think about.

MERE HOURS AFTER THE battle, Deagan doused the cook fire, wearing his pack and weapons in readiness for travel. Kellen finished his own preparations then mounted his horse. Rory, who had nothing with him in terms of provisions, helped where he could, tidying up the battlefield and aiding the towermen as they rallied for another late night of marching. He still rode high on the success of Oscar's rescue and on the thrill of flight, so it felt to him that nothing he attempted would go astray.

"Deagan," Kellen said in a hushed tone. "Do you really think this is the right course? Our motley band will never be able to survive Haven's army, let alone break through it and *kill him*! I have a bad feeling about this."

"Take heart, old bandit," Deagan comforted his friend. "It is not the city's army we must conquer, it's the undead. They have no order! They have no discipline! All they know to do is charge and devour what they may, with no heed for how many they have lost. I have faced them before, and now, all of us have. We have the Dragon Riders, Kellen, and no rotter could hold a candle to that."

"I hope you're right. Though I use hope only in the most figurative and insignificant sense of the word. The road ahead spells doom, Deagan."

"You're a seer now? How can you be sure? We have Gwyn! She knows the Royal Lord like no other. She has his secrets locked in her head like a store of weapons that we'll unleash when we reach Haven."

"Really? What kind of secrets?"

"Even *I* don't know, Kellen. That's how secret they are."

There was a pause between them in which Deagan peered into Kellen's face and Kellen looked down at Deagan's boots. "Keep me safe, Deagan," Kellen said.

One of Deagan's big hands landed softly on Kellen's shoulder. "I will, my friend, as long as I live."

They were interrupted by Durvish calling the group together for the final words before they departed. "Come here, you! Gather in! We are ready to set out for Haven, though not by any known road . . . at least not known to most. There is a track over the mountains that will take us to the doorstep of Haven's outer realm. From there we will make for the South Towers, which by that time should have been cleared out by the Dragon Riders." He gave an appreciative nod to Sir Oscar. "You have all fought hard for your very lives, and yet there is something wretched lurking in our own home that must be driven out. So as much as we'd love to rest, there is no time. How long until the sarcophs' ruler finds out that they have failed? How long until this cave is once again crawling with the things?

"I for one intend to be long gone before we get the chance to find out!" He laughed. Others joined in. Then the seriousness of their situation again settled upon them along with a taut silence. "We can rest when Saxus is overthrown," he said with sadness as he stepped down from the rock he'd been on and led the group down from the cave and into the jungle.

B Y DAWN, THE LARGE group of combatants led by Gwyn Androth, had made it into the close fitting forest of the upper mountains. The succulent jungle plants of the lower reaches had given way to a prickly and stunted forest of evergreen trees. The soil was full of hard rocks and in the cracks there were stagnant, pollen edged pools and tufts of dry, dormant moss. They had been on the march for hours and had crossed the farmlands on the outskirts of Darkwell while the farmers slept entering the trees that would shelter them from sight all the way to the outskirts of Haven.

"We must be close to the top now," Kellen breathed, as he looked up to the stony surface ahead and the sky above it.

"You've been saying that for over an hour." Deagan replied, even more winded than his friend.

"So it's truer now than it used to be," Kellen said.

Rory was breathing deep too, for never before had he climbed up to experience the mountain air. No smoke! He marveled at the wild fragrances and nearly made himself light headed just trying to take it all in. He could not stop smiling and looking to his companions as if to say, *can you believe this?*

"Slow down, cabin boy!" Kellen said. Rory did as he was asked and perched on a rock above them, waiting at ease for the two older men to catch up.

"Look behind you," he invited them. When they reached his rounded stone outcrop, they turned to follow his gaze. Darkwell sat in the valley, steeped in its own shadows. The morning light caressed its parapets and flying banners. To Rory it looked utterly clean from way up here. To Kellen it looked full of wealth and promise. To Deagan, it finally looked far enough away. He was out of its clutches and the shackles of his past. He was with an intriguing and beautiful new woman and the only friends that truly mattered to him. He had a quest, and he had his freedom. He was overjoyed to be alive for the first time since his first campaigns for the king.

Stretching out from all sides of the city were the safe lands where farmers dwelt, under the constant patrol of Malagor's forces. Beyond the farmlands the jungle crouched, its greenery made alive in the brilliant sunrise. Wind played on the treetops as the creatures woke up and began to call and sing. The day held promise. In the distance, other mountains rose to greet the dawn and lend their great shoulders to the endless task of holding up the sky.

The three of them looked at each other and with the hard work of mountain climbing, they were giddy to see bright sunlight in these dark times. They laughed without truly knowing why, and all of them would remember the view from here. Then as they still looked out, they saw a host of flying shapes sail toward them from near Darkwell, figures that they would have thought were hawks, if not for the occasional spurts of fire that sparked in the dawn air.

They plunged forward into the climb again, focused on the stones beneath their boots and the branches whipping them in their faces until finally in an hour's time they had reached the end of all trees. Above this mark there existed only wind, blue sky and stone. The company scrambled up to the mountaintop, which afforded them a view of both cities, Darkwell and Haven. Haven, to the North and West of them looked decrepit and care worn; its imperfections revealed in the now intense light of day, rather than hidden by the shadows and hues of sunrise, and its impurity was just as apparent as its lack of life.

A column of smoke rose from the heart of the city and as the group mounted the peak, the Haven folk came alive with a stir and commotion at the sight of it. Still the stragglers topped the mountain and by the time all were assembled, a new council had been formed there: a ring of people around a single grassy meadow filled with jutting gray stones.

"What can we do if the city is burned to the ground?"

"What about our homes?"

"And our families! Some of us had to leave them behind you know."

"Family? Ha, I wish I was so lucky, mine were all eaten alive."

"I was a beggar even before the raid, when we get back to Haven, I couldn't be much worse than I already was." Those from Haven were now arguing loudly about who had it worst—who had sacrificed the most and suffered the greatest losses.

It went on for too long. Deagan and Gwyn exchanged looks.

Deagan now spoke up, "Whoa, whoa, whoa! Shut up! These are not the days of cream and honey. These are days when you take what you can get." An offended silence greeted his unpopular words. "When the rotters came, did you think they'd shake hands and walk home at the end of the day? No. You knew it was only the beginning.

"So don't look so surprised. Slap yourselves across the face and get ready to do what you came here for. You can turn back whenever you want to. But all of us climbed these mountains for a reason. Saving your lives cost me more than you think, but I knew there was *a reason*. Because now, we alone have a chance to change things." He pointed to Darkwell. "Do you see any great column of men marching to Haven's aid? No. And I hate to shock you, but a group of rebels with a couple of outlaw ex-knights aren't likely to get any help from the likes of them.

"So we can sit on our laurels like a bunch of lazy cowards and complain about everything, or we can get up and stop it from happening again." He moved the straps of his pack further up his shoulders and walked away. I'm going to Haven," he said.

"Are all knights of Darkwell so rude?" one of the villagers asked in the direction of Deagan's back.

Kellen answered for him when Deagan wouldn't turn around, "There are two ways I could answer that question, young lady. The first is, no, Deagan's the rudest one. The second is, he's not a knight of Darkwell."

T HE HIDEOUS BLACK FORM trailed behind the group of flying dead. After a time they sank to the grass and approached two distant lights, that looked to the monster very much like stars, but as the demon closed the distance, his eyesight confirmed his suspicions that these lights were the guardians of the Warriors Hall.

He slinked closer, hidden in the tall grass, peering over it with his misshapen and drooping eye only as needed to stay on course. He was disgusting in this form, even to himself, but power always had its price. He drew close enough to hear their conversation. The grand and mighty talk sickened him. Warriors and their epic speech! Bah. To the monster in the grass it sounded like this:

"O great pony, I bow before your mighty snout in deference and respect. I have traveled farther than the bravest gryphon, I have slain more evil monsters than the noblest king. Blah blah blah, valor. Blah, blah, blah, courage. Blah, blah, blah kneel humbly before you."

And it continued laboriously until all were duly flattered and the sycophantic men were allowed through the threshold to the Star Country. A dark, polished braid of leather hung from the sturdy door and the white stallion clasped it in his teeth to pull open the portal under the freestanding golden archway. The monster drooled, for this was his way in. This was his chance. The fire-bright spirits flowed into the beyond and only the wariest of them bothered to serve as rear guard and survey his surroundings before entering behind the others. The horses stood by to watch them go. When their flanks were turned, the rag-monster sprung.

It was the mare who saw him first, a powerful wave of thought accompanied her alarm. *CLOSE THE DOOR BROTHER, AND TURN YOUR MIND TO KILLING! WE ARE UNDER ATTACK!*

The rag-monster dodged a sharp-hoofed kick from the mare, becoming a puddle of oozing blackness. He slithered between her legs, attacking them each in turn. She stomped, but his liquid nature rendered him invulnerable to it even though she shook the very ground of death's realm. She tried to get away, her legs now bleeding, but like a plague of flies, the mass of evil cloth and flesh stayed underneath her, leaving her with nowhere to run. The door now closed again, her brother turned to fight. He was larger than his sister, and more stoutly built.

DIE, THING! Thought the stallion. And so powerful was the thought that the monster almost considered obeying. The stallion dipped his open mouth into the mass that was the monster, tearing at it with his perfect and ivory-hard teeth. He came up with a mouthful of bloody, black rags that disintegrated as he spat them out. He reared up in agony, for the flesh of the demon was a deadly poison that he had taken in.

Still his sister stomped on her foe, but no blow would pin or break him. He then rose up, all bloody teeth and pale flesh, to sink his maw into her vital belly. This growling, rending bite was how the star-horse lost her life. In weakness and defeat she collapsed.

I TOLD YOU TO DIE! Repeated the stallion. He again bit into the rag-monster's cloak or body, whichever it was. This wound left a chunk missing from the creature's form, and it howled in pain. Its wraith like shadow gathered in upon itself into a tight roiling ball. The monster retreated a number of yards for it was a near mortal wound that he had sustained.

Dripping from the stallion's lips came a black ooze full of red foam. He staggered in pain and his nostrils drew in huge gulps of wind. Soon blood dripped from his ears, his nose, his eyes. *You came here to do evil,* he managed. *And evil, you have done.* He took a faltering step toward the monster and the monster retreated. *Die now and be satisfied.* With his last effort, the mighty horse charged forward on shaking legs, he fell on the villain with his poisoned mouth open wide, bent on revenge for his sister, no matter the cost. He landed upon his foe, but already the poisonous flesh had sent him to his death, and his corpse gurgled as the acid continued to consume it from the inside. Then in triumph, the monster rose up in the form of a man. He was ragged and bloody still, and his face held no human quality, but from afar his outline would seem man-like. He reached for the strap of leather that hung from the door to the Warrior's Hall.

THE PATH CARRIED THEM down a long reaching ridge. There were steep sections that required them to climb down hand over hand, at times even lowering ropes to assist the elderly. They caught glimpses of the burning city every now and then and each time the sight was closer revealing more grisly detail at each vantage point. The company snaked through the mountains single file. They gathered for a midday rest; waiting to make sure all were accounted for before setting out again. Provisions were shared sparingly. There was not enough to fill everyone's bellies, but any attempt they made to forage or hunt would only slow them down, and these were farmers, not survivalists. Their knowledge of plants was confined to the borders of their garden plots back home.

Grim thoughts played through their heads, some of them even thought of this brief and meager repast as being their final meal. Deagan watched their morale bend under the strain. Then a rush of air went over their heads and they were shadowed under the wings of dragons. "Look, there they are!" the people cheered.

Deagan's speech hadn't made him any friends among the villagers, but it had stirred them to action. His words hung heavy in his head for once again he had let the purple sickness rise up and blind him. At least Durvish and the tower men understood. They knew that fretting on a mountaintop would gain them nothing and some even patted Deagan on the back, or thanked him for his speech. But he still wished that he hadn't shamed them so.

Now on the north side of the mountains and thus, in their shadow, the company descended into Haven's valley. The jungle engulfed them as they climbed down. Again they gathered in the evening. It would be their last rest before arriving at the South Towers.

Rory still seemed in high spirits. He was thinking about dragons and gallant heroics. He seemed to have added a dashing swashbuckler's lean to his butler's repertoire of poses. He leaned on trees and on rocks whenever he got the chance. There was a confident fire in his eyes that seemed to say, *who's the cabin boy now?* He made friends with the towermen and the villagers along the way. He even carried a young boy for a time as they went.

It was through a thick hedge that the company first glimpsed the South Towers and the countryside that they protected. They had climbed down the mountains and it was now almost sun set. The group waited at this natural barrier, peeking through the foliage to spy on the abandoned farms and gloomy towers that jutted up at odd angles through the sod. They saw no sign of movement.

Kellen, Deagan, and Rory volunteered to scout ahead. As they made ready, Rory pulled his weapon from his pocket and brandished it gingerly to be sure he could still use it when needed. "Not much use against the undead, that," Deagan remarked looking down at the sock full of stones hanging from Rory's hand. Rory looked up at him nervously.

"What am I to do?" he asked. "It's all I have, sir."

Deagan was by now bristling with weapons after searching the group of rotters as he dragged their severed limbs to the death fires. Also, the short swords of the fallen towermen were still of some use. He furnished the butler with one of these, a belt and scabbard, and then gave him a naked battle-axe lifted from a rotter corpse. "It's a pity we can't outfit you with armor," the warrior apologized.

"I have never worn it before, and I think it would weigh me down, though I thank you for the consideration." Battle-axe in hand, Rory separated the branches of the jungle before him and stepped through.

Deagan looked back into Gwyn's masked face and smiled. What a mystery this woman. He then left as well with Kellen close behind him. The three of them first made for the farm ahead of them. In the failing light, the field of grain stood as a sea. They crossed it carefully then came to the vegetable patch. It was full of weeds, but intact. They passed an animal pen. All within it was carnage. Pigs, and a cow lay mostly devoured in the mud. It gave them pause, but soon they were at the building. Deagan led them past it after one brief circle around the outside.

They moved on to the next farm, always walking onward to the nearest tower, which appeared at this distance to be no larger than Deagan's hand. Kellen was worried that they would be accosted at any moment, but it never happened. The gray tilted pillar that was the nearest tower grew ever closer, until finally they crossed the last expanse and approached within yards of the sentinel.

Unfamiliar with its layout, the men didn't know how to enter the tower, so they circled around it seeking a gate or doorway. They found neither, but as they searched, a night wind arose. It filled their ears with noise and chilled them. Kellen ran his hands along the craggy stone, looking for some hidden latch or handle. After seeing the ingenuity of Durvish's defenses back at the caves, Kellen did not think the captain would be hard pressed to conceal a door, especially if he had enough time to build it. Rory on the other hand looked up to the ramparts. Deagan scanned their surroundings incessantly watching for attackers.

Finally, Rory called out, "I say! I just saw something." Deagan drew his sword and Kellen turned about with his back to the tower, then, imagining a secret door opening up behind him he turned back around to face it again. "Up there," Rory pointed to the very top of the tower. Deagan looked, but at first saw nothing. Then all three of them jumped when they saw a flicker of movement.

"What is it? Kellen asked.

"I don't know," Rory answered. He backed away to get a better view. Deagan, ever the protector followed him closely as he went. From here they could see that the movement had been the tail of a long triangular banner. And though the sun had set, the sky was still light enough for them to see what it was. "Let's tell the others at once!" Kellen said. Deagan and Rory agreed and the three of them hurried back to join the company that awaited them at the edge of the jungle.

T HE MONSTER TUGGED THE braided leather thong
that served as the door's handle, but it wouldn't
budge. He pulled again and still it was fastened
as tightly as ever, anchored as it was in the fabric of both the
death land and the Star Country. The pony-thing had opened
it with such ease. He wondered why. He sat and thought. He
searched the door for runes, or secret locks. He examined
the horses to find any detail on their hide that would give
him a clue.

He found nothing in his long searches. But, finally he
had a thought. He grabbed the stallion around his neck and
dragged him inch by inch to the arch and the door. With
great effort, he pulled the beast's head up to the thong and
clamped its teeth around the leather. Holding the mouth shut
he tugged on the door and with no effort at all, it came open.

He slid inside the door and found himself on a marble
staircase suspended in a starry sky that swallowed him on
all sides. It led ever upward, and he climbed it. Letting the
rush of success carry him swiftly. Finally he heard voices
ahead, and firelight, not starlight gleamed from an arch in
the distance above him. He reached this doorway, and on the
other side of it, was a vast mead-hall. Silently, the black shape
slithered into the feast, and he dwelt in a dim corner. Some
warriors looked ancient indeed, he knew that if he brought
them back to fight for him, they would be so decayed that
they could never even walk, but there were plenty of other
dead warriors he could claim.

But he needed to choose the ones that would be near enough to Haven to avail him in time. That meant, men who were buried in Darkwell, Haven itself, or in the nearest lands to Haven's North, the ruins of Tianna. So the monster waited and watched the men mill around. He sought men in garb that would mark them as from these three places. And he schemed about drawing them away, one by one to tempt them back to the living world. He knew that hundreds of thousands resided here. Some at least would fall prey to his haunting.

Some of the men were colored with the red glow of fire, these he would not be able to take. Even if they were tempted back to life, their bodies made of scattered ashes would not avail him. So he would have to settle for those that died dishonorably far from home perhaps. He would have to settle for those whose sides had lost the battle, and whose enemies had not burned their bodies properly, but left them rotting on the battle field. He knew that coming into his service would only add to their dishonor, and this thought gave him pride. He chuckled in the realization that he was truly, purely evil. He hoped that he would be remembered as the most evil villain of all time.

He winced at the pain in his wounds. He had paid dearly for entry to this place. He'd best make use of what he'd sacrificed for.

S IR LUTHAN SAT IN the courtyard eating a loaf of bread, pondering the sunshine, and imagining his old friend Deagan challenging him to a game of sticky in the courtyard. He imagined how quickly he would rise to his feet to join the game. But what now got him to his feet like that? Nothing. The sun was warm, but held no joy for him. After finishing the bread, he forced himself up to go do something—anything. Then the heavy gates opened and in rode a nobleman seated on a chestnut horse. His silken tunic was belted over a shirt of mail. And a helmet sat upon his head. It was Duke Worth, dressed for battle as usual, though Luthan thought his outfit to be more of a costume.

Nevertheless, he bowed before his superior and greeted him.

"Get up Luthan," Worth said. "A messenger from Haven has arrived."

"I saw no messenger," Luthan countered.

"Be that as it may, sir Knight, one arrived. He brings tidings from Haven and he seeks Darkwell's aid. Saxus is in dire need. It seems that sarcophs have overrun the city."

"These times are cursed!" Luthan sympathized. "Will Darkwell respond to the need of our neighbor, my lord?"

"Yes. And you will lead the effort, Luthan. It shall be you, on horseback commanding the knights, and it shall be me, commanding the footmen."

"Do we have a plan?" he asked.

"We set out at first light tomorrow. I will lay out the plan for you tonight when you have made your arrangements with the knights."

"Aye, sir," Luthan nodded. "I am known to the messengers from Haven, sir. Pray, what was his name? The man who asked for Darkwell's aid."

The duke balked, and did not reply at first. He held Luthan's eyes in a contemptuous stare. "This is no time to seek out old drinking companions and rehash your misspent youth, Luthan. This is a time for action. It is none of your concern whether or not you know who the messenger was." He advanced his horse within arms reach of the knight. "Your concern is whether or not you know what your duty is." Again the duke fixed Luthan with a dark stare, which the knight gladly returned.

"My duty is clear, Duke Worth. I apologize." He nodded slowly and the duke rode away. Now Luthan again had a purpose at least, he suspected however that it was a dark one. It was time to muster the knights.

WHILE THE THREE SCOUTS were away, Gwyn brought some of the towermen together along with Durvish, to make them aware of some tactics she thought might be helpful for any further engagements with the sarcophs. They had experienced the way to form a shield wall, but now she added levels of complexity. They numbered only ninety swords now, and she sought to accomplish their task while keeping as many of them alive as possible.

She chose Durvish and a few other towermen. She explained to these new-dubbed marshals how they could form a shield wall into a chisel-like wedge and drive their foes off of a bridge with a single charge. She explained how best to defend a narrow corridor, and she drilled them on a proper retreat. She taught them the most basic elements of the Royal Guard hand signals that would allow her to maintain command even when there was need for silence. Silence of course was what she was used to, and her throat grew sore from so much talking.

The men were mesmerized by her lilting, yet authoritative speech, and while she looked up into their eyes to ensure they were paying attention, half the time she saw the look of respect and understanding, the other she saw the thinly veiled look of lust. She was not used to such looks, for men rarely knew she was even a woman. But now, with her oaths broken, she revealed her beautiful face and hair, the mask left to rest on the ground as she explained the tactics her men would need. She couldn't deny that she liked the attention, but she would never say so to anyone else. Besides, none of these men showed the courage or the skill that Deagan had. He was the one she would rather get looks from. Her thoughts drifted to his scouting mission.

"Well, that should be enough for now. Go and teach these things to the others." She dismissed the semi-circle of men and turned to look through the hedge at the now darkened countryside. She lifted her spear as she heard a noise approaching. It was Deagan and the others she was relieved to see, unhurt and weapons at ease.

Kellen smiled and leaped onto a tree stump to address the group. His voice was loud and unafraid unlike the hushed conversations that had been held since the scouting group's departure over two hours ago. "Well, my friends, it seems the Dragon Rider's have done their work. Their banner flies over the nearest tower, being a dragon keeper myself I should recognize it I would think. It should be safe to approach. Let us make for the South Towers, re-stock ourselves, enjoy a true meal and plan our next move!"

"Hear, hear!" cheered the group, and at once they all departed through the hedge.

"Did the Dragon Riders tell you what had befallen them? Was their conquest difficult?" Gwyn asked Kellen as the mass moved away.

"We didn't speak with them, M'lady. They were locked away in that tower no doubt."

"Why didn't you go up to greet them and be sure that it was safe?" she asked somewhat accusingly.

Kellen replied under his breath, "We couldn't find the door." He smiled at her in the shadows and clapped her armored shoulder before gallantly jumping down from the stump. He sang a sea shanty of good food and a safe harbor after a long voyage. The refrain had a lot to do with the happy maidens that could be found in the tavern.

"All right, Gwyn?" Deagan asked as they walked together. "Any trouble out here?"

"No trouble, Deagan. I took the opportunity to explain some tactics to the towermen . . . how about with you? Any trouble? Other than finding the door that is."

Deagan chuckled at himself, "No, lassie. I mean, *lady.*" He corrected himself with a horrified look on his face. Now it was Gwyn's turn to laugh.

They reached the tower in full darkness, and Durvish led them to a small shed rather than to the tower itself. It stood fifty yards from the base of the leaning tower. He threw open the door and pulled a key from his pouch. He unlocked a hidden hatch in the floor and led them in. This was a tunnel that went under the earth and then up into the rock of the tower. The timber-supported soil gave way to a corridor of hewn rock, and they climbed a finely built stairway in torchlight. Another locked door opened before them, and they were then inside what looked like a normal guard room. Armaments, supplies, and tools were arrayed neatly. "Hello?" Durvish called.

No one answered. Durvish grinned back at the group then touched the flame of his torch to a black filament of twisted rope attached to the wall. Immediately the chord showered sparks as it burned up. When the sparking end reached the next torch in the hallway it burst into flames with a pop. *Pop! Pop!* Soon the fuse had lit five torches in the circular room and then the sparks receded up a flight of stairs that led to the next higher level of the tower. The group traveled up the stairs only to see the sparks, like a shy kitten retreat around the next corner.

Durvish led them through more locked and hidden doors, through the traps and through mazes always finding a well lit chamber, the torches burning before they set foot inside. Only the tower men knew how high they had ascended, but now they reached the floors of the tower that housed hidden arrow slits which were so difficult to notice from the outside that the arrows would appear to fly from the solid rock.

Deagan peered down from one of these, and found that the drop below was a dizzying height. The fuse that had traveled through ahead of them a harbinger of the return of the tower's rightful owners, left a telltale scent as it burned.

More chambers equally clean and dotted with torches greeted them as they climbed through the stories of the tower until finally they emerged into the open air. A trap door led them to the top of the tower and Durvish peeked through. Sure enough a sleeping dragon lay there, and a Dragon Rider, under a thick blanket slept with his head on the beast's toe. At the creaking of the trap door, rider and dragon both awoke. It was Sir Goodsing and his green scaled mount, Warmaker, two of the beneficiaries of Kellen's hospitality.

The dragon squealed and stood up, spreading its wings impressively as the Dragon Rider mumbled, "Who goes there?" and struggled to free himself from the blanket. Warmaker opened his mouth and a glow of fire showed from within. Durvish retreated so that only a sliver of an opening remained through which he peeked with one eye. "Dragon Rider! It is I, Captain Durvish of the South Towers! Please, tell your dragon I am a friend so I may live another day."

Those assembled below heard the dragon and the man hold a brief conversation, and then Goodsing called down, "Come up here, Durvish, he won't harm you." And Durvish did.

The villagers and the six towermen who had been stationed here made ready the fires and the provisions and when a hot meal was prepared, everyone was made comfortable for a night's rest. Goodsing had related to the men that his comrades, the Dragon Riders had scoured all the towers, leaving only one knight in each one, the rest of them had traveled on to a roost outside the city, known as a Hutch, where they could rest more fully, it was not far from here. When he had supped, Goodsing mounted Warmaker and made for the Hutch to get Sir Oscar.

Deagan made quite a show of helping all others before he helped himself. It reminded him of his days as a knight. Chivalry. He hoped that Gwyn would notice. Finally he was the only one awake apart from her. He went over to her and said, "Quite a day."

"Yes it was. Tomorrow may be even more eventful. A bit of mountain climbing can wear you out, but as we both know it can't compare to a day of battle. We shall sleep soundly indeed."

"I can never sleep the night before battle," Deagan said. "There's no use in trying. I take comfort now, though, knowing there are others here to watch over as I lay awake."

Gwyn laid her blanket down in the dark chamber and loosened her armor, but kept her weapons by her side. "Suit yourself," she said. "Still, you should rest awhile, whether or not sleep takes you."

"Perhaps I shall," he said. And he went to get a blanket from the pile and laid it down next to Gwyn, though with a decent space in between.

They said no more to each other that night. But thoughts of battle were not the only thing keeping Deagan awake. Her presence pulled him like oxen in a yoke, a force he could barely resist. He tossed and turned thinking of how tonight could be his last, and did he really want to die without kissing her sweet mouth? The hours drifted slowly by, and the warm dark twisted his reasoning. Eventually reaching out to hold her was the only thing that made sense to him, and the fact that he didn't have the courage to do it tore him apart. It was a sweet pain that gripped him. He tortured himself with the thought until dawn, but never moved an inch closer to her.

The light of pre-dawn dispelled his certainty, and as others began to stir, he deemed his opportunity lost. As if admitting defeat, Deagan sniffed and rose. There were dragons on the roof. He thanked himself for staying under control. If he died today, he needed to accept that he would die without declaring his love for her. Well, he'd better not die then.

SIR OSCAR WAS WITH them again. The towermen and villagers all thanked the skinny old Rider heartily and asked him for news.

"By the gods, this city has been ravaged," Oscar said. "The South Towers were easy enough to secure, but the undead are truly entrenched within Haven's streets and I fear it will be much more difficult to get them out of there.

"There are survivors within the oldest portion of the city, which for those of you not familiar with Haven," he turned to Deagan, Rory and Kellen, "Is fortified with a wall and a moat of its own and raised above the city on a hill. The survivors in Old Haven have no leader, but among them are several tribes from the outer lands and many families from the outskirts, some of which have chiefs or captains of their own. They are armed fairly well, and they have provisions for the time being. The scourge of undead hasn't gained entry to this sanctuary yet, but they know they cannot survive there forever, and escape would mean a battle that would either cost them dearly, or utterly destroy them.

"It may be that we can find a way to get them out, but I do not know."

"Get them out?" Kellen protested. "Let them remain I say. I like their chances better than ours." For this remark Deagan slapped his arm.

Oscar continued with a sigh, "My Dragon Riders will fair well against the sarcophs, but it will be only a matter of time before they learn to defend themselves against our strikes. There aren't enough of us to wipe them out. As for Saxus, we have had no sign or word. The survivors haven't seen him any more than we have.

"They did report to me however that every now and then, the sarcophs will all turn at once to look up at the bell tower in Haven's center. After that they will move in new ways, as though they had just received new orders." At that, his audience perked up.

"Are they being commanded from there?" Deagan asked.

"It would seem so. But who or what commands them remains a mystery."

"Something vile, no doubt," Rory said with a sneer. The entire story made him feel utterly unclean.

"Quite," Oscar replied, sharing Rory's sentiment.

"Anything else?" Gwyn asked, her voice drawing all attention.

"No, I have told you all I know. All that remains is for us to decide what comes next."

Gwyn took the floor, "My friends," she addressed them, "Saxus has always been greedy, and he has always been harsh. His people have tolerated him only because he kept them safe in dangerous times. Now that safety has been shattered like glass. I guarded him for half my life. I know him. I studied his lies as much as I studied those of his adversaries, and as wise and calculating as he is, no one can deceive forever without making a mistake. I have pieced together his secrets and his weaknesses. I saw his downfall coming on the horizon and left before it could happen. The rest of the Guards are undoubtedly dead, now—killed for knowing too much—as I would have been had I not escaped.

"He has other lairs than his throne room. He has other passages than the halls of his castle. I haven't mapped them, but I know where most of them lead. Since the coming of Jatham Holmin, he has used them more and more often, until finally he disappeared into them completely. While I waited on him from outside his throne room, I was guarding an empty chamber. He had vacated it to dwell in secret places within the city.

"I know this because I was the last one to see him after he secluded himself. I saw candle light from cracks between the stones of the city wall. Only Saxus travels that path. A hollowed tunnel in the wall that leads to places unknown. The bell tower has no chamber within it, only a cavity for the bell to swing in, and a chain that leads to Cloud Tower.

"There is something going on inside the tower, unseen from the outside. I think I can bring us there, but we'll need to fight our way in to reach one of the entries to the tunnel system."

"Are there any entries in Old Haven?" Oscar asked. "I could drop you in there if you'd like."

"I don't know. There probably are, but I don't know where. They are very well hidden and I don't know if there is enough time to search."

"If there was a way into Old Haven through these tunnels, why wouldn't the monsters have already used them to get in there?" Deagan asked. "I wish there was a safe road to enter the passages, but we must do what we must do."

Durvish added, "These entrances could be well guarded"

Gwyn nodded. "If I can get to one, I can find my way to the bell tower and see what is there. Hopefully whatever it is can be stopped and the rotters will have no orders left to follow, and will be easier to destroy."

Kellen said, "It sounds dangerous. I'm sure Deagan will go with you."

"Of course I will," he said.

"Then let us decide on a plan."

THE NORTH GATES OF Darkwell were pulled open wide to allow the assembled troops to pour out of them. Those going about their business in the streets paused to watch them proceed out and onto the road to Haven. So impressive a force it was that cheers arose from the people, though many of them knew not what campaign was being undertaken. Rumors washed through the crowd and fingers pointed north to the column of smoke coming from Haven.

On his way by, Sir Luthan rode to greet the guards in the gatehouse. "Hail, men. How goes it?"

"Well, enough," said the guard.

"Did you let a messenger in recently? A man from Haven?" the knight asked.

"No, sir. He didn't pass through this gate. Few come from there now, in fact in months no one has. Save for one." The guard finished and the two of them looked at each other.

"Who is this one?" Luthan demanded, not sure of his question's importance.

"On this we'd best speak no more," the other guard jumped in. "Good luck in battle Luthan, and good day."

Luthan dismounted and approached the barred opening to the gatehouse. "You'd *best speak no more*, eh? What dribble is this to be speaking to your superiors? Need I remind you it's the same king that we both serve?"

Intimidated and alarmed, the two guards again shared a look of confusion. One of them spoke up, "Pardon us, m'lord. It's a man outranking yourself that bids us to silence on the matter, and fearful though we are to upset the leader of the knights, it's a deeper fear of this other man that keeps my tongue behind my teeth. I mean no disrespect, Luthan, but for my own sake, I'll say no more."

"You're silence tells me more than you think, friend." Luthan wondered now if it was Duke Worth the man referred to who had been traveling to Haven. But he thought it more likely it was Jatham Holmin. Why else would the wily adviser have readied his horse in such haste the night before? Didn't he ride directly to the North Gate? Luthan clutched his wounded hand into a fist. Certainly they would fear Jatham more than they'd fear a knight. It was Jatham who'd had the Dragon Rider imprisoned after all. "Yes, I do believe you've said enough," Luthan finished and then mounted and galloped away to head up the column of mounted knights.

Why would the Duke lie about the messenger? Why was Jatham traveling to Haven? Why all the secrecy? I'll never understand. If any good comes of this march, it will be in spite of these clandestine dealings, not because of them.

His thoughts were clouded and sorrowful; he was unable to concentrate on the upcoming battle because of them. He called one of his fellow knights to come ride with him in the front and they spoke of these things. The man's name was Tieg, and he was a good friend, though never of much importance to the king. He told Tieg about his dark suspicions and about Jatham's attempt to kill him. Tieg was at a loss for how to unravel the cords of the story, but it helped Luthan think it through. He found himself thinking of Deagan again. *Now there was a man who served with dignity*, Luthan thought. *Even though he never could hold his tongue, or follow orders.* He chuckled to himself and Tieg looked over.

"What's so funny?" Tieg asked.

"Remember Deagan Wingrat?" Luthan replied. The other knight smiled, knowing that Luthan was referring to their mutual friend's rebellious side. "Maybe I'll be taking a page from his book sooner or later."

"Insubordination?" Tieg asked.

"Not if I can help it," Luthan said. "But, tell the others, old Luthan smells something fishy on this march, make sure they know as much as they need to, tell them about the fake messenger, Jatham's attack, all of it. And tell them that no matter what they are to follow my orders, not the Duke's. Even if he yells charge, they wait for my word, got it?" Luthan's heart was racing even as he tried to keep his face calm and reassuring.

"Got it," Tieg answered, but instead of beginning to spread the tale, he rode beside Luthan for a few steps more.

"See to it, Tieg. The road to Haven is not so long that we can tarry."

With a deep breath, Tieg said, "I fear the consequences, sir."

"I know you do, Tieg, and so should we all. But more than that we must fear the Duke. Besides, we have done nothing yet. Only warn them and tell them it is my command they follow. In all likelihood I am completely wrong and I will echo everything that the Duke will say."

"Aye, sir," Tieg said, but he didn't like it.

THE WARRIOR'S HALL WAS loud with the din of voices; songs and poems were recited, tales were told and above all, there was laughter. Truly this was a paradise for those who reveled in feasting and drink. The monster in the corner rather liked it as well, for here were the soldiers he needed to finish his conquest of Haven.

Already he had tempted many. He sought the shy ones, those who limped, and those who stayed to themselves. His whispering promises had taken them one at a time to become his slaves, and he sensed that in the living world they were marching to Haven. Of course he couldn't command them from the death world, but so much could be gained that he lingered to swell his ranks before returning to assess his troops.

Hours or days went by as the rag-thing picked its victims to be taken back to the living world. *My sarcophs,* he thought to himself. *My dead men. My rotters.* Across the feasting hall, a helmet made a quiet rasping sound as it turned to the left. The black masked helmet of one of Saxus' Royal Guards fixed the demon with an expressionless stare. The Guard, with its long spear, gold star, and black breastplate was joined by others dressed in the same fashion and silently they all watched the demon intently. Their helmets showed the image of the cloud tower, and they were identical in their confident and aloof bearing. The monster knew they were recently dead, and would love to have them for his army, for already their bodies would be in Haven, lying somewhere or other in the rubble where they had been dumped after the poison set in to end their misguided lives of service to the Royal Lord.

The demon was hideous in his current form, but at least his disfigurement served as a disguise. These Guards would recognize him for who he was if they met in the living world and they may even suspect that their deaths had some connection with him. They may know far too much, in fact, which scared him deeply even though they could not harm him in the Star Country.

Come to me, he thought at them. The Royal Guards crossed the feast hall and formed a ring around him. He drooled to think they would be so easily won over, but as always he was still suspicious that they knew his designs.

Noble warriors, he thought to the five Guards, *Do not waste your talents in this endless and meaningless place. You can come back to the living world. You can be forgiven for your mistakes.*

In reply the Guards only stared. He was accustomed to their kind, and had spent much time under their silent vigil in the living world while he held council with Lord Saxus. Even though he should be used to it, their resolve to remain anonymous always irked him. Their urge to uphold their oaths was appalling and foolish. Perhaps that would be a way to win them over . . .

Silent as you are, you can never be happy here. You cannot even remove your masks in order to drink! Come back where you belong, where your oaths may yet have some meaning. The Royal Lord still needs you.

Still they stood resolute, boxing him in. His thoughts had attracted another warrior though, an impressionable one who looked thoughtfully at the specter.

"What say you?" he asked. "Is there a way back to the living world?"

Yes, the rag-thing answered. It tried to smile with its mangled, dripping face. *The way is through me. I will take you back.* The man set down his goblet and looked to the Royal Guards with hope. They returned his gaze and said nothing.

"Is it true?" he asked them. And though they didn't reply, he took their silence as affirmation and stepped closer to the monster to become only one more victim after thousands that had already succumbed.

One more step and you will awake in your old body, free to rise again and right your wrongs. The Royal Guards looked back and forth from the rag-thing to the man-spirit. The warrior stepped forward and spread his arms wide.

"Take me there!" he said eagerly. Then the dark figure lunged forward to envelop the warrior. Like lightning, the Guards were upon him. Their spears crossed and braided as they stabbed the monster again and again, but their steel was incorporeal and had no effect. The man was swallowed piece by piece, though his face was a mask of horror, he felt no pain as his body was taken apart. At last, one of the Guards stepped forward, and stabbed the warrior in the neck, killing him just before he was devoured completely. The partially eaten man disintegrated into smoke as the demon gurgled with disappointment and outrage. The Royal Guard placed the butt of her spear on the stone floor, waiting.

In a rage, the rag-monster lunged forward, but the Guard was too fast. The group of Guards moved in concert staying always out of reach. It was a stale mate, but a raucous one. One of the Royal Guards jumped onto the table to avoid the thing's reach, spilling a plate of food and several mugs of ale. The warriors around her stood up.

With all his might the demon sent forward a message to all the warriors in the hall. *Join with me! Slay them and be free to return to life. You will be rewarded!* For some it was a command, for others it was a challenge. Either way, it was the Warriors' Hall, and fighting was not uncommon. The Royal Guards prepared to kill as many as they could, while dodging the wicked monster that menaced them from within their formation.

Those who obeyed the demon's urgings drew steel and descended on the Guards, but none could overcome them. Unlike the Royal Guards, the miscellaneous combatants did not fight as a group, but attempted to break through as an unorganized mob. Soon, the fray spread and those who had no idea what was going on were fighting each other. It was a good day in Warrior's Hall, but it was a day that was far from over.

The Royal Guards thought of their old companion and leader, Gwyn Androth. They suspected that somehow, the longer they held out, the more they would aid her and so they fought with all they had. In the afterlife, they never grew weary and felt no pain. It would be some of the most enjoyable battle they had ever had. Barbarians jumped down from the rafters, soldiers from ancient wars charged them from below, duelists advanced on them from the table tops, but none could get the better of them as they twirled, parried, and slew their way through the throng. They were thankful for their armor on more than one occasion for its hard plates deflected potentially dangerous blows, but despite these close calls none of the Guards were yet harmed.

As the bubbling, putrid face arose from the depths of the black cloth, one of the Guards looked over her shoulder to glance into its eyes. She recognized some aspect of its face that reminded her of a dark and horrible man she'd seen in Saxus' chambers. She didn't know if that glimmer of recognition was accurate, or just some strange memory, but there was no time to ponder it for sooner or later she feared that they would fall. *There must be a better solution to this mess than this all out brawl.* The smoke of the twice-dead rose all around them as the Royal Guards dealt mortal wounds to the spirits of the warriors. As the melee continued, one Guard cast about in her head, searching for a better way.

A PLAN DEVISED, GWYN, Deagan, Rory, Kellen and six towermen, crept closer to the town of Haven. They had already traversed the lower quarters and left the refuge of the last tower, and now at a good distance behind them, a group of three Dragon Riders followed. The beasts stalked along on their four strong limbs, slinking low to the ground to avoid detection, while their Riders walked beside them.

The buildings grew closer together as the outbuildings, animal pens, garden plots, and open lawns of the rural swath around coalesced to begin forming the outskirts of the city itself. Even outside the urban center, the stench of death gathered heavy around them. The laughter from the other world played through the alleys and streets like the distant echoes of a mirthful crowd sitting in a playhouse. After a few more minutes the dirt roads gave way to the cobble stone paving that marked the edge of the city, and as they crept between bits of cover: stoops, doorways, statues, piles of crates, they became completely surrounded with buildings, and the remnants of slums.

But unlike Darkwell, Haven's putridity came from *lack* of life rather than its *excess*. Dismembered corpses lay in corners and grisly scenes awaited inside every broken shop window. Surprising to all of them, except Deagan, it appeared that of all body parts, the rotters didn't care much for feet. There were severed feet everywhere, some bare, some still encased in their shoes. Many of them were still attached to the shinbones, or even to the entire denuded skeleton from which the rest of the flesh had been stripped away.

Gwyn was in front, showing no reaction to the carnage, and as she darted past an alleyway, she saw a shambling horde of corpses on the other end of it, they were not coming closer, but only moving past and clutching weapons like some sort of patrol. The ten of them stopped, pressed against the walls, allowing the group to travel on. The dragons following behind them took the cue from Gwyn's hand and halted as well, and flattened to the ground. When they had passed, the terror of the laughter diminished and the company crept forward to the end of the alley. They had to wade through a pile of bodies, most of them eaten alive. Deagan covered his nose.

Gwyn looked left and right, scanning all the windows of the buildings and finally took a deep breath and sprinted across the cobble stone street. Her nine companions followed, weapons bared. Into the shadows of another alley they passed, but the dragons were now farther behind. Here there were piles of bodies indeed, but the stink was not that of normal decay . . . and the corpses still possessed their flesh. The laughter was suddenly loud in their ears.

The piles of corpses began to rise and quake as rotters pulled themselves up from the mound with deliberate, yet clumsy movements. They had been so still; as though acting like proper dead men would convince the Gods to end their torment and bring them back to the death world, but the scent of living flesh had awoken the uncouth hunger inside them, and unwillingly they were diverted from their masquerade, and forced to carry out the grisly purpose they had been summoned for. As reluctant as they were to stand, Gwyn and the others harbored no doubt that these were rotters like any others, and would stop at nothing.

With a signal, Gwyn formed them into a shield wall. The bodies crashed against them, hard. It was with mercy that the company tore these sarcophs apart, for they had all sensed their forlornness, and doing them in one by one seemed to be releasing them from their servitude. Before long the rotters were taken down. Writhing limbs littered the street and the group was dismayed at being unable to burn them properly and finally undo whatever evil had animated them, but though they had torches, they didn't have time, and it would not be worth it to signal their presence to the entire city.

They broke their formation and traveled on. Deagan waved for the Dragon Riders to follow. One at a time, the dragons leapt and glided across the street to land in the shadow of the adjacent alley. So far they hadn't raised an alarm. This alley took them to a street where the buildings were taller, and stone bridges connected elevated walkways that gave access to second story shops on either side of the street.

Gwyn opened a side door in the alley and led them into a ransacked shop. In it were clay trinkets, drinking vessels and pots. Some of them were smashed. The shopkeeper still stood behind his counter, but his jaw was missing, and his eyes were mostly closed. His skin was covered in a thick layer of dust as though he hadn't moved in weeks. Move he did however. He advanced on them, but before he could react, Gwyn had him off balance and on the floor with a sword in his back. Another swipe took his head off. She picked up a pitchfork from the ground and pinned him down with it, much as Deagan had done on Flag street in Darkwell.

Blazes, I love this woman, Deagan thought, but "Well done," was what he said. They climbed the back stairs and made for the third story. The stairs brought them to a crooked wooden door, with a mug painted on it. Inside was an abandoned bar that was eerily intact. There was no broken glass or clay, and the stools had all their legs.

"I favor a drink as much as the next man," Deagan said, "But this hardly seems like the time Gwyn."

"Killing rotters is thirsty work," Kellen laughed in agreement.

"It's not the tavern I'm interested in," Gwyn explained, favoring Deagan with a slight smile. "these walkways should bring us to the entrance of the tunnels. The Rotters so far have all been on the streets, so I thought we might avoid a little fighting if we went over the bridges."

With an effort, Deagan kicked open a stuck door that led to the raised walkways they had seen from the alley. The walls of the building still towered overhead, and they stood in the shadows of more elevated walkways and bridges above them. A flicker of movement caused Rory to clutch Kellen's arm and point to what he had seen, but before the other man had time to make a comment they both saw that it was a dragon tail. The three Dragon Riders were hanging upside down in their saddles as their mounts clung to various bridges and window ledges high above them, keeping a watchful eye on their companions. Gwyn now took the lead again, for Haven was more familiar to her than to any of the others. They reached the bridge and crossed it, crawling on their bellies, invisible from the level of the street. The arch of the bridge ended at the elevated walkway on the other side of the street. And they stood up in order to move quickly along the boardwalk passing several shops, before coming to the corner. Gwyn peered around it quickly, then gestured for them to get down. They all crouched or took cover against the wall.

Gwyn gestured and they all inched backwards the way they had come. Gwyn led them into a shop door and all ten of them hid inside. Moments later, an undead host stomped past them, walking boldly along the raised walkway outside. It was a small pipe and leaf shop that could barely hold them all. The tiny, smoke-stained window was shaded by head after corpse-like head that shambled past until one of the shadows did not go past, but remained. The glass was too dirty to see any more than a silhouette, but the head surely turned to look into the shop. Rory was face to face with the door, and gripped the handle tightly, knowing they had been sniffed out or heard.

The mass of dead men gathered around the entryway, and Rory began to sweat. They were trapped, and with his friends all behind him, the butler was as good as alone against the horde. Deagan put his hand roughly on Rory's head pressing him into a crouch, then turned and nodded to Gwyn. Her spear loudly shattered the glass and caught the sarcoph in the forehead. She pulled the spear out and the corpse was scraped off against the door, two more stabs, two more pulls and another death visited the monster, this one permanent.

Though there was no room, Deagan managed to shoulder Rory aside and take his place, he squared himself in the doorway and took a low stance, then as a roar of protest and hunger grew outside, he kicked the door down, sending two of the creatures over the edge and splattering them on the paving stones below. The battle began.

Deagan, a stalwart and impenetrable barrier, Gwyn's spear a battering ram against their skulls, the rotters were soon dealt with. Some of them flew off the edge and joined those that had fallen to the street, others collapsed on the raised walkway or found the sharp clamp of a dragon's maw, but one way or another they were all disabled, though their creeping limbs lived on.

"We are close to the entry way now," Gwyn said. "Stealth has brought us as far as it can." With that she left the pipe store and continued along the walkway. She led them up another stairway to a higher level on the lattice of pedestrian byways, and then through a broken window into one of the haunted buildings. A dull groan issued from the street below and the laughter of the dead grew bold in their ears.

Before disappearing into the window, Deagan yelled, "Now, Riders! Now!" And in moments, the trio of Dragon Riders rose up from their hiding places and winged into sight. Ranger the yellow dragon flew in first with a squeal. As the company on foot descended through the dark building, bursts of dragon fire lit their surroundings through the windows.

They were in a marvelous and ancient building, seemingly a rich mansion. Within it there were portraits, tapestries, rugs and sculptures. Another ornament that adorned it was an insidious horde of sarcophs milling about on the first floor. Surely whoever commanded them was aware of the entry to the tunnels concealed in this building and had set these additional guards to keep it safe.

"Go and alert the Dragon Riders that this is their target! Tell them to burn the first floor, then let us do the rest!" Gwyn commanded. One of the towermen went back up the stairs. "We'll keep them down there until the dragons take care of them."

As Kellen and Rory looked down the stairs at the sea of living corpses, they were shocked when a large stone urn flew over their heads from behind them and clattered loudly down the wooden stairway. "Are you crazy?" Kellen yelled as he spun around to face Deagan.

"All we have to do is slow 'em down!" Deagan explained as he picked up another priceless artifact to throw at the undead.

Kellen quelled his indignation, seeing it would be wasted on his brutish friend in his state of battle frenzy, though several insulting quips queued up in his brain only to remain unsaid as Deagan tossed an upholstered armchair down the stairs with a laugh, knocking two rotters backwards. Then the others got the idea, and helped the former knight barricade the stairs while their compatriot relayed Gwyn's command to the Dragon Riders. They threw statues and furniture down the sloping stairway to keep the monsters at bay, but in their haste, couldn't form an effective wall. Instead they were only able to make climbing difficult. The towermen shot crossbow bolts at the rotters and though the bolts do very little to hurt rotters, it did slow them down a little. Seeing that they would be coming up sooner or later, Deagan formed a shield wall across the top of the stairs with the remaining towermen. There were high vaulted ceilings, and the room below lay open like a great hall. What sort of building was this?

The shield wall held, especially thanks to the uphill advantage, but a worm-ridden sarcoph lurched forward, seized a tower man's ankle and pulled him down to be devoured by the rest. His cries of anguish died with him before long, for the unlucky man and the teeming horde of sarcophs on the ground floor were engulfed in blast after blast of dragon flame that gave him a quicker death than he would have hoped for at the mercy of the hungry dead. The rotters cried in dismay as they died. But their moans didn't last long.

Gwyn dipped a torch into some of the still burning woodwork on the main floor. Some of the rotters were still standing after the blasts having been shielded behind cover as the fires surged in. The monsters still sought to kill them, but now they were out of time to fight back. The whole city would be alerted to their presence now, and the best thing to do was disappear.

Gwyn led them deeper into the building at a run, and the others had no choice but to keep up. She took them by torchlight into a winding corridor edged with bookshelves. She turned down another hall that was lined on both sides with doors. Her torchlight revealed what looked like a hundred doors, when finally she grasped one of the handles and pulled it open. An endless dark tunnel stretched before them, and into it they marched.

RAVE DAYS I TRUST," Duke Worth greeted Luthan when
he caught up to the old knight. Their horses were out
of synch, causing first one man then the other to lunge
slightly ahead. The knight's greeting coming from Worth's pompous
voice disgusted Luthan, but as always he replied cordially.

"Aye, what an honor it is to ride with the likes of Your Lordship,
sir. We are not far now from Haven. Are the footmen still able to
march, or do they need rest?"

"They are well and eager, Luthan. No rest will be needed until
we gather our ranks at the doorstep of the enemy."

"Haven's men will be eager to see our coming. I am glad that
the army is able to keep on. It wouldn't do to keep Haven waiting.
I am sure that if what you say is true, *they* have no opportunity
for rest," Luthan mentally warned himself not to be too snide. He
should not have said, *if what you say is true.* He bit his tongue.

"Indeed," the Duke replied. And though he stopped talking, he
did not take his eyes off the knight. "Is something bothering you,
Luthan?" he asked.

"No, M'lord," he lied. What he wanted to say was, *you are.*

"Good, I need you at your best today. Listen, I know not what
may come next," the Duke went on in a conspiratorial tone. "But I
need you at all times to follow my commands, though they may not
seem to make sense. You must trust that I know what is best."

Luthan's heart was pounding; he hoped that his anxiety was not
apparent. "Why does M'lord need to remind me? It is ever so, Duke
Worth." Luthan thought his laughing tone covered his true feelings,
but like many other knights, his lying lacked practice.

"The undead are a deadly foe, Luthan. I need your word that you will follow my orders, the safety of Darkwell depends on it."

"You have my word," Luthan replied. It drove him mad to give a false oath; a conflict of chivalry.

"Good," the Duke said. And he lingered for a moment, a conflict playing out on his clean shaved, and weathered face. He had tears in his eyes. The next thing he said was: "You're a good man, Luthan." Then he rode away.

THE TUNNEL WAS DAMP, but not wet. It had a musty smell, that for some reason Deagan found refreshing. So much of what he was used to was the scent of all things dry and hot. The cool of the deep soothed his sun-beaten skin, and relaxed him. Of course he couldn't relax completely, for there was much to do, and a lot of it had something to do with blood shed.

There were no turns for a long time. The tunnels were not built apparently to confuse those within them, but to allow quick and reliable passage to different parts of Haven. They came prepared with enough torches and even a little food, but eating was the last thing on their mind after scooping the reeking guts off of their weapons.

They then came to an intersection. It was a room with a shaft of light from above shining down into it. There were five tunnels joined here. And on the floor was a five-pointed star. Each point indicated a different passage and each was labeled with a symbol. A cloud on one, a bear, a shield, a stone wall, and a burning fire marked the direction they had come from. The dust was thick here, and in the sunlight, they could see their footprints after stepping on the floor.

Kellen looked at the stone for tracks. "Which way?" Deagan asked.

Gwyn considered for a moment then said, "The wall. That was the last place I saw movement. The candlelight through the cracks."

"Slow down, my people," Kellen said. He pointed at the floor. The way they were about to go, the passage of the wall, was littered with shuffling footprints in the thick dust. "At first I just thought someone had decided to sweep the floor in this section, but it looks like there are so many footprints, it amounts to the same. They come from the passage marked with a cloud and they go down the one with a stone wall."

"Master Kellen?" Rory asked, "How recent are they?"

"How should I know? I may be master Kellen to you, but one thing I'm not is a master tracker. Let's hope they're old," Kellen finished.

"What's the point in hoping?" Deagan asked with a smile. "we'll find out soon enough."

"I love you, Deagan, but your sense of humor is—frankly it's offensive," Kellen said.

"I love you, too, Kellen."

"For crying out loud, must you? In front of Rory? All I meant by it is I'd rather not hack and slash our way through a hundred foes to reach the bell tower."

Rory said, "There is nothing wrong with expressing love at a time like this—this hour which could be the end of us all. Love could never offend a butler, sir." He laughed knowingly, "Not in a thousand years. If these monsters await us at the end of this tunnel, then so be it, there is nothing we can do, but try to prevail."

"I'm all in favor of prevailing, you know, and vanquishing and all that. But let this be the last I say about it, if we can do so without another blood bath, it's more to my liking, and what's more, I'll buy the first round when all this is over and done with."

Deagan replied, "And if it's a blood bath after all, the first round will be on me."

Fixing the straps of his pack, Deagan stepped down the path toward the stone wall. As the torches burnt out, they lit new ones. They had no fear of running out. The tunnel traveled straight and direct, taking them at last to a right hand turn that led them up a stairway.

The stairs were unadorned, narrow and steep. They climbed for several minutes, and then emerged from the dank stone of the underground, and found themselves inside the wall of Haven, flecks of sunlight splattered the stacked stones on either side of them in the places where the stones were not completely snug. They could now turn in either direction. Following the wall either clockwise or counterclockwise around the center of Haven.

"Which way?" Kellen asked. Gwyn glanced through the cracks, trying to find one wide enough to see the bell tower through, but she was disoriented, unable to find it through any nearby.

"I can't see the tower from here," she said.

"Oy," Deagan grunted. "Check the floor, *master* Kellen. If we find more tracks, let's follow them."

Kellen bent his nose close to the floor and brought a torch within inches of the layer of dust. He examined both possible paths, and soon had no doubt which way the troop had gone. "Would you believe me if I said they went that way?" he asked gesturing to the route with no tracks. In answer Deagan laid a meaty hand on the back of Kellen's neck and pointed him the other way with a chuckle.

"No, I don't believe I would," he said. "I told you I'd keep you safe, Kellen."

"I know," he said. "I think it's safer back there."

To that, Deagan had no real answer. "Be quiet now," he said. "I think we're getting close." With Gwyn in the lead, they crept on through the dismal passage. The flecks of sun did little to raise their spirits, but instead accentuated the feeling of being trapped, able to see fragments of the outside world but still at risk of dying without ever reaching it again.

Then they came to another stairway, this one leading down. A stone above the stairs had an eye inscribed on it, and an arrow pointing to the left, they looked that way and saw a sizable crack in the wall, left deliberately no doubt when the wall was built. Through it they could see the column of smoke that had so bothered the Haveners from the mountain top, but still they couldn't see what was burning. They looked and looked, but did not know what they were supposed to see. Then Gwyn snapped her fingers. "Yes!" she said. "Behind that smoke the bell tower lies. I can see the top of a building I recognize for it is shingled in red clay. That building lies between the wall and the bell tower. You were right Deagan, we are getting close."

The tracks in the dust appeared to descend the dark, narrow stairs so down they went. At the bottom of the stairs they could only follow the tunnel one way. They walked forward until they came to a single right hand turn, when they came around it, what the tower man screamed was, "Holy Blazes!"

Now Luthan and his host of knights rode forth through the outer region of Haven known as the Lower Quarters. They didn't know they were being watched by Dragon Riders who perched on the tops of the South Towers. With a furtive look over his shoulder to make sure Duke Worth was not near, Luthan got Tieg's attention again.

"Have you spread the word, Tieg?" he asked softly.

"Yes, there are many questions that your tale leaves unanswered, but I told them to be patient. A few don't believe it, but I think they understand at least that they must follow your orders and no others."

Luthan sighed, "Alright, it's the best we could ask for. Curses, I wish I knew what was going on. I must tell you about the Duke's latest command. With tears in his eyes he bade me to follow his orders no matter what happened. He made me give him my word. I don't like the look of this one bit, sir Tieg. It's dark business, and no mistake."

"Well, what are we to do about it? These aren't our decisions to make," Tieg replied.

"Every shot of your sword is your decision, Tieg. Don't forget that. I almost did in all these years of trying to get ahead. But when Deagan went against orders to free those rebels, I realized that I always have a choice." He took a deep breath. "I gave my word to Duke Worth that I would obey, but I make another oath now. No evil will be done through me this day, so say I, Luthan of Darkwell."

"Witness," Tieg said, smiling. "I hope the Duke leads us rightly."

"Is that the vain hope of a man who hopes to escape responsibility? Or is it the hope that at least among our own people good still outweighs evil?"

"It's the vain hope that Duke Worth is more than a pile of snot! Ha! Tears in his eyes or no, he's lost all sense of honor and rightness. I, too take your oath, Luthan. No evil will be done through me this day, so say I, sir Tieg Alfburn! Fearful though I am, it is the only thing to do. We will swear the others to it! Again I ride back to spread your words. This time they shall unite under Luthan's oath!"

"Luthan's oath?" the knight said. "Call it that if you will. Or call it the oath of horse shit if you like so long as you meant what you said. Off with you, man, we are almost to Haven!"

S IR OSCAR, ASTRIDE PETE'S saddle, soared high over the city of Haven watching the advance of Darkwell's army. Yet another mass came from the other side of the city. Instead of in shining columns, this troop was dark and mob-like, scattered over the road and the countryside. He swooped low over them, and what he saw was the newly risen dead from the North, descending on Haven. Already matters were getting worse. Oscar knew that while Darkwell's forces would be there soon, they had many streets to fight through before reaching this new horde. Also, from the North, Old Haven was much more vulnerable. If the undead stumbled upon it, they may chance to find a heavy-gated tunnel that led into the interior walled city, passing even under the moat. As much as he would have loved to meet with the troops from Darkwell, he knew he had no time.

Back to the roost he flew, to muster the dragons as swiftly as possible and soar them to meet this new enemy—a shambling horde from Tianna—and stop them if they could. "On, Petey!" He cried with the wind in his long white hair.

I N THE WARRIORS' HALL the battle went on. One of the Royal Guards had fallen, the smoke of her spirit rising to mingle with that of the others in the beams overhead. The monster still lunged at the Guards when possible, but had given up most of its hope of catching them. It knew it should return soon to command in Haven, but it couldn't bear to leave with so many souls it could collect! His wounds grieved him, but he knew they would be worse still in the living world and that too kept him here.

One of the Guards who had striven to find another solution to the problem finally thought of a new way. She broke her oath to the Royal Lord and hollered as never before. Hearing the timbre of her woman's voice, the host of warriors broke off their attack momentarily giving her time to speak.

"I am Wynna, daughter of Haven! Cease this madness and hear me! This monster seeks to devour you! His promises are false! Who will you believe? A demon in black rags or me, a fellow warrior? I know not what his intentions are, but I know that he is evil as none here can comprehend. Speak now if you think I lie!"

She dodged an axe that flew through the air, then leapt aside from the lunge of the monster behind her. "Look how hideous it is!" The battle didn't stop, but it slowed as many combatants considered what she said.

"If he is here, then he is only another dead warrior like us!" protested an old ghost. "I am Gurda, son of Phoe and I say this. If he seeks to devour us, let him try! In this hall such battle is but a game, and all of us will arise in the morning as we are now!" He illustrated his point with a sword thrust at her stomach. She dodged, kicked him in the knee, spun away.

"Gurda, Phoe's son, you lie! Look at the demon and tell me he is a warrior. It is not so. If he eats you there is no coming back!" A large man tossed another man into a group of large men. A brawl ensued and Wynna lost their attention. Warriors who felt no pain and would come back as easily as they were slain were a hard bunch to captivate, for the thrill of battle was ever their sport of choice.

Do not believe her lies. Come here, spar with me Gurda, you are right. I am just another warrior, the monster's thoughts insinuated themselves into the minds of all those nearby.

"Listen to its fell words!" Wynna protested, "Why is it that he speaks not, but instead thinks in our own heads? No warrior here can do this."

This argument impacted the man. Others seeing he was considering her words also paused. The battle again lost some of its ferocity. "It is better to die on my spear than in his mouth." She declared. "Stay away from him, for I will not let anyone get close." In solidarity the other Guards crowded closer, keeping all others away from the rag-thing.

It seemed that now the warriors understood. By keeping them away from the demon, the Guards were helping them. "Well I have one test that will tell us for sure what he is," Gurda said. And he picked up a javelin and threw it forcefully into the rag-thing's middle. The weapon passed through as if through liquid and clattered to the floor. "She's right!" Gurda declared. "Let none of us near him! Some evil has brought him here."

Then a murmur arose asking how he got into the Hall. What of the star-horses? What of the golden arch and the unbreakable door? For the first time since their deaths, these warriors felt fear. They were not alone in their paradise.

It gave the monster satisfaction to see these immortals in such terror, but he could see that now it would be impossible to harvest any more of them, cautious as they were in avoiding him.

Finally he would leave, for there was nothing more to gain here. He closed his grotesque eyes and reached a hand up to an object within his robes. He clasped it and spoke the words.

When he opened his eyes, he was still there. All eyes were still on him. The world shift didn't work in this place. This would complicate matters.

"HOLY BLAZES!" SAID THE towerman. He drew his weapon instantly, but felt no strength in his sword arm. After all they'd been through, this was the worst he could imagine. He didn't have much time to think about it though, because a club knocked him out and he fell to the floor. On the other end of the club was a corpse-hand. Attached to it was the arm of a large rotter with no face. Behind this rotter was an unending horde of rotters, packed so tightly together that further progress through the tunnel would be impossible.

Gwyn immediately defended herself from the dead man's next swing. In an instant Deagan was beside her, their shields touching. A towerman filled in next to Deagan, and Rory and Kellen were behind them. "Get him out of here!" Deagan ordered, referring to the clubbed towerman. Those in back pulled him free giving Deagan better footing, and he needed every advantage he could get.

The rotter with a club went down, behind him, three more rushed forward, Kellen reached over Deagan's head and cut off an arm. Rory stabbed over the towerman's shoulder to catch a dead man's hand with the tip of his sword. Meanwhile, Deagan and Gwyn hacked, eviscerated, and maimed several more. The pile grew quickly at their feet. Kellen lit torches and flung them over their heads and into the horde. Unable to maneuver, the sarcophs endured the burning under their feet until flesh crumbled away.

"Nice work, Kellen!" Deagan cheered.

"Well, I'd say we're in the right place, they're definitely guarding something!" Kellen replied.

"There are so many of them!" Rory exclaimed as he reached forward to block a sword. They were doing well, but outnumbered as they were, it would be a long, hard fight. The pile of fallen rotters writhed and reached for them; Deagan had a vision of digging their way through the bodies to reach whatever was on the other side. Eventually the things would cram themselves into the passage trying to get at them, and they would have to get through an un-living wall.

"Gwyn," Deagan said, blocking a blow aimed at his leg. "We have to press forward." He returned the one he blocked with a shot of his own, cutting off the monster's left leg at the knee.

"Forward?" she asked in disbelief. "We'll never get over them." She stabbed unendingly, sticking a dead man on the end then flinging him against the wall.

"He's right," Kellen admitted. "I don't like it anymore than you do, but if we don't advance we'll get stuck here." He lobbed a torch. The smoke of burning flesh was getting to be a bit much. It clouded their vision and hurt their lungs.

"Why not fall back?" Rory asked. "Lead them to the stairs and get the advantage like back in that building."

Deagan killed another one, (head shot, arm off, leg gone) and thought about the idea. A slobbering, panting corpse on all fours rushed forward, it lunged at the towerman, bowling him over. Rory landed three heavy blows with the axe on its back and head, but it did not stop.

"Get it off!" Deagan ordered, and Kellen helped lift the thing from their friend, covering their hands with gore. Its fast hands latched onto their arms and it sought to bite Kellen. The towerman it had bowled over lurched up with a swipe and severed its biting head as he pounced to his feet. Rory kicked the thing backward and again returned behind the tower man. "All right, friend?" Deagan asked.

"Fine," the towerman answered.

"In answer to your question, Rory, I think we'll have to crawl over them eventually, whether we make our stand here or at the stairs, they'll pile up to the point of forming a wall unless we advance, killing them as we go. Those in back can keep an eye on the ones under our feet, keeping them dead."

Disgust resonating thickly in her voice, Gwyn said, "He's right." She took a step forward until she was over the corpse of a still moving, but armless sarcoph. Deagan matched her, and the Towerman followed suit. A stray hand grasped at the towerman's thigh, trying to claw him. "Kellen!" Gwyn yelled. "Keep them dead, damn you!"

Snapping to his senses, Kellen against his will, plunged into the carnage just behind his allies. The previously unconscious towerman was back on his feet, and the other towermen guided him forward. Rory and Kellen kept their attention to the floor, hacking apart anything still capable of doing harm. Gwyn was now at the highest part of the wall they had already made. There was no floor to stand on. She carefully stepped up with one boot on a dead man's back. Blood gushed from its sides, and the one below it squirmed in anger.

Deagan followed suit and the two of them balanced together on the pile of dead, trying to be brave for the others. The towerman balked and hung back. He didn't realize how vital the shield wall was. Even the man in back was in greater danger than those in line. He glanced down, wanting to follow the others, wading into the dark and the death before him, but he couldn't build up the courage. He looked for safer footing, but this distracted him. Deagan tried to stop the bloated rotter that descended on him while his shield was down, but couldn't. The towerman's throat was ripped out by a knife, then feasted on by the creature's foul maw.

Rory and Kellen hacked it apart, then looked up. Deagan was screaming at them to fill in the hole. Rory moved forward, but Kellen held him back. He picked up the fallen man's shield and jumped into line. "Keep 'em dead, Rory." Kellen said. "You always were good at cleaning up after me!" and with that he set the blade of his saber into the spoiled flesh of his opponents.

"Front lines, eh Kellen?" Deagan goaded him. "How's it feel?"

"Squishy."

The group moved further in. Rory, saved them more than once hacking the heads and arms of the undead that crawled about their feet. The mush and gore that they left behind, after all eight of them had passed by looked more inert and somewhat safe to cross. It was horrific, but still better than what lay ahead. Kellen narrowly dodged a slash, and the tip of a blade scratched his cheek, and nose. In response, Deagan laid that rotter low, and gave Kellen time to regain his composure. "You're alright, Kellen, shield up, now. Getting tired?"

"Ha! I've been tired for days. Why should I let it stop me now?" Kellen replied and redoubled his efforts. The group of them pressed on, hacking and slashing into the horde before them, there was still a lot of killing to do.

L UTHAN AND THE MOUNTED knights of Darkwell approached the outskirts of Haven itself. The pillar of smoke loomed above them, and on their faces was the grim resolve of warriors traveling into the unknown. Duke Worth called a halt and Luthan echoed him. The company came to a stop on the road. It took the knights another minute or two to line up their steeds in orderly fashion. Luthan rode to Duke Worth.

"What is our plan then? The men are arrayed as you explained to me this morning, and here we are at the edge of battle. Already in the midst of those haunted streets I can see the shambling dead who await us."

"How well do you trust your men, Sir Luthan?" Duke Worth asked after a pause.

"They would follow me to the end, Duke."

"Good," the Duke replied. "For now you need no other orders, nor will you receive any until the time comes. Simply remain ready."

"Aye." The knight rode away without any of the honorifics or pleasantries to which the Duke was accustomed. He rejoined his knights with more doubt than ever in his heart about what he might be asked to do and he hoped that he would have the resolve to rebel.

T HE RAG-MONSTER RECEDED INTO the shadows. All the heads of the dead warriors turned to follow his movements. The spirits held their weapons at the ready, it was all they could do, and yet they knew that this creature had somehow breached the sanctity of the hall, and that their weapons were as good as broken. And though they weren't conscious of it, they shied away from the hall's entrance for pouring in from the fields of death came a cold draft. The door that held this place secure may have been unbreakable, but unfortunately it was left open. The cold from outside was alien to the dead men. Though their forms were now immortal, the wind of the death plains somehow reminded them of life's toils and problems; it chilled them as though hot bath water was being drained from around them, or like the sad waking from a happy dream.

Disturbed as they were, the Royal Guards, with Wynna at their command continued to ward the rest of them from drawing near the intruder. They didn't know however that the monster's purpose had now shifted. Now he only wanted to escape.

He slid across the floor in the shape of a man, stumbling now and again, collapsing into rags then re-forming. He went slowly, watching all those around him. The Guards moved with him in a ring threatening to slay any foolish enough to approach the thing. Then he backed toward the open door, his cloth blowing in the winds of the death plains.

"Stop," Wynna ordered and surprisingly, the monster did. Hearing her voice heartened the rest of them. "Where are you going and why?"

I'm going where you can't follow. Back to the land of the living; a place where your only chance has already been spent. Thought the voice inside their heads.

"Who are you? Were you ever a man or is the thing before me the only form you possess?" She thought perhaps she could stall him.

Who I am does not matter, thought the voice in her head. But inside, all the monster could think was, *she knows. She knows and it will ruin me. But how much does she really know?*

"Does it sadden you to know that it is only through treachery that you would ever gain entry to this place?" Wynna asked provokingly.

I do not envy you in this place. Ale and blade do not interest me in the least.

"What about fellowship? Do you admire that?"

Enough of this. You've said enough, wench. His anger was apparent. He was bristling with rage and she could tell that her words were working. But, he was now moving towards her instead of trying to flee. Could she avoid him if he truly tried to catch her?

"I see you are trying to leave here. A wise choice, for our weapons may not harm you, but we may find a way to do you in if you linger." A single bark of laughter echoed in their minds. "But if you can come in here, then I can leave. And I shall follow you to insure your evil is contained, I have had enough of paradise. If one more tour of battle means you will do no more harm, then I'll march gladly. I care not if others decide to follow. Lead on then, thing. Let me see where you would travel." It was Wynna's time to step forward. She walked until she was in arms reach of the monster. It was revolting to her, but she did not let it show. Then in a display of fearlessness she removed her helmet and let it drop to the floor allowing the assembled spirits to see her beautiful face for the first time.

If you come with me you will die—the thing thought in her head.

"Walk," Wynna commanded and now others were behind her, the Royal Guards were at her elbows.

All of you will perish Came the thought, but she again interrupted with a single word.

"Leave," was what she said. Others added their own orders. "Get out." "Be gone!" "Go back where you came from." And so on. The mob grew louder and now that they spoke for her, Wynna resumed the comfortable silence she had observed for so long in life.

The monster tried to speak again, but they found that if they yelled in response, they could drown it out.

In fury and frustration, it leaped forward and cursed them, but the throng dodged aside, and a war song rose from their throats. It was an ancient song and Wynna did not know the words, but the verses did something to her heart. Again the thing lunged at the crowd with its bloody mouth open. Wynna fell to the side but kept her eyes on the devil before her. It was in that moment that she noticed a glint of gold inside the rags it wore. A medallion rested in the folds of its body. *Strange,* she thought.

After being urinated on, cursed at, and drowned out in song for long enough, the monster finally backed away through the door. He wondered if this unruly throng would ever tire of harassing him. And he thought only of returning to the plains below. The stars gleamed in an endless sphere around them as the warriors followed behind the monster down the long white stairs. They left the Star Country; the wind of the plains blew past them. Dust was in the wind. Then they could see a gleam at the bottom of the stairs, the unbreakable door that stood open below its golden arch. The grey light of the death fields shone in. It was through this door that the monster led them, and not knowing what would happen to them, they followed. Singing.

THE KILLING WAS STILL underway below Haven. Many feet of the passage lay covered in gore behind them, but just as many feet ahead were packed with the undead ready to destroy them at the slightest opportunity. There were missing eyes, broken in skulls and foul decaying hides. There were oozing boils and lolling tongues and reaching fingers. There was also steel. And a blade or an axe in the hands of the twitching and gnawing dead was something most menacing and unpredictable. Of all the bouts of sticky that Deagan had fought, none could prepare him for the way a corpse wields a sword. This unorthodox and sadistic way of doing battle was to blame for the wounds Deagan had sustained. He blocked a wild shot by slicing the inside of the thing's elbow, and this would normally have stopped a swing, but feeling no pain, the monster followed through and connected with Deagan's shoulder, just below the hard plate and severing several links of his chain mail before drawing blood. He was grateful for his hide of hard rings, but it would only keep him alive as long as he had energy to wield his blade and shield. His other wounds were just as painful; a scathing gash on his right leg. A bite that might have broken his toe, a severed head had managed to latch on and stayed there, gnawing throughout several minutes of fighting before Gwyn stole the opportunity to pry it off and shatter it with her sword back in the caves.

He thought of using the experience to create a new warrior's saying. Something like, "When there's a rotter on *its* feet and a rotter on *your* foot, kill the first one first . . ." He claimed no mastery of language and had never attempted saying-making before let alone the more conventional modes of poetry, so he resolved to pose the question to Kellen if they made it out of this alive.

Gwyn had now drawn her sword and still held her massive rectangular shield. Deagan hadn't heard her yell out in pain so he didn't think she was wounded, certainly she was still fighting like a king's champion at a tournament of mere squires, but the former knight would not rule out the possibility of his new friend being injured—another thing they'd have to see to when the fighting was done.

Kellen delved into his reserves to keep up the fight. His armor was light and his sword was swift, but he was not well versed in holding a shield and it now drooped dangerously low. Deagan wondered how long before he dropped it altogether. His face was locked in concentration and splattered with the blood of the dead men. He looked almost asleep, dreaming an unforgettable nightmare no doubt. Deagan called for him to switch to the back.

"Off with you, pirate! Take a rest in the back lines," he ordered. And without protest Kellen stepped back. Rory was about to step forward, but instead one of the towermen did so, and he fought valiantly beside the more experienced fighters. He was big and strong, and his form was solid and defensive. He was called Hunch, and his advance gave greater support to Deagan and Gwyn than Kellen had. In fact, they started moving more quickly now through the sea of undead.

The end of the horde lay in sight now, but it wasn't over yet, and likely it wouldn't be even after they broke through. Deagan knew that unlike Kellen, he would never step to the back row in this fight or in any other.

Hunch said, "I see the end of them!" and he cheered like a howling dog. His fellow towermen laughed and joined the howl, but just as the call was loudest, a heavy war hammer in the hands of a decrepit and dark looking rotter swung down onto Hunch's head. He went limp before he fell to the ground, dropped to his knees then toppled forward, the rotters descended on him, their mouths taking chunks from the back of his neck and shoulders. Another voracious, wide-eyed dead man threw a knife into their midst. It dug into Rory's chest, burying itself only an inch or so, then it fell to the ground, in all likelihood disease ridden and filthy. Rory sprung forward with his battle axe in hand. Unarmored and with no shield he strove to kill all his foes with a flurry of chops. He was aggressive and tired quickly, but now they picked up speed. He ducked a blow and severed the arm that delivered it in one fluid movement. He chopped three times into the monster's skull before it could recover and then moved onto the next one.

Their pace stabilized and they progressed steadily through the packed hall. After this day Rory owed Deagan three un-payable debts.

One: Rory had moved too far ahead of the line, his heart was pounding with anger and fear and he lost all his patience. Soon he was pitted against three enemies at once. As they were about to descend on him, bearing him to the floor, Deagan reached forward, letting his shield hang ineffectually from his elbow for a moment and pulled him back, while chunking off the spindly neck of the wretched thing that would have drooled on Rory's face as it devoured him.

Two: A huge, grotesque rotter that was so wide it took up half the hall threw a strike with its club that knocked Gwyn against the wall. Then, faster than lightning he swung back at Rory. The blow sent the butler down to one knee, possibly breaking his femur. The beast raised his club a third time, but Deagan broke from his post in the center of the shield wall to take the hit on his shield. It was like a battering ram hitting his arm, but his stance held. The club came around again, attempting to sweep out Deagan's feet. He reacted just in time as he turned and fell to his knees, bracing the shield against the floor and his side. The swipe clocked off the shield, but it hammered into him still. The weight of it numbed his leg. But when he looked up to this foe, as Rory and Gwyn regained their feet, he found that his sword had instinctively found its way into the creature's gut. He did not remember putting it there, but like finding extra coins in his pocket when he changed his breeches, he was glad he did. Now the thing looked stupidly down at its wound and Deagan didn't hesitate, he wrenched the sword down, spilling its stinking intestines, then he rose to his feet and chopped at the side of it's neck. His sword met Gwyn's in the middle of the monster's neck and the head fell forward. Rory then helped them dismember the corpse so it would pose no more threat.

Three: This instance had actually happened earlier, when they had hiked in the mountains. Rory had been about to step in quicksand and Deagan had said, "Hey, quicksand."

Nevertheless, the battle raged on with Rory, Deagan and Gwyn taking the front line with Kellen and the remaining towermen destroying the remains as they went along. It was a span of several more minutes until finally, the last sarcoph fell. Breathing hard, staggering from the prolonged exertion, the company stumbled a few paces past the writhing carnage and rested. They were covered in blood and exhausted. Deagan never sat down, and taking his lead, neither did Gwyn. "Holy shit," he said and they all laughed, it was a welcome release after so much danger. "Well, we're here to kill whatever's in that bell tower right?" he asked.

"We think that's where they are being commanded from," Gwyn replied. "If more killing is what's needed then that's what we'll do, but right now all we have to do is get there."

"Then let's get there," he said, and Deagan, as exhausted as he was, set out with a smile on his face to the unknown of the dark tunnel ahead.

D UKE WORTH ORDERED THE advance. It wasn't a charge, for there was no assembled enemy yet. But men blasted on the horns, and many who were having their first taste of battle no doubt felt the heroic dread descend on their hearts. Their prayers went swiftly to the Star Country and their minds were overcome with the sensations of the moment, the smell of horseflesh, the feel of leather, and the crunch of their own boots on gravel.

For Sir Luthan, there were none of these pre-occupations. He had battled the undead before and did not fear them. He only wanted to know what was going on. And all around him he sought clues. Was Duke Worth riding stiffly? Was he whispering something to the man riding beside him? Was he glancing too often at the skies, seeking some signal? His heart raced in anticipation of what deeds might follow for he'd made his oath, and he intended to keep it. He thought of when Deagan met him in the courtyard for a game of sticky and brought news that there were rotters in Darkwell. How much of this did Duke Worth already know? Was there some part of it that he helped to arrange?

Like a dog pulling on its leash, the men under Luthan's command picked up their pace without his command. It began in fits and starts, then as the more collected knights sought to maintain the lines, they too went faster.

"Steady!" Luthan yelled warningly from Luka's back at the head of the unit. Still they rushed on. Unwilling to yield his command, Luthan kicked his heavy warhorse into a gallop and rode down the line chiding the men. He had them arranged so that the most experienced knights were spread out in order to lend their leadership to those around them. He called them by name in reproach, "Rogar, keep these men in line! Jason, hold them back! What's the matter with you, Brother? Control this company!" He sounded calm and scolding like a disappointed father. Many of these men looked up to him in such a light and, fearful of losing his approval, they rallied their men to hold the line. None challenged him or gave him lip. He did not give them the chance to do so. Instead he rode on, arranging his men how he saw fit. Only one part of the column called for more than one correcting remark. In this group he made eye contact with a man, not the commanding knight, but a lesser one several rows back. His challenging stare corroded Luthan's facemask, but the old knight's ego had withstood such impudence before, and he matched the man glare for glare. It became apparent that this was one of those who pushed the group forward, and still he urged his steed out of synch with the rest. Until Luthan clearly and indisputably held him in his stare saying, "Slow. Down." He said it loud enough for all to hear.

Then he rode off to his position, satisfied that the group was still under control—*his* control, not Worth's. He hoped that the condition would persevere, for already Duke Worth was eying him with something that looked like disapproval. The Duke's men hadn't budged, and they were simple footmen, not knights. Why had he momentarily lost control?

His thoughts returned to the challenging knight a few rows back. He was an imposing figure, both brawny and tall. His face held a confidence that would make him dangerous on the battlefield, and damned difficult to lead.

"Still no enemy force opposes us, Sir Duke," Luthan said so no one else but Worth could hear. "They are disorganized, the way we are grouped . . . we're ready for a ditch battle, a fight of shield walls and cavalry. They are scattered through the streets, not lined up across the field. What the devil is that!" He interrupted himself to look up to the skies. What he saw there was the muster of the Dragon Riders. They swirled over Haven, a cloud of screeching, howling beasts capable of disintegrating Darkwell's army. After the imprisonment of Sir Oscar and the subsequent attack on the spire and jail break, Luthan did not count himself lucky to be marching toward the city the Dragon Riders were sworn to protect.

"Worry not, Sir Luthan." Duke Worth said. "We are prepared for the likes of them. You were saying something about the enemy being scattered in the streets."

"Aye, commander," Luthan said, his visor lifted in one hand, revealing his deeply lined face and the long white hairs that somehow escaped his hood of chain. Still he watched the dragons and his heart grew sore. Weren't they here to free the city? Why then should the duke be ready to slay them? Then Luthan remembered the bounty for their heads. Gods this war was confusing. "Let me send outriders. A force of one hundred to rout the nearest streets, to ride down any stragglers and find any signs of a larger army ahead."

"Make it so, Luthan. We'll be better off seeing the enemy first hand. Reliable men, Luthan, it seems you're struggling to keep them under control as it is."

"Thank you, sir," Luthan said. He'd never had the pleasure of meeting the Dragon Riders, but he had never thought that their first introduction would be through the opaque, death dealing veil of dragon flame. Truly these worried him more deeply than the rotters, no matter their number. He sent the outriders forthwith. They galloped ahead, leaving an impressive plume of dust. Lances held at the ready and swords strapped to their sides, they rode onward into the streets to what end Luthan didn't know. He expected them back in less than half an hour. Once they watched the group ride past, appearing through the gaps in the buildings in predictable fashion, then disappearing again behind the urban cover. Luthan called for horns to be blown, and within minutes the men returned, their numbers dwindled not at all.

Their leading knight said, "They wander about the streets in groups of ten to fifty. We met no challenge on our ride. The nearest streets are clear, and there is no sign of a larger force."

"Well done, Brother," Luthan said with a congratulatory pat on the back. "Now join the others and await my orders. There is more going on here than we yet know."

And indeed Luthan was certain that there was.

BEHIND WYNNA AND THE Royal Guards in their black plate mail, the great horde of warriors rolled out from the door, for the first time inviting the chill of adventure back into their bones. They left their sanctuary for no longer did it protect them. And as warriors must, when the safety of home is in jeopardy, they left it behind.

The door stood open, massive and unmoving, and now at their feet they saw the two white horses, brother and sister lying dead by the door, a trail of dark red blood leading from the belly of the stallion showing how he'd been dragged.

"The fell demon owes its wounds to these two no doubt," Gurda son of Phoe said loudly. "But surely we must be careful, for if he can slay these two, there is dark power in him indeed."

"Aye, keep your distance," another warrior advised. Some of the spirits gathered around the horses, trying at first to move them in more reverent positions, but realizing they lacked substance, they instead only bowed their heads and wished them well. They thanked them for their eons of service. In this distraction, they almost lost track of the demon thing, but faithfully the Royal Guards encircled him, stalking in agile caution to track his every movement. Wynna with her long hair in a braid that lay on her back in perfection, left her companions briefly and she swiftly returned to the open door.

"Gurda, look out upon this great crowd of men, each one bloodthirsty and ready to serve. They have all left paradise behind to seek justice in this world between worlds and they may be stuck here for all time, or waste away, we know not. And yet, we leave the door open in hopes that we might return even though I believe we never will. We must send them back. Not all these warriors need to accompany the demon. The Royal Guard will be enough, for it isn't in strength of arms that we will prevent his evil, but through watching, learning his ways, and by warning others of his tricks.

"Bring them back in, and close the door behind you. Set a watch on the stairs in case another intruder comes back, but do not throw away the bliss of the Star Country for a task that only needs a few."

In answer Gurda said, "I too have had enough of paradise, Guard. I, at least, will go with you. Whether any go back or none, I agree that the door should be closed, even if the rest of warriors of the ages leave it behind with us. I will spread the word and consult the others." She nodded to him and jogged back to join her group.

The rag-thing stumbled now, its wounds apparent, for blood trailed behind it on the tall grass, gathering on the stalks and blowing in the wind like wisps of black thread and scraps of cloth. Always it looked behind it, sometimes with a grotesque twisting of its horrible neck, sometimes by moving its figure like clay so that an eye appeared in the middle of its back, and every time it did, its gaze was fixed on the open door. The stars that shone through it, and the crowd of warriors that grew now to the thousands.

Wynna caught another glimpse of the gold medallion in the monster's robes and wondered what it was. After each look behind it a sickly hand reached for the medallion.

It's not too late, brave warriors. You could return to life, you could right your wrongs, the thing thought in their heads. It was tempting. On some level they all missed life—yet the temptation was not so much one of reason, but something unnatural, insinuated into their heads, growing inward like icicles. One of the Guards shook her head.

Yes, come here. The monster thought. As they walked his voice grew stronger and so did the vile temptation to allow him to devour them.

"I'll kill you where you stand," Wynna warned, and the Royal Guard maintained her distance from the thing.

"I'd do the same for you," the other Guard replied at last.

"And so would I," said another. And thus they formed a pact of death.

Gurda finally caught up to them. "Hail Guards!" He greeted. "It has been decided that the door will be closed once the Hall is emptied. There were none who wished to stay behind while others were banished, and there were none who would risk the Hall being taken by other demons. So it shall be closed, and stay that way forever, until perhaps another being is born who can open that door. Before, only the star-horses could do it, now any can close it, but none will open it again."

Wynna sighed, but her only response was a nod. In the distance, the warriors still poured out of the door. Tens of thousands swarmed on the unending fields. The battle songs that rose up were loud and mighty.

The rag-thing reached up and clasped the piece of gold. *Death behind me, life ahead.* The thing thought softly. And its form wavered, shrank a bit into the center and became faint. But it returned quickly, then hurried onward away from the door with a growl.

After what felt like years later, the last warrior emerged from the door. All eyes turned to see the ending of an age, the closing of the Hall. And then a thought occurred to Wynna. Why was this thing protecting that medallion in its robes? While she had already been operating under the assumption that the talisman was what would enable him to disappear, she hadn't until now thought that unlike the rest of its grisly form, the golden trinket might actually be vulnerable to attack. She gripped her spear tightly, watching for her chance.

Far behind her, the door was shut, and the boom of its closing rattled her mail, still she didn't flinch.

Death behind me, life ahead. The words were already playing through her head as she saw the gold. The thrust of her spear would have shot the gold disc across the grass for yards and yards because it was perfectly aimed and forceful as could be except, by the time her jab fell, there was no more substance to the thing, and it receded into the shell of gold just before her spear tip connected. As the door closed, they all became suddenly aware that some force that had been spilling out from the Star Country was now gone. They all felt heavier and more vulnerable. Still this place was bereft of pain, but also it was bereft of sacredness.

Still hanging in perfect stillness, Wynna's spear tip hovered over the ground and in the skin of her hand, she seemed to recall the sensation of her weapon connecting with something slightly, and the metallic sound of a coin being struck had traveled up her arm and into her ears. Was it a false memory? Hope was kindled in her anew and she explained her findings to the other Guards. They all agreed to stay there, and if the thing appeared, they would aim for its trinket and see what happened. There was nothing else to do, so the Guards stood guard, in the land of the dead.

DEAGAN, KELLEN, GWYN, RORY and the towermen marched forward through the catacombs. It was only a straight tunnel now, and there were no obvious tracks on the ground. None that Kellen could find anyway. If Wer the Gigant had been among them, he would have easily found a set of tracks leading in the direction they now traveled. Wer would also have told them the height, weight, dominant hand, mood, and overall health of the one who'd made the marks in the dust of the floor. But Wer didn't know Deagan or the others, nor was he aware of the troubles in Haven, and he would have a hard time fitting in this tunnel in the first place, Gigant that he was. A good friend he would have made during such times as these.

Had he been there, Wer would have told them that the footsteps in front of them belonged to a frightened and hopeless man who looked over his shoulder at every chance. He was not a tall man, but not short, and his gait told of weakness. His shoes were of fine quality, and every so often, on the left side, a cape brushed the floor, on the right, a sword tip. That made him left handed. He had a nervous tick of rubbing his head. He was tired, and his legs were sore from riding. These were things that Wer would have told them in either the sign language of his people or a badly accented and broken version of Deagan and Kellen's, but of course he wasn't with them so he didn't.

Instead the only clue they had of what lay ahead was the sudden scream of a man's voice that echoed down from above them. They all shushed each other and Rory ducked. It was a scream of pain at first. Soon it became the scream of orders being given. Kellen was no master tracker, but he had keen ears: the ears of a career thief always listening for signs of trouble.

Kellen explained, "He sounded badly hurt, but somehow surprised by it. Then he said, 'Come here, bind my wounds,' I couldn't tell what he said after that," And from this tid bit, he had an inclination that the man was a weakling, that he was dangerous nonetheless, and that he wasn't alone. Which was a detail that for all Wer's tracking skill he couldn't have told them.

The group came to an opening in the tunnel. It was a circular chamber of stacked stone, and they were glad to have found it. There was an opening in the ceiling, but no obvious way of reaching it. From the bottom of it there emerged an iron bar, perhaps the bottom rung of a ladder.

They all paused at the sound of more talking above, they were closer now and must be quiet. This time Kellen only made out the word, *sassis*. And he didn't report it for fear of being heard. He held his breath.

"Hold this," Rory whispered, handing his battle axe to Deagan. And with a running start, he pranced to the curved wall, took two steps on its surface, then leapt out from it toward the rung, which he gripped with one hand and stuck. They all cheered in hushed tones. He easily hoisted himself up into the hole and disappeared.

A loud screeching sound surprised them from above. "Rory!" Kellen called, and he was by the hole in an instant looking up. What he saw was a metal ladder lowering from the opening above, grating across the stationary piece that was already in place. The ladder stopped and the sound died away. But so had the sound of talking from above. Of course whoever was above had heard the sound, it had been so loud.

Then a bit more talking came down from above in hushed tones. A low moan, perhaps the moan of the undead, answered the voice above. Then there was silence followed by a thump, like a door closing.

Then the deafening, bone jarring sound of the great bell.

GONG! GA-GONG! GONG! GONG! GA-GONG! Its peels were irregular and jostling, not the even tones that would signal the alarm in the city, but something frantic and unruly. They clawed at their ears to somehow rid themselves of the din.

Rory lowered the ladder faster through the hole, its screeching sound was soft and raspy next to the great bell. Rory's hands appeared through the hole, and he fastened the hooks on top of the ladder to the bottom rung where they appeared to fit snugly. Kellen was climbing already, and soon behind him the others followed.

"Well done, Rory!" Kellen yelled. "Now what?"

In answer, Rory pointed up. Now that their torches had been carried through the hole, they could see that the ladder extended upward through the long hollow tube of stone above them. The inside of it was painted with foul markings and it wreaked of old blood. The signs of the occult were here, littering the beauty of the white stone with their curses and promises of death. None of them understood the markings, but a sense of foreboding dwelled in this place, and it soaked into them with each new tolling of the bell. The sound grew louder as they climbed the ladder. But it became less frequent. The sound eventually grew weak by comparison, but still their ears rang from its intensity, then it died out altogether, and the shaking of the ladder decreased, relieving their hands from the unpleasant buzzing that seemed to numb their very bones.

At last Rory reached the top of the ladder and fearlessly hoisted himself up through a trap door and disappeared. As he opened it though, he moved into a world of light again, and it alarmed him more than the relative darkness below simply because his eyes were assailed with sensation. The chamber, however, was empty. Whoever had screamed earlier was now gone. The bell made an imposing presence in the center of the room and was now only barely swinging. A chair of beautifully worked silver, that was drenched in fresh blood sat beside the bell and some food in boxes and bags lined the wall.

The room was circular; its walls were a glowing stone. It appeared that the rosy glow came from the sunlight outside, and it shone through the thinly sliced slabs of rock, which formed opaque, yet luminous windows. Deagan gave a hand to the last of the towermen as they got inside the chamber. Deagan was faint and weak from the height of the ladder. And still his heart raced because he was unable to trust the stone floor below them. He stayed close to the wall and did not look down. Attached to the bell there was a chain. It disappeared through a hole in the wall. Gwyn walked over to the hole, her gloved hand running along the chain.

"Where did they go?" one of the towermen asked.

"And who were they?" Kellen followed. "There is blood on this chair and on the floor. It looks very fresh."

"Look," Rory said. "Scraps of thread and cut cloth on the floor. They look like rich silk, the dress of the nobles."

Kellen took it in his hand. "This could very well have been the stuff that I shipped to Haven not long ago; this hue of purple, this quality of weave. Indeed, I would guarantee that this fabric came from the caravan of Jorn Kahorne, his last trip, no less. Do you think it was cut to make bandages for whoever was bleeding?"

Deagan finally got up the courage to look down at the floor and it appeared solid enough. He relaxed a bit, trying to pretend the precipitous drop below him did not lurk under his feet. "If they were bandages," he managed mopping sweat off his brow, "they didn't work. Look, the blood trail goes over there."

They looked where he indicated, and since the scarlet glow of the sunlight passing through the stone that encased the bell chamber made the entire world around them look red, they did not at first see the trail of blood. The veins through the rock were dark lines through the rosy stone. It looked as though they were inside a body, searching by the light shining through living flesh. The trail led to the outside wall, near where the chain disappeared out of its hole.

"Well, that doesn't answer the question of where the blazes they have gone to," Deagan said. "What do we do, climb back down the ladder and try something else?"

Gwyn was looking through the hole. "The reason there are no doors on the outside of this bell tower is that the bell can be rung from Saxus' tower. This chain spans the distance from here to there, and it is left up to the servants to pull the chain from Cloud Tower. I can see a little through this hole, but I can't quite see the other end of the chain. But I know this because I was one of the Royal Lord's servants, and from time to time, I rang the bell myself if the need arose."

They all thought about this. "Can I see?" Kellen asked. Gwyn moved aside and Kellen took her place. Sure enough he saw the downward arc of the heavy chain that stretched from the bell to the Cloud Tower, the bastion of stone after which Gwyn's helmet was fashioned. Just as she had said, the chain stretched upward and out of view. He looked around for a while. The throng of undead made a dark and cohesive mass in the streets below. Wisps of black smoke crossed his vision so he couldn't be sure, but it looked like all their eyes were turned to Cloud Tower.

"I say," Kellen said.

"What is it?" Deagan asked.

"Unless I'm wrong, the teeming hordes of evil appear to be gazing somewhat avidly at the upper reaches of . . . Cloud Tower itself."

"Are they?" Gwyn asked. "Does it mean their receiving orders again?"

Kellen looked quizzically at them and leaned against the wall. He shrugged and raised an eyebrow. "Well look!" Deagan ordered, losing his patience.

Kellen jumped and turned, stooping to see the sarcophs below through the small hole. "Now fancy that!" he remarked. "It's actually somewhat comforting to see them like this. They're turning around all as one. It made them almost look alive for a moment. Oh that's a disgusting one! And now they are . . . yes they're marching away. They seem to be taking up arms and . . . yes indeed marching right along now. Oh! And who's this character?" even without seeing his face, they could tell Kellen was alarmed.

"Who?" Deagan asked.

"This beastly undead knight, calling down to them from the balcony, that's who. He's got a cape, a great sword, a crown. I can't make out a bloody word he's saying!"

Gwyn pushed Kellen aside and set her eye to the hole. An unvoiced gasp escaped her. "It's Lord Saxus," she said. "He has become the king of the dead."

T HE DRAGON RIDERS, CRISS-CROSSED in a predetermined, but undecipherable pattern. Oscar was at their head, astride Pete with his well oiled, azure scales gleaming in the sun, and reflecting the blue sky twofold back to the heavens. They dipped and careened back and forth over the scattered batch of rotters that had unearthed themselves and begun the march to Haven from parts unknown.

Then as Pete carried him upward with a howl, for a moment, the sarcophs all stopped and looked forward in the same direction. They stood there for a time, giving the Riders pause.

"If they're going to stand still, then they can die standing still!" Oscar bellowed. "Give them no quarter!" and with that he dove back to the fray. Pete did not echo his war cry with a roar. His throat burned from so much dragon breath. And steam rose from his back sending lines of disturbance through the air. It felt good to drive his broad wings through the cooling air, but as soon as he slowed he grew hot again. He longed to plunge into the water of a lake and sleep at the bottom for an hour. But he was as devoted to Haven as was his Rider, and would not rest until this scourge was destroyed. His wing beats grew weaker. His maneuver's grew clumsier with his fatigue. But he scorched the standing rotters all the same.

Oscar's legs burned and his white mustache was singed. He too would suffer for his city. To the South, in the city of Haven, the undead moved as one, drawn as if by magnetism to form ranks and march away to the city's defense. Then the rotters below him started moving again, but in a new direction. They were headed straight for the gated tunnel that would lead them into Old Haven, the last sanctuary of humankind. The Dragon Riders harried them and burned them to the ground, but their numbers were great, and soon they were clinging to the gates, shaking them on their hinges. The gates came down, and the horde filed into the tunnel of stone where they would be protected from the assault. Oscar was glad that their numbers had dwindled, but an unexpected attack at the heart of the resistance might do massive damage whether there were great numbers or few.

"Sir Johan!" Oscar called. It was his dragon, Ero who answered the call rather than the Rider himself, but it amounted to the same. "Fly with all haste into Old Haven, warn them of the coming hordes. We will meet you there!"

Ero wheeled over, and shot straight to his destination. Oscar and the others took a more relaxed, but still urgent pace. On the way, Oscar spoke with his men and saw how each was faring. Each of them was blackened by the char of fire, and the mounts drooped in their tired flight. Unfortunately now was the time they would make mistakes and lose men and beasts. Now, when it mattered most in the heart of their city. It would be less than half an hour before the rotters appeared in Old Haven, perhaps they could rest a bit before their coming.

LUTHAN HAD SENT ANOTHER band of outriders to clear the next streets while his main force advanced. When Duke Worth gave the order to hold, Luthan echoed it just as loud. The Great Bell of Haven rang out through the air and then, figures appeared. Gray, staring figures that numbered first in the hundreds and then in the thousands crowded on the rooftops, and then the streets too were filled with undead, marching outward from the heart of the city. Luthan had the horns sounded again. And the outriders started back, but this time, their numbers were few. Luthan rode out to meet them.

"What happened?" he asked when he reached the lead rider though it was not the man he'd left in charge.

"Sir Gillfur is dead. They swarmed us, sir. The bell rang. They all looked at the tower then turned to kill us." On his clothing, this man carried the putrid scent of the undead. In the distance, sickening laughter could be heard on the wind.

"Join the others." Luthan said, then turned Luka on a course for Duke Worth. He sidled up next to the higher ranking, though slightly younger knight, and his steed bumped into the Duke's.

"What say you, Duke?" was all he said as he gestured with his chin toward the mass of un-living flesh.

"They aren't advancing," the Duke observed. Luthan turned and saw that he was right. "I know it's impossible, but its as though they are displaying some sort of discipline. They are acting in concert, Luthan. Have you ever known their kind to do that?"

"I haven't seen this before, sir. What do you think it means?"

"This might be our last battle," the Duke replied with a sad smile.

It was pathetic and disgusting to see the Duke so overwhelmed. As far as Luthan was concerned, lined up in rows or no, they were still only rotters. Killing them took patience, but if you were careful, and Luthan was, they would come out on top. "Duke Worth, we are here for a reason." The Duke turned with wide eyes to face him in surprise. "To save Haven from this menace." The Duke looked suddenly relieved as he nodded. "We aren't here to die, we're here to kill. Do we charge or wait?"

The Duke looked into the heart of the enemy force. The dragons now came back into view flying low, and coming straight for them. "I suppose we charge. Send the cavalry around to flank. We will go in head on."

Luthan stared at the duke for a minute, looking for other motives within his plan. Did he want them separated so some other foul deed could be done? Did he want them divided so they'd be more easily confused and crushed? "Yes, sir," Luthan said. "When all is ready we'll flank."

Without giving Worth another chance to correct him, Luthan left, glad he'd bought himself the ambiguity that he did. That way he hadn't committed to flanking at a certain time. He would watch first, then act as he saw fit. Once the battle was joined it would be chaotic enough that he could order his men freely, and he wouldn't have to worry about the duke until it was over.

He returned to rally his men. As he spoke quietly to each leading knight with a warm and eager smile and firm words of encouragement, the message was passed through the group. They would charge soon, then fall back and possibly circle around to flank. When he rode past that same dark haired, muscular man that he'd seen before, he heard, "Luthan! You led us astray! Too many of the outriders died. Why should we listen to you?"

He pretended to ignore it for a moment, looking to the battlefield ahead instead of dealing with the man. It was true that those deaths were unexpected. But long ago, Luthan learned to hold the enemy responsible, not himself.

"Look, how he ignores me. It is because he has nothing to say!" the man called. Now Luthan turned to face him, he pushed his way through the lines, his steady warhorse butting his way back into the mass to be face to face with the man.

"It is cowardice, not bravery that urges you to speak so. If you have not seen such deaths then you have not seen battle. The only thing I would change would be to send you with them, sir knight." At this the ugly knight only smiled. When he opened his mouth to speak, Luthan cut him off. "Not another word, boy,"

"What are you going to do about it?" the long-haired man asked, still grinning. Luthan was seeing red. How did this man become a knight? He wondered. Luthan felt that at the edge of battle, and at the edge of his patience, he had little to lose. He looked down at the man's horse and he furrowed his brow. It was Maggie! Deagan's steed. He remembered now Deagan's last goodbyes to the beast. How sad it made him to let her go after so many victorious rides.

"That's not your horse," Luthan growled, and slapped the knight across the face with his glove. "If you live through this battle, you'll have me to deal with on the other side. If you make one false move, I may not wait until the battle is done. Do you understand?"

"All too well, old man," the knight replied. Luthan turned Luka around roughly and left, a shocked murmur hummed through the assembly. When Luthan was far enough away, the younger knight continued, "I understand that you'd kill your own men for disagreeing with you." At that some of the other knights rallied in agreement—not many of them, but enough to worry Luthan.

Tieg rode forward to Luthan's side, there was a fresh scratch on his brow, a small token to remind him of his foray into the city streets as one of the outriders. "Pay them no mind, Luthan. He knows not what he says. A new knight that one. Fresh from some raid in the Border Lands and thinks he's some kind of hero. Used to be a jailer," said the smaller man.

"Then he should have stayed a jailer," Luthan replied. "Let's hope for his sake that I don't live out the night. If it comes to a duel between us, I'll try to kill him swiftly. Even as bad as he is, a man shouldn't have to suffer long." He took a deep, calming breath.

Between the soldiers and the undead there was an elaborate garden, maintained perhaps by one of the monastic orders in Haven, but now gone mostly to ruin. It was small, but it was terraced upward, a pillar of wild green in the city. At its peak, sad and careworn, there grew a stand of fruit trees that were adorned with white blossoms. The ivory pedals sailed to the west on the breeze, each one transformed into a shining bird by the bright sun.

"What is the Jailer's name?" Luthan asked.

"Colstin."

"First or last?"

Tieg paused for a moment. "It's what he goes by." He was convinced that neither one of them were still thinking about this Colstin any longer, but only about the battle ahead, and whether they would live through it. Worth's footmen worked to assemble a dozen ballistae. The parts came out of the wagons, and like spears, the bolts were arranged beside each one.

"Those men woke up as city guards this morning. Tonight they'll go to bed dragon slayers," Tieg mused. Sure enough the Dragon Riders still flew toward them. Luthan looked back at the lines. Their numbers were impressive. With all the refugees on the streets of Darkwell, soldiering became one of the few trades that would put food on the table and the army had swollen massively.

A flash of fire erupted from the belly of a soaring dragon over Haven, distant as it was, the men under Duke Worth flinched. Memories of their attack on Malagor's spire were still near the surface. Then, the Dragon Riders swooped down, presumably to land somewhere in the city. Luthan did not know if they waited in ambush, or if they would emerge again in an instant, bearing down on Darkwell's force. His wondering was cut short however. For then Duke Worth called the charge, and the footmen clamored forward to the enemy.

The horses stayed still as Luthan looked back at them to hold them in check. "CHARGE!" he yelled, and as a single block the horsemen broke into a gallop, lances lowered, to flatten the first of their enemies. Luthan rose in his stirrups, allowing Luka to smoothly surge over the street, his heavy breath blowing through both flared nostrils. The horses had a battle cry of their own—the sound of their hooves like ten thousand drums.

"WELL, SAXUS IS COMMANDING from the balcony, and we are in here," Deagan said, trying to force the discouragement from his tone. Kellen peered out the hole again, and stayed there motionless. Rory, prodded at his wound, but kept a stiff upper lip, and even as the blood drained from him at a drip, he maintained a butler's posture and stayed out of the way. Gwyn paced around and around the bell. Deagan, for a few moments, had been staring at the blood trail, leading from the chair, to the wall.

The towermen spoke in hushed tones, exhilarated, yet unsure how to proceed. They kept watch down the ladder. The silver chair was similarly marked with symbols of the occult. The top was adorned with thin, flat spikes of silver, symbolizing perhaps the rays of the sun or moon. The back of it was inlaid with the images of stars in the sky. The seat was textured like fur or grass. The legs were shaped like thick leg bones, and the arms were decorated with sigils of death.

"Did they disappear from here using magic?" Deagan asked. Gwyn paused to consider it, but then kept pacing, locked into a familiar silence. Then, slowly, the bell tipped to one side, then swung back. No one reacted to the movement, except Deagan who looked at it like it was haunted.

"Get out of the way!" Kellen said through the hole.

"What is it?" Deagan asked, terrified of what he might see.

"Just a bird, a big bird at that, but just a bird. It landed on the chain and now I can't see Saxus."

Deagan shoved Kellen out of the way and peeked through. He was right. There was a large brown bird with a curved beak swaying back and forth on the chain. "They escaped by the chain!" Deagan said, squeezing Kellen's arm and turning to face him. "If they could get to it, they could have climbed across the chain to Cloud Tower!"

Rory, who had rushed to help Kellen up from the floor, paused and smiled, convinced that this was true. Gwyn stopped to consider it. "May I see?" she asked. Deagan hurried out of her way and she crouched beside the hole to look through.

"Just because a bird landed on it?" Kellen asked, wanting to believe, but not seeing the connection.

"When the bird landed on the chain, the bell moved!" Deagan exclaimed as though that explained everything. Then seeing that it didn't, he went on. "When we were at the bottom of the ladder we heard the bell ringing. If a man crossed that chain, it would be more than enough to ring the bell. The bird moved it, but it didn't ring. A man is heavier than a bird."

"That is a very *sizeable* bird, though Deagan. How can you be sure?" Kellen asked.

"Sizeable is it? Well, you said the man up here wasn't alone. Do you think that bird weighs as much as two men? Or three?"

"I think he's right," Gwyn interrupted. "I see no other way out."

"What do you mean no *other* way out?" Kellen whined. "There is no way out period. How did they get to the chain? Unless there is some secret door." He cut himself short. "On second thought, after all these passages, a secret door wouldn't surprise me in the least." And then, grateful for something to do, Kellen scrutinized the walls for a seam, latch, or mechanism. The others did the same.

"Look where the blood leads," Kellen advised. The group concentrated their search at that point on the wall now. As Kellen slid his skilled fingers down the luminous stone, something slipped. A brick shaped slice of rock moved slightly to the side. He slid it further over, alerting the others that he had found it. Underneath the stone, there was a keyhole.

Kellen pushed on the wall on both sides of the key hole; he tested above and below. One thing was certain; this door was locked. "Go on, then, brigand. A locked door never stopped you before. Would you like us to turn around so we can't see your criminal ways?" Deagan urged him with a big warm hand on his shoulder.

"Criminal? Hardly. A misspent youth perhaps." Kellen retorted, glancing at Gwyn nervously.

"You and your misspent youth," Deagan moaned. "Just get it over with. Time's wasting."

"Of course he's referring to my brief stint as the apprentice to a locksmith," he assured the group. "But, sadly, a tradesman needs tools. And I gave up the craft long ago."

A stink arose from below. The laughter of death echoed up to them through the hole in the floor.

"Well, you worry about those tools, Kellen. Me and the rest, we'll worry about whatever climbs up this ladder."

"Right." Kellen patted down his clothes as the group circled around the entry hole at the ready. Of course he found nothing, for his days of burglary were long behind him, and his "locksmithing" tools were stored away in his mansion, only Rory knew where. He pulled a dagger from his belt and toyed with the lock, The blade was too wide and too thick to be of much use. He looked into the lock to determine what tools he would need. It was a simple enough lock, though well made, and he would need only two tools at a minimum, though it would be easier to have a third. One would be his torque wrench, simply a piece of metal, bent at the end, with which he could apply pressure onto the lock. The other would be a long, thin, pin. A third, which would help was a similar pin, that would be curved on the end, instead of straight. If only Gwyn was the type of woman to hold her hair up with pins. He guessed she'd be quicker to lop it all off with a broadsword than get it out of the way with something as paltry as that. He didn't have his hat, which had a pin through it for style. He didn't have his cloak, which was held together by a brooch. What did he have? These damned dueling clothes were little good for much else. He shook his hands out, tired as they were from fighting.

He looked around at the clothing of his companions. Could he bend a ring of chain mail into a pin? No it would be too short.

The groans of the undead greeted their ears. Deagan cast about for a way to detach the ladder and be done with it. He still had a war hammer that he had picked up from one of the rotters. Maybe he could knock the metal bolts out of the stone, but that left them with no way down. Mostly he was tired, and wanted an easier way to avoid these things than killing each one as it topped the ladder. He sighed. "Well, maybe if they're sending this many after us it means we're on the right track!" he said hopefully.

"Indeed, sir," Rory agreed, always a yes man.

"Be that as it may, I still have no tools. Do any of you have a pin or a fork, or anything? Blast, I'd take a writing quill if I had to." Kellen said urgently. Now they could hear dry, groping hands clapping on and off of the metal rungs. Deagan sighed again as he glanced around looking for something to help, but he couldn't spare his eyes for long, because now the sarcophs were here. He sent the first one back where it came from with a downward chop. They would need to be careful not to hit each other in such close quarters.

Kellen looked about. The chair, the bell, the chain. The chair, the bell, the chain. The chair, the bell, the chain. The chair! The sun beams on the top could be taken off with some effort and bent into the shapes he needed. They may be a bit too thick, but it was all he had. Back and forth, back and forth he bent the silver, and the first tine broke free.

A gurgling belch came from another dead man as it fell. The group had settled on taking turns by the hole. The next one in line assisted if needed, but with such an advantageous position the need was rare. The rotters put some pressure on them, but endangered them very little. One thing they did though, was block their escape, at least by that route. It made Kellen their only chance, and Deagan didn't mind reminding him.

"You're our only chance now, Kellen," Deagan said. "We aren't getting through these bastards any time soon."

"Ah, Deagan," Kellen said calmly as he snapped off another tine confident that his plan would work. "How many times have I saved your life, now?" he chuckled knowingly as he set to work bending the tine into a torque wrench. Satisfied, he moved to the lock and got to work. He placed the torque wrench low in the socket, and twisted it slightly to the right, just enough to bind up the pins. Then he stuck his other tool in above it. But the two would not fit into the lock together. He tried again, and decided it wasn't worth it. "I chose the wrong day to leave my hat pin behind—damn you Gwyn for your manly ways." The two thoughts were joined uncouthly in one sentence to the bafflement of all the others.

Kellen immediately walked back to the chair. He looked for other tines that might provide thinner tools, but he wasted precious time doing it, for they were all the same. He rolled up his sleeves and began to rub the silver on the stone floor, trying to wear it away and make it thinner. "I'm going to kill you, Kellen," Deagan muttered under his breath. "What are you doing this time?"

Kellen heard him, but said nothing; he only rubbed the metal raw then checked it to see his progress. One side was now flattened and he had left a gray streak on the floor, but it would take more than that to get both pieces to fit. He ground the metal even more. He checked again. Not enough. He took both tools in his hands and slid them simultaneously across the stone as rapidly as he could and with as much pressure. "Rory, do you have a moment?" He asked.

The butler came over with a hurried bow and Kellen continued, "If you don't mind, would you please grind this piece of metal on the floor for me? It would be a great help."

"Very good, sir," Rory said, and he took the piece in his hand to commence the task. The two of them working together, Kellen thought they now had a chance.

"I already killed this one!" a towerman said as he regarded the wounded sarcoph that now showed itself through the hole.

"Well, kill it again my good man," Kellen said over his shoulder. "I don't know what you want *us* to do about it." He lifted the pick to his eye and deemed it ready. "Thank you, Rory," he said snatching the torque wrench from the younger man's hand and stepping to the lock. He set the tools into the keyhole and got to work. This time they fit. He tried to rush through it in all the excitement, but then he lost his grip and had to start over. On his second try he took his time as much as it pained him to do so.

"Grab his arms," Deagan said, as he held the monsters head in place by stabbing it with his sword. "Good now let's do away with those claws of his. We'll see if this one climbs back up to get us!" A few chops of Rory's axe and the hands were gone. Gwyn brushed them down the hole, and then they dropped the rotter after them. His fall brought the next two down as well and it was utterly satisfying to watch.

They gave the same treatment to the next sarcoph: skewer the head, grab the arms, chop off the hands and drop him down the chute. The next several all got the same.

The lock moved a little further as Kellen tapped the third pin into place. If he lost it now he could get back to this point fairly easily, but he was close to opening it so his excitement grew. *Three more pins.*

Gwyn stepped back from the ladder, she was not needed at the moment so went to the hole that the chain exited through. She squinted out into the sun and after a moment she saw what lay before her. Still standing on the balcony was the crowned figure of Royal Lord Saxus. Arrayed at the base of Cloud Tower there rambled a host of undead serving as some sort of guard, but they were the only ones left in the square, the rest of the mob having moved somewhere out of view. Standing beside Saxus was a dark clad man, clutching the stump of a missing arm. His head was bald, and Gwyn recognized him immediately. He was the last one seen with Saxus in life. In Haven he was called Lord Othar, but in Darkwell they called him Jatham Holmin. Her blood ran hot. Never had she trusted him. And now she wished only that she had a crossbow and a clear shot. Clearly he was somehow involved. The missing arm would explain the blood on the floor of the bell tower, but what of the chair? And how did he cross the chain so wounded? Perhaps she would never find out.

Kellen grunted with effort to her left, getting her attention. A rasping sound followed. The lock spun to the side and the door swung slightly outward, admitting into the bell tower a warm wind. Now they could clearly see the outline of the door and it was very small as far as doors go. "Ha ha! Success!" Kellen said.

"Gwyn, give me your shield—I mean, may I please use your shield?" Deagan said.

Wordlessly she handed it to him. During a lull in the monsters rising from below, he placed the curved rectangle of metal over the hole in the floor, sat on it, and said, "That should do it." A thump from below lifted him momentarily and his face looked shocked. He prepared to fall to his death. When he didn't, he laughed instead. Two of the towermen sat down beside him. Now the thumps didn't lift them at all.

"The door." Gwyn said. And they all looked over to see the slim box of sunlight shining in.

"Now what?" Kellen asked.

E RO THE DRAGON AND his rider Sir Johan landed in the
square in the center of Old Haven. It was raised high,
walled and heavily gated. A moat also bordered it on all
sides. Unfortunately, the tunnel that bypassed all these defenses was
now filled with sarcophs coming to kill them.

The townsfolk gasped to see the dragon, and they gasped again
when he snaked his long neck down into the well, as sir Johan
dismounted. Steam rose with a hiss from the drink below.

A man in medium weight armor and carrying a sword stepped
forward bravely to meet him. "Greetings wind rider! I am Hazen
Raiche." His face was an honest one, and his spirits seemed high
despite all that had happened; Johan liked him already.

They stomped toward each other and clasped forearms in the
manner of warriors. "It is an honor to meet you, Hazen. And I am
Sir Johan Sibard."

"I knew that dragons breathed fire, but I didn't know that the
Riders gave off heat as well! Truly you feel like my hearth at home,"
the other man said as he pulled his hand sharply away to keep from
being burned.

"If you wish your family's hearth to be safe, then listen, friend.
There is little time. There is a gated tunnel that leads from here
to the North of Haven. Now, gates are one thing and tunnels are
another. Being a flying man, I've little use for either one so I can't
tell you where this one is"

"I know such a tunnel exists, but I know not where. Why?"

"A force comes by that path to meet you today. Don't worry,
you've all lasted this long and from the bandage on your brow I can

tell that it wasn't easy. Find the entrance to the passage, and soon the rest of the Riders will be here to defend it. I will assist any way I can. My mount will rest for a while though, for he made great haste to come here."

Hazen's eyes filled with tears. "Thank you for your message. It will be carried out at once. You rest yourself, knight. It's been too long a rest for these people anyway, and they'll be eager to find the tunnel you speak of. There is a chance that one of them already knows where it is and can lead us there!"

"Hurry, man." Johan said.

Hazen set to the task of spreading the word; he stood up to address the crowd and within minutes the search was begun. Ero pulled his still steaming face up from the water. "Rest, friend," Johan, uttered. "I will be back." With that, he climbed a stairway up to the top of the wall and looked out over Haven. The war was joined now at the edge of the city. The flash of sword and shield from the south met the thick mass of gray from inside the city, and horns were sounded. It would be simple enough to ready Ero for another ride and aid the Darkish army, but those were not his orders. He'd wait until Oscar caught up and they'd decide what to do.

LUTHAN SLASHED TO AND fro while his warhorse Luka instinctively brought the knight in striking distance of his enemies. Their lances were now shattered, but sword work was much more favorable to the old knight anyway. His shoulder ached as it always did, age rather than injury had dealt that blow to him, but in the heat of battle, his body remembered its old ferocity and forgot much of the pain that it usually endured.

He looked across the battlefield wary of both the enemy and of Duke Worth's motives. He had been ordered to flank at some point, and as the battle wore on, he worried that soon he would be seen as insubordinate if he did not comply.

Loud thuds to his left and right interrupted his thoughts. Then came the shocked yells and death screams of his fellow knights. He looked around, but saw nothing at first. Then a swift shadow flashed before him and something struck him leaving a bloody streak on his pauldron. He reeled and looked up. "The roofs!" he mumbled to himself. "THE ROOFS!" he cried.

More dead men hurled themselves onto the horseman from thirty and fifty feet high. They fought with such abandon, like mindless insects following the orders of their queen. The corpses careened uncaringly through the air, crushing knights under them even as their decayed forms broke apart in oozing chunks.

Should he flank now? Well, at any rate he should avoid these buildings. "Fall back!" he ordered, and his knights turned as they got the opportunity to do so. They regrouped farther away from the rooftops while the undead gave chase, breaking away from their mass.

"Form a line! Make a line!" Luthan ordered. It took a little longer than he wanted, but it was ready in time. "Now charge!" he yelled and they fell upon the enemy like jackals on a wounded calf. The disorganized ranks of undead fell easily.

"No!" *"Save me!"* Came the screams from up ahead. The rotters now fed on the horses and knights that had fallen under the plummeting corpses from above. It angered and sickened him. Even if the bodies of the falling sarcophs were too disfigured to function, the jaws still worked open and shut, gorging themselves on the bloody remains of Luthan's company.

Looming behind the undead, Luthan saw shapes, tall figures, brawny and heavily furred. They were Giants, he supposed, tempted by coin perhaps to join this fight. Many believed Giants to be immortal, but Luthan knew it wasn't so. He'd killed one.

He rode over to Duke Worth who overlooked the battle from a vantage point on a small hillock. "Duke, Giants." He said.

"I see them," he said and he turned to one of his marshals. "Ready the spearmen, move them forward, but not too close." The rider acknowledged the command then rode away to carry out his orders.

"Your men are waiting, Luthan," the Duke said. "Were you stopped by the undead on the roof tops? Or did you only grow weary of your orders?"

To this, Luthan had very little answer. "Neither, sir," he said. "We are moving to flank now, I only wanted you to know about the Giants."

"Go, then," the Duke said. Before he was finished, Luka already turned and carried Luthan to his men.

He called his marshals together then rode into their midst yelling, "These monsters are slow, if they stop us in our tracks, they can drop onto us from above. But if we ride fast enough, even death won't catch us! So we array ourselves in a narrow column, narrower than a street, leaving plenty of space on the sides so they can't jump out to get us. We'll flank from the side. Don't wait to kill one, just strike as you ride through. Trust the men behind you to finish them off! Tell the others, and form a column with me, over there."

He rode to the appointed spot, and in moments his column was formed. It was ragged around the edges, but he could either wait for perfection or act quickly and he decided on the latter. Still his numbers were impressive to look out upon. He arranged for the second half of the column to split off and attack another street. He ordered the charge, himself at the head of it, Luka bearing him into the tide of the enemy.

The rotten heads swiveled to watch them, but they had no reaction other than to raise their weapons. The horses slammed into them, sending rotters spinning, trampling some under foot, and knocking others to the sides. Luthan's sword flashed again and again as they raced through the streets. They broke through one of their ranks to a spot where the rotters were thinner. The thickest mass of them was at the front lines. So Luthan led a charge from one side of the city to the other. It was like riding at a gallop through the crowded streets of Darkwell on a market day. It was exhilarating and terrifying, but once started, there was nothing to do but finish.

Luthan's knee collided with the open mouth of a staggering dead man, and the teeth somehow lodged into his leg. The pain was immense, his knee was weak in the first place, but still Luka carried him boldly through the mass and he had no time to think about the wound. His sword carried off the heads of three ghouls in a row. The last one made him laugh with joy. This was a ride to remember. Finally they made it to the other side, and no more sarcophs stood before them. Luthan waited for the entire force to join back together before giving new orders.

When they all got there, they exulted with glee. They cried out in triumph. The plan was well executed, for even though bodies plummeted from above, very few of them hit their mark, and most landed on fellow ghouls. Luthan saw no reason not to try the same tactic again, so without delay he formed the columns anew and they plunged into the city.

"**B**LAZES, THOSE ARE THE same sorts of things what came after us in the cave! You see them?" Durvish asked as he handed the spyglass to one of the towermen. They had been hiding out in a building on the outskirts of town. They were removed from the battle itself by less than four hundred yards, but no one seemed to have noticed them so far.

They were unsure of whether or not to help, because the memories of the raid in the Border Lands were all too fresh in their minds. And it had been Darkwell's own men that had attacked them. Undoubtedly some of the same men were here in this battle.

"Not over there, look, behind the rotters. Great hairy beasts."

"Aye, so they are. It's too bad we don't have any of our traps built right in the very streets," the towerman replied.

"Well, Keal, there might be something we can do," Durvish mused, taking back the spyglass. Keal went back to whittling, turning the block of wood over in his hands.

"Those horse are impressive aren't they? Look what they're doing now!" Durvish went on.

"Look at that column. Mighty thin wouldn't you say?"

"Mighty thin, mighty thin," Durvish answered. "There they go!" The two of them watched in silence as the cavalry plunged into the city. Durvish leaned forward, held his breath as they left view.

Keal whittled.

"There they are!" Durvish said at last. "Didn't lose a man looks like! Ha ha, these Darkwell chaps aren't half bad, supposing they kill rotters and not you."

"They charged clear through did they?" Keal asked.

"Looks that way. Clear through. Oh their getting ready to do it again! Heh heh, that one doesn't want to go back! Sorry, friend, back in line with you!"

"Are they charging again?" Keal asked as he watched through the window.

"Yep, there they go," and Durvish smiled in anticipation, waiting for the troops to come clean through the other side. He waited and waited. His smile started to fade.

"Not out yet, eh?" Keal asked.

"No sir, they might have turned to the side in there. I'll wager they're headed straight for Cloud Tower! Ha ha! This cavalry won't quit! They just won't quit!"

They waited again, and Durvish took a draught of water. He looked into the quiet rooms of his men most of them carrying out conversations such as his own. He heard one of his men exclaim from the other room and he looked back out the window. "Oh there they are, Kealy," he said with a downtrodden tone. "But, where's the rest?"

L UTHAN AND HIS KNIGHTS congratulated each other again on a successful ride. They rallied outside the battle, at the edge of the city where there was enough room in a grassy field. They waited for a time. The other column of the cavalry never arrived. Instead a single rider came out of the city, dust trailing from his clothes, his white horse splattered with blood.

"Giants, sir!" he said. "The knights aren't dead, but the Giants stopped us!"

Without hesitation Luthan charged his men forward to aid the other knights. From behind him he heard a voice that he knew to be Colstin the Jailer's, "Great gods, you just can't keep your men alive can you?" Luthan spurred Luka at the front of the charge, the other steeds unable to keep up with him.

Back into the racing tunnel of the streets they rode, the shops and windows flowed past them on either side. Luthan ducked a rope that held up a shop sign, then they came to the rotters. The gallop brought them into the heart of them. They were in something of a town square, a bloodied font of water stood in its center, limbs and heads of the undead littered its purity. From this square, Luthan could see the raised walls of Old Haven. He glanced to the sun soaked battlements, and there he saw a man watching them from above. He had no time to ponder this, for now the battle had begun, and the throng of sarcophs that lay before him was gathered like ants on spilled honey, lapping at the shores of a sea of knights. Among the walking dead, there stood behemoths of muscle and fur: Giants who looked unbeatable.

"It is a good day to die, brothers," Luthan yelled. And he stabbed his broadsword with all his strength into the expansive back of one of the beasts, ignoring the rotters around him. The blade must have reached his heart, for the Giant clutched his chest then fell dead. He was only the second one to fall, however. Now, though the knights had them surrounded and hopefully the tables would turn. *I'll make them turn.* Luthan thought.

K ELLEN PUT THE FINISHING touches on his contraption. It was a thick padding that he made to cover the tongue inside the bell. The food stores that lay in the room contained a number of sacks and he had stuffed these with as much food as possible before tying them to all sides of the clapper. Deagan's idea of strapping a headless rotter onto it was voted down six to one.

Deagan and the towermen who had sat on the shield, were now off it, having used the supplies and the silver chair to weigh down the metal well enough to keep the monsters at bay.

"That's Lord Othar over there," Gwyn explained as she looked again through the hole, "I'm sure of it. He's missing an arm. Although you three would know him as Jatham Holmin." Deagan had known Malagor's adviser was a snake, but didn't have him pegged for pure evil.

Then as she spied through the hole, Gwyn said, "Okay, now's our moment. Jatham just grabbed Saxus and ran inside. I don't know why, but this is our chance. Are you sure you can do this Rory?"

Rory was about to answer, but Kellen interrupted, "Have you seen the man climb, Gwyn? He can do it with one hand tied behind his back."

"Thank you, sir," Rory said. "Now let's see to it." He opened the door to the outside. It was a sheer drop of over sixty feet to the cobble stone streets below. He exhaled sharply, and drew back.

"You don't have to," Deagan said. "We can fight our way out of here."

Without answering, Rory blew out another preparatory breath and took the chain. The bell swung, but not far enough to make a sound. Then he took the plunge and he was out over a surely fatal drop. He swung a leg over the chain and began to inch toward the other side. Grim determination lined his brow, and then he picked up speed, gracefully swinging himself closer and closer to Cloud Tower.

"That's one hell of a butler," Kellen said in awe. Then he turned to Deagan. "You realize we're all doing this, don't you? Take your armor off, but by the Gods, do not leave your sword. I think you're going to need it."

Deagan knew that he was right, and he added his armor piece by piece to the pile of materials holding the shield down. Next, Kellen disappeared out through the door and crossed the chain. Then the towermen, and Gwyn. Where they ended up, Deagan didn't know. Apparently there was a chamber in Cloud Tower on the other side, but it was up and out of view. Now alone, Deagan's terror grew. He looked down at himself. Out of his armor, his figure took on a more human shape, a vulnerable one. He looked like an average man, losing the struggle to stay young and fit forever. He was not a hero in his normal garb, but a fearful man. His wounds ached anew and his legs grew weak. The bell swung violently behind him, thumping instead of tolling impressively, but he did not watch it. Instead his eyes looked down at the drop, to what looked a whole lot like death to him.

From here at the door, he could see the other end of the chain. It led to a window just a little higher than the bell tower. Gwyn had just made it there and the others pulled her inside. Across the divide, he saw her face turn to see his progress. Now, added to his fear, was the shame of fear. He was hungry. He was glad he was hungry though. It had been a lack of hunger that made his belly so big, and difficult to carry across insane chasms of doom.

He adjusted his sword to be sure it wouldn't fall out. What was worse, the shame or the fear? Gwyn beckoned to him. He shook his head. She beckoned again. He took a step back. Damn Rory and his strength!

He heard the voice of a woman long silent calling to him from across the gap. Gwyn yelled to him, "We need you!" Deagan suddenly wrestled his doubt to the ground and the fear inside him shut its mouth. It was Deagan and another task before him. That was all.

He grasped the chain, but hesitated. His heart nearly stopped and he felt weak. He squeezed the metal tighter, held on with both hands and struggled until one of his legs was over the chain. Then with great effort he went hand over hand across the deadly drop.

The chain sagged greatly under his weight more so than it had done under the weight of any of the others. He toiled on, looking only at the sky with both legs wrapped around the lifeline. His ungraceful climbing, shook the chain violently and back in the chamber, the clapper struck roughly against the side of the bell. Kellen's knots loosened, the food in the bags shifted. Finally the bag slipped off, revealing the metal of the bell's heavy tongue and instead of the dull thuds from before, the bell rang out in full. GONG! GONG! GONG! GA-GONG! Deagan yelled, "I told you a rotter would work better!"

What none of them knew however, was that the sagging bag of food that had silenced the bell, now swung back and forth hanging lower than before, knocking into the barricade on top of the shield. A crate fell off, then Deagan's armor. Soon all that remained was the chair lying on top of the shield. The rotters on the ladder below, who had never stopped pushing on the barrier, now met less resistance and lifted it off.

Deagan was almost to the other side of the climb, his grip loosening as he fought to hold up his weight. Then the first of the undead exited the door of the tower. It plummeted to the ground below and was followed by two more. "Look out!" Kellen yelled, and Deagan looked back to see the monsters trying to follow him. He laughed to watch them fall, but then, one grabbed hold of the chain. Without a leg over the chain, it swung toward him, surprisingly quickly. He doubled his efforts, but the monster still advanced. Another gripped the chain and came forward. *GONG! GA-GONG! GONG! GA-GONG!*

He now got to the steepest part of the climb and his hands were sweaty and slick. He could see the looks on his friends' faces as they leaned out the window toward him. "You should have closed the door, Deag!" Kellen yelled, drawing another laugh from Deagan's lips.

Deagan was almost to the window, his hands were just feet from the edge. But the chain was held tightly to the stone, and his slippery hands didn't know how to grab it. The rotters were still gaining. Being so close to the wall of Cloud Tower gave him perspective on the drop below. A flock of pigeons flew by below him and a wordless, exasperated grunt of fear escaped his throat.

"Almost there," Kellen said. "Come on!" Deagan inched closer, then stopped.

"I can't do it," he said.

"Shut your mouth," Kellen said, and reached for him. He grabbed his forearm with both hands. Rory leaned out farther and grabbed him under both arms. Gwyn's strong hands clutched his belt.

"I can't do it," he said again, ashamed, but no longer able to control his fear. The rotters gained, rattling the chain and making his grip even more questionable. *GONG! GONG! GONG! GA-GONG!* Though he had the support of three of the others, he feared that if he let go of the chain to let them pull him in, he imagined they'd all fall out the window together. "I'm too fat."

"Deagan! Deagan, listen to me," Kellen said. "Look right there. Do you see that rotter? He wants to kill you. He knows you've killed hundreds of his friends and relatives and he wants to eat your *daft, foolish* brain! But I for one, I'm not going to let that happen! Do you hear what I'm trying to tell you, man? Climb!"

At that, Deagan knew he owed it to his old friend to try, for now he had little to lose. He hoisted himself up, trusting the others to bring him the rest of the way. With lots of groaning from all involved, they pulled the man in and all tumbled onto the floor. Deagan lay there a while breathing heavy. Rory had his axe at the ready and stood guard by the window.

He had made it. Living through it gave him a euphoria that made him want to make hundreds of promises. Deagan's sense of duty eventually overcame his sense of relief, however, and he took to his feet, sword in hand. His eyes met Gwyn's, she too was out of her armor, and looked less the titan that she had seemed. A woman merely, but this made her more beautiful and more impressive than ever. She did indeed have wounds from their battle, though most were superficial. She seemed to favor her right leg. "Thank you," he said.

The sarcoph screamed as it fell off the chain, fingerless due to Rory's axe work. Deagan said, "Let's go kill this king of the dead. Where do you think he'll be, Gwyn?"

"Throne room."

"I don't suppose you know of any secret passages that might lead us in do you?"

"If Kellen didn't drop his lock picks on the chain crossing, then there might be a way," she said. In answer Kellen displayed his hand made tools.

"They're locksmithing tools, not lock picks," he said defensively.

"Watch out!" Deagan said as he pushed Rory aside. A claw raked the air where the butler had been. Then a few hacks of Deagan's sword sent the monster out of the window. It appeared to be the last one coming across the chain.

Deagan looked out to the open door high up on the bell tower. The sunlight shone in from outside, illuminating an interesting scene. Two rotters were working together to lower the silver chair through the hole in the floor. "What do you make of that?" he asked the others and they all gathered to look and wonder.

A towerman said, "I am sure that whatever their task, it will come to some evil end. I'm almost tempted to go back across and try to stop them." The others silently agreed with his sentiment, but all of them knew that their task lay ahead not behind, and they could not do everything at once.

HAZEN RAICHE'S SEARCH SOON turned up an old woman in their midst who knew about the secret way into Old Haven. Any who got close enough to listen to her heard the story of how she used to sneak through it to meet with a lover when she was young. Everyone nodded, laughed and smiled, but few believed her, except her husband, who of course had been the young man in her story, the object of her girlhood affections.

So she brought them to the stable where the tunnel opened into the heart of Old Haven, Ero flying overhead, leaping from rooftop to rooftop, to stay abreast. As Johan watched them, he thought he heard the laughter of the dead, but then assured himself it was only the people chattering below.

"Look at the sky!" someone yelled. The other Dragon Riders arrived casting impressive shadows on the cobble stones. They landed one by one falling more than flying out of the blue. Some of the Riders had to be harsh with their mounts to keep them from landing in the wrong places where they might ruin roofs, or get in the way. Every one of them sought shade or water, any relief from the heat. It was all they could do to keep themselves from brushing the burning saddle from their backs, rider and all, just to be rid of the temperature and the confinement. They were trained well enough not to do that though. Like Ero, other dragons now took their turns at the well, and another group of them found another one. Plumes of steam came up, and Johan knew it would be a few minutes before they were sorted out so he stayed with the armed villagers of Old Haven and protected them.

The stable they sought was a square building made of stones as old as those that comprised the walls and streets. On one wall, a great stallion reared up, depicted in colorful tiles. The building was sunken into the ground and each door led to a wide ramp, down which large wagons could be brought in order to reach the spacious stalls and workspaces below. Horses must have been shorter in those times, though. People generally believed that the makers had built the old stable into the ground to allow the horse's to escape the heat. It made sense, but it made the stable dark at all times, a perfect hiding place for a secret door.

Looking satisfied the old woman walked up and pointed into the darkness as she stood partway down the ramp. And then foul arms reached out to snatch her and she was carried into the darkness. Her old husband hobbled in after her, yelling at the monsters, and as he did a handful of warriors lurched forward to hold him back. A mass of unruly dead men poured out of the stable and up the ramp. The Haveners were just a little too late and most of the villagers panicked as the undead poured into what had been their last sanctuary.

Ero roared a song of war and Johan in his saddle urged him forward feeling weightless as the dragon dropped from the rooftop onto the street below. "Out of the way!" He bellowed, as Ero paced back and forth, the dragon fire close behind his teeth.

No one could hear him, and Old Haven's defenders were just as disorganized as the marauding sarcophs. Instead of working as one, forming a shield wall, they were separated and picked off. Some rotters fell, but just as many villagers did too. Some of them were city guards, but none of them were ready for this. Clearly it was only the advantageous position of this part of the city that had kept them alive so long and their survival had not relied on fighting prowess. Ero the red walked forward, swallowing his fire. He nosed his way into the battle and swept the living away with his wings. He boxed the undead into the ramp, but still there were a few living men endangered by his deadly breath. A few combatants remained in the way, so he reached forward with his talons to pull them free. The man, surprised, chopped at Ero's finger, his sword somehow finding its way between the scales, which drew a shriek from the dragon's maw.

Ero pulled him out and set him down nevertheless. As he turned to put the man on the ledge of the ramp, sarcophs lurching from the dark of the stable swarmed him. He roared again this time calling for help. Rusty swords were lodged in his wings and he tried to pull free, but pulling made the wounds rip wider and the pain was too great. If he leapt to safety, he knew that his wings would be torn so badly that he would never fly again.

Now it was only the dragon, the Rider and the enemy on the ramp and all the others stood by to watch. Sir Johan reached down to hack at the rotters, but there were too many. They began to gnaw on the leathery flesh of his dragon's wings. "Torch, 'em Smokey!" he commanded, but Ero shook his head, and howled. He tried to reach for Johan, to get him off of his back and put him safely beside the other man he had picked up, but Johan pushed his talon away. Ero clawed at the dead men, but some that tore at his wings were out of his reach. He slashed his tail and it drove them away, but they came quickly back.

Sir Oscar appeared sitting astride Pete the blue. They landed nearby, but hesitated, innocent people surrounded the scene and he couldn't urge Pete to breathe, risking so many lives, not to mention his dear friend Sir Johan. He was determined to help, but didn't know how yet.

"Torch them, Ero!" Sir Johan commanded again. But he knew that the dragon would not risk hurting his rider no matter what the cost to himself. There was one trick that all Dragon Riders hated to use for it was a breach of trust and it caused some harm to the dragon when it was done, but now Johan saw little other choice.

He pulled on Ero's reins speaking reassuringly to him. Ero resisted, but the reins held him fast. Ero felt his head being pointed to the ground at his feet. "Easy, boy," Johan said. "It's alright." The dragon protested again, but his Rider was determined to hold his head steady, there was nothing he could do but whine.

"Johan! No!" Oscar yelled, and Pete's wings opened in surprise. The blue dragon stomped his feet unsure of how to join the fray with nowhere to land other than on top of the surrounding villagers.

Johan pulled the wooden rod out from beside his saddle, the implement he'd been trained to use, but that he'd never needed before now. With both reins in one hand, he lifted one of Ero's scales on his lower throat. He hesitated for a moment, but then looked down into the mob at his feet. One of the rotters looked up from chewing on Ero's wing to look into Johan's eyes, and Johan smiled grimly back.

In a violent movement, the knight jabbed the rod under the lifted scale and into the flesh below. The red dragon gagged, and lurched forward. Johan jabbed again, and this time the fire came. It exploded from the dragon's mouth in all directions, slamming into the ground at his feet and spreading to the sides. The rotters fell away, those farthest away holding on longest. But Johan wouldn't let go of the rod. He held on for as long as he could, causing a bath of flames to engulf him from below.

"Goodbye, old friend." Johan said as he lost consciousness and slumped in the saddle. At last the horde of undead was no more. Those closest to the blast were nothing but blackened skeletons, those at his wings were well charred, but still looked human. Ero backed away chomping his teeth. He no longer heeded those around him, but limped up the ramp, and walked to the shade forcing the Haveners to make way. His body was painfully hot, but he was alright. Dragons hated the heat, but they were invincible to it. Dragon Riders on the other hand, were only human. And Johan was no different.

Oscar ordered four Riders to surround the stables. They were positioned at the gaping maw of each ramp when Oscar aptly yelled, "Fire!" Each of the four ramps was bathed in flame to rout out any additional rotters that waited inside and Oscar left the dragons to wait there in case more emerged. The thin knight then took some time to think. He decided that the source from the North was dealt with, and the only remaining threat was outside of Old Haven, so without removing the guards around the stable, Oscar sent the other Dragon Riders to aid Darkwell's army while he tended to Ero and Johan.

When he got there, Ero had gently gathered Johan in a talon, and laid him on the cool stones. Smoke still rose from his body. Ero breathed heavy, and each breath let out a high and pathetic whine. Oscar ran to his friend's side, sweat dripping down his sooty face. "Johan?" he asked. "Old friend?" There was no answer. "He needs his rest," Oscar said lamely. "Let me have a look at you."

The old slender knight stood and stretched the dragon's great wing out to its limits to see the damage. Bite marks, slashes, and holes made up as much of the surface as flesh did. He stretched the wing just a bit further and the beast shuddered in pain flicking droplets of hot blood like a light rain. Oscar heard a snap, and the whole wing quivered. The dragon pulled it back to his body and out of the knight's grasp. He was done being inspected, and all he needed now was to wait for Johan to wake up. He petted the knight on the ground. And he laid his chin on his rider's chest as he purred deep in his thorax and tried to sleep.

Oscar left him there. He had seen it before, not that it made this any easier. "Farewell, Johan." He said quietly.

Tears welled up in his eyes as he stood. There would be time for tears later. The opportunity for revenge however was fleeting. He mounted Pete, and sternly commanded him up. The dragon latched onto the stone wall that shaded the fallen knight, and climbed it swiftly. He reached the top, spread his wings, but stopped to look down at Ero and his rider.

"On, Pete," Oscar barely whispered and with a whine, Pete swooped down from Old Haven, ready to deliver his fire to the fell creatures below.

J ATHAM HOLMIN LIMPED AS he paced through the dark room, groaning through clenched teeth with veins in his neck on the verge of bursting. He examined the stump one more time, and cursed the star-horse for biting him so. In the death world he had, like a puddle of muck, no differentiated body parts, so he hadn't been sure what he would look like when he used the world shift to return.

He fondled the gold medallion around his neck, working his thumbnail into a slight indentation that marred its otherwise smooth surface and thought back to that cursed Royal Guard. Her spear tip had left a mark. He was not certain that he could still world shift now. Though the attack hadn't stopped him from disappearing at the time. With so much to do, however, Jatham didn't necessarily want to go back. Not now.

The army he had raised was most impressive so perhaps the missing arm was worth it. He was now ruler of Haven after all. But something nagged at him still. Who had climbed the tower below him when he first returned from the death plains?

He had just appeared in the bell tower where he'd hidden the chair, and had suddenly experienced the full pain of his mortal body. When he at last overcame the initial shock, he distinctly heard the sound of the ladder being lowered in the tunnel below. Escape was his first directive so he did not oversee the extermination of his pursuers first hand, but he wasted no time ordering his legions of sarcophs to swarm the tower. Had his minions killed the intruders or did they somehow escape? Did they find the chair—the chair that provided the anchor point he needed to survive the world shift?

Jatham spun around as if someone had snuck up on him when he heard a terrifying sound: the ringing bell.

It had been so loud when he had commanded Saxus to take hold of the chain and carry him across to safety that it threatened to deafen him! The peeling of Haven's alarm bell was not so loud now as it had been then and he knew the difference in volume had an explanation other than his now greater distance from it. It sounded muffled.

A dragon flew by the high narrow windows of the dark throne room. Jatham jumped to the nearest shadows. Three more sailed past. He was glad he'd prepared for the likes of them. He clenched his remaining fist around the medallion and used its power to see through the eyes of his army.

Turbid visions pounded through his head. His heartbeats sounded like booming tympanis, and each one brought the perspective of a different sarcoph. Some vantage points through which he peered were still speckled with the dirt of the grave, others lacked depth perception due to a missing eye, and all of them looked foggy and contorted. Just as the limbs and bones of his sarcophs did not function as well as they had in life, so too with the eyes.

Doom Boom! He saw through the eyes of a rotter looking down at his feet, holding a dead rat in one hand and a pitch fork in the other.

Doom Boom! The next sarcoph was looking out a shop window at the battlefield, spikes of metal obscuring his view.

Doom Boom! He saw through the eyes of a sarcoph just before its head was cut off by a mounted knight of Darkwell.

Doom Boom! Distant shadow. Scales and claws.

The dragons were coming, but were not there yet. Jatham's troops were so pliable, so useful. He loved them. They had accomplished so much.

He opened his eyes emerging from his strange reverie. Standing before him was the Royal Lord Saxus, the one he had made into the king of the dead. Saxus was the only one who could hear commands in the spoken speech. He was the only one who could send those orders to the rest. "Listen, I have work for you."

"Yes, master," Saxus breathed.

"I heard the bell ring. Do you remember the bell?"

"Yes master."

"Then bring some men to the bell room to find what has happened. Leave none alive. And ready the jumpers. Tell them the dragons are coming."

"Yes master." The armored ghoul bowed and walked away, but before he left, he turned.

"What is it, Saxus?"

"Th-ank . . . you."

A smile played on the bald man's lips for the first time since returning to the living world. "For what?" Jatham asked.

"Pow . . . er," Saxus pronounced carefully. "It was all . . . I wanted . . . but could never . . . have enough."

"I know the feeling," Jatham said. "But you have enough now, thanks to me."

"I . . ." Saxus began, his lidless eyeballs staring into Jatham's own.

"What did you say?" Jatham asked smiling, expecting more praise from his prized creation. Saxus was elegant as though laid out in honor in preparation for his death, but his face was shriveled and skeletal and when he ceased moving, he did so utterly, leaving onlookers with the sense he was dead.

"What were you saying?" Jatham asked, stepping closer.

The standing dead man still said nothing. His eyeballs only stared bleakly into Jatham's. Jatham went closer, examining his creation to see if the monster was somehow broken. Then the one armed man gasped when Saxus finally inhaled.

"I . . . Could kill you," Saxus said. And unmoving, he stared at his master.

Chilled to the bone, Jatham felt instantly alone as if in a nightmare. Saxus stood half in and half out of the secret door.

Staring. Jatham was paralyzed, horrified at his vulnerability in the face of what he'd created. He looked down to his bloody stump. He tried to think of something else to say, to make sure that the thing wouldn't kill him. Had he imagined these last words? He couldn't remember. He forced himself to stand up.

"No, Saxus," Jatham said. "I don't believe you could." He lifted the gold medallion in front of him. "I command you to carry out my bidding, Saxus. Now!"

The thought of speaking frightened him so deeply that he barely forced himself to do it. "*Carry out my bidding,*" Jatham whispered. Instead, the undead lord, came closer and drew his sword. Jatham backed away into the dark corner. There was a flash of silver, but the blade came up short.

The dead king pushed upon the quivering blade, but as if it had hit a wall it went no further. He wheeled back for another strike and again Jatham's aura repelled the sword and he began to laugh. Saxus reached for Jatham with a gauntleted, skeletal hand, but this too was frozen in mid-air feet away from Jatham's slight frame. Jatham stepped forward toward Saxus' grasp and the knight flew backward onto the floor.

"Will that be all, Saxus?" Jatham laughed. "Now go! Do as you're told."

L UTHAN CROSSED SWORDS WITH a dead man in the middle of Haven. The reason for this was simply that the rotter stood between the knight and the Giant he intended to kill. This wasn't his own sword either, but one picked up from the armaments of the fallen. His was still lodged deep in a Giant's back. Several more Giants lay dead now. So did many knights. One of the Giants had picked up a piece of rubble from the street. He pulled it back for a throw.

"LOOK OUT!" Luthan screamed, and he broke the engagement with the sarcoph short so he could move away from the boulder. By the time it flew, however, he hadn't moved far. It was only luck then that it took the life of another knight instead of his own. The man who fell under the rock was a brave one. It was Sir Tieg. Gone as quickly as that, and with no chance to say goodbye.

A spear stood up from the body of a corpse. Still on horse back, Luthan yanked it free and charged the Giant who hurled the stone. Once he was within range he hurled the spear, and drew his sword. The spear connected, and it certainly got the monster's attention. "Die, thing!" Luthan yelled as he swept at the Giants massive arm with his blade. The edge caught, and drew thick blood, but the Giant was quick to riposte.

His club came around and found Luthan's shield at the ready. The blow numbed his arm, almost unhorsed him, and his shield dropped lifelessly to his side. His brave horse, Luka carried him away from the battle. No matter what he did, the arm would not move, and behind him, his massive foe stepped over the dead men and horses to come chase him down. Luthan struggled to tear the heavy shield from his shattered arm. Finally it clattered to the ground. His men were flagging. Progress against the Giants was slow, but their numbers were few, so each kill was important and gave hope. There were four more of them. But so many knights were dead. Then a shadow passed overhead. *Dragons.*

Now this was a battle that horsemen could not win. "Retreat!" he called to his soldiers. "Scatter, and meet on the plains. We will regroup there." As they were ordered, the men scattered. The first belch of fire came from above, and Luthan shielded his eyes with his good arm. He would not turn to see which of his fellows had been consumed by it for witnessing those deaths would do him no good.

The knights escaped, and indeed they gathered outside the city. Luthan's face was set in a grimace as though the tightness of his frown could lock the pain in a cage. "You need help!" one of the knights told him. "You'll do no good in this battle now."

"I may yet," Luthan answered through gritted teeth. They watched the dragons swoop and swerve heaving flames into the ranks of . . . the undead. Could it be? They weren't attacking Darkwell at all.

When the flying reptiles came close to the footmen, the ballistae were shot, sending bolts like spears against them. Two of the dragons went down. Crushing sarcophs and humans alike as they plummeted onto the fray. The rest of the Riders turned back in retreat.

As they soared low, scorching the undead host in the streets of Haven, shadows fell from above. Spiked demons descended from the rooftops. They were living corpses like the others, but pierced throughout with sharpened iron spikes that emerged from them at all angles. Most of them missed, impaling and crushing the sarcophs below, but whenever a dragon went too close to a building, the full rooftop of the spear laden rotters jumped down, and en masse they took dragons down.

"Whose side are they on?" Luthan asked the man beside him quietly. "Whose side are they on?" he asked louder. "They aren't killing men! They're killing *them*. Do you see that?" He challenged, hollering to his men. Grudgingly they nodded, not sure whether they should believe their eyes.

"Step forward if you took an oath on the ride today!" he ordered. Slowly, most of the men, stepped forward. There were only one or two hundred left. "Then we must not stand by while our allies are slain. Gather around me! Listen, and you shall hear the plan."

After brief discussion, the men departed. New energy invigorated them even though at their cores they knew that they were about to commit unthinkable crimes. But an oath was an oath and knights were no strangers to them.

They dismounted and entered the ranks of the footmen while Luthan rode out to meet Duke Worth on his hillock. He gritted his teeth as each of Luka's jolts shocked his arm with pain.

He finally reached the smug duke's position and reined in his steed. "Call off the ballistae! The dragons are helping us!" Luthan shouted. "Can't you see that? Look they're burning the enemy! Why kill them?"

The duke turned to face him. "Something's wrong with your arm. Were you hit on the head as well? They are just as much our enemy as the sarcophs are."

"You lie! Call off the ballistae, now!"

"What is the matter with you?" The duke demanded hotly, "You gave me your word that you and your men would follow orders no matter what they were. Have you forgotten that? If that isn't something you can handle, then perhaps you aren't cut out for this!"

Luthan winced as he pulled the gold chain over his head. The symbol of his knighthood dangled from his clenched hand. He remembered when Deagan had relinquished his own chain not long ago and he cursed himself for being a part of it. "Perhaps you're right," he said solemnly and he dropped the chain onto the ground. Duke Worth met the gesture with a blank stare, motionless except for the twitch in his left eye. Then from his belt, Luthan pulled a horn, raised it to his lips and sounded three notes.

At once, the knights who he had positioned at each of the Duke's giant crossbows set upon the ballistae with axes, swords, and whatever else they had, rendering them useless in less than a minute. They slashed the thick chords that served as bow strings, hacked at the wooden limbs, and smashed the ammunition. The footmen cried out in defiance, but were so surprised by the sabotage that they could not react and the knights rode back to regroup before one of the footmen even made his way to the duke to tell him what happened.

"I pity you, Duke Worth," Luthan said. "King Malagor has given you a hundred reasons to desert him, and still you pretend there is something noble in Darkwell. Something worth defending."

"There is, Luthan. There is a king! The people of Haven never fought bravely in history. They have no spirit of war, no pride. These things come from a king, and they soak down to the people. There is no hope, or pride in a Royal Lord. It takes a king to rule the great cities and keep evil at bay.

"There will be consequences for your actions on this day, Sir Luthan."

"It's just Luthan now, Duke."

"You have chosen wrongly Luthan. Goodbye." Duke Worth turned back to watch the battle and Luthan left. Duke Worth called some of his marshals to him.

Before he left, Luthan said, "Look not to the cavalry for help this day, Worth."

The fighters who had triumphantly disarmed the ballistae returned and exchanged congratulations and praise. Then one of them, sweaty and battle worn hushed the others, his mouth agape as he looked to Luthan who rode back from his confrontation with the duke.

"Sir Luthan! Where is your chain?"

"Its just Luthan now," he said. "My chain is at Duke Worth's miserable feet and I hope he trips on it." He looked up at the men with a wily grin on his face. "I am just a man now. I do not have the favor of the duke or the king. I know that I ask for much, but I only do so because I must. If you will still follow me willingly, we still have work to do. This battle is not yet over. And there are many questions unanswered."

D EAGAN, KELLEN, RORY, GWYN and the rest set out. The secret passage that they sought was in the larder in a lower level of Cloud Tower, so they went downstairs. Gwyn was in front, she led them through the twists and turns of the palatial fortress she had lived in for most of her life. In an effort to gain his bearings, Deagan made a point of remembering most of the turns that they took; Kellen remembered all of them. Rory straightened things up a bit as he went.

Suddenly an animated corpse lunged from a closet, and without a second though, Deagan punched it in the jaw, spinning its head around backwards, and knocking it back in the closet. Kellen knocked over a statue in front of the door and they kept going.

Then they made a final turn through a richly carved door and into a room with chandeliers, a balcony that ringed the outside overlooking a grand ball room from a height of ten feet up. There were two staircases that led down from the balcony to the stone floor below. It was a feasting hall fit for an emperor, with tables and chairs, tapestries, and the skins of large predators, and both the balcony and the room below were lined with doors.

At the bottom of the stairs before them, there was a menacing throng. They looked ghostly and recently exhumed, as though they were members of a different and more dangerous breed of sarcophs. They were strangely intelligent looking, and reminded Deagan of the stories he had been told as a young man of epic heroes from elder days. Dirt caked their armor and shields and they were dressed like warriors from the north with horned helmets and high boots.

They moved forward expressionlessly as though they were characters in a tapestry stepping off the wall, but not yet fully alive.

Then from another door on the balcony, shadowed under a windowless portion of the room where no candles burned, there appeared more shambling figures advancing to meet them where they stood.

The group was set upon from both sides, the laughter and stench were both present, but also there loomed a dark will. It was a foul power that seemed to choke the senses with its malice. The towermen, who had been in front of Deagan, lost heart and turned back, muttering unintelligible complaints and protests. Deagan caught two of them by the scruff of their necks and dragged them back. "Just one more battle lads, that's all it is. Nothing to be afraid of," he said.

The towermen relented and turned back to face the enemy, with sweat pouring down their faces. The rotters on the balcony advanced into the light of the windows, and the hazy yellow illumination shone through the foremost one's clouded eyeballs. His hair was tousled and brown, and he looked recently dead, hardly decayed at all. His face was slack, but even so, Kellen remembered him. It was Jorn Kahorne, one of the men on his caravan to Haven that never made it back alive. Beam had warned him that this had happened, but now he had the proof. Behind Kahorne followed his other waggoners, their skin clammy, but not tight over their bones, their movements clumsy, but not frail.

"Jorn Kahorne!" Kellen called. "So good to see you. What brings you to Cloud Tower today?" In answer, Jorn's mouth opened slightly, and he brandished the bloody dagger in his hand. "Look, old friend, I didn't know the road was dangerous. I didn't know that you'd be . . . attacked. I sent you with guards didn't I! I can't be blamed for this!" And Kellen backed away, his breathing rapid.

"He can't even understand you Kellen," Gwyn said. "Just be strong."

But a thousand thoughts rushed through Kellen's head. *I knew the road was less than safe. I knew that others hadn't made it home from Haven and that news from there had all but ceased. Now it seems that this invasion of undead must have been the cause of that lack of tidings, but at the time, safe in my accursed mansion with my butler to provide for me, I never bothered to find out!*

Kellen moved behind Gwyn and Rory. The Northmen started up the stairs, moving as one in a shield wall. "Kellen," Deagan said. "Come help me with these. There's no need to worry about your men."

But Kellen found he couldn't turn his back on them, for he felt they would leap and kill him at any moment no matter how far he inched away. Behind them walked a steady form. At first he looked human rather than undead because he looked so strong and vital. But in reality, he was anything but alive. It was Lord Saxus, with his unblinking orbs shining in the sun. He was momentarily shadowed by a dragon flying past the window.

Gwyn tightened her grip on the sword and looked at Rory. They lifted their weapons and went to meet the dead waggoners. Deagan formed up with the towermen across the stairs in a tiny shield wall. "Steady," Deagan said. But he was the first one to disobey his own order. The dead warriors were still steps away yet he pounced on them slashing like the devil. His sword stung their faces, and in a fury, he struck three of them in his initial attack, before any of them could raise a shield to defend. Deagan snarled and barked, he grunted and growled. He was tired, but he wouldn't let this horde pass him, with the dead king in sight, he thought this might be his last battle anyway, so he held nothing back. The armor of his foes was corroded and old, but it held up to his strikes, these were the toughest dead he'd fought so far, for his blows would not knock them aside. Finally he severed a sword hand then shoved another one over the railing. But there were plenty more of them to fill in the gaps and his struggle continued.

They jabbed at him and gave him war, but he wouldn't be pushed back. The towermen now stepped forward to help, terrified and weakened. As one of the Northmen stepped up, Deagan broke his advance by kicking him in the face to knock him off balance. There were some perks to taking your armor off. The dead man fell back into his fellows, but they caught him and forced him back into position.

Above, Rory and Gwyn stepped through the fray. The butler knocked a sarcoph onto the railing then wrestled the thing's bony legs over the side, dashing him to the stone floor below. Gwyn did battle with Jorn Kahorne and Kellen's caravan. "Look away, Kellen," she advised. She didn't look back to see if Kellen had taken her advice, but she couldn't delay any longer, and Jorn's head was cut in half from above, his arm lopped off, and a kick to the center of his chest brought him down.

They advanced, but so did the ghouls. Rory and Gwyn didn't know whether Kellen recognized any more of them, but he still wouldn't join the fray. He hung back in fear and guilt. Rory glanced away to check on Kellen, and took a slash to his arm while distracted and cried out.

Gwyn felt another wound open on her shoulder, and in retaliation she felled the sarcoph with a chop that buckled his knee. She descended on him savagely, taking him apart. Chunks of gore flew out from over the railing and fell down to where the towermen fought on the staircase. The sight of these flying body parts disgusted the towermen and they blanched, but they didn't run.

Deagan held the stairs, but the progress was slow. He beheaded two of them, but stalled out, wasting his strikes against their armor and shields. A jab found its mark on his shin and he stumbled, but he pulled away in time and cut into his attackers wrist, leaving the hand limp and mostly severed. Still the monsters advanced.

Then the battle worsened for the humans, for the Royal Lord stepped in to fight. His sword was long, his armor thick. He wielded his blade swiftly, but Gwyn noticed that his technique was basic. He was impressive next to the other undead, but compared to her knew friend Deagan, the dead man looked clumsy. She engaged him, ducking under his sword and getting in close, where the advantage of his reach would be diminished. "Kellen, help us!" she said.

And finally, Kellen got up, drew his sword in a shaky hand and stepped closer. The look on his face was proof enough that he wasn't yet ready to fight. Gwyn blocked three heavy blows from Saxus' sword making an opening to drop her blade onto his forearm, but the metal there deflected her attack. Saxus' weapon spun around and she stepped back out of the way, losing the benefit of her positioning.

Behind her, Jorn Kahorne clawed his way toward Kellen. His head was still attached, but hung in two pieces giving him double vision of the worst kind. Gwyn had severed his arm, but it must have been the one that already lacked its hand thanks to Beam. Kahorne still held a dagger and he crawled closer to Kellen who stood at the ready, but was too afraid to be of much use. He was too ashamed to ask for help after being unable to give help to others.

"Jorn," he whispered. "Look what's happened to you. This wasn't supposed to happen."

Deagan glanced up to the balcony, just long enough to see Kellen's predicament. "Kellen, I love you, but don't try my patience. You know what you have to do, now get in there and do it." With a grunt, he dispatched another of the Northmen, withdrawing his blade from its spilling guts just in time to block a shot aimed at the top of his head.

"Listen to me Kellen. I would help you, but I can't right now. No one can help you. You have to help yourself. Quit running away and fight." He crossed swords with the sarcoph, and a towerman slashed the same one's gut, links of chain fell, but he made no wound.

Gwyn was face to face with the Royal Lord, his eyes held hers, and she thought he might remember her from all her years of service in his throne room. He raised his hand and faced the palm to her, and a wave of unnatural fear swept over her. Another rotter attacked, and it appeared to be more than she could bear. Rory felt it too, and backed away, panting. Before Deagan's eyes the warriors in front of him became nightmarish and horrible as Saxus' power swept over him. Their faces became terrifying enough that he stepped back and shielded his eyes.

But then he shook his head and remembered the chain crossing. He relived the moment of paralysis he had felt, frozen at the last leg of the climb. He remembered the words of his friends, urging him to keep trying. After that, nothing could turn him back. He fought on, frightened, but in no more danger than before. The towermen turned and ran and where they went, Deagan would never know.

Saxus said, "I am Lord here. There . . . is no . . . escape."

Kellen heard Jorn's voice. *Why did you send us there, Wayfield? You knew we would die. You knew.* But he convinced himself it wasn't real. Even still, he was paralyzed as the grotesque figure came closer.

Gwyn lashed out at his upraised hand, but he drew it away swiftly, meeting her sword with his own. The fear diminished, but did not disappear. Cold sweat still soaked Deagan's brow. Gwyn moved to attack Saxus, but two rotters intercepted her, gibbering and frantic, the first one latched onto her arm, trying to sink its teeth into her living flesh. The other one swung with a battle-ax, its head was hooded in chain mail. She spun, and put the rotter on her arm in the path of the axe, which descended on the dead man's back, causing it to flinch. She pushed it away, and Rory cut its head off. The hooded sarcoph and another two of them forced Rory to the edge and had him leaning off the railing. Finally this got Kellen's attention.

"Rory!" he said. Jorn came closer and Kellen would have to deal with him soon. Still he couldn't move to attack, but he raised his sword tip.

Rory was forced farther over the edge while Gwyn was engaged with Saxus and could not help him. He was about to lose his balance. The butler rolled to one side to dodge a sword stroke, but still the hands pushed him. Kellen heard Jorn again, *You should have died with us. You sent us to die!* With Rory in danger, Kellen had had enough. "Sorry, Jorn. My mistake," and he cut off the other arm, leaving the man unarmed.

He then found the rope holding up a chandelier and unhitched it from the wall. He sheathed his sword and drew his dagger, clenching it in his teeth. He took three swift steps then soared out from the balcony in a wide swing. He avoided all the dismembered corpses that would have snatched at him, he avoided Saxus, and he landed on the railing beside Rory. Then he grabbed his friend under the arms and pulled him free, swinging back the way he had come. Rory's strong grip found the rope above Kellen's hand, and they landed on the railing farther from harm.

Deagan cheered as Rory and Kellen got onto the balcony and let go of the rope. The chandelier fell rapidly and landed on the mass of Northmen occupying the stairway.

Kellen and Rory rushed to help Gwyn who was momentarily alone. Deagan cheered again. His growls and barks grew louder, for now he felt invincible. He held the stairs, one against many.

Now Kellen and Rory took care of the rest of the rotters for as much as Kellen avoided battle, he was skilled with his sword and the two of them seemed to work together in concert more gracefully than hunting lions. They dispatched the undead until all that remained was the Royal Lord locked in combat with Gwyn Androth.

Kellen saw his chance, and pulled the knife from his teeth to take aim. Then with a smooth and forceful movement, he hurled it at Saxus. The blade stabbed into his forehead, and they all paused, to see if he would die.

"No . . . blade . . . can hurt me," he said. "For I . . . am lord here." He lunged at Gwyn, chopping at her relentlessly until his strength overcame hers, and her blade was broken in two. She backed away, her footing was unsteady on the slippery dead. Kellen watched as the undead lord pulled the blade from his forehead. Not a drop of blood decorated its silver sheen. The king of the dead then turned and threw the dagger back at Kellen. The length of it plunged into his upper chest, close to the joint of his shoulder and blood spurted from the wound. Kellen fell back against the railing, clutching it.

Rory was filled with new strength and he charged. Saxus blocked half of the blows with his great sword, but let the other half land on his body. This time the laughter was not otherworldly, but very real, as the Lord displayed his invulnerability. He caught Rory's ax blade with his hand. Rory's muscles bulged as he tried to tear it away, but the steel was clamped firmly in the monster's grip. Saxus slashed into the butler's side and kicked him away.

Deagan raced up the stairs, and knocked a statue down onto his assailants hoping it would keep them at bay. Gwyn was alone with the invincible opponent, and he did not know whether Rory and Kellen would survive. Deagan ran to challenge the Royal Lord and shouldered his way in front of Gwyn. He did not charge foolishly into battle, he stayed six feet away, raised a shield, crossed his sword calmly over the top and looked through the gap as he took a deep breath. He was a shield wall of one. Saxus laughed again and struck at him. Deagan blocked it. He was relieved to be fighting only one opponent.

"He may be telling the truth, Gwyn." Deagan said as sparks flew from his shield under the glancing blow of his enemy's sword. "Maybe we can't kill him. We *can* get away, though. Bring Rory and Kellen out of here. I'll hold him off."

Saxus spread his arms wide inviting an attack, but Deagan saved his strength. He waited in a defensive position. Gwyn went to Rory and Kellen. They were both alive. But their fighting was done.

"Get them out of here Gwyn." Deagan repeated. Blood dripped from his wounds and onto the floor. Even more blood flowed down his sword, soaking the ground. Saxus set upon him with vengeance. He swung and swung, and his blows were heavy, but he could not get through Deagan's defenses.

Kellen could walk on his own, so the two of them helped Rory out through the door. They tied rags tightly around his wounds and he did not complain. "It hurts," he said matter-of-factly. "But it won't kill me."

"It would take more than that to kill my Rory," Kellen agreed. Gwyn led them to a separate room, where they could no longer hear the fighting, or sense the evil. Sun streamed in. Kellen winced as he slumped against the wall beside his friend. "Can you imagine getting your own knife thrown back at you? It's the worst," he said. He looked down at the hilt of his dagger, bristling from his upper chest. The two of them sat together in the room, and Gwyn closed the door behind her.

She rushed to Deagan.

Deagan stood steadfast before his enemy. He never swung his sword except to block. The Royal Lord had stopped laughing. He groaned with frustration.

"I . . ."

"I know, I know," Deagan interrupted. "You are lord here." He rolled his eyes.

Gwyn came in. She armed herself with the weapons of the dead, including the largest shield she could find. The effort of lifting it forced blood from the wound on her shoulder, but nevertheless she stood beside Deagan, adding her defense to his.

"Deagan," she said. "This can't go on forever."

S IR OSCAR YELLED, "To the sky! To the sky!" and Pete boldly repeated his words in Dragon. They lifted up and away from the enemies, out of range of the nasty ballistae, and above the falling, spiked corpses. He had lost too many this day, and Oscar was ready to put an end to it.

The other Riders flew up to greet him. None of them were pleased. The battle had turned out badly. Oscar did not know what to do. After being attacked by the Darkish, he had no allegiance left to them. But the undead were invading his home. He wanted to do something about it without risking more lives.

The Dragons soared in rising circles. They flapped their wings little, and they stayed silent, resting not rallying. The meditation of flight always cleared Oscar's head. He shifted in his saddle to ease the burning on his legs, but it was no use. The tactics he had in mind were simple: take out the spiked jumpers first, then attack the rear flank of the undead army. When the Darkish army came into view they would simply leave, perhaps never to return. He feared that the Dragon Riders would be forced to live in exile, with no acceptance from humankind, the great cities no longer friendly to their presence.

Somber musings aside, Oscar knew that the reason they had lost lives was simply due to the element of surprise employed by the enemy. *Well*, he mused, *that and the back stabbing betrayal of Darkwell*. Now that the surprise was sprung, it would be easy work to incinerate the spiked jumpers on the rooftops, then sink down to continue raking the rear flank of the horde.

The question that plagued him, however, was where would they go after their part in the battle was done? To the South their lay another of the great cities, Pillar, ruled by Everach the young barbarian king. He was said to be just. A king like that could have need of these men and beasts. But dragons were not seen as friendly these days, and whether they'd be allowed in the city at all would be a gamble.

With a deep breath, he cleared his head. Whatever happened would happen, and he knew that however the battle went, he still had his brothers, the knighthood of the wind that still survived. Whatever fate befell him, Oscar would not have to face it alone. "Riders!" He cried wearily, but with gusto. Pete echoed him in Dragon. All ears were on him. Only the soft wind and the dragons' wings interrupted the silence. He thought of sharing his thoughts of exile, and he opened his mouth to begin, but instead he yelled. "DIVE! DIVE ON THE ROOFTOPS! LEAVE NONE ALIVE!" And before any could respond, he had already followed his own orders, Pete's wings folded into his sides as the pair shot downward like a stone, hurtling to deal death to those who had missed their chance at it once already. The slim knight was in a war-crouch, one hand on the hilt of his prized sword. Rapidly the enemy grew as he fell. He could sense the determination in Pete's soul, the roaring silence of his concentration as he adjusted a wingtip to bring them closer to the mark.

Then all at once, the fire erupted from his throat, his wings flared out and bodies toppled from all sides of the rooftop. The dragon's four feet landed on the hard surface of the roof, and instantly spun. His tail knocked enemies away behind him, Oscar's sword slashed at those in front. Then, with a leap, the pair was gone, and the smoldering undead perished in the flames of their clothes, even as their assailants attacked another rooftop.

Pete jumped from the first one to the next, stonework crumbled from beneath his mighty claws, and he roared his song of battle. The explosions of his comrades descending on other rooftops like comets from the sky sounded from all around him. Pete clung to the side of the building. Oscar let go of the reins and locked his fist around a loop on the saddle. Pete peered above the edge of the roof and swept it with fire. He ducked below the plane of the roof, and undead toppled from above him. One of them fell over his back. And Oscar clung tighter to the saddle. The spiked monster fell to the ground, spreading the fire. Another blast of flame annihilated the rest of them, and Pete was airborne in moments.

As weary as they were, the dragons picked up speed, and the rooftops were cleared in minutes. They then rose up and formed an airborne line. Oscar ordered the attack on the rear flank. They dove as one and each street was bathed in fire. When they got close enough to Darkwell's force, Oscar pulled up on the reins and the dragons all followed the arc of Pete's flight. Then they landed on the streets, wreathed in the aftermath of their own assault. Edging the line of their breath ever closer. Pinching the dead men against the forces of Darkwell.

"Halt!" Oscar cried. And Pete barked as he nipped at another dragon's neck in a signal to stop. Though they were enemies still, their fight was done. For on the far side of the sarcophs' ranks, Darkwell's men stood in shield walls. And though the Riders could do much to help, could save many lives, Oscar ordered them to turn back, and leave these former allies to whatever fate awaited them. He was not willing to risk any more of his kind. Some of the rotters turned to blankly stare at the quiet dragons. The dragons stared back then turned around and leapt to the sky.

As the dragons lifted up, some of them carried the bodies of their dead. It took two to carry one, but the toil was worth it to them, to prevent any further feasting on their kindred's flesh. One of the dragons was little more than a skeleton, but it held together well enough to be carried away.

"Wait," Oscar muttered through his mustache. "Sir Goodsing, who is missing?" Oscar looked over his shoulder, but he couldn't find them. He wheeled Pete around with Warmaker close behind, the green fan at the tip of his tail flashing in the sun. Back and forth they ranged to find the missing Riders. Then from between two smoking buildings, there rose not three but four dragons. The fourth was one who had fallen to a ballista shot during the first attack. She didn't have a wound, though her brave Rider was nowhere to be found. She was a yellow dragon, small and sleek. One of the other riders held her reins from a long way off, having tied extra length to the ropes.

Ranger, she held something in her claws. She did not want to be led as she was, but the other three dragons surrounded her, and a dragon below her prevented her from landing, and the reins kept her from turning to either side for this was how unwilling dragons were customarily escorted.

"Conner," Oscar breathed. He turned back to his course. They would land next in Old Haven. Tears flowed down his cheeks, leaving clean streaks in his soot-blackened face. He knew that Ranger's talons held her dead rider. Oscar nearly turned back to rain death on the Darkwellians. He dreamed of soaring over their heads and attacking the city itself. But these dark thoughts would remain fantasies.

Forlorn and crestfallen, the Riders left their task undone. They retreated while their enemy still threatened Haven. The dragons keened and wailed. They coughed and wheezed, choking themselves on their bridle straps. They turned back to the battle and had to be reined in, for they didn't understand that the humans would betray them or that this was something Oscar would not risk.

The three others escorted Ranger up and over the walls of Old Haven where she gently placed her dead Rider on the paving stones, then alighted and coiled around him, whimpering her own name for him that we humans would fail to say

J ATHAM HEARD A THUMPING on the doors of the throne room. It sent fear through his blood at first, but soon he heard the groans and the disembodied laughter of the undead, and knew they were some of his minions. He opened the doors, and a group of sarcophs came in, carrying his silver chair. It was a bit worse for the wear, two tines were missing from the back, and it had a few dents in it, not to mention the red patina of his own sticky blood that coated it. The servants placed the chair down on its side.

"Not like that!" Jatham whined and he picked up the chair and wrestled it onto its four legs. Then he grasped his dented medallion and said imperiously, "Guard."

The servants scattered throughout the room and then stood still. He regretted not having the control that Saxus had over them. One-word orders were all he could get them to follow, but the royal lord was able to give complex commands and he could order them with or without being in range of their hearing. He was a good commander for the troops, but he lacked vision and needed Jatham to provide that for him.

Jatham strained as he closed, locked, and barred the doors to the throne room. He needed no disturbances now. He felt the stump of his missing arm, and his hand came back bloody. It would be difficult to heal from this. He felt faint from blood loss. The sensation gave the world a distant appearance, as though he was removed from the physical reality around him.

He was dizzy, and he sat in his chair to rest as he looked through the eyes of his troops. *Doom Boom! Doom Boom! Doom Boom!* The dragons had taken their toll, but had since retreated. This battle may be his after all. And after it was done and he was no longer needed to command the sarcophs, he could return freely to the death world and harvest all the fallen to swell his numbers even further.

D EAGAN, GWYN AND SAXUS all stood still contemplating their stale mate. Saxus walked to the other side of the balcony, but they mirrored him and he was still barred from passage. He ran at them suddenly to break through, but just before he reached them, Deagan shoved himself forward with his powerful legs, catching Saxus while he was between steps, with one foot off the ground. It felt like colliding with a tree, but nevertheless, the Royal Lord was lifted off his feet and thrown backward. Lying on his back, he looked up at his enemies. Then he groaned and looked to the dead Northmen, still baffled on the stairs, each one clawing at the statue that blocked their way. They all turned to look at him. Then as one, they lifted the statue and threw it over the railing. It smashed on the ground, and they advanced up the stairs.

"You see . . . I am . . . lord here." Saxus said as he stood up.

Gwyn stayed in her guard, but she was thinking hard.

"Come on," Deagan said to her. "We don't want them behind us." She followed his lead, and they backed up quickly to the doorway through which they had entered this room. *Snick! Thwack!* The first slashes of the Northmen narrowly missed them, and one blade lodged itself in the doorframe. Deagan ignored the fatigue and weight of his sword arm. He ignored the fact that he had no armor. Those thoughts would only distract him. He took the head of a Northman.

Gwyn said, "Saxus!" The undead lord looked at her but did not reply. "You say you are lord here, but you know this isn't true." Deagan glanced over, confident in her, but still not sure what her plan was.

"You answer to another. You follow his orders. What would happen to you if he were to die?" She slashed at the rotter in the doorway. It was a good position to defend and if they were pushed, there would be another doorway to fall back to. Saxus stopped in his tracks and said nothing.

Gwyn turned to Deagan, "It might be our only chance, and it might not be a chance at all. But one of us needs to go up to the throne room and find that crooked adviser Jatham Holmin. We need to kill him."

"If you say so," Deagan answered. "You go. I wouldn't be able to find it, I'll hold them off down here to give you time. Good luck."

"Be careful," Gwyn said as she let Deagan slide her out of the way so he could block the entire doorway. He heard her footsteps leave, but he wouldn't let himself turn to see her. Then he was alone. A striving, hideous mass tried to get past him, but he would not be pushed back. Hands, feet, heads all flew from their rightful places, but still the sarcophs pushed on him. A stray blade found his shoulder, crossing another wound that already dyed his tunic red. He retaliated with a thrust to the eyes, blinding the one in front of him. He didn't need to kill them, just slow them down long enough so Gwyn could kill her man Jatham Holmin. So he left the one in front of him able to swing, but blind. The others waved their weapons behind the one in front, but it was no use, the doorway was only wide enough for one.

GWYN RUSHED UP THE stairs, feeling light and energetic without the weight of her armor. She hoped that her hunch was right, and that she might be able to put an end to this with one slash of her sword.

She forced her way through another door and rushed through the passageways. A group of rotters that had lingered in a side chamber became alerted to her presence and gave chase, but she sprinted past and was at the far end of the hall and through another door before they spilled out to follow her. She raced up another flight of stairs and then turned right. The thought of Deagan's struggle below, spurred her on. Even if they got past him however, he had already given her enough time, for she was almost there.

She stormed into a pantry then felt around for the latch to a secret door. *"Come on Gwyn."* She found it behind a braid of garlic. She flicked the metal hasp to the side, kicked the door open and burst through it into the final dark stairway that would lead her to the throne room.

T HE OTHER NORTHMEN, DRAGGED the blind one out of the way and two more reached through the doorway, flailing their weapons. Between them, Deagan could see much of the balcony behind them, but where was Saxus? He was gone. Fears and questions filled Deagan's head. He imagined the royal lord coming up behind him and running him through. He imagined the royal lord chasing after Gwyn and stopping her before she reached the throne room. Was Gwyn correct in her guess that killing Jatham would put an end to this? Was she throwing her life away for a bluff? There was no one to answer his questions. All he could do now was try to live. With Saxus gone he no longer needed Northmen alive to keep the dead king at bay. So his stance shifted.

"Hey, did you see my foot move?" he asked.

"Ungggg" the rotter moaned. Right before his teeth were bashed in by a sword hilt.

RORY AND KELLEN SAT side by side in the chamber. Kellen spotted some jugs and bottles so he went over to investigate. It felt like the blade of his own dagger was almost poking out the other side of him. He wanted to feel faint, but he didn't. He felt awake and alert and fully aware of the wretched situation. He finally found a corked jug of wine, and he leaned on it as he let himself down uncomfortably next to Rory again. Then they drank and they laughed, even though it hurt.

"So, Rory, is this what you thought the adventuring life was all about? Getting slashed by a sword and dying a slow and drunken death in enemy territory with no chance of rescue?"

"No, sir," he said. "I'm happy though. If we are going to die, and I admit that it looks that way, it will be a good death."

"You're happy?" Kellen asked incredulously. "You're happy to be mortally wounded and lying in a pool of your own blood behind enemy lines? Ha!"

"That's not what makes me happy, master Kellen. What makes me happy is this," he pointed to the wine, "this," he pointed to the sunset out the window, "and this," and he pointed to Kellen then himself, and the short distance in between them.

Kellen smiled, and winced as he tried to take a deep breath. "I suppose it could be worse," Kellen admitted. He took a long draught of wine then gave the bottle to Rory who followed suit.

GWYN BURST INTO THE throne room through a hatch in the wall. She beheaded two rotters before they could react, then half a dozen others came toward her. A figure in black sat on the silver throne. It was Jatham.

She avoided the sarcophs in the large room then said, "Call them off and keep your life"

"What are you talking about?" he asked innocently. "I was just about to thank you for coming to rescue me. They've trapped me here for days! Thank you, thank you! Are you here to get me out?"

She said, "My name is Gwyn Androth. First Guard. I know a lie when I hear one. But then you already know that."

"I'm not lying. They've got me kidnapped. I didn't know what to do," he complained.

She peeled away from the group so that only one could attack her at a time. One on one, a sarcoph was no match for her, so she dispatched the next one quickly, leaving him legless and with his brains leaking onto the floor. "Why would they kidnap you instead of eating you?"

"Don't you see? They have eaten me! But slowly, my dear, just an arm today, who knows what they'll take tomorrow? These things are under someone's control! They are under orders." He stammered a bit now. "I admit that I was a bad adviser, I only truly looked out for myself, and I was involved with both Haven and Darkwell. But I did it for the king! Malagor put me up to it! And since I'm the only one who knows about his treachery, he's got to keep me quiet, that's why I'm up here."

There was a bang on the door. Then another. The lock and bar held in place, though. "Maybe it's someone here to help us, Gwyn! Lift the bar, and turn the lock!"

She did not move to do so, but instead fought off the last of the corpses. While she was occupied, Jatham moved to the door. By the time Gwyn turned around he had it open and standing tall in the doorway was lord Saxus. He pressed into the room with his sword raised instantly upon seeing her.

Jatham closed the door, smiling. "Remember her Saxus?" he purred.

"The one . . . that got . . . away." Saxus rumbled.

"I trusted you!" Gwyn barked as she easily blocked a heavy swing.

"I . . . trusted you . . . too." The fighting paused The two combatants waiting just out of reach with swords raised.

"How many times have I saved your life?" she asked, trying to appeal to whatever remained of his humanity.

"You . . . should . . . have saved me . . . from him." He looked at Jatham who stood by the door.

"But she didn't, old friend," Jatham said. "Now, kill her." Gwyn ducked the dead king's two handed sword and it crashed into the torso of a sarcoph behind her.

DEAGAN HAD KILLED THE last of the rotters that assailed him. He had been hit in the foot and the side, but there was nothing serious—at least nothing as serious as the need to help Gwyn. He had seen no sign of Saxus since he lost sight of him. He had worked out a plan now. He couldn't follow Gwyn, but he could follow the blood trail that led from the bell chamber. Before they ran into Saxus and his goons, they had been making their way to a passage Gwyn knew of that started in some kind of pantry.

After only two wrong turns, Deagan made his way to the bell chamber they had climbed into at the start. He found the trail of blood that came from Jatham's arm like paint dripping off a brush on the ground, and he followed it as quickly as he could through the tower, thinking only of her sweet, black and silver hair.

N OW ONE OF LUTHAN's men had bound his arm firmly in a sling that left him permanently hugging himself around his blood drenched armor. The battle against the rotters raged on even now into the night, but the Darkish forces no longer had the ability to attack any dragons that might swoop near enough to the ballistae. None did however. It seemed that the days of alliance between Darkwell and the Dragon Riders were done. At this Luthan sighed in disappointment. He never thought he'd live to see humans turn against one another, presuming that the wars against the monsters should be enough to satisfy the warrior spirit that dwelled eternally in the hearts of men. The thirst for violence however, seemed as difficult as ever to quench even in these dark times.

The footmen of Duke Worth were still embattled at their shield wall. The cries of dying men were as haunting as ever. They called out for their mothers, wives and children. They called out to the gods in the Star Country. And all those they called to were equally unable to come save them. Such was battle, Luthan knew; suffering for many, glory for few.

He could not allow good Darkish men to die unnecessarily, at least not without his own blood mingling with theirs on the battlefield. He turned back to his men to order another charge, but as he did so, already a group of knights thundered past him. At their head was Colstin, the man he'd challenged to a duel. He rode on Maggie, the great gray warhorse, trained and cared for by Deagan, Sir Deagan then, for twelve years.

The tall, frightening man glared at Luthan as he rode past. He went forward on Maggie's back, sword drawn. "Why do you sit idly by?" he chided Luthan. "There is work to be done. I suppose we know who are the men to do it, right boys?" he said calling to his fellow riders. Other men glared at Luthan.

Luthan turned to see his other knights—an equal force to that who had just deserted him—who still held the oath of following Luthan's word alone. They sat on their horses in unease, cautious to speak out. Some let their support of Luthan show on their faces. Some let their trepidation and uncertainty overpower their sense of loyalty, and that too was evident even through their helmets. "That man is no knight!" Luthan finally said to them. "Not in my opinion. He has a bent and twisted sense of honor. Nevertheless, I will not let his impudence prevent me from doing the right thing. Charge we shall, my knights, oh yes. But it is not through his prodding that we do so. It is out of duty." He raised his sword, feeling weak in body and in command. Without another word he charged into the fray, and just as silently, his knights followed. Soon the battle lust was on them again and thoughts of weakness were forgotten.

Luthan now harbored no false hopes that Colstin and his followers were still under his command. He wondered how long the rest of the knights would be. As he cut through the organized ranks of the enemy, in a formation he would not have thought was possible, he pondered the possibility that after being un-knighted just as Deagan was, he'd simply join Deagan as an outcast. The thought gave him courage, for Deagan's was a life of freedom now. It was as a free man then, that he dropped his heavy sword into the flesh of his foes.

S AXUS' ATTACK WAS LIKE the rush of a savage mother bear. His blows fell like hammer strokes on her shield and sword, ringing her bones with thudding vibrations. But Gwyn dauntlessly flung these attacks aside, an expert in combat. She struck at Saxus' head and knocked it off balance for a moment. It felt like striking a dusty carpet with a stick. She hit his head again, and knocked off the crown, which clattered on the stones.

He advanced again and she backed away, turning ever so slightly so that she could maneuver herself closer to Jatham. When she was within ten feet she sensed him starting to back away. She faced Saxus, the two of them dueling mightily, and sending great *cracks* and *clangs* resounding through the throne room.

She forced Saxus away with a few quick strokes then with all her speed she rushed at Jatham, hoping desperately to kill him swiftly even if her death quickly followed. She hoped that all the undead would fall down inert. But Jatham avoided her, he cried out and dropped to the ground under her blade, then Saxus was on her again, his lidless eyes staring down into hers. She spat on his feet. She battered his chest with sword blows. Though they didn't harm him, they unbalanced him enough for her to escape.

On equal footing again, they continued to duel. His hand shaking, Jatham drew a glistening dagger from inside his black garments. The only hand he had left was weak from blood loss, but he didn't need strength to get rid of the Royal Guard, he needed opportunity. He crept closer.

As he approached her from behind, she suddenly stepped to the side, and slashed the weapon out of his hand, sending it sliding across the floor. Jatham looked at both sides of his weaponless paw in fear, seeing it was whole he looked up in time to see Gwyn's boot connecting with his chest, sending him backward into his silver throne. He gripped the gold medallion at his throat.

But Saxus lunged on her in her distraction. He locked his sword against hers and managed to slam a fist into her stomach, doubling her over. With all her willpower she tried to force herself back into a defensive stance, but Saxus had knocked the wind out of her, and she could not lift herself up fast enough. In only a moment the king of the dead swung his sword around in a great circle, and brought it down on the back of her neck.

There was a flash of movement. Gwyn heard a crash and a grunt in front of her as she tried so desperately to breathe. And it took her a moment to realize that it was Deagan who had slammed into Saxus, took him off his feet and now stood over him as he lay on the floor. He stepped to the side and placed his right boot on Saxus' dropped blade, and he waited.

"Kill him," Deagan said through heavy breaths. Gwyn did not wait for this command however, and she already strode toward Jatham with her sword raised before he finished his words.

"Life behind me, death ahead," Jatham said as he clutched the gold trinket in his hand. The medallion inhaled him, and he vanished, leaving Gwyn's sword with nothing to bite into but the back of the chair. His form flickered for a moment in the seat, sparks flew from the broken tines of the sun beams that Kellen had taken for lock picks.

They looked at each other, confused.

THE ROYAL GUARDS STOOD in a circle in the plains of death. A beautiful gray sky wheeled about them. They were never hungry, thirsty or tired; simply committed to a task as they had been in life. Wynna breathed the cool air. The grass swayed in the middle of their circle.

Then a flickering shape appeared before them. In its center there was a vague and moving circle of gold. Without hesitation they thrust their spears at it, knowing the rag-monster had returned.

The spear tips jabbed in unison and sparks flowed thickly from the medallion's wounds. As if hanging on a chain, the medallion swung violently from the impacts. More sparks bled from its surface, and then finally, Wynna ripped it out of the air with a slash of her razor sharp spearhead. The flickering shape of the rag-monster winked out, and the medallion laid smoking on the grass.

J ATHAM APPEARED ON THE chair in full. He grasped at his neck for the medallion, but it was no longer there; instead smoke rose from the center of his chest. Gwyn slashed again. Her blade still hit the back of his chair, but this time it traveled first through his neck, making his head fall severed to the floor.

Saxus stood up, and took a staggering step closer to Deagan. The former knight stepped back, sliding the sword further away with his boot. Saxus kept coming, his hands outstretched, he didn't look down at the sword. Instead he only followed Deagan with his lidless eyes.

"You are defeated, Saxus," Deagan said, not sure if he was right. The corpse didn't answer him; instead it lunged with an open mouth. Deagan got out of the way and chopped at the side of his head. It did not harm him. Savagely, Saxus lunged at Deagan again and still Deagan dodged away. Then Saxus' eyes swerved to the ground and a worm crawled out from the corner of his mouth. Blood was rushing from Jatham's neck, and he now ignored Deagan and Gwyn. The king of the dead dropped to his knees before Jatham's body.

Deagan and Gwyn stood back grateful to have a moment's rest as their enemy stopped his assault, seemingly to mourn the death of its master. And why shouldn't he? He was invincible after all. Saxus laid his hands on Jatham's shoulders, then pulled his maimed body up. He hugged the corpse to himself. Deagan lowered his weapon. Then Saxus sank his teeth into his master's flesh and feasted.

Deagan ripped a tapestry off the wall that depicted the siege of Old Grayhelm. If Deagan wasn't using the tapestry for fully utilitarian purposes, he might have taken the time to appreciate the relevance of the image to today's warfare and hope that the day would turn out much as it had when the Helmers had defended their city for twenty one days before finally forcing the Gigants back where they had come from in the mountains.

If only Old Haven could hold its defenses so long. There was a *flump* sound that accompanied Deagan's trapping of the Royal Lord. The folds of the artistry entombed him, and despite his strength, the weight of the woven cloth overwhelmed Saxus, while the two battle-weary warriors rolled him in its stifling woolen mass.

They found a rope to tie the bundle tightly, and Saxus still struggled. He would free himself if he had enough time, but neither Gwyn Androth nor Deagan Wingrat would give him that luxury. They did not pity him as they threw him down the stairs. Gwyn knew of a certain royal fireplace that they could throw him in.

Finally they carried the heavy squirming roll into the banquet hall, and started a fire as fast as they could. There was plenty of dry wood stored in large bunkers on either side of the stone fireplace the opening of which was twelve feet across and six feet tall. The heat was unbearable by the time they deemed the inferno ready. At times, entire trees were fed into this blaze to show the Royal Lord's wealth at feasts. This time however, the only log that mattered was the woolen one containing a dead king, still kicking to be freed.

He had not uttered a word since Jatham's death. His supernatural durability remained, but all his intelligence seemed drained away. He behaved now like a normal rotter, soulless and hungry. They wrapped him more firmly with the ropes from a chandelier then fed him into the blazing fire.

They watched in anticipation as the fire ate the dry cloth, the ropes. They saw no signs of struggle and heard no cry of pain. Would Saxus simply wait until the fire burned his bonds then stand up to eat them both? They had to stay and watch over him, not once did they sheath their swords as they did so.

O
UTSIDE, ON THE BATTLEFIELD, Luthan saw the line of sarcophs disintegrate all at once. Instead of fighting, the dead men dropped onto the fallen and wounded and gorged themselves. They wandered about, turned around and they allowed their hungry instincts to take over. Luthan did not question the change. These were the type of sarcophs he had dealt with in the past. The Giants were dead. Their bodies were still smoking from the dragon fire.

The Darkish army rallied and Worth's marshals urged the troops forward in organized charges that soon dispatched a great number of the enemy. Many stragglers however took refuge in the buildings or disappeared into the alleys and gutters of Haven. It would still be dangerous to travel the city, or to try and return to live there. Luthan rode through the streets, his wounded arm sending surges of tight pain through his side, and up into his neck. A column of horse followed. They routed another street but met no opposition as the eager sarcophs feasted on the entrails of Darkish horses and men.

Duke Worth's men cheered in victory, but Worth gathered his marshals to him once more. A few minutes later, the men advanced again, toward the raised draw bridge of Old Haven.

There were piles of dead in the cobblestone square. The great walls of the inner city were cast in the light of the dwindling dragon fires that had caught in the debris of the streets. Small waves lapped against the muddy bank of Old Haven's moat. And nearby Cloud Tower loomed taller than tall, with a single chain reaching from its side to a smaller tower of rosy stone. The Darkish army was diminished from its initial strength. Those who remained had seen things that they would long wish to forget. But for now, all that mattered was the promise of safety and comfort that would greet them when the draw bridge of Old Haven let them in.

Something disturbed the water. "*Gods*" someone cried. "*Not again!*" Up from the moat climbed some two hundred rotters. Who knows how long the had been standing inert at the bottom of the now filthy water.

Again the fight was joined. Luthan hung back this time. The pain in his arm had worsened in the last engagement and as unorganized as the enemy was, the men were able to handle the fight without many losses while figures watched from the walls above.

When victory finally seemed certain, the drawbridge was lowered. It cranked down and down on its thick chains, then thumped onto the near bank of the moat. Armed troops went out from their sanctuary of Old Haven to join the fray, and with their help, the Darkish forces were soon rid of the soaked rotters.

The Old Haveners quickly returned to the drawbridge. They were apparently under the command of a man with a bandage on his head. He alone remained on Luthan's side of the moat to discuss matters with Duke Worth. Hazen was his name.

He nodded much as he conversed with the duke, then he clapped the man on the shoulder and he returned to his men at the drawbridge. Duke Worth did not look so happy. Instead, he looked as though all his anxieties were coming to a head. He frowned deeply as his horse carried him slowly back to his men.

He raised a hand to indicate that he was ready to speak. "Men of Darkwell, you have come this far in glory and honor!" They cheered. "But our work is not yet done. We have freed Haven from the scourge of the undead!" More cheers filled the square. "But it is with great dismay, that I say this: these men are not as they seem. They show signs of the plague; of this I am sure. By the end of tomorrow every one of them will rise again as undead, possibly infecting some of us as well." Luthan's breath stopped short in his chest. So this was the order that the Duke feared so deeply to give. But order it he did, so he lost all sympathy from Luthan.

"LIES!" Luthan yelled from the ranks. Only a few of the men heard or comprehended what he said.

Duke Worth continued. "We have no choice, but to end their suffering. We must thank them for the sacrifice they have made and the heroic charge they made from the drawbridge. Even as doomed as they were. Look in their eyes and you will not see men. You will know that they are already losing what humanity they had. Even their leader had the look of the damned. We act now! Ready yourselves for the last charge!"

Solemnly the footmen formed fresh ranks. Colstin and his followers did the same, putting on airs of sad nobility as they lined up. Luthan too arranged his men, but as disciplined as they were, it took less time, and he charged them to the drawbridge, where behind him they formed a bristling wall.

It was Luthan's turn to yell at the assembled men. "Unlike the duke, I have fought these abominations before! The *plague* as he calls it does not spread! It does not affect the living. Only the dead may fall prey to its clutches. We have more to fear from our fallen brothers that we left on the battlefield than we do from the survivors inside these walls! The duke is mad! He killed the dragons, now he'd kill innocent men women and children! Tell him no! I at least will do no such evil."

"Nor I!" answered some of his knights, loud enough for the first few ranks to hear.

"You *will* not?" Colstin asked from the other side of the battle line. "Or you *can* not?" There was quiet consideration for his words. "I for one will not see these people suffer and turn into unthinking monsters and ghouls. I am with the duke."

Luthan sent a rider back to Hazen's drawbridge guards as the banter continued.

The messenger was a knight, not a herald. His blood ran hot with fear and urgency and the words that would have made his point eluded him. "Raise the drawbridge, you fools!" he said. And then the duke's men charged in, and the drawbridge was so weighed down with embattled horses and footmen that they could not now have raised it if they tried.

Sir Colstin was at their head, a group of eager footmen, and some of the duke's horsed marshals were in the fray as well. Luthan did not want it to come to this, but he was resigned to fight it out now. What other choice was left?

F ROM THE DOORS OF cloud tower, emerged Deagan, with Kellen leaning on him for support, and Gwyn with Rory leaning on her. They did not know what to make of the scene before them. Deagan could see Luthan on the drawbridge. He looked hurt.

"Easy, Kellen. I'll put you down right here. Looks like I'm still needed," Deagan said. He then saw a group of knights charge at Luthan.

"What are you going to do?" Kellen protested. "Fight the entire army? There's nothing you can do!"

Rory agreed. "He's right, sir."

Gwyn set Rory down beside Kellen. "You're likely right," Deagan said with a sigh. "Especially after using up a lifetime of good luck climbing across that damned chain." As he said this, his gaze stayed squarely on the drawbridge and his hands worked on their own to tighten his sword belt. "Oh well." He started toward the fray at a weary trudge that turned into a painful trot. Gwyn was close beside him.

THE CHARGE HAD BECOME a disorganized brawl. Some of these men knew each other and were unwilling to draw steel and slay outright. When Deagan saw this he was relieved. This may not be as bad as it looked. He heard Duke Worth threatening his troops with docked pay, whippings for insubordination and so on. Deagan forced his way through the ranks, and got to the drawbridge.

Then an ugly and familiar face rode into his sight. Long greasy hair hung about his broad shoulders that bulged under his chain mail, and a wicked curved sword lay naked across his lap. It was the jailer from the raid at Oxham. Around his neck hung a golden chain. And around his waist, was wrapped a belt of white leather; the marks of knighthood. Deagan, with nostrils flared, got his blood up.

The menace before him rode the armored gray mare named Maggie. And he worked his fingers into her mane absent mindedly as he watched the battle, looking for a place to drop in and fight.

"You!" Deagan roared, unable to come up with anything more severe.

"Me," the jailer agreed. All thoughts of rescuing Luthan were washed from his mind. He wished he could forget his pain, but he could not. Despite his years of experience and his many victories, he entered this fight with fear in his heart. It was fuel for him though. He took a deep breath and locked his eyes on those of the jailer. Gwyn was attacked by some footmen, and turned to defend herself. She punched one of them in the jaw, knocking him with the basket hilt of her broadsword.

"Get off my damned horse," Deagan growled. Colstin only laughed. He kicked Maggie hard in the ribs and she jumped forward into a charge. Deagan, on foot charged as well with a crazy look in his eyes. The jailer swung his sword in a circle over his head. Deagan's boots shook the planks of the sturdy bridge.

They slammed into each other. Maggie veered aside at the last second and the jailer swung his sword. It bounced off of Deagan's shield. And Deagan swung back. The blow hit Colstin's mail, sending rings flying. The warhorse bounded a few lengths farther, but then stalled. She reared up against the rider's will, and Deagan smiled. A man ran at Deagan, sword raised. He ducked and threw himself into the man's legs who toppled over in a fabulous flip, and Deagan rose to charge the jailer anew.

Even though Maggie protested, the fierce digging of Colstin's spurs in her sides urged her forward, but he could not get her to charge. He wrenched on her bit, and blood trickled from her sides where the spurs dug into her with each hard kick.

Deagan moved within ten feet of his walking mare and never took his eyes off of the knight on her back. Then all at once he jumped into her side, and pressed his shield as high up into Colstin's face as he could. The knight grunted in surprise, trying to wrap his sword around the large barrier, but he was kept so off balance that he could not get a shot.

Deagan said, "Okay Maggie, let's call it a day!" She remembered the words and held still for him, reaching her nose around his great shield to sniff his arm. He dropped his sword and shot his hand underneath her belly.

"Move, horse!" Colstin yelled. He jabbed the spurs in her again. His sword still lashed weakly around the edges of Deagan's shield. One of the whipping attacks found Deagan's forearm, another wound for today. But by then, Deagan had undone both of the two straps he was looking for, and he latched his meaty hand onto the edge of Colstin's leg armor and pulled both rider and saddle off of Maggie's back.

The Jailer dropped his sword in the fall, and it was swallowed by the bawl. He dropped his shield as well and he was on his feet in an instant. Deagan threw his shield at the knight hard. It hit him in the arm as he tried to catch it and Deagan was upon him. He flung himself at his enemy, his knee found the jailer's gut and his fist pounded into the side of his head. The Jailer seemed to feel it not at all. He got his hands on Deagan and struggled to wrap him in a squeeze. He was terrifyingly strong, and Deagan felt his body compress and Colstin's armor dug into his skin.

Deagan couldn't breathe. He heard low popping sounds coming from his ribs. He struggled silently and groaned in breathless pain. Then finally he got a hand free, scraping his skin against the chain mail to get it loose. He dug his thumb up into the man's armpit and squeezed hard. The nerve pinch elicited a sharp bark from the knight. Deagan applied more force, up and into the armpit. The jailer let go and brought a hand to his aching underarm.

Deagan caught his breath as the world spun around him. He knew that his time for recuperation was short. So he made a feint and then sent a firm punch to the jailer's nose. Blood flowed down into his teeth. Deagan punched again and the jailer caught his fist in an open palm. Deagan's wrist was bent backward in a painful contortion, but he delivered three punches to the man's hard stomach, then an uppercut that finally broke the man's hold. It sent him reeling back. Deagan took two running steps forward then drew back his foot.

"Forgive me," he said as he swiftly swung his boot into the jailer's groin. Colstin fell onto his back, clutching his crotch. Deagan slammed his boot into the man's temple and his head snapped all the way to his shoulder before bouncing back. The jailer's eyes looked dull as he lay there. He barely held onto consciousness. Deagan, quite worse for the wear, staggered and clutched his ribs as he swayed over the man. It took him several moments to realize that part of his unsteadiness was due to the ground actually moving under his feet.

The moat below him lowered farther and farther from the bridge. He heard the cranking of chains. The planks that were flat before, now sloped down toward Old Haven, and Duke Worth's army was trapped on the far side of the moat. Deagan trotted wearily down the ramp, catching Maggie's reins as he did so. Colstin rolled down the ever-increasing slope along with other unconscious and lifeless bodies.

He scratched Maggie on the withers, and talked softly to her. His happiness at having her back was immeasurable and he giggled as he held her cheek against his own. He was eager to get her some food, and take her somewhere that had proper bandages for her spur wounds. This time, no matter who told him to do so he would not give her back. So he was a horse thief, stealing the king's property. Well the king was a lying murderer.

"Maggie," he said as though he was about to begin to explain how much he'd missed her. After such a hard fought day and so many wounds Deagan wanted to melt. He wanted to sleep for hours with someone watching over him. His mind was a throbbing blur of exhaustion and the words he sought as he laid a hand on the horse's neck wouldn't come. "Maggie," he whispered again.

He held her for a long time, almost dozing off with his face buried in her shoulder. She wrapped her neck around his back and pulled at his sleeve with her lips. She smelled the same as ever, like cut hay, sunshine and sweat.

His body told him that it was time to be done. The aching muscles, the open cuts, the bruises, all delivered their individual sensations of pain in concert with his heartbeat. The red waves lapped against his brain, lulling him to sleep. And then a drop of water splashed on his shoulder. Night rain fell on him, waking him up. His first thought was for Kellen and Rory, sitting out in the streets with no shelter from the weather. He looked up to see around him.

Men were groaning in pain, mortally wounded but denied the comfort of death until some point in the days or weeks ahead, the rain made the city look ugly and full of emptiness. There was so much history that was hewn into the rock of the buildings and the curves of the streets, but the scene before him, made it look like that history's end. The dark sky would provide the only burial for some of these dead. Besieged by Duke Worth, they would never find a bare patch of ground to perform a better one.

Thoughts like these flowed under the surface in Deagan's head, but at the forefront was a concern for Gwyn. He searched around, Maggie walking beside him, for any sign of her. The Old Haveners had surrounded the Darkish men who still survived, or who slid into the city due to the raising of the drawbridge. Hazen had commanded his men to take them alive as prisoners. The surrender was complete and Colstin was tied together with several other men. Their hands were bound behind their backs and their necks were fitted with tight loops.

"Gwyn?" he called, but she didn't answer. He went to the base of the drawbridge where many weapons had gathered. Under a shield, Maggie's saddle lay. He picked it up and put it on her. The rain let up, and then stopped. He checked it to make sure it was centered then stepped back to look over her. There was a pillar of steam rising over one of the rooftops. He rode closer.

He rounded the edge of the building and yelped with surprise, instantly pulling up on the reins to keep Maggie away from what lay there. It was a dragon with tattered wings. It did not appear wet for even as the raindrops splashed on its hide they boiled into steam and floated away. The dragon looked up at him and bristled. It gathered something closer to its breast with a scoop of one paw. There was a body there. Deagan knew to leave them be, but he stood and watched a while longer, fascinated by the beautiful creature.

He turned Maggie around. In front of him the blue dragon Pete, steaming and breathing heavily was perched on a rooftop. Sir Oscar was singed, but seemed unhurt.

"Ho ho! You made it through the fighting eh Deagan? You shall have to tell me all about it." Oscar greeted him.

"And you shall have to spin your tale as well, sir. Perhaps we could trade accounts over mugs of ale?"

For all the world it looked like Oscar wanted to give a hearty yes, but something held him back. "I cannot, old boy. I've sent the other Riders away, to find refuge and make camp in the mountains. They'll be needing me and Pete before long."

Deagan looked up at him squinting in the rain. Firelight flickered on Pete's polished blue scales as people lit torches in the streets. Oscar went on, "I stayed here, but only for a little while. To keep vigil with them."

"I'm sorry," Deagan said. Oscar nodded and looked at the dragon Ero, who still curled around his fallen master.

"There's a bounty, you know," Oscar said with a sad smile. It meant the Riders would be hunted. Deagan thought to suggest they find refuge in Pillar; there would be no bounty there. But still the hunters would chase them. Deagan nodded in understanding for there was no realm still standing that they could call home.

Then a wailing howl rose up from behind Oscar. Ero perked up to listen, but he didn't join in, instead grunting in annoyance before arching his scarlet neck to watch his fallen master. Pete turned to look down from his perch at the street behind him from whence the wailing sound came. "Is there another dragon there?" Deagan asked.

"Ranger is her name," Oscar said in agreement. "It was anyway. She won't answer to it anymore. That's the way dragons are, their name dies with the one who named them. I don't understand their language well enough to know why that is, even though Pete has tried to explain it to me many times." Pete cocked his head to look at Oscar and grunted. "She won't leave. Her Rider was run through by one of Darkwell's ballista bolts. She carried him back here, only because three other dragons forced her to. Now even if we pull her reins she won't fly. So I'll stay until she is ready to leave, I'll keep her safe until then. If she chooses to come with me I'll take her to join the others, but if she goes off on her own I won't stop her. Ero here will never fly again I fear. He may live a while, but he can't join us where we're going with his wings in tatters and rags. He may just walk off." Oscar looked at the dragon. The steam cloud had ceased billowing from his back and wings. He looked asleep.

"It may be a lot of work, but could his wings be patched?" Deagan asked. "Bits of leather and stout sinew chord?"

Oscar considered this. "It may work," he said. "It is worth a try." He was not naïve enough to put much hope in the idea.

"Oscar I have a large favor to ask you. Have you seen Gwyn?"

The Dragon Rider shook his head, "No, but I'm sure she's safe, though."

"Yes," Deagan said. "I can keep an eye out here if you could fly to the other side and bring her back. If you get Rory as well he can try to mend the dragon. If you bring Kellen back he'll be nothing but trouble, but you may as well bring him anyway. I'd go myself, but Maggie never quite got the hang of flying—and I'd not ask them to lower the drawbridge."

"Of course," Oscar laughed. "Well I would, but they may try to shoot me down again, and if I land, they may hurt Pete. I'm not sure how much I can do, but I will fly over to see what I can see."

"Thank you, sir Oscar," Deagan said and he described where Rory and Kellen were left sitting against a wall close to the battle on the drawbridge. Pete took off flying and Deagan moved to the intersection of the two streets so he could watch over both Ranger and Ero. Ranger was younger and smaller. Her bright yellow scales glowed like buttercups, her color was the only thing not sullied by the night rain. She moved about, pacing around her Rider, squealing and nuzzling him. When she saw Deagan, she belched fire. The heat of it hurt his eyes, and burned his whiskers, but he wasn't consumed by the fire. He backed away, heeding her warning. She stopped her attack, but did not take her eyes off him.

He talked softly to her as he waited for Oscar to return. A group of boys came running in to see the dragons. They were loud and obnoxious enough to elicit a low growl from Ranger. Ero opened his mouth and a faint glow emanated from behind his teeth. Deagan grabbed one of them by the scruff of his neck and sent them all away. They argued, and tried to get past him, but he maneuvered Maggie to stop them getting too close and he chased them off.

Pete alit on the roof again, and Oscar waved. He was not carrying anyone in the saddle or in the dragon's claws. "They weren't there," he said. And Deagan nodded, but did not give up hope that they were alive. "All I found was an empty bottle of wine where you said Rory and Kellen were waiting."

Deagan laughed. "Thank you anyway, I'm sure they'll turn up."

"Yes, I am certain that they will," Oscar said. He and Pete got down to look at the other dragons. He deemed the yellow one ready to fly. She was more relaxed now; she had given up on pacing to and fro. Oscar gently took her reins and then mounted Pete. He clicked with his tongue, and Pete spread his wings.

"Well, Deagan. I'm sure our paths will cross again. I wish I could wait for this one to be ready, but the shouts of those men outside the walls were none too kind when I rode down to find your friends. No we're not welcome here. But if you do patch up his wings, he can take you to our camp. He knows where it is. He'll want a chance to bury Johan, maybe you could help carry the body for him to a patch of ground. And if Rory turns up . . . Give him this." From a leather case, Oscar produced a sealed scroll.

"I'll get it to him, Oscar," Deagan said. "Good luck. I'll keep an eye on this one for you."

"Thank you. Good luck yourself, Deagan. I don't believe I can even count the number of ways you're an outlaw these days. I don't know where you'll go, but good luck all the same." Then Oscar took off and the yellow dragon followed. The red dragon with the tattered wings didn't even watch them go. He just lay curled around his master. The rain let up, and all Deagan could do was wonder what would happen next.

THAT NIGHT THERE WAS a council n the center of Old Haven, where Hazen and a few others gathered. Deagan kept his distance for watching over the dragon was his prime concern, but he did hear much of what they said. At first there was some debate about whether Duke Worth's undead plague was real. A familiar voice spoke up, "Don't be daft," the voice said. "There is no such plague. I told the men outside the walls the same as I'll tell you now. It's the dead that rise up and turn wicked, not the living. I've been fighting rotters since before some of you were born, and never once have I seen a living person turn into one. Of course you'll see that for yourselves in time so I need not prove my point. Besides, it would make no difference the plague were true. You wouldn't allow yourselves to be killed either way."

The voice belonged to Luthan. Deagan couldn't see him, but he chuckled to know that he was there, that he was safe. The survivors had set a bonfire in the courtyard and some of its comforting light reached Deagan. He had brought some hay and water over for Maggie, and she had eaten some of it. He sat with his sword in his hand. The council went on.

They discussed what to do about the force of Darkwell surrounding Old Haven. "There's no chance of defeating them!" one man said in a tone that brooked no argument. Deagan racked his brain for a way to beat them. He imagined challenging the duke to single combat. It would be utterly satisfying to knock him around, and his knuckles ached for the chance to connect with that smug jaw, or perhaps that ache was only the pain that remained from his slug match with Colstin.

Thoughts of the jailer only fueled his anger. He wanted to ask, *'how could you choose* him *over me?'* They had been at the same raid, the raid that would have claimed Gwyn's life.

The gears were turning fast now in Deagan's mind. If he hadn't saved Durvish, Gwyn and the others in that raid, there would have been no one alive outside of Haven itself who knew that the city was overrun. King Malagor had ordered the raid, the slaughter, and now his army stood ready to wipe out the innocent people of Haven. With the sarcophs wiped out there would be nothing stopping King Malagor from claiming Haven as his own and sending the refugees in Darkwell here to rid his own streets of them.

Had this entire massacre been the result of an old man's greed? Had all these lives been taken in the name of Malagor's play for power?

Deagan tried to think of another way, wrestling with the facts and events leading up to now. He tried to prove to himself that this was not what it seemed. Yet this story explained everything. There was more evil in that man than he could imagine.

"You can take care of yourself a little while, can't you?" he asked the dragon. It didn't respond, but he stormed off to join the council. With Deagan's back turned, the red dragon stretched its long neck out and snatched some of Maggie's hay, the pile that Deagan had been sitting on. The warhorse backed away and let the badly wounded dragon eat his fill. Deagan had much to tell them. He sheathed his sword just as he entered the circle.

"**R**ORY, UNTIE ME YOU blubbering infant!" Kellen whispered.

"Indeed, sir," Rory answered in an impatient tone. "I will make a point of it."

"...Well get on with it then," Kellen said.

"Of course, master Kellen, but you must understand–"

"Understand *what*, man? I understand that I'm sitting over here in the dark with next to nothing on. And that I'm tied to a blasted *anvil!*"

"Right you are, sir." Rory said as calmly as possible.

They sat in silence.

"What do you mean *right you are*? Get over here and untie me you worthless slime!" Something hit Kellen hard in the arm, it upset the dagger slightly and he called out in pain. "What was that?"

"What was what, sir?" Rory said.

"Was that your boot?" Kellen asked.

"Was what my boot, sir?"

They sat in silence again. They had been dragged by Darkish men into a blacksmith's shop and tied to the anvil. The furnace had not been stoked in weeks so it was not warm, but the smell of smoke and hot metal permeated the place. It had still been light when they were dragged in, so they saw the hammers and tongs that hung around them.

The reason they were whispering, was that a pair of guards were standing outside the door on the street. "If they find out who I am, I'll never see the light of day again, old friend," Kellen said in a melancholy whisper. "Which is why I would appreciate it if you would please get over here and untie me."

"I will sir," Rory said. Then Kellen heard the sound of teeth clicking against each other.

"Thank you, Rory." He whispered. The clacking sound continued for several minutes.

Kellen asked, "Rory, *when* were you planning on untying me, my lad?"

"As soon as I gnaw through this rope, sir. It won't be a moment."

"Ah," Kellen said with an understanding nod. "Gnaw away then by all means."

The sound of clacking teeth continued.

Kellen tried as hard as he could to be patient. Patience did not come naturally to him however, and after only a few more minutes he was irate. "Rory, I'm getting cross," he whispered.

"Hmm," Rory grunted, still gnawing.

"Getting anywhere?" Kellen asked. No answer. He cleared his throat. "Getting anywhere, I said."

"I heard you," Rory said.

"Well, are you?"

"Master Kellen," Rory whispered warningly. "Would you like to talk or would you like me to gnaw? I can *not* do both."

Kellen took a deep breath, thinking about it. Then as if he was indulging a child he said, "Oh you can keep gnawing I suppose. It wouldn't kill you to let me know how you are doing every now and again."

"Thank you, sir," Rory said and kept chewing away. The butler chewed on and on in the dark, and Kellen waited with his hands tied behind his back. Every minute or so, Kellen yawned or sighed. Then a commotion broke the tedium. There was fighting outside the building. There were *thumps* and *crashes*, and muffled grunts. The clash of arms didn't last long, though, indicating that the fight was quickly won.

The smithy door opened letting in a meager beam of light that silhouetted an armored figure. He came toward them and sheathed his sword. "Come on then," he said. "We'd best get marching." It was a voice that they knew belonged to Captain Durvish.

He quickly untied them and whisked them out the door. They hustled down the shadowy street and joined the other towermen who waited in the dense shadows of an alleyway. Gwyn was with them.

"She did better than you two," Durvish laughed. "By the time we showed up to *her* cell, the guards were the ones in bonds. But unless you'd like to fight through the whole Darkish army, put your clothes on and follow me."

Kellen struggled to put his trousers on and said, "Where are we following you to?"

"First things first," Durvish said, referring to Kellen's trousers. "Just get yourself sorted out then we'll be on our way." Kellen and Rory gladly obliged, but injured as they were, the task of getting dressed was a painful process. Kellen left his shirt open so as not to disturb the dagger in his chest, and Rory left one arm in his shirt, afraid to lift it away from his wounded side.

Gwyn kept a watch on the street and then turned to Durvish. "It looks like this is our chance," she said.

"Right," Durvish said, "Hoist it, boys!" And the tower men picked something up off of the ground and onto their shoulders, then went further down the alley. Gwyn helped Kellen and Rory along as they lagged a few paces behind the towermen and the object that they carried.

As one, they moved through the streets of the city, now creeping, now rushing across an exposed street, until they were a good distance away from Darkwell's army and had moved close to the high wall of Old Haven. They climbed a grassy hill and then they were standing at the edge of the moat. Without a word, the towermen lifted their burden and leaned it against the wall so that now Rory and Kellen could see that it was a ladder. It reached perfectly to the top of the wall.

Then, some with more difficulty than others, they all ascended the rungs until they were safe atop the walls, and the towermen pulled the ladder up behind them.

"**T**HEY HAVE US OUTNUMBERED even now," Hazen said to the makeshift council that had gathered around the bonfire.

"And they'll have catapults here by tomorrow—not to mention conscripts from Darkwell. If they want us dead, it's dead we'll be."

"Hail, Haveners I am Deagan Wingrat, former knight of Darkwell, and survivor of many wars." Never would an ex-knight be permitted to speak in a war council in Darkwell, such talk was left to the nobles, whose lands were at stake, but not their lives. This was no noble war council, this was a bonfire and a circle. It was a gathering of survivors, trying to escape death for one more day. As informal as it was, the strength of one's words held more meaning than any title. The assembly turned to regard him and ceased their nay saying to listen. Luthan crossed the circle at a forceful limp, and embraced Deagan with his one good arm. They exchanged the old greetings and then Luthan urged Deagan to speak.

Deagan went on, "For good or ill this whole mess has had me tangled up in it since the beginning. With your permission I'd like to spin my yarn, so to speak. I would tell it in full if you'd listen. There are parts of it that fit together, and parts of it that don't. I'm hoping that someone wiser than myself may be able to make sense of it," the group laughed. And urged him to speak. The elderly wrapped blankets around themselves, the young clutched to their parents. The warriors stared into Deagan's eyes or the fire or fed the pipes clutched in their teeth.

"It began with a raid in the Border Lands of Darkwell . . ."

"It began before that, my friend," Durvish interrupted. Rory, Kellen, Gwyn, Durvish and the towermen entered the circle. "Or have you forgotten about the South Towers?" The crowd welcomed the newcomers with open arms. Deagan greeted Kellen and Rory with great relief.

"I sent sir Oscar out looking for you two, what happened?"

"'Tis a long story, Deagan. I appreciate the thought, but by the time he flew down we were tied up and locked away. As for me, I'd fancy a stiff drink and it would be nice to get this blasted dagger out. Of all the lousy wounds, to get my own knife chucked back at me. Well, I'm off to find a barber."

"Rest well, my friend," Deagan said. Rory and Kellen supported each other as they stumbled away, and from the smell on Kellen's breath, Deagan knew there was more behind that clumsiness than the wounds they had sustained.

"Well this was a happy meeting," Hazen said. "Always good to have someone coming through our walls who isn't here to kill us. Never thought I'd be grateful for something so simple, but now I don't suppose I will take it for granted again. Now, on with your tale, Deagan, if it concerns us and if you think we have the time."

Deagan almost had to grab his chin with his hand and turn his head in order to tear his eyes away from Gwyn's face beautifully aglow in the firelight. She smiled at him and he spoke, "Aye, Hazen, we'd best make the time for it. Though at its end, I suspect we'll be better served leaving as quick as we can." Through the murmurs of assent, Deagan continued. "Durvish was right. It started in the South Towers."

Then the tale began. With help from Gwyn and Durvish, he told how the Royal Lord Saxus took a new adviser with a bald head, a man who was also adviser to King Malagor, though the opposing courts did not seem to know this. They told of how the undead overran the lower quarters, and the towermen were forced to fend for themselves, and how when they sent for help, the royal

Lord Saxus sent no one, and as a result, Gwyn Androth became their silent leader and taught them to take their fate into their own hands, by setting out on an adventure for Darkwell.

Gwyn explained how Saxus sent the Dragon Riders away, though they could have easily removed the undead threat. He ordered small groups of men to fight the undead, attacks so insignificant that they would be easily beaten and then devoured by the enemy, essentially forfeiting the city. Saxus and his new adviser would take secret walks together at night and Gwyn followed. She learned of their use of the hidden passages.

Then the Royal Lord disappeared and no one was allowed to enter the royal chambers. Gwyn received an invitation to a closed-door banquet to all the Royal Guards. Never before had such an invitation been given. Gwyn had pleaded with the other Guards to defect, to go against orders and leave the city so they could keep their lives, for she smelled a trap. She had seen Saxus' dealings too many times to believe this banquet was what it seemed. The other Guards still unconvinced, Gwyn left his service before the banquet occurred, and was sure that they were all dead.

Then Durvish told the story of how Gwyn came to the South Towers and led them away from Haven. They fought through the undead to make it out to the road to Darkwell where they would seek refuge and appeal to the king. Durvish admitted that at that time he still believed Gwyn was a man, for she hadn't broken her vow of silence, and had not taken off her mask or armor. The group laughed. The secret of the Royal Guard was out, but there were no guards left, no Lord to serve, and very few Haveners alive to care. Gwyn told of how the towermen, the refugees of the lower quarters and herself had reached Darkwell and she gained an audience with King Malagor.

She explained that she sought refuge in the city and cruelly, Malagor decided that she and the other refugees would not be admitted, that they were to move out to the Border Lands where they would rebuild a small village called Oxham.

Now Deagan told his part of the tale and it was impossible to keep the contempt out of his voice. He told them about the fateful raid. For this raid, Malagor's orders had been delivered by Jatham Holmin, and all they were told to do was *rape, pillage and burn.* "I *was* a knight you see. But I couldn't do it. Against my orders . . . I let them go."

Gwyn nodded at him with a smile. "He means he saved our lives," she corrected him.

"And for that they took my belt ad chain." He told about his duel against Gwyn, and how he too was convinced she was a man, and indeed, a mighty knight, for she had him on his back with his helmet off.

"It would take a mighty woman indeed to get you in that condition, Deagan," Luthan laughed. "That must be why it happens for you so rarely!"

Nevertheless, Deagan continued. He told of how he joined the towermen in the cave and the battle there. He told of sir Oscar being captured and Rory's heroic rescue. He told of their council and decision to kill Saxus. He told of their entrance to the tunnels and their assault on the hallway that led to the bell tower. They saw Saxus in a state of undeath, commanding the rotters, but he seemed to answer to Jatham as though under a spell. He told the hunt for Jatham, and the battle with Saxus. And finally he told of Gwyn's brave attack on the throne room through yet another secret door, the attack that ultimately resulted in Jatham's death.

The group agreed that Jatham's death had been the turning point in the battle for his devilry had been the cause of the invasion at the outset. The rotters ceased to follow any discipline or order, and stopped their assault to gorge themselves on the dead of the battlefield.

Then it was Hazen's turn to continue from what he knew inside Old Haven. They had been driven inside the walls of Old Haven several weeks ago, and they had been safe since then. A Dragon

Rider came and gave them warning of a sarcoph attack through a forgotten tunnel. Deagan interrupted to warn them that if the rotters found this tunnel, Duke Worth's men may find it as well, and they may have even less time than he thought.

Hazen continued, telling about Johan's great sacrifice to save Old Haven from the incoming horde. Deagan looked over to the red dragon, lurking just outside the firelight. He proposed that Johan be buried inside Old Haven, and the Haveners agreed to erect a monument for him in the square to remember his heroic deed.

"If all of this is true," Luthan grumbled, "then my part of the tale is explained at last." Luthan told of Duke Worth's treachery, his backstabbing attack against the Dragon Riders, and the evil of his orders to kill the Old Haveners. He explained how he stood against the duke, and dropped the tokens of his knighthood to the ground. He told of the Giants in the city, and how they seemed to be carrying great sums of Haven's treasure. He also told of the skirmish on the drawbridge which all of them had seen. How he and his loyal knights, many of whom were now in this circle stood against the army of Darkwell, prepared to die in Haven's defense. Someone called for hearty cheers and joyous noise in celebration of Luthan's tale and in thanks for his leadership against the evil of Darkwell.

With all the stories told and the pieces of the puzzle finally assembled. They could not ignore the involvement of King Malagor. His motive was clear: the destruction of Haven. Smoke rose in a pillar outside the Old City. It was the food and supplies that were piled by the rotters to help starve the inhabitants. It was a smoke that signified the desperation of the times and the evil of the so-called Great Cities.

They agreed on a plan, which would risk much, but would at least begin to repay the damage that was done. Those in attendance had little left to lose anyway, and with somber faces they shook hands and parted ways to make ready.

D EAGAN FOUND KELLEN AND Rory in a first floor
barber's shop not far from the council fire. They were
asleep and bandaged with white cloth. Jars of clear
well water sat beside their bed. He decided not to wake them. A rush
of exhaustion swept over him. And though he knew he should be
making himself ready, his body would not let him leave this spot. He
knew that his own wounds could use some tending anyway so what
harm would it do to stay here a while? He sat on the floor beside the
bed and leaned back onto the mattress of packed straw. He closed his
eyes for only a moment. But they wouldn't open again.

It felt like only an instant later, but it must have been longer
because the sun was up. Deagan woke up not on the floor but up
in the bed with the other two. He sat up and found that his wounds
were bathed and bandaged as well. He faintly remembered waking
up to a dim figure muttering and caring for him. He was glad that
he had slept, and had every intention of rising up to get back to his
duty, but instead he fell back asleep.

Finally Rory stirred, he sat up to drink some water and the
movement pulled the blanket and rocked the bed frame. Kellen
woke up with a groggy yawn, and then Deagan sat up as well.
"Where did you come from?" Kellen asked.

"I just came in to give Rory a letter, and I fell asleep."

"A letter?" Rory asked.

"I think so," Deagan said, "I don't know what it is. It's from Sir
Oscar. Here."

Rory reached a weary arm to take the scroll, and he began to
read,

"Dear Rory,

This is for your extraordinary service in my moment of deepest need. Your bravery and cunning at the dungeon of Malagor's spire will be remembered forever in the stories of the Dragon Riders. If not for you, I never would have seen Petey again, and I would have died in there, with no one for company but the common outlaws and the spiders and rats. I am indebted to you beyond any hope of repayment, but there is at least one token I must offer in hopes of making it up to you.

There is a red dragon in Old Haven who once lived with us on Kellen's roof. His name was Ero, but will answer to that name no longer. He was wounded in the sarcoph war, but he will live. If you are willing and able, you may have him. He may never fly again, but you have an uncanny way with the beasts, and he would be a true companion to you if you take him under your wing. If he is too much of a burden to you, you can set him free, and he will find his way back to me, he knows where we are camped. Have him bring you along for a visit some day. Deagan, if Rory is unable to receive this, please consider the offer extended to you and Kellen. Perhaps we will see each other again! Beware, there is a price on your head if you ride a dragon these days.

Sir Oscar, Dragon Rider"

Kellen's eyes were wide. "Well blow me down, Rory, this is incredible!"

Deagan said, "I kept a watch with the dragon as long as I could, last I knew he was over near the fire last night, watching over sir Johan. Oscar said we needed to bury him. Also, the dragon's wings are badly tattered, but I asked Oscar if they could be mended with patches of leather, and he thought it might work. He might fly again, Rory."

Rory was speechless, but he got out of bed and took a deep breath. He got dressed and so did the other two. After a long time he said, "I wonder where I can find some quality leather in a town like this."

G WYN AND DEAGAN MET up in the square. They had
both outfitted themselves with new armor that Hazen's
men had taken from the fallen Darkish soldiers.

"Everyone's ready," Gwyn said.

"Good, we'd best be going then. I was relieved to see you last
night," Deagan said.

"Were you?" she smiled.

"Aye, I was. It's been a pleasure fighting beside you, through all
this."

She laughed like a kind mother, "It's clear you've spent more
time in war camps than you have courting women. Men have
praised my sword arm before. It won't win me over."

"Win you over?" Deagan said, feigning ignorance. "Courting
women?"

"We both know it's not the fighting beside me that you would
miss if I were gone," she said.

"Don't talk about that,"

"Are you *that* shy of a man that I can't even hint that you might
have more to you than steel?"

"You misunderstand me," he said. "I don't want you talking
about being gone.

"And why is that?" she asked taking her helmet off.

He looked from her eyes to her lips and back. His cheeks grew
hot, and he fell apart inside, dying to say something romantic, but
too nervous that he'd say the wrong thing. He promised himself
he'd say it, but he bargained with himself that he didn't have to say
it while looking in her eyes. "Because you're the most beautiful

woman I've ever seen." She smiled. He went on, "Because your voice is like a song about sunset over the ocean." Her breath caught in her throat and her eyebrows shot up. "Because you're all I can think about, ever since I saw you."

She kissed him and the softness of her lips awakened him despite all the pain and fatigue. He held her in his arms, and forgot about the mission, about the dragon and about the siege. When they parted he said, "Also, I saved your life from Lord Saxus."

"So I owe you?" she asked.

"Aye, you owe me your life," he said.

"Oh I see. Do I have to save yours?" she asked, "or can I share mine with you for a time?"

"For a time," he answered, "until you get tired of me."

"Until I get tired of you then," she said.

"Well I suppose that will have to do," he said. Then their group was ready. Luthan, some of the knights and a few of the native Haveners stayed behind, but all the rest of them left through the tunnel that Johan had given his life to defend. Kellen, Deagan, Gwyn, and Durvish were in the group that left, but Rory said farewell to them at the secret stable entrance. Kellen wished him luck, and told him to take care of himself. He said *very good sir*, and took his bundle of leather scraps under his arm, a sewing kit in the other.

Luthan tightened his belt—a black one now—and made ready to withstand the siege. His knights, Hazen, and a few stalwart men were with him, and that day they made ready, setting watch fires on the walls and preparing spears and arrows.

D EAGAN'S GROUP EMERGED FROM the other side of the tunnel, helping each other across the fallen gate, and they moved out around Haven, careful to avoid the watchful eye of Duke Worth and his army of footmen. They kept their distance and looped wide around the opposing force to evade detection during the dark of night. They stealthily gathered some supplies from abandoned farms and guard towers on the western outskirts of the city.

At midday they were almost out of view and into the mountains over which they would travel to return to Darkwell. A small group of men pushed handcarts they had found in the surrounding farms into the edges of the battlefield. Remaining unseen took some maneuvering, but with Kellen's expertise and leadership, they returned an hour or two later with enough suits of armor and weapons to outfit, or at least disguise the entire group of refugees. They dressed fully then continued to Darkwell over the mountains.

As they traveled down the South slopes after a hard uphill climb, they reached a vista that afforded a view of Darkwell and the North road. They saw another company of men traveling the road away from the city. Horses in tack and harness were hitched together in fours to pull the king's catapults up the road to Haven. They would make it there by nightfall, and Deagan hoped that Luthan would be ready.

When the siege weapons had gone by, they slipped out of the jungle and onto the road. Then Deagan formed them into ranks, and marched them to the gates showing their faces as little as possible.

In a gruff phony voice Deagan called up to the gatehouse window, "Ho there guardsmen! Open up and make it snappy!"

"Who goes there?" the guard asked. Deagan recognized the voice, but couldn't place it. He coughed into his fist then gestured to the mass of refugees behind him.

"We're just weary soldiers, returning home after hard . . . dangerous fighting in foreign lands," he said, begging for sympathy.

"What is your name?" the familiar voice demanded.

If Deagan knew the man's voice, he couldn't risk sharing his real name. "Er . . . You wouldn't know it if I told you, sir. We're wounded, and seek refuge in the city."

The guardsman turned to some others behind him and held a hushed conversation. Then the man called down, "Sir Deagan Wingrat, is that yourself?"

The gatekeeper's tone was hard to read so Deagan struggled deciding whether being Deagan was a beneficial trait or a malignant one. He hesitated and pulled his helmet down tighter as he glanced back at Kellen who he deemed far more adept in the realm of deceit. Clutching his dagger wound and lying in a wheelbarrow, Kellen gave him a slight nod.

"'Tis," Deagan said, pulling his helmet off. Gwyn stepped closer to him defensively. Again the guards up above held a secret meeting and Deagan shuffled uneasily, not sure if he had just ruined these people's last chance at refuge. What if these guards were under orders to kill him on sight? What if they slaughtered them all where they stood with a volley of arrows from on top of the wall?

There was a loud thud inside the gatehouse and Deagan jolted, putting a hand out in front of Gwyn to usher her behind him. The huge gate swung out toward them, allowing light to soak the well-trodden road in a widening column. The former knight loosened his sword in its sheath and stepped back, squinting into the sun.

When the gates were open, no one came out to meet them. "Thank you!" Deagan called up. "Thank you very much." He waved those behind them into the city, and they marched in on Deagan's orders.

Men emerged from the alleys to bother them, but they insisted they weren't in the mood for story telling or revelry. Deagan nodded to Durvish who took a crow bar and six towermen, and went up to the gatehouse.

"Remember, if you need anything, just meet at the third level of the Queen's Street platform, by the old tree," Deagan hissed to the surrounding escapees. "Otherwise just disappear and fend for yourselves. It's a big city, and once you take these clothes off no one will give you a second glance."

Armor and uniforms fell into piles of straw, in dark alleys, and in dusty corners. Anything valuable would be picked up and sold within minutes, and even Deagan lost track of the people he came in with. Hazen with his headband pulled low to block some of the harsh sunlight gave Deagan a grateful nod before disappearing with his people into the throng. Deagan was sure that he'd never see them all in the same place again, in fact, he wouldn't recognize most of them, but he and Gwyn stuck together. And they both followed Durvish up to the gatehouse with Kellen close behind.

"Lemme in," Deagan grunted. The gatehouse was a mess, with the guards' weapons strewn about the floor and the guards themselves tied up in the corner. It was crowded, especially with the machinery that moved the gates. "Get that gate closed will you?" he said. Durvish and his men, who had covertly captured the gatehouse, hurriedly sorted out how to operate it, and with the captain's ingenuity, the massive doors soon boomed to a close.

"Deagan?" a voice asked through a cloth gag. It was the voice he had recognized calling to him from the gatehouse window.

Deagan turned to look at him. "Korvis!" he said, and he immediately untied him. "I haven't seen you since that raid. Are you alright? Boy do I have a lot of explaining to do."

"I should say so," Korvis said, frowning and furrowing his brow as he accepted Deagan's hand up. "I've had to answer a lot of questions about you since you've been gone."

Then Deagan explained in full the situation as he knew it. With Gwyn, Kellen and Durvish verifying the tale, Korvis became a believer. The other guards that were in the gatehouse also agreed to help with the plan and not interfere so they were untied, but kept in the gatehouse.

"Well, I trust you boys, but I'm going to leave Durvish here with you anyway. And I want you to go about your duties—just as normal as ever except I'll give you only one order; do not let Duke Worth or his men back in this city."

K ELLEN WAYFIELD LIMPED BESIDE his old friend through the shadows of an overcrowded housing platform. Deagan said to him, "How are you holding up, burglar?"

"I'm . . ." Kellen began and then sniffed back his tears.

"Kellen?" Deagan asked putting his hand on Kellen's shoulder. They both stopped in the street as Kellen quaked. "Do you think he'll come back?" Kellen asked. "Rory, I mean."

"Of course he's coming back, Kell. Of course he is."

"I'm sorry," Kellen said with a gasp of laughter, regaining some fraction of his composure. "I have much to do. Inciting a revolution can be a lot of work, I hear."

"Sure?" Deagan asked.

"Positive," Kellen replied wiping the corner of his eye with a fingertip. "I'll just be off home to clean up and then it's down to business. And when I get down to it, you won't want to be anywhere near by. The sorts of men with the ambition to take over the throne after Malagor has his little accident are not to be taken lightly, (and I expect that's just how an oaf like you would take them) so it's off to bed with you two. I'll meet you by the oak tree when all is ready and not a moment sooner. Good bye, my friend."

"Good luck, Kellen," Deagan said. "And be careful."

Kellen winked over his shoulder at them and continued down the street toward his manor. A few more turns through the labyrinthine cobble stone streets brought him to the scaffold attached to the façade of his manor. The Dragon Manor sign still hung proudly over his door, a memento from less troubled times.

His key turned easily in the lock of his front door and the pirate made himself at home. The banister felt sticky and smooth under his palm as he climbed the magnificent stairs.

Kellen stopped on the landing by a painting, first resting a hand on it then removing it from the wall to hold it out in front of him. It was a framed portrait of the *Daring Rover*, a sailing ship on a stormy sea. He carried it with him to the entryway of his bedroom, where he sighed and leaned it against the wall on its side.

Outside the bedroom window refugees living on the platform were going about their chores so Kellen closed the curtains and changed his clothes. Before putting on his finest tunic, he ran his hand over the wound on his chest. It looked somehow lifeless, the raw flesh was dry and dull like meat, and lacked sensation. He dressed himself in his finest tunic and breeches, donning a leather vest, a rich purple cape, and a wide brimmed hat. Now dressed, Kellen lifted a glass and filled his belly with wine, then filled a flask with spirits, and with a dagger in his boot, he set out for the streets, leaving the manor well locked.

He turned to look at it as one looks with pity on his sick father, so strong once, but now buried in artifices that obscure the original identity of the man. Yet enough of the figure is recognizable to induce admiration, even though the infirmity that is so apparent will surely force you to say goodbye to him at last. That is how Kellen looked at his manor as he walked away, with pity and love and admiration, but he did not know why.

Shoving his emotions aside, Kellen buttoned his cuffs and smoothed his hair behind his ears with gloved fingers. He checked to see that his flask was well hidden and then stepped out from around the corner, and into a secluded courtyard. His eye was trained to pick out deception, so already he could locate the rat-like man on the bench who was surely keeping watch rather than reading. Kellen made as if he was there to shop for books from an antiquarian store window, watching the lookout on the bench with his peripheral vision. When the man turned around to investigate the entrance of a carriage pulled by two heavy horses, Kellen dropped the book he was holding and slipped down into the street through a crack in the surface of the ground that served as an entrance to the trenches.

He was under the city, in a shallow trench that was sunken into the streets. There were grates under his feet that dirty water poured down into. Despite this attempt at drainage, foul waters lay stagnant in the walkway, and this is why for all Kellen's fine attire, he wore his scummiest traveling boots.

Side alleys branched from the one he walked in, and he jumped every time someone was standing there. He asked questions, he handed out coins, and he charmed his way deeper and deeper into the undercity. Within half an hour, he stood at the feet of two burly bodyguards that blocked a door.

"Gentlemen!" he greeted them, "Let your man know that Kellen Wayfield is here for a visit."

"Wayfield?" the one on the left asked. "Right this way." His name was like a password here. What would his mother say if she knew of her son's notoriety?

The room was lit with scented candles and fine cooking. A large bearded man sat on a cushion on the far side of the room. He had beautiful attendants and imposing bodyguards surrounding him.

"Plucky!" Kellen said jovially with his arms spread wide. His face showed no fear because his heart felt none. The man he addressed was Pluck Wiley, a fellow smuggler who had done business with Kellen for years.

"Kelly," he replied, "What brings you here? Taking up piracy again or just saying hello?" His voice was husky and heavily accented. In Darkwell he was a smuggler, but before that he had been a nobleman from a coastal city. He once had land and wealth beyond Kellen's wildest dreams, but the city was taken over by the teeming forces of evil, and his fiefdom with it. Now the king he once served was in a watery grave and his title was meaningless.

Pluck was lucky he had a gift for self-preservation, because if he hadn't, he'd be just another refugee living in the slums of Darkwell. He had risen to be the local chief of all the refugees from his city. He took care of them and they took care of him. He was their protection when the city guard ignored their needs, he was their source for goods that were banned under Malagor's decree. And he was an overall nice guy.

"I have some news for you, Pluck, that's all," Kellen said.

"That's never all, but go ahead," Pluck said.

Kellen laughed, "No, I insist, it's only news. His majesty is sick these days. Very sick, maybe. And as I understand it, he has no heir."

It was Pluck's turn to laugh, "Everyone knows this, Kelly, get to the point here. Would you like a drink to loosen your tongue?"

"Sounds grand, Plucky," Kellen said. "But like I was saying, he's *mighty* sick."

"And how does Kellen Wayfield hope to profit by this?" Pluck asked.

"Oh yes, he's been coughing a great deal in court they say."

"Has he been sneezing as well?" Pluck asked, "and if so what's the point?"

"Sneezing a bit here and there I'd say," Kellen said. "Sneezing a bit."

"And would you like me to send him some flowers? Would you like me to pray for his health? Or drink to it?" Pluck said.

"A drink wouldn't hurt," Kellen said and clinked his glass against his old friend's.

"Well, you could get a drink in any tavern in Darkwell, yet you come to me. So I'm left very curious about your interests,"

"Not my interests at all, Pluck. Yours are the interests at stake here, you see. You're more respected in this town than you think. If you made a bid for the throne, you might actually get it."

Everyone in the room except Kellen laughed. Kellen sipped his drink. "Well, I'd better be going," he said. "It was nice seeing you."

"And you, Kellen," Pluck said. "What's gotten into you, my friend?"

"I just wanted to share the news. The king might not last the week," Kellen said, then brought a hand to his lips in mock surprise. "Oh did I say, *might* not? Well, anyway I'd best be going."

"Well, well, well, you bring bigger news than I thought. The king dies by the end of this week?" Pluck asked, the room silent again.

"See to it that you are ready for it when it happens, Pluck. You're a good man. The city could use you. Oh, and of course you didn't hear this from me . . . If you ever mentioned it anyway, it would raise very serious questions about your own involvement," and with that he set his half finished drink on the table and walked out to go have the same conversation with someone else.

DUKE WORTH ARRANGED HIS catapults by torchlight. He ordered them to be aimed at the wall in one spot where the moat was narrowest. He rode forward to the edge of the moat, and looked up to the top of the walls to see men patrolling the balustrade and tending the watch fires. He called up.

"Lower the drawbridge, or we will pummel this city to dust!"

"What?" called a man.

"I said lower the drawbridge or we will pummel this city to dust!"

There was a long pause then someone said, "I have no idea what you're saying."

"Go and get your commander!" Duke Worth demanded.

The man called down, did he call to Luthan? Worth wouldn't put it past him, fool that he was. The minutes wore on before Luthan came to the top of the wall.

"So you've defected entirely have you Luthan?" The Duke yelled up to the wall.

"It isn't too late, Duke!" Luthan yelled back. "You can stop this! You know as well as I that these people are no threat!"

The Duke didn't break his gaze. "They have the plague, Luthan, and now you must have it as well."

"There is no plague, Duke."

"Lower the drawbridge," Worth ordered.

"And let you come in and slaughter them? Never."

"Then come out and we will speak face to face," Worth said.

Luthan stopped to think about this for a while. The minutes rolled by. "No, Worth. Even if you offered me all the gold in

Darkwell I would not open this drawbridge. I'll die before it's lowered."

"So be it," said the duke. And he breathed a sigh of regret as he ordered the catapults to attack. If Luthan had heard that sigh of regret, he would have felt no pity for the duke, because sighs of regret do not mean you are changing your mind. "Kill them," said the Duke.

The rocks flew slowly through the air. They were huge chunks of stone, mesmerizing to watch at a safe distance. *KA-KRACK! BWACK!* went the stones against the wall. "Look out!" a man called from below as a boulder hurtled over the rampart to shatter the roof of an inn. Luthan ran along the top of the wall away from where the stones were aimed. He fled down the inner stairs nearly losing his balance as the fortifications shook with the *SLAM!* of stone on stone. He joined with the rest of the meager number of men. Luthan's wounded arm didn't allow him to do so, but the others picked up their longbows to shoot arrows blindly over the wall. They all yelled continuously, as loud as they could. "Louder lads! As if all the men of Old Haven stood beside us!" Luthan urged.

Outside the wall, Duke Worth watched the boulders chip away at the ancient fortifications. The first one bounced back without noticeable effect, the second sailed over the wall without making contact. The duke ordered the aim to be lowered before another shot was wasted. Though he mused that the rock must have done some damage on the buildings or the people inside. The third rock hit lower than the first, and it left a light colored circle on the stone face. It was the shot, not the wall, however, that shattered and splashed into the moat.

Still Luthan watched through an arrow slit while the remaining men showered arrows over the wall, shooting as fast as they could. It was dark, and Duke Worth himself found it hard to tell if the arrows were hitting anything and how many archers they were up against.

The second volley of stones fared a bit better, this time the catapult that had thrown its ammunition high, connected with the very top of the wall, knocking the battlements in. Almost simultaneously two other rocks cracked into the surface and fell down into the moat. Now some damage was visible, but one of the catapults had struck farther to the left.

The stones continued to hammer in, and the arrows continued to pour out. Luthan hoped his arrows were missing their mark, for there was only one man among them who he wouldn't mind piercing with one. But for this to work, he had to keep them here as long as possible.

Now the top of the wall was crumbling and the Darkish army cheered. A large wedge shaped section was now cantilevered out over the water, hanging on by only the luck of one stony crag caught behind another. Duke Worth watched as he saw victory drawing near. Two more volleys and the chunk plummeted into the dirty water, forming a shaky bridge across the moat. The lower part of the wall crumbled away, bit by bit. There was now a notch carved in the wall, and some of the stones soared through the gap that they had made. Raining destruction on all sides of Luthan's few.

Luthan's men were picking up their final arrows. "Save 'em, lads." Luthan ordered. "Up to the wall, quick!" He knew the catapults were aimed at the notch and they would take several minutes to re-direct. It was time to take a chance. They crouched behind the battlements that still remained. Luthan told them who to look for. He told them where to aim. Then he gave them a wicked smile and stood up beside them yelling. "FOR HONOR!" and the archers stood too and loosed their arrows.

Duke Worth froze in place when he saw the white haired ex-knight stand up on the wall, unarmed and wounded with a war cry in his hoarse old throat. *FOR HONOR!* As if with an arm in a sling he'd take on Darkwell's army by himself. But he wasn't alone. Twenty-odd archers took aim and let their arrows fly. He wanted to run, but couldn't see the arrows in the dark. He fumbled for his shield, but already the shafts were upon him. Several struck the sand and stones around his horse's hoofs with a *thwick!*, but one of them passed right through him before hitting the ground. Blood bubbled out from his chest, and he felt himself deflating. Another one slipped through his neck. One of his marshals who was nearby, but was watching the catapults rather than the archers said, "M'lord?"

The Duke allowed his weight to fall from his horse and down to the earth. He hated himself for the many evils that had been done through him, but he was thankful for the swift death that would surely come. The hot red nothingness that comes with losing consciousness swarmed his vision on all sides. A gloved hand gripped his shoulder. "M'lord!" the marshal said again, only now seeing the blood in the dark of the night.

"Charge," was the last word the Duke ever said, for after he breathed it out, his lungs refused to do anything but gurgle and hiss.

"Yes, M'lord," the Marshal said, and signaled the men to carry on, half wading through the moat, half climbing across the stones that had fallen into it. But of course, when the army entered the citadel of Old Haven, they found no one left, but their own men, tied up and naked in a store room. They searched almost until dawn, but with Duke Worth dead, the marshals were at each other's throats about who should be in charge. And they turned up no sign of Luthan's band, nor the secret tunnel they had escaped through.

KORVIS HAD RISEN TO the station of head gate keeper of the North gate and as such he had keys. He could access the gates, gatehouses, and several other closets and rooms nearby, but also Malagor's spire. Deagan asked if he could have that one. Korvis said he wouldn't miss it; he didn't go there often anyway.

Deagan at least did him the service of not explaining why he needed it. That was best left secret. Deagan did a lot of brooding in the following days. The first night he and Gwyn visited the third level of the Queen's Street platform by the old tree. And they met Haveners there, wondering what to do next. They wanted to know how they were supposed to survive here when they didn't even have the money for food. Deagan told them all the cheapest places to buy bread, but didn't offer any of his own money. He knew that if he did his coffers would be empty too soon, and he would go hungry. He waited until Kellen would arrive. He didn't want to be responsible for all these people, but unfortunately they knew where to find him every night, and he thought they would probably keep coming to ask the same sad questions. But he would endure the questions until Kellen arrived. Then he could continue with the plan.

Horns sounded at the edge of the city. The Duke was back. Deagan wanted to be nowhere near the confrontation. The Duke would sniff him out like a rat and have his head. No, the men would have to wait, they would have to hold strong and keep the gates closed. At least until Kellen showed up at the old tree. And Deagan hoped it would be tonight.

KELLEN WALKED TO HIS manor and changed his clothes for the third time that day. He was not disguising himself, he was just having one of his "me days" in which he changed his clothes whenever he wanted to and carried rum or whiskey in a flask. He pulled back the curtains in his bedchamber to the surprise that he was completely in shadow. It was a sunny day, why should he be in shadow? The platform adjoining his house had been completed. Right now he was looking out his window at a shirtless man swabbing himself with a wet rag over a tub of water. The man looked at Kellen. Kellen looked at the man. He wanted to say, "Rory, who is this man?" over his shoulder to his faithful butler.

It made him feel powerful to ask questions about other people who were present, particularly when these questions were directed to his butler and even more particularly when he spoke over his shoulder without breaking eye contact with the person.

Kellen decided the man outside the window couldn't necessarily tell that his butler was missing, so he said it anyway, "Rory, who is this man?" and of course no one answered him. The man went back to his washing and Kellen could tell he had not been properly intimidated. So he opened the window.

"Excuse me sir," Kellen said.

"Yes," the man said. His accent was horrible, his voice went from low to high on every syllable and he hissed.

"Who are you and how long have you been living here?" Kellen asked.

"My name is Dib. Live here three days." Said Dib.

"Are you from Banwick?

"Yes, yes," he hissed, smiling broadly.

"When did you come to Darkwell?" Kellen asked.

"Came here four years back," he said.

"Do you know Hevestraud?" Kellen asked.

"Aye, yes," Dib said approvingly.

Kellen smiled. "Will you take me to him? I'd like to speak with him."

"Sure, yes." Dib said. And Kellen went inside to get him a bar of soap. He climbed out the window and handed Dib the soap, and a clean shirt.

"There you go, my friend," he said. Dib tried to turn them down, but Kellen wouldn't let him. By the end, Dib had said many thank yous and they were off to see Hevestraud.

Hevestraud was a small man, he wore clothes that would have been fine when they were made, but had grown somewhat worse for wear. Nevertheless he presented himself as a gentleman and Kellen could not deny that. Kellen had heard of the former lord of Banwick during his trader days. He had no idea whether he was still alive until a few minutes ago when he met Dib.

He bowed before the former Lord, who like Pluck Wiley, had lost his lands to an invasion. However, among the refugees of Banwick he was chief. "Greetings, Lord Hevestraud. I am Kellen Wayfield, humble traveler. It is a great honor to finally make your acquaintance after hearing your name a great many times in conversation."

"The honor is mine, Wayfield, I am sure," Hevestraud said. His accent was much more pleasant. In fact it was soothing and low. "What pray tell have you heard about me, nothing damning I hope." He rested a hand adorned in gold rings on the railing of his meager balcony. The place they had met was a shabby building, but it was a building nonetheless, and it was a mark of status nowadays in Darkwell to have a proper roof.

"Not at all, M'Lord, not at all. What I have heard is only of your glory in the days of Banwick and your unavoidable misfortune that followed it. I have heard only of your generosity and grace. I have heard only of the lordly fashion in which you have conducted yourself for the betterment of your people here in Darkwell."

"You are too kind, Wayfield. Would you like a drink?"

"It is you who are too kind, but how can I refuse." Kellen replied. He sipped the pink liquor from a short glass and made a show of rolling the taste in his mouth. When he sensed that Hevestraud was about to ask him why he had come to chat, he said this, "M'Lord, I've come to make your acquaintance and to share a bit of news . . ." Again, Kellen engaged in the swordplay of language. He revealed enough to draw his opponent in, then he retreated and left him with little more than another question unanswered. He feinted and parried without revealing his interests—without saying too much.

At the end of the conversation, Hevestraud understood however that King Malagor was at his end. And he understood that if he played his cards right he could profit from it. And he was thankful to Kellen for the information, so he silently resolved that this Wayfield man would be his ally.

One last conversation, and Kellen could meet with Deagan tonight. He bid farewell to his new friend and found his way back to his manor. He then changed his clothes and this time he didn't open the curtains.

In a blue cape and a wide brimmed hat, Kellen went to a friend and client's house. It was a certain noble named Rond Hollow who he'd convinced to house dragons on his roof. That had gone so well, that he now thought he might be in good shape to convince him of something one more time.

Kellen knocked on the man's door. "Good day to you, sir!" Kellen said seizing the man's hand and barging into his house before there was any opportunity for objection. "What a gentleman you are answering your own door like that. I'm such a shut-in I always just make Rory do it! Anyway, how are you? How are you doing with the draconic pursuits? Where is your wife? Tell me everything!"

"Wayfield! What the devil's gotten into you? You seem possessed."

Kellen had never been accused of being possessed before and wondered if he might be, it gave him pause, but then he lied, "No, not possessed. If you must know I'm in love, man! I'm in love, isn't it wonderful?"

"Oh yes, yes splendid, can I get you anything?"

"Tea my good man, tea!" he said. And when the nobleman turned around he sipped from his flask. "Mm, terrible shame what's become of those Dragon Riders wouldn't you say?"

"What's become of them? More like what they've become!" Rond retorted smartly. "They attacked the tower causing all manner of commotion and turmoil and before you knew it they were gone, and me with seven roosts packed onto my building and grounds. I knew they were brutes but I never knew they were treasonous! Attacking the king and all that."

Seeing he wouldn't change Rond's mind, he settled for warping it. Kellen said, "A shame it was a shame it was. It was a shame, indeed. But rest assured there is no connection between the Dragon Riders and the attack on the tower. I was there, and as you can imagine I know the Riders quite well. The dragons were hijacked you see, hijacked by a gang of kids out for a bit of excitement on the old dragons if you know what I mean," Kellen drew Rond into a fed up and very adult laugh. "I couldn't believe it when those young hooligans took off like that. Where were their mothers one must ask!"

"Shining boots in the streets I would only imagine," Rond said in a pitying tone. "Or worse. Was it really a band of hooligans, Wayfield?"

"As I live and breathe before you, the dragons were hijacked. And what could I do? What could anyone have done? Look at the tower itself! It's half burned to the ground and bedraggled as a wet cat, and not one dragon was taken down. Not one sir Hollow! And doesn't that tell you something about the power of the beasts."

"Doesn't it just?" Hollow agreed. "If all the men in that tower couldn't even take one down then what could you or I have done eh Wayfield?"

"Mm," Kellen grunted, apparently looking back in regret. Then he allowed his face to brighten once more. "But you and I were man enough to tame them while they were here eh, old boy? No gang of kids can take that away from us."

"No," Hollow said with a phony smile. "No they certainly can't." What he was concealing with his phony smile was that he had never gotten the chance to ride or even touch one of the dragons. The Riders had been doing all of that sort of business. And whenever he did see the Riders which was not very often they always said things like, "thank you for letting my dragon sleep on your roof." And "Terribly sorry, but it might be best if you try to avoid the dragons," and worst of all. "Maybe you can brush him when you get a little less shaky and pale looking."

But Kellen needn't know any of that. As far as Kellen knew, Rond was nothing less than a Dragon *Master*. "Well besides my being in love I do have a snippet of information to pass along," Kellen said.

Delighted to change the subject, Rond said, "Ooh! Snip away, Wayfield, snip away."

"I'm going to be blunt, Hollow. Can you take bluntness?"

"If I can take a few dragons on my roof I can take any bluntness, I should think," he lied.

"Good. Because I'm going to be even blunter than you expect."

"Well go on-"

"There is a plot to murder the king," Kellen said, his posture unmoving. Rond looked like he was about to die. He got up and strolled around the room and rearranged some things on a table. He made sounds of surprise, something like the sounds of horses. "That's right there's a plot to kill him and I have nothing to do with it. But when it happens and mark my words it will (and soon) there will be many people vying for the throne. There are displaced nobles from all over the world camped out in this city. There might even be a few former kings. Rond, hold it together, man I warned you I'd be blunt!"

The nobleman took a few deep breaths and forced his red eyes to face Kellen's. "Now there could be a lot of bloodshed over this as you can well imagine," Kellen said.

"Of course there could, I have no doubt about that, ha ha ha," Rond said.

"Right, and think of it, man I'm warning you now because of your station. You're wealthy, you're powerful, you have land in the city. You are going to be a wanted man. Everyone will be wondering if you are going to make a move for the throne."

"They will? I don't know about that," Rond sputtered.

"Well while you're still thinking about whether you will or you won't someone is going to come in here in the night and do you in, you hear me? And once your done in what good will that be? I don't want to see a good man like you *done in*," Kellen said.

"Thank you, Kellen, thank you, but what can I do?" he asked.

"I'll tell you, but I won't guarantee that it's going to work."

"Blast, I'll try anything. I'm a dead man already it sounds like," Rond laughed, sweating.

"Well, when the time comes, and dozens of powers are going after each other trying for the throne, you sir are going to be the voice of reason. You alone will suggest a new way. You will not try for the throne. You will suggest a council of equals."

"A council?"

"Yes, Hollow, a council of equals, and everyone will realize that you aren't trying for the throne at all and they won't kill you. And then if the council does form, you will be forever remembered as the man who said it first."

Hollow turned it over in his mind. "Now that I know what you have told me, I cannot ignore it. I must act."

"Yes, you must act to save your skin. You must act natural for now, but soon you must act like a fearless hero who desires peace. The council, Rond. That is all you desire."

"I shall try it, and I hope that it keeps me far from trouble. But if trouble comes knocking perhaps I should be ready."

"Perhaps you should," Kellen said. Then with a sunny smile he dismissed himself and headed to the streets.

He went over his work in his head. He was tired from it, and he knew that if anyone would ever be caught in this web of lies and deceit that it would be him. Fortunately he currently felt like a spider, standing on the strands of silk without getting stuck. Everyone he had talked to had some reason to keep his name a secret. Rond would want to claim the council idea for his own. Hevestraud would want to protect him because he was a valuable informant for the future and a nice guy. Pluck was an old friend and his reputation was dirty enough that if he admitted to knowing something about the murder before it happened he would be called a conspirator. There were others that he talked to as well. Soon Darkwell would erupt and Kellen did not know what was going to happen.

With a final swig from his flask, he walked up to meet Deagan.

THIS IS AN OUTRAGE!" shouted Duke Worth's marshal. "I'm tempted to load these catapults and send a volley at your impudent face!"

"No entry!" Durvish repeated between laughing to the towermen behind him.

"Sir," a footman said, "you ordered the ammunition be dropped in Haven, you said we'd travel faster without it."

"It was a bluff, you idiot. Now he knows it too," the Marshal replied. The men were growing restless waiting on the road. At least they had enough food to wait this out, but not if it lasted forever.

"Duke Worth! Lay your weapons down, and we shall think about it," Durvish called, because he did not know what Duke Worth looked like.

"I am not Duke Worth!"

"Where's Duke Worth?" asked Durvish.

"He's dead. Killed by rebel arrows at the moat of Old Haven," said the marshal. "And we will not lay down our weapons! We are Darkwell's own troops returning victorious from Haven! We may carry our weapons in the city if we like!"

"Oh so you're the same troops that charged in to kill the innocents of Haven? You're the same army that let Haven be overrun by undead monsters without lifting a finger to help? Are you the same men who swooped down to kill my people when we camped in the Border Lands? *That* army?"

The marshal made as if to explain but as soon as he started with *yes,* Durvish cut him off, "That's what I thought. In that case, you'll be better off down there where I can't get my hands on you!" and with that Durvish slammed shut the window that let him peer down on them. The towermen cheered and congratulated each other inside the gatehouse.

T HE NEXT MORNING IT was already common knowledge that Malagor was dead. His body was found on the cobblestones surrounded by stained glass shards. He was in his night gown and his crown lay beside him. His funeral procession wove through the streets and no one knew whether he jumped or he was pushed. No one wept at his passing; no one keened in anguish. Silently and dry eyed the populace watched as the guards carried his body to the underground resting place of his forefathers. The torchlight disappeared into the tomb and Malagor's line was utterly extinguished.

All the old songs were sung in the courts, grieving the end of an era. The same songs were sung in the taverns, in the streets. Deagan sat atop his barstool with his back to the warm stone of the city wall. From forty feet up in his usual location, he had become part of the ring of dirt, that circled the worn out washtub that Darkwell had become. Maggie was tied up down below, waiting for him, and Gwyn was by his side.

Clunk. They toasted, "Long live the king, and all that."

"Whoever that may be," Gwyn replied.

"I still wish sometimes that I'd been a blacksmith," Deagan said. "Not a care in the world except how straight the iron was, how clean my smithy."

Gwyn took a long drink from her mug of stout. Deagan went on, "But if I had taken one step different in life, or said one word apart from what I did, maybe we wouldn't be here together now. You might be off with some other man."

"I've thought the same thing. I have so many regrets. Or I did. All the suffering . . . ha! I don't even think I believe in regret anymore. All this madness has shown me that some things are worth fighting for."

"You're worth it, Androth-"

"Call me Gwyn,"

"Gods I can't believe you're with me. I don't deserve you." As he looked into her blue-gray eyes, it was like she didn't even know how beautiful she was.

The balcony over the smoky city gave a good vantage point to see the somber proceedings following Malagor's death. It was the loss of *a king* not the loss of king Malagor that saddened the streets so heavily. Though most of the peasants had no memory of past kings, the stories about them began to light the taverns and courts with nostalgia and sadness. It was a celebration of the heroic deeds of all time, a celebration of chivalry, of history, of human potential symbolized by Kingly grace.

From the bottom of the ladder down below that stuck in through the tavern window, there came a beautiful song. Deagan leaned over to get a view. The singer was the lad who worked here. Holding a rag in one hand and standing on a chair. His voice was fine like nectar and Deagan smiled.

"What is it?" Gwyn asked.

"Good thing I scared him off of being a knight," Deagan said.

Her weathered hand slid on top of his. "Well, good thing I don't scare so easily," she said.

At midday, Durvish took pity on the troops encamped miserably outside the city and he opened the gates. They marched in and they were welcomed home from their campaign with kisses and hugs and gifts of little worth, but great meaning. They took off their helmets and they formed a parade through the streets. The marshals had been confused about what to do once the Duke was killed. Now with the king dead, they were utterly lost. The parade gave them something productive to do until they could all go home and weep.

They finished their pints. "Well, there will need to be a new king before I even have a chance of being knighted again. I may as well save what little money I have left, and look for work," Deagan said.

"Maybe your dreams of blacksmithing aren't completely over with now are they?" Gwyn asked as they climbed down the ladder and into the noisy bar window then out onto the street.

R ORY, WALKED BESIDE THE Dragon out into the sunshine North of Haven. Sir Johan all shrouded in a sheet was on the dragon's back. His red scales glistened brightly, for Rory had brushed him and oiled him. Rory had sewn sturdy patches of leather to the beasts torn wings. The stitches were thickly enforced with sinew, and he polished the leather with some of Kellen's red boot polish which he had carried with him on the adventure knowing that Kellen's boots would need it after all that mischief and tromping around.

Rory had a shovel over his shoulder and when the dragon stopped and found a spot, he put his shovel into the earth to dig. The dragon dug as well, his great claws each larger than a shovel, and much more powerful. He carved into the earth sending great showers of soil flying between his two legs. Rory stood back and watched. The grave was dug in minutes and Rory helped pull Johan gently from the dragon's back. He lowered the knight into the ground where he would quietly rest forever. Then the dragon screamed fire into the sky. Rory had to step back from the heat. But he watched the magnificent display in awe, unable to turn his eyes away even though they could hardly bear it. The dragon spread his wings and sniffed at the patches.

When his sad grieving was done, the dragon pushed the mound of fresh brown soil back on top of the deep grave. Rory said, "You'd like to go back to your fellows I should think. Wouldn't you?"

The dragon looked at him, but didn't nod or shake his head. Rory knew enough about dragons to know they understood human speech, but could not utter it themselves. They looked at each other a long time. Rory sat down, and so did the dragon.

"I've seen much to tell me that you are a wise beast, so I'll speak to you plainly. I got a letter from Sir Oscar, thanking me for helping to free him from the dungeon. Do you remember that night?" he asked smiling. The dragon nodded. "He said he would have died there if it weren't for us. So he wanted to thank me for it by letting me . . . how can I say this? By letting me *have* you—take care of you. He said that if I didn't want you or if you were too much work that I could send you back to meet the other Dragon Riders at their camp—he said you'd know where it was." Again the red nodded. "Well, I don't know what to say, I'd take you if you were willing, but it won't be easy for either of us. And there will be a bounty on our heads. And above all this I could never force your decision in one way or the other. I suppose the question is will you have me, or will you go back to join the others?"

The dragon took a step toward him and grunted. "You'll have me?" Rory asked. The dragon nodded. "You'll need a name, now won't you. Oscar told me you won't answer to Ero anymore." The dragon whined at the sound of his former name and shook his head, taking two steps backward.

"I suppose I'll call you . . . Ragwing. Seems fitting, unique as you are after my tailoring job." The dragon nodded sharply. The two of them stood together for a time, and when Rory turned to leave, Ragwing didn't follow. He curled up over Johan's grave and closed his eyes, though Rory didn't think he was asleep. Rory sat some distance away and waited. He knew that all the dragon needed was time, and rushing him would do no good. So they let the sun sink toward the treetops in the west, but they didn't wait for sunset. Rory climbed into the saddle and for the first time since his wings were torn, Ragwing flew up into the sky. And it was Rory's turn to wail with emotion.

Epilogue

IN THE HOUSE OF the healers, a gnarled pair of hands encircled the pool of blood. The blood boiled, though no heat source could be seen. Four women watched as the fifth one performed the ritual.

"The way he repays us for what we gave him, is this?" asked the one holding out her hands.

"If so, he has repaid us not at all, trinket. Not one bit," said another holding a doll.

"I will go to him. I will get his payment."

"It is not easy postponing death, giving back the power of speech to a cold corpse, is it sisters?"

"Not easy, no, but for us, not impossible. Just one more trick, one more trick to help the needy."

"I will go to him, I said."

"Go then, sister. Find out if he forgot about us, or if he thought we forgot about him."

"I said I would go, I'll let him know that our memories are long. We didn't forget, not yet." With that she stood up, and walked out the door of the house of healers and with a bag over her shoulder she went through the streets of Darkwell looking for Kellen Wayfield.

"She is young, this one. She wants to prove herself."

"What of it, sister? We were all that way once. Young and pretty and oh so eager."

"You should have told her. You should have told her about the other debt."

"We made him strong, sisters. Long ago. Do not forget that we made him strong."

"He still owes us, trinket!"

"The candle that burns twice as bright, only burns half as long, sisters." A middle aged one agreed. "Will he hurt her?"

"Who can say?"

KELLEN WAYFIELD STUMBLED DRUNKENLY to Rory's exercise room. Its weights, bars, ropes and contraptions looked lifeless without the strong butler to wield them. Kellen found out that the old adage was true, you really never knew what you had until it was gone. He gingerly picked up one of the weights with both hands. He strained with his arms to lift it, but it got the better of him. He fell to the floor in dismay, succumbing to one of his very rare fits of melancholy. He usually never felt daunted by the world, and always carried himself with a carefree confidence that betokened a survivor, one who would always overcome the odds. But tonight, after all that had happened, he let himself fall apart and he ran his drunk fingers along the barbell in memory of his missing friend.

He felt alone in the most acute sense of the word. His body hurt more from the weight of solitude than from the knife wound in his chest. In fact, it didn't hurt him at all. He walked to his books and papers, arrayed on the fine wooden desk that was the center of his study. He opened and scanned the pages, sipping from the bottle of wine. There were too many debts. If he paid them all, he would be thrown in the poor house. If he neglected them all, he'd be thrown in the dungeon. With the dragons gone, and his caravan business below water, Kellen didn't know what to do. And what about his minions—or workers? They would miss their wages for certain. He'd already docked Rory's pay; that may have been the single worst mistake he'd ever made. He saw the butler's handsome face in his mind.

He was so addled by the wine that he couldn't even focus on the task at hand. This was a decision best left for the morning, he decided. But before he turned the page, an entry in the book got his attention. It read like this:

Creditor	Service	Debt Due
The Healers......................*Revived my minion*........................*two favors*		

Kellen knew when he enlisted their help that the healers would not be easy to swindle. If there was one debt in the book he was sure to repay it was this one, but those witches had mysterious ways, and he had no desire to rush into any further agreements with the likes of them. They would have to catch him first. He closed the book and walked away.

He held a candle up to his map of the Knowne Worlde. The dark cloud surrounding the great cities, labeled "Teeming Forces of Evil" loomed mere miles from where he stood. He looked at the three standing cities on the map. Pillar in the south with its stone and its young king was still there. Darkwell, packed to the gills with population, pollution, and poisons of all kinds still remained unblemished. Haven with its jaunty watchtowers remained as well, but Kellen knew that this wasn't the case. It was decrepit, inhabited now by corpses alone. He lifted a quill with ink. He illustrated the map yet again. Smoke rising from Haven, an undead hand reaching up from the soil, an X over the road to get there, and a zombie king standing on top of the wall. He smiled with approval at his work. His eyes went into and out of focus so he closed the left one so as not to confuse himself.

The candlelight that fell on his rich study flickered a bit, drawing his attention. Had someone opened the door downstairs, causing a draft? He picked up a statue in his hand, and hid behind the door, waiting. His heart pounded. If he had misjudged and told the wrong person about Malagor's death . . .

The danger on the borders of which Kellen had always danced may now have caught up to him, but Kellen wouldn't be taken easily.

CҺE ENO